"Celia Martin is an engaging storyteller. I absolutely loved And the Ground Trembled. It is beautifully written, entertaining, and a lot of fun."

- Vonda Sinclair USA Today Bestselling award-winning author of Scottish historical Highlander Romance Novels.

I see fans of the historical romance genre flocking to Celia Martin's *And the Ground Trembled*. Lush descriptive passages, a vivid rendering of the historical period, and strong characterizations highlight this novel. Martin feels a strong personal connection with this era in history. The book shows her familiarity with even the smallest of details about its fashion, a keen ear for human speech of the time, and more than a nodding acquaintance with its history.

Martin's characters are not cardboard cutouts. The protagonists and supporting casts of romance novels are often one dimensional, but Martin succeeds where others do not in creating fully three-dimensional characters with credible emotions, motivations, and genuine depth. She handles the connections between her characters with a steady hand. Convincing dialogue makes this possible. The verbal exchanges crackle despite the archaic language, reveal character, and advance plot points. She develops her characters in such a way they evolve and hold readers' interest as the book progresses.

The book is the right length. Martin allows herself an expansive canvas for the novel's story and never overreaches. Her talent for invoking the historical period never fails her and she avoids overwrought histrionics. She builds her plot along classical lines. *And the Ground Trembled* boasts solid Aristotelian construction throughout and its three-act structure frames the story in memorable fashion for readers.

The chapters flow into one another without a hiccup. Her novel unfolds in a continuous flow rather than as an assortment of episodic set pieces and builds momentum as it nears its conclusion. It's another of the book's many elements showing off her talents as an orchestrator of tales; she hears the music of the novel in a way too few authors do.

She handles the love scenes with artful tastefulness, yet her forceful language fills them with passion. This is illustrative of the novel's prose overall. Martin is an experienced author who has honed her skills to a sharp edge and readers will be hard pressed to identify any dross throughout the book. The confidence and unwavering focus she brings to the novel strengthens the reading experience.

She nails the historical facts of the time. Her familiarity with the era of King Charles allows her to incorporate such references without sounding like someone straining for effect. It is an uneasy time in English history and Martin does a sparkling job capturing the tenor of those times without ever belaboring them. Such material, in the hands of a lesser writer, would fall flat.

And the Ground Trembled has a satisfying ending. Martin ties up the plot's loose ends and her main characters finish the novel far removed from how they began the story. This novel is a vivid example of what a talented writer can accomplish with the historical romance; skeptics who deride the genre as formulaic nonsense miss the point. Celia Martin proves, beyond any doubt, the genre can serve as a gripping vehicle for invoking human emotion and filling us with a sense of adventure. Longtime fans of this style will love this book.

- Mindy McCall, Reprospace Reviews™

And the Ground Trembled

To Andi —
I hope you find
this a fun book —
it was fun to write.
Celia Martin

Celia Martin

KITSAP
PUBLISHING

**KITSAP
PUBLISHING**

And the Ground Trembled
First edition, published 2020

By Celia Martin

Book Layout: Tim Meikle, Reprospace

ISBN-13 Softcover: 978-1-952685-10-1

Published by Kitsap Publishing
P.O. Box 572
Poulsbo, WA 98370
www.KitsapPublishing.com

Also by Celia Martin

To Challenge Destiny

"Exquisite passion and breath-taking action! A historical romance feast!"
Curt Locklear - Laramie Award Winner

"Martin proves she has the vision and talent to make bygone times come alive for modern readers."
Anne Hollister, Professional Book Reviews

A Bewitching Dilemma

"A willful heroine cornered by a relentless foe and a dashing sea captain tormented by his past cast their lots against the tides of a history dark with treachery. A compelling read cover to cover."
Michael Donnelly - Author of False Harbor

With Every Breath I take

A love story laced with fun and surprises

Taking A Chance

"I've no hesitation to recommend this five-star read to new or old readers of historical fiction."
Trisha J. Kelly - multi-genre award-winning author of children and middle school books, and of cozy mysteries and crime thrillers.

"Celia Martin captures the complex landscape of people dealing with Puritanism which squelches the fun out of life for ordinary people. A great backdrop for the heroine to shine as she strives to marry the man she loves"
C.A. Asbrey - author of the 19th century murder mysteries, 'The Innocents' and of articles on history for magazines and periodicals.

Precarious Game of Hide and Seek

"Celia Martin's historical romance ranks as above average fare in the this genre.

- Jason Hillenburg, Reprospace Reviews™

Fate Takes a Hand

"Each character, lovingly written, pulls the reader into the story, contributing to the elegance of this beautiful work of fiction. Love stories like this are timeless. If you are looking for a wonderful historical romance with a truly satisfying conclusion, I highly recommend Fate Takes A Hand."

Kristen Morgen - **Author of Behind The Glass**

""Celia Martin's Fate Takes a Hand provides a reading experience any devotee of historical romantic fiction will enjoy and holds up under multiple readings."

- Jason Hillenburg, Reprospace Reviews™

cmartinbooks.kitsappublishing.com

To lovers of history, romance, and adventure
— thank you for your support.

A Collection of Romantic Adventures

Follow the romantic adventures of the D'Arcy, Hayward, and Lotterby families, and their captivating friends in seventeenth century England and the American colonies. In And The Ground Trembled, Lady Elizabeth D'Arcy goes to London to find a husband. But does William Hayward, the man she falls in love with, love her, or is he after her large dowry? Be sure to watch for Perfidious Brambles when Lady Timandra Lotterby accompanies her friend, Eliza Tilbury, to Northumberland and meets the man of her dreams, Gavin Merritt. But while striving to win Gavin's love, she and he must contend with mysterious ghosts, a hidden staircase, and murder attempts on Eliza' two little brothers. Can Lady Timandra and Gavin solve the mystery before Gavin or the two boys are killed?

Excerpt from

Perfidious Brambles
At the end of the book.

Visit my web site at:
cmartinbooks.kitsappublishing.com

Chapter 1

England 1681

Elizabeth D'Arcy could not remember when she had last been so excited. Her stomach fluttered and her pulse danced a jig. She had been presented to Queen Catherine the previous morning, and this afternoon she would be attending a ball where King Charles was certain to be in attendance. She had heard many tales of his attraction to pretty women, and her Aunt Phillida had warned her not to flirt with him should she catch his eye. Even so, she had hopes the monarch would ask her to dance. She wanted to tell him how as a child she had thrilled to tales of his heroism and his daring escape from the treacherous roundheads. She thanked God he had survived to return to England as the rightful heir to the throne.

She had heard too many horror stories of the joyless life under the Commonwealth and Cromwell's rule to ever want to experience life without their merry monarch. She had been born in sixty-one, the year after the Restoration, but two of her brothers and several cousins had been born during the years of the harsh Puritan constraints. Her father and uncles, strong supporters of the King, had been amply rewarded for their devotion to King Charles.

"Elizabeth, you dawdle. 'Twill not do to be late. I have no wish to offend the King."

"Yes, Aunt Phillida." Elizabeth tried to stand still as her serving girl, taking great care not to muss her hair, helped Elizabeth slip the skirt of her gown over her head. Elizabeth's dark hair, pulled starkly back from her face, cascaded about her shoulders in a mass of finger-size ringlets, but tiny curls clustering about her forehead softened the severity of the coiffure. While her maid attached the skirt to the gown's bodice, Elizabeth licked a finger and ran it over her eyebrows. She had plucked them

1

so they formed perfect arches over her blue-green eyes. Lastly, she bit her lips and pinched her cheeks to heighten their color. She wanted to use red ochre to redden her lips and kohl to darken her eyelids, but her aunt had forbidden the use of such embellishments.

"Your own youthful beauty enhances you more than any fake ornamentation. However, you are welcome to wear some of my rose water. I think in the crowd, we will need it."

Elizabeth glanced into the parlor at her aunt. She was instructing her maid to have their beds turned down and fires in the hearths upon their return. With another furtive look, Elizabeth pulled the puffed sleeves of her gold silk bodice lower on her shoulders. Tucking her red gauze pelisse about her shoulders, she hoped her aunt would not notice she was displaying more of her bosom than might be deemed appropriate.

Getting anything past her aunt's watchful eyes was never easy, all the same, she loved her aunt almost as much as she loved her mother. She should. She had been fostered with her and Uncle Berold since she was ten. She understood the practice of sending adolescents to relatives to be educated. Parents were seldom strict enough with their own beloved children. Her mother and father were seldom able to deny her anything, especially after the deaths of her two older sisters. She had learned that early in her life – long before she had been sent to Aunt Phillida's.

The practice was growing less common. Her younger brother, Garrett, had not been sent from home. Her parents hired a tutor for him until he turned twelve. They then engaged a seaman to train him to sail so one day he might captain his own ship. Her brother loved the sea, and as he would inherit no properties, seafaring would provide him with an honorable mode of support.

Elizabeth wished a girl's education could be more like a boy's, except for having to learn Greek and Latin. But learning about the world, its history and geography – that she had always thought she would enjoy. Then to go on the Grand Tour and travel around Europe. How thrilling! But no. Girls were trained in the social graces and how to manage a household.

Elizabeth feared she had not been the most responsible student. She loved the dancing, archery, riding, and especially the music – she could play the lute quite well, and all said her singing was lovely – but oh how she had hated the needlework, the nursing, and the household chores, in particular butter churning and making soap. Aunt Phillida insisted she must know how to do all these chores, including bed making and serving at the table, in order to properly train and supervise her servants when one day she would be the lady of her own household.

At least she had had the comradeship of her cousin. Flavia, two years her junior, had often conspired with her to escape the drudgery of their tasks. They would hide out with Flavia's brother, Ewen, and go fishing or hunting. Ewen taught them to swim, though he received a bottom tanning from Uncle Berold when they were discovered. Ewen was Elizabeth's age, and she guessed he would have preferred the company of other boys had any been fostered with them, but sadly for him, he had but his sister and his cousin to offer him companionship.

She would enjoy having her cousins with her now. What great fun they could have. But Flavia was headed home for a visit with her parents. And for the past four years, Ewen had been at Oxford. His father wanted him properly educated to assume management of the three manors he would one day inherit.

Elizabeth knew she had been brought to King Charles's court to find a husband, but what she wanted was adventure. And love. She wanted to find a man she could love as her Aunt Phillida loved Uncle Berold and as her mother loved her father. Of course, she wanted to be loved in return. Her father, the Earl of Tyneford, had sent three suitors to court her at Harp's Ridge Hall, Uncle Berold's primary residence, but she had not been taken with any of the three. The first, a boy two years her junior with a pimply face and dirty hair, had been shy and rather sweet, but he had certainly not set her heart to cart wheeling even if he was, in some way she could not remember, related to the King.

The second suitor, heir to two Earldoms, had been in his mid-twenties and in appearance, she had found him fair to look upon, though he was a tad on the stocky side. However, she had discovered he had a cruel streak. She had seen him slap a serving girl and use his whip on one of the stable boys. When she told Uncle Berold about his behavior, young Lord Macon had been hastily, if politely, asked to leave.

Her third suitor, the Viscount Abercar, she had actually liked. She even allowed him to kiss her, but no trumpets blared, no goose bumps clamored up her arms, she had felt no flush of exhilaration. After the kiss, she looked up into the Viscount's genial blue eyes. "Lord Abercar, felt you the ground shake?"

Smiling at her, he shook his head. "No, I felt no such tremor."

She frowned. "Nor did I." She thought him quite handsome for an older man. Surely he was in at least his mid-thirties, but he looked to be fit, no paunchy stomach or spindly legs. She had no idea what his hair might be like for he wore a wig. He could have had his head shorn. He had a strong chin and delightful crinkles about his eyes when he smiled. And she knew him to be a fine horseman. They had been out riding several times. But she could in no way believe herself to be in love with him, or he in love with her.

"Does it matter?" He brought her attention back to the kiss. "I mean, that the ground failed to shake?"

"I know you will think me silly, but yes, it matters to me."

He took her hand in his. "My dear, sweet Lady Elizabeth, I do believe we would deal well together, and that we could build a happy enough life for ourselves. Yet I cannot fault you for wanting the ground to shake. In my youth I had such hopes myself."

She thought he looked sad. He had looked past her, almost as if he was seeing someone else. She wondered if he had once loved someone and then lost her. His eyes came back to hers and his bright smile returned. "I shall tell my grandfather that you are most charming, but that we failed to suit. He will be disappointed, as he was a great friend of your father's father, and he hoped to unite our families. However, he has survived many other disappointments; he will survive this. Now, I should go find your uncle and tell him I plan to depart on the morrow."

So Abercar had departed. And here she was in London, on her way to the King's ball. Matching her stride to her aunt's, she glanced out of the corner of her eye at the beloved woman's profile. Elizabeth thought her Aunt Phillida, though in her mid-fifties, was still a handsome woman. Her dark hair tinged with strands of gray, parted down the middle and pulled starkly back from her high forehead, was not softened by curls as was Elizabeth's, but her clean, straight jaw line and high cheek bones, combined with a slim, straight nose, and curvaceous mouth, gave her a regal, yet winsome appearance.

"Step lively child," Aunt Phillida said as they hurried out a side door and down the covered passageway that connected the residence where their lodgings were located with Whitehall Palace. They were staying at her Uncle Ranulf's apartment suite. It consisted of a parlor, a dining chamber, and three bedchambers with adjoining servants' closets, but meals had to be ordered from a central kitchen on the ground floor that served all the apartments in the building. Her uncle, a favorite of the King's from their days together in exile, made frequent command visits to London, so he kept his own rooms close by the palace. Soon immersed in a throng of people hurrying into the already crowded Banqueting Hall, Elizabeth and her aunt locked arms that they would not be separated. People of varying social rank and title, all dressed in their most resplendent attire, all hoping to be noticed by the King or at least by one of his minions, pressed in through the wide doorway.

"Close your mouth, Elizabeth, you look all agog," Aunt Phillida hissed, and Elizabeth dutifully snapped her mouth shut, a flush creeping up her face. She did not want to be thought a bumpkin, yet she had never imagined such splendor nor such a host of people. She could not help but be impressed with the beautiful tapestries and the carved and inlaid paneling, the lifelike statues on tall marble pedestals, and the velvet draperies patterned with silver and gold threads. But the ceiling murals and huge hanging candelabras near took her breath away. And the gowns on the women – vibrant in incredible hues of greens and blues, oranges and reds such as she had never before seen. The fabrics were as astounding, bombazine blends of silk and wool, elaborately designed damask, deep-piled velvets, brocades, satins, fine cambric linen, and gossamer lawn linen. She was in awe.

Aunt Phillida took her elbow and directed her to a less crowded area. "How anyone is going to find room to dance is what I am wondering," Aunt Phillida said with a shake of her head. "I had forgotten how much I dislike court life, or I would have never allowed your father to press me into bringing you here."

Elizabeth knew her aunt had acquiesced because Elizabeth's mother was too infirm to accompany her daughter to London. Years of consumption had sapped her strength. Thoughts of her mother momentarily dampened Elizabeth's spirits, but she pushed the thoughts aside. Her mother would be pleased did she find a husband, and that she intended to do.

"Why you could not have found a husband close to home as my Vivien did, is beyond my understanding," Aunt Phillida said, and Elizabeth smiled, and giving her aunt's arm a squeeze, said, "Vivien, and Timandra, too, are fortunate to have found wonderful and loving husbands. I will count myself fortunate do I but find a man I can love as my cousins love their husbands. Of course that man must love me as their husbands love them. I could ask for nothing more."

Aunt Phillida returned her smile and patted her hand. "You will find such a man. I but hope you find him quickly. We have been here little more than a week, and I am ready to return to Harp's Ridge." She brought her scented lace hanky up and fluttered it under her nose. "I do believe some of these people have not bathed all winter. I cannot understand why His Majesty fails to command his subjects to bathe regularly."

Elizabeth shared her aunt's disgust with the odor of unwashed bodies in the too compact space, but it seemed a minor annoyance in comparison to the excitement that filled the air. She watched the people bowing and nodding to friends and acquaintances while she looked around in the hope of spotting the only person of her age she had thus far met. She and her aunt had been so busy with fabric selections, fittings, and sightseeing that she had had little time for socializing except with a couple of Aunt Phillida's friends who were once ladies in waiting to the queen.

Elizabeth was not surprised when she finally caught sight of her new friend backed up against a wall and almost disappearing into the drapery. Annis Blanchard was small, exquisite, and timid. Elizabeth first met Annis when she had come across her crying in a doorway of a dark secluded corridor. The girl had eluded her guardian in her need to seek solace away from prying eyes. Elizabeth, returning with her maidservant from a fitting, had heard the heart-wrenching sobs. Sending her serving girl back to their rooms, she tried to console the youthful maiden whom she at first mistook for a child, so small was she.

"Are you lost," she asked. Certainly since her arrival in London, Elizabeth had already turned down several wrong passageways in the maze of buildings that surrounded Whitehall Palace. She could understand how getting lost could be terrifying to a youth. But the girl shook her head and cried harder. "Well, all the same, I must insist you come back to my rooms with me. 'Tis not safe for you to remain here in this lonely corridor." She took the girl's arm and urged her toward her lodgings. Only when the girl looked up from the handkerchief she had pressed to her face, had Elizabeth realized she was a young woman near her own age.

Once back in the parlor, Elizabeth, after asking her maidservant to bring them some wine, convinced her aggrieved guest to sit beside her on the only modern piece of furniture in her uncle's lodgings, a blue tufted couch. Every other piece of furniture from beds to dining table dated back to the Restoration and was of heavy, durable oak. Having coaxed out her guest's name, Elizabeth learned between sobs and hiccups that Annis was being forced into a marriage she could not endure.

Elizabeth was indignant. "Why do you not refuse to marry the fiend?"

Annis pushed back a lock of her golden hair and turned her lovely, tear-stained face up to look at Elizabeth. Her vibrant blue eyes were still brimming with tears, and her moist golden lashes sparkled in the candle light. "I cannot refuse to marry him," she answered, her bow-shaped mouth curving downward as a teardrop slid off the side of her dainty, little nose. "King Charles himself has given his approval of the jointure."

As they sipped their wine, Annis calmed enough to relate her tale. Her parents had died when she was but a year old. She had been raised by her grandfather. Now he too had died. Ever a loyal supporter of the King, her grandfather had lost a portion of his landholdings during Cromwell's reign. Though those holdings had not been restored to him when King Charles returned to the throne, her grandfather had borne the King no ill will. However, he had never forgiven the man, who by trickery, had taken his land. It was that man Annis was now expected to marry. A man near old enough to be her grandfather. In marrying Annis, her grandfather's sworn enemy would take control of the remainder of her grandfather's wealth and landholdings.

Incensed, Elizabeth assured her new friend she would help her find a way out of her terrible dilemma. What she would do, she had yet to determine, but she did not believe any woman should be forced into an unwanted marriage. After all, this was the seventeenth century. They were no longer living in a barbaric society. She had asked her Aunt Phillida's advice, but her aunt had told her she must not meddle in court intrigues, especially if the King was involved. So she was on her own to think of a solution. And she would, she knew she would.

Chapter 2

William Hayward did not need the nudge to his ribs from his friend, Lord Albin, to know the beauty who entered the crowded hall and made her way with her stately chaperone to a more secluded area was the much discussed Elizabeth D'Arcy. Word had spread rapidly that not only was she an enchantress, but as the Earl of Tyneford's only daughter, her dowry was bountiful.

"Did I not tell you she could outshine the sun?" Lord Albin said. His round face with its perfectly trimmed chin beard and mustache fairly beamed.

William nodded in agreement. His plumpish, affable friend had first seen Lady Elizabeth when he had passed her in the corridor outside his aunt's lodgings where he had just taken his leave. She and her aunt were but arriving. Initially, Albin stated, he had been able to do little more than gawk, but he had roused himself in time to hear his aunt's serving maid announce her lovely visitor. He had yet to receive an introduction to the fair maiden, but he and others were raving about the lady's multiple virtues. Hearing their exalted acclamations, William determined, even before setting eyes on Lady Elizabeth, she met the criteria he sought in a bride.

He had had no plans to wed any time in the near future, but King Charles changed that. The King had commanded he marry – and soon. "Young Hayward, you are too attractive to the ladies. Indeed, far too handsome for your own good. We believe we have even seen the Queen cast a glance in your direction. 'Tis time you wed. Find yourself a young wife who can keep you satisfied in your bed so we need not worry that you are corrupting the thoughts of our ladies."

"But Your Grace!" William had been taken aback, but the King dismissed his protests and stalked away. Decree issued, subject closed. William believed himself fortunate to be one of the King's favorites, but he had not expected to have his majesty direct his personal life.

He had first caught Charles's notice at the horse races at Newmarket where the King was a frequent patron. William prided himself on his keen knowledge of horse flesh, and he rode well. Consequently, he won several races when the King was in attendance. He had, of course, set out to be noticed. And when Charles lauded him, William had bragged of his skills at tennis and pall mall. Everyone knew the King to be a vigorous sportsman, and William had cultivated the sports the King was known to most enjoy. As he had hoped, he had been invited to play the King at tennis. The match had gone well – he allowed King Charles to beat him but only by the slightest margin. Soon he was being invited to other sporting events – riding, boating, bowling, and in no time, he found himself a member of the King's courtiers, an enviable position, especially for someone who was naught but a knight's son.

That had been two years past, and the King's patronage had helped him immeasurably in his fledgling enterprise. He gained more favor with the King when he remained steadfastly loyal to Charles during his troubled bouts with the Whigs in the House of Commons. It had been a trying time for the King when even his mistresses met with his enemies, and Charles's beloved illegitimate son, Monmouth, plotted against his own father. But now they were celebrating. King Charles had triumphed over those who sought to exclude Charles's brother, James, the Duke of York from succession to the throne because of his Catholicism – Charles having no legitimate children as his heirs. Charles's enduring patience and reasonable stance had eventually won the moderates to his side, and he had prevailed. The Bill to exclude James had been defeated in the House of Lords, and Parliament had subsequently been dissolved.

Now King Charles was more popular than ever with his people. England was prosperous and trade was flourishing as England remained at peace, while her rivals on the continent were at war. With that same vigorous commerce that was helping the King pay off his Crown debts, William was building his own fortune. He had become a broker in the expanding maritime trade. Acting as an agent to a diverse number of clients, he made the perfect intermediary. He had access to the nobility and the gentry and was equally comfortable with merchants, guild members, or even laborers. Anyone with money to invest, he welcomed.

He frequented the coffee houses which were becoming important centers of commerce for businessmen who preferred the quieter atmosphere to that of the Royal Exchange. He also visited the coffee-houses that were political in nature, both the St. James, which catered to the Whigs, and the Cocoa-tree, which was home to the Tories. He talked trade, while the Parliament Members argued politics. But he also listened and reported back to King Charles any machinations being plotted against the King that he might happen to overhear. That he had highly profitable business dealings with any number of Whigs, who were the dominant party in the House of Commons, never swayed his devotion to his King.

William's fealty was of longstanding. His father had fought for the King; risked his life for years in nefarious activities to help support Charles while he was in exile. Consequently, upon his restoration, Charles had knighted William's father. Knighthood had come with an ample land grant adjoining the small holding near the Welsh border that William's family had held since the time of the Conqueror. Land that William, as his father's only child, would one day inherit.

They were, in fact, members of the gentry. They owned their land outright; did not lease it from a larger estate. But to William, their income was but middling, and most of the time, his father worked the land himself; more like a yeoman farmer. From an early age, having seen his father slighted by a nobleman of the parish, William had determined he would better himself. Never shy nor in doubt of his own capabilities, he had applied himself to his studies, though he had not neglected sports or social deportment. But his provincial upbringing in rural Cheshire, which included his early schooling by the village vicar, aided him in his dealings with the humbler rank and file.

Once William had gleaned all he could from the cleric, his father sent him to a private school in Chester. An apt student, at the age of sixteen, he moved on to the University at Oxford. He distinguished himself at Oxford and was offered a fellowship, but he had greater goals in mind. After graduation, he went on a two-year Grand Tour of Europe with his friend, Albin, who covered much of the expenses. Upon his return, he spent a year at home with his father, reacquainting himself with country life and the agricultural and animal husbandry practices of the region. Then for the next three years, until he became a member of the King's entourage, he resided in London or with Lord Albin at one of his three principal family estates.

Now at the age of twenty-seven, he was to take a wife. He could, of course, ignore the King's wishes, retire to the country, give up his burgeoning business, but that he would not do. Besides, his father had been after him to wed. He wanted grandchildren to sit upon his knee. And perhaps 'twas time he settled down. He glanced at Elizabeth D'Arcy. He could look far and not find a more suitable mate. She would do. He had but to woo her and win her. He would have competition for her hand, lords as well as wealthy members of the gentry, but he was confident of his success. He was yet to meet a woman of any age who was not susceptible to his charms.

Decision made, 'twas time to act. With Lord Albin at his heels, he began making his way through the crowd toward his future bride, for such did he consider her. He would meet her and begin his courtship this very evening. He had drawn close to hand, but before he could contrive to introduce himself, trumpets blared, and King Charles's arrival was announced. Men bowed and doffed their hats, were they wearing them, and the women sank into low curtsies. William was in the fortunate position to be treated to an unobstructed view of the provocative mounds of Elizabeth D'Arcy's creamy white bosom daringly flaunted above the bodice of her golden gown. He was certain King Charles would appreciate the tantalizing display. He would no doubt halt before the charmer. His King was not one to miss welcoming a pretty new maiden to his court.

And indeed, though the King spoke to several courtiers as he advanced down the aisle cleared for him, he did not stop until he paused before Elizabeth D'Arcy and her aunt. "Do our eyes deceive us or have we been graced by the presence of Lady Grasmere?" he said.

"Your Majesty." The lady sank into a deeper curtsy.

The King put his hand under her chin. "Rise, dear lady, and let us look upon your face. We think we have not seen thee in near ten years, or are we mistaken?"

The lady raised remarkable blue-green eyes to look up at the King. "No, Your Grace, you are not mistaken. Lancashire is far from London and travel can be perilous, plus my bones are grown old. I fear I have not sojourned here as often as I might wish."

King Charles laughed, "Ha! We think you have little wish to visit us as you prefer your humble hall to our grandeur." He swept his arm out over the crowded room. "But you are forgiven your absence as you have brought this lovely young maid to grace our court."

William was not surprised when the King turned from Lady Grasmere to Elizabeth D'Arcy who was still sunk in a curtsy at her aunt's side. Putting his hand under Elizabeth's chin, he urged her to rise, though he still addressed Lady Grasmere. "Your niece, we believe, so the Queen has aptly informed us."

"Yes, Your Grace, my niece, Lady Elizabeth D'Arcy."

Elizabeth looked up at the King with eyes identical to her aunt's. She bestowed upon him a smile so brilliant it made William blink and take a step backwards. By God, she was a beauty! King Charles also seemed impressed by her loveliness. He took her hand and raised it to his lips.

"Your beauty, Lady Elizabeth, enhances our poor court," the King said, and William saw his future intended blush a becoming pink extending from her breasts, up her neck, to her face.

"Oh, Your Majesty, you are most kind. I cannot begin to tell you how thrilled I am to be here." Her voice sounded breathy, and she appeared awestruck. William smiled to himself. A bit of a bumpkin, but he rather liked her naïveté. And certainly, meeting the charismatic King for the first time could be spellbinding. He had been mesmerized himself at his first meeting with the dashing Charles. Now in his fifties, the King, though never considered a handsome man, was riveting. Where once his own thick dark hair adorned his head, he now wore a wig. Clean shaven but for a perfectly trimmed mustache, he displayed a winning smile, and his dark eyes danced with merriment. Still fit, he needed no padding to fill out his blue bombazine woolen frockcoat with matching breeches and silver hose. The lace cravat at his throat appeared to be tied in a new style. William had no doubt, by the morrow, courtiers would be copying it.

"Do we understand you are here to nab a husband?" the King inquired, an obvious twinkle in his eyes. "We would have thought a beauty such as you would have no trouble attracting numerous suitors."

Lady Grasmere answered for her niece. "She has had suitors, Your Majesty, but our Elizabeth is a romantic. She insists she will not marry but for love. And her adoring father has acquiesced, so here we are."

"Ah, yes," Charles nodded his head, "love has its merit as long as one is not blinded by it. We wish you good hunting, and we look forward to seeing more of you as you grace our court."

"Thank you, Your Majesty," Elizabeth said as the King turned from her to her aunt.

"Lady Grasmere, do inform Lord Grasmere his steadfast support for us in the House of Lords was not unnoticed."

"I will so inform him, Your Grace," the lady said, sinking into another curtsy as the King turned and continued through the maze of courtiers vying to catch his eye.

With the King's departure, William was ready to make his move. Elizabeth whispered something to her aunt and turned to look in his direction. He smiled boldly and stepped forward, but the young lady pushed past him without looking up. Her indifference to his charms took him off guard. He stumbled backwards against his friend Lord Albin.

"Ow, watch the feet, Hayward!"

"Sorry, Albin," he said, but he did not look at his friend. He was staring after Elizabeth. She pushed her way past any number of smiling and bowing courtiers without acknowledging any of them with anything more than a nod as they stepped out of her way. She made her way to a back wall where she embraced a small young lady who looked more like she should still be in the school room than at the King's grand ball.

Intent on making Elizabeth's acquaintance, William edged his way past the same courtiers his quarry had ignored. He acknowledged some of the men by name, others he offered a cordial smile. Never knew when someone might become a paying client. He stopped beside a young man who was staring so fixedly at the two young maidens he did not bother to look at William when William apologized for bumping into him.

"No offense taken," the youth said, his obsessed stare never wavering.

"You seem quite taken with the Lady Elizabeth D'Arcy," William said, assessing this possible competition for his lady's heart.

For the first time, the youth looked around at him. He was a handsome lad with large, serious, brown eyes, light, brown hair that floated loosely at his shoulders, and a sensitive mouth. William guessed he could barely have gained his majority. He was not a man used to wooing and winning women's hearts. William could not believe him to be of any consequential competition unless he had some great inheritance. And was the lady true to her word, and meant to marry for love, not wealth or title, then he could not think the youth to be much of a rival.

"I beg your pardon, sir. What was it you said?" the youth asked.

"I said you seem quite taken with Lady Elizabeth D'Arcy. Have you met her?"

His youthful rival looked confused. "I am sorry. Who is Lady Elizabeth D'Arcy?"

"The young lady you are so bemusedly staring at," William said, a laugh in his voice. The youth did not know her; did not know her name. He must simply be besotted by her beauty.

"I stare so bemusedly, as you have put it, sir, at my wife. I know no Lady Elizabeth, unless she might be the lady speaking to my Annis."

William looked back around. The small girl at Elizabeth's side was staring as fixedly at the youth. "Your wife! You mean the tiny lass in the blue gown."

"Yes, that is my Annis, my love, the very beat of my heart." The youth's gaze was again directed at the lady he claimed was his wife.

"For heaven's sake, boy, why do you stand and stare at each other? Let us go greet her, and you can introduce me to her friend, Lady Elizabeth." William had his hand on the young man's back. "Oh, allow me to introduce myself. I am William Hayward, and you are?"

"Sir Jeremy Danvers," was the answer William received, but his attempt to push young Danvers forward met with instant resistance.

"No!" came Sir Jeremy's adamant declaration. "I may not go near the lady."

"You may not go near your wife? Or near Lady Elizabeth?" William thought he must have heard the statement incorrectly.

"My wife. Do I go near her, she will be kept in confinement, and I will not be allowed even a glimpse of her."

"Sir, your words make no sense."

The youth dragged in a ragged breath. "She will not be my wife for much longer. Even as we speak, the annulment could have been approved. And my reason for living will be at an end."

William could not remember when he had heard such pain in anyone's voice. For some reason these two young people, so apparently in love, were to be separated. Had they eloped and been caught before the marriage could be consummated? He did not feel right in prying or in adding to Sir Jeremy's suffering. He would have to contrive his own means of meeting Elizabeth. But he would. Why even now, he would swear the young maiden was staring at him.

Chapter 3

Elizabeth had been chattering on to Annis about her presentation to the King for several minutes before she realized Annis was not looking at her, nor even listening. Following the direction of her friend's riveted gaze, she saw the most absurdly handsome man she had ever seen, did she not count her younger brother. He was tall, at least as tall as the King, mayhap taller, and broad shouldered. He filled out his plain, black, velvet coat quite handily. And in this day of chin beards and mustaches, he was clean shaven. His face had a classical look to it, prominent cheek bones, strong, clean jaw line, and a mouth so sensuous it made her lick her lips.

"Who is that man you are staring at, Annis?" she asked her young friend.

A catch in her voice, Annis answered, "My ... my husband."

"Your husband!" The surprise pronouncement hit Elizabeth like a blow to the stomach. The man she had been admiring was married to her friend. Her surprise turned to bewilderment. "How can that be? You said you are to marry Lord Creighton. You cannot have two husbands."

Tears welling in her eyes, Annis heaved a harsh sigh. "My marriage to Jeremy is to be annulled. Lord Creighton but waits for that annulment. Otherwise, we would already be married."

Elizabeth wondered Annis had not made her privy to her marriage sooner, but her friend answered, "I was about to tell you of Jeremy when your aunt returned to your lodgings. Then, when you and your maid escorted me back to my rooms, you talked of naught but this ball, and your insistence I should attend. Indeed, I am glad I am come. I can at least see my Jeremy."

Incensed, Elizabeth stared down at Annis. "This makes your forced marriage to Creighton even worse. On what grounds do they seek the annulment?"

"Jeremy and I were married by proxy shortly before my grandfather's death. When my grandfather realized he was dying, Jeremy was in Europe on his Grand Tour. Grandfather obtained a special license and had a neighbor stand in Jeremy's stead. With Grandfather's physician and solicitor as witnesses, the parish priest performed the ceremony. Jeremy and I had been pledged in marriage since we were in our puddings and hanging sleeves."

Annis turned back toward her husband, but Elizabeth was attempting to make sense of this new twist. She had to help Annis be reunited with her husband, yet her heart was saying nay. She had to tamp down the attraction she felt for Annis's husband.

"No sooner had my grandfather been laid to rest," Annis related in a small voice, "than Creighton appeared with a writ stating I was, at King Charles's command, to accompany him to London. He had my mother's Aunt Beata with him to act as my duenna." Annis nodded her head at the small, round woman in a dull, brown, damask gown who stood pressed against the wall. The woman seemed as much in awe of the court as Elizabeth had been when she first arrived. Her round mouth was open and her small black eyes slithered back and forth in rapid motion.

Elizabeth had met Mistress Beata Underhill but briefly on the day she walked Annis back to her lodging, and though she could not say why, she did not trust the woman. Pulling Annis aside to continue her questioning, she asked, "Why did King Charles send for you?"

"I believe Creighton offered him a goodly sum to have my marriage annulled that he might marry me." Elizabeth had heard tales the King was perennially strapped for funds owing to his indiscriminate lavish spending on himself, his favorites, his mistresses, and his many illegitimate children. Mayhap there was more truth to the tales than she wished to believe. "Creighton told the King that Jeremy was but a boy and could hardly be expected to properly manage the property my grandfather left me," Annis supplied. "And as Jeremy was not there for our wedding, was in fact still in Europe," she blushed, "our marriage has never been consummated, making it easier to obtain an annulment."

Annis looked up at Elizabeth, and for the first time, she looked angry, not defeated. "King Charles told me he was doing me a favor. I needed a man, not a boy to care for me, to see no one took advantage of me and my estate." Knotting her tiny hands into fists, her voice rose. "Not take advantage of me! By all that is holy, what is Creighton doing but taking advantage of me?" Then her anger ebbed away, and she bowed her head and sobbed, "I want my Jeremy."

A few people looked at them questioningly, and Annis's aunt stepped forward and put her hand on her arm, but the girl shook her off. "Oh, leave me be, Aunt Beata. I have no care who may hear me." But when Elizabeth put her arm around her friend and pulled her close, the girl did not shake her off.

Elizabeth patted her shoulder. "You must not give up hope. We will find a way, I swear we will. I do think the fact you are already married could well be a help." She looked back at the man who was staring fixedly at the two of them. "I find it hard to believe such a man could be considered a boy. He looks a capable man to me. Nor does he look like someone who would so easily allow Creighton to put him aside. How long has he been returned to England?"

Sniffling, Annis pulled away. "He started for home as soon as he received word of my grandfather's death. I saw him but for a moment yesterday before Creighton saw us together. Creighton told me, did I dare talk to Jeremy again, he would have me locked in my rooms until our wedding. I think he threatened Jeremy as well, for he has not come near me."

"Hmmm. Looks like that is going to change. Here he comes now." Elizabeth watched the man she had been admiring shoulder his way past the party revelers and advance toward them.

One arm slightly extended, he bowed at the waist. "William Hayward," he said, "with a message for you, Mistress Blanchard, from Sir Jeremy. He sends you his love and life-long devotion, and he vows he will forever remain true to you."

Elizabeth's chin dropped. The man she had been staring at so overtly was not Annis's husband. Her gaze darted to the youth she had not given so much as a second glance. Mouth downturned, shoulders drooping, he appeared as love sick and broken hearted as Annis.

Elizabeth looked at the man towering over her friend. Giddiness surged through her. He was not married to Annis. She smiled blissfully as Annis breathily said, "Thank you, Mister Hayward. You are kind to deliver his message. Please take a message for me, that I feel the same."

William bowed. "I would be honored."

"Annis," her aunt interrupted, "Lord Creighton would not like you talking to strangers."

"Oh, but he is not a stranger, Mistress Underhill," Elizabeth asserted. "Allow me to present a new acquaintance, Mister William Hayward. He has but stopped by to greet us. Surely Lord Creighton can find no fault there." Elizabeth turned her most charming smile on the drab little woman. Mistress Underhill started stammering and looking about as if to see if Lord Creighton might be near, and if he might be watching. Elizabeth guessed she had been given strict orders not to let Sir Jeremy or any other man near her charge.

"Well, ah ... indeed ... ah, Mister Hayward, I am pleased to meet you, ah ... ah, sir." Beata Underhill curtsied, and William took her hand and bowed over it while offering her a beaming smile. "The pleasure is mine, Mistress Underhill."

"Oh, my ... well, yes," Mistress Underhill gushed and stammered again. "I suppose if you are known to Lady Elizabeth you are certainly welcome to stop and chat."

"Yes." Elizabeth's aunt's cool voice sent a cold shiver up her spine. She turned to find her Aunt Phillida, eyebrows raised questioningly, standing behind her. Her mouth in a thin line, Aunt Phillida turned her frigid gaze on William Hayward and stated, "As you are known to my niece, I do think I should make your acquaintance." Before Elizabeth could form an answer, William stepped forward.

"Ah, Lady Grasmere, you have made my acquaintance, though I fear I have no memory of it, only what my father told me of the occasion."

Aunt Phillida looked down her nose at William. "Indeed. When might that have been?"

"First at my birthing, and then my christening, Lady Grasmere. Your husband stood in for my Uncle Cyril as my God-father. My mother's sister was named my God-mother, but you stood in for her as we were in your home. Indeed, I was born in your home. I am William Hayward, Lady Grasmere, and my father is ..."

His sentence went unfinished for Aunt Phillida interrupted him. "Your father is Caleb Hayward. I should have known you by your hair and your eyes." His eyes were magnificent Elizabeth thought – wide set under straight, dark brows, they were a turbulent green, the color of a storm-tossed ocean when she looked down on it from the heights of her home at Wealdburh on the coast of the Irish Sea. "And though you resemble your father," her aunt continued, "I think you inherited your mouth from your lovely mother. How fares your father?"

Elizabeth was thrilled by this sudden revelation. This incredibly handsome man was known to her aunt. Not just known to her. He had been born in her home. She would have to learn more about that.

William bowed his head. "Father does little but work his land. After my mother died in sixty-one, giving birth to a brother who died two weeks later, my father said my mother could not be replaced. He never remarried."

"I am sorry, Mister Hayward. I lost a dear friend when she died. Your mother was beautiful both inside and out, and I know she loved your father dearly. She had to, with him constantly on the run. Then, her seeing to his care despite her condition. A courageous woman."

The crush of people squeezed them into tighter contact, and Elizabeth felt a pleasurable shiver race up her spine as William Hayward pressed closer to her. She was pleased her aunt was ignoring the constriction and seemed to be enjoying calling up a long-forgotten memory. "I can still remember my brother and his motley bandits arriving at our door. And there was your mother, ready to give birth at any moment." She put her hand to her face. "My, what memories. 'Tis God's will we all survived to see Charles again on the throne where he rightfully belongs."

Joining the others of their small group in a chorus of, "Amen", Elizabeth stared wonderingly up at William Hayward. He was the son of one of her Uncle Nate's gang of highwaymen who had harangued and robbed the roundheads then sent their plunder to Europe to support their exiled King. Upon his restoration, King Charles had pardoned them and amply rewarded them. She sighed. Members of her family had benefited from their King's generous largesse. Other Royalist squires, as well as nobles, who had had heavy fines levied against them by the Commonwealth for their support of the King, had not fared as well, though unlike Annis's grandfather, many had managed to hold onto all their lands.

"Well, then," Aunt Phillida said, interrupting Elizabeth's thoughts, "now that I have learned of our early acquaintance, how is it you know my niece?"

"He is friend to a dear friend of mine," Annis said, surprising Elizabeth with her temerity.

"I see." Elizabeth's aunt's face softened as she looked at Annis. "I will accept that," she said, but she turned her eyes on Elizabeth. "We will talk more later."

"Lady Grasmere, would you permit me the honor of dancing with your niece?" William said, and Elizabeth turned pleading eyes on her aunt. To dance with this handsome stranger who was not exactly a stranger, could hardly be more thrilling. Her heart raced at the thought of his hand touching hers, or resting on her elbow as he steered her toward the dance floor. Oh, please, she silently begged.

"Very well, but bring her back here to me after the dance. I, in the meantime, will become better acquainted with Mistress Blanchard's aunt, to whom I have yet to be presented."

Elizabeth and Annis stammered out introductions, then Elizabeth set off with William for the dance floor. William stopped to introduce her to Sir Jeremy Danvers. She thought Sir Jeremy a sweet and pretty boy, and she gave him a sympathetic smile as William passed on Annis's message. Then she and William were on the dance floor, mingling with the other dancers. How well William danced. Every footstep, every toe point, perfect. She was now glad for all the lessons her dancing master had made her practice over and over again.

"I feel so sorry for Annis and Sir Jeremy," she said as she and William took their turn about the floor. "I cannot but think that if King Charles were to know ... if he were to be told the true circumstances, he would never agree to this evil annulment. If I could but talk with him."

"Oh, no, Lady Elizabeth. When the King makes up his mind, it can seldom be changed." He knew from firsthand experience, he assured her. "Best not to question the King's decisions."

Elizabeth gazed up at the man she found so handsome he near made her forget what she wanted to say. Finally she managed to stammer out, "But I ... I spoke with the King tonight. He said he believes love has its merit. The problem is, he has not been told all the facts. Surely he would not otherwise dismiss true love."

"He could, and he would. I beg your pardon, but I happened to be near enough to overhear his conversation with you. He also said one should not be blinded by love."

"Annis and Sir Jeremy are not blinded. They are equally in love. You can see that."

"I can see it, but King Charles is not apt to see it because he will not be apt to see them."

"But if Annis and I were to get an audience with him."

"Hold it." William led her back to their spot as another couple took the lead on the floor. They would wait their turn until time to separate, then again step forward. She would curtsy and they would come together once more and take the lead. In the meantime, they stood very close together, his shoulder touching hers, his extended forearm brushing against her rib cage and almost grazing her breast as she rested her hand on his arm. Tingling sensations rushed up and down her spine, and with the stays hampering her breathing, she feared she sounded the fool as she gushed, "Mister Hayward, pray thee not try to dissuade me, for I am determined I shall help Annis escape a horrid marriage to Lord Creighton. 'Tis wrong, and the man is evil, and this shall not be borne. I will get an audience with King Charles. I know I can do so."

Before William could answer, it was their turn to separate. She could breathe easier without his body tantalizing her senses. This phenomenon she found most interesting. No man had ever left her tingling and craving his nearness. This would merit thoughtful consideration once she was in her bed, her head resting on the soft down pillows, the fluffy quilts pulled up around her chin. She could not think about it now. Now she needed to concentrate on the dance steps and revel in the thrill of dancing with the most handsome man at the ball.

Chapter 4

The ball lasted long into the evening, but the food provided had been substantial. Servants had somehow managed to set up trestle tables amongst the throng, and the tables were piled high with miniature pastries filled with beef marrow or fish or chicken liver, bowls of bite size pieces of meat in a cinnamon sauce, slices of eels in a thick sauce flavored with savory-scented sage and parsley, chunks of boiled mutton, beef, and pork, as well several different fish dishes and venison accompanied by frumenty and jellies, plus large dishes of blank-mang garnished with almonds and anise seeds. Elizabeth had eaten little for her stays had been laced too tight. But once back in her room, she feasted on a plate of cold sliced beef, chunks of crusty bread with a side dish of quince marmalade, and some curds and cream her serving girl had awaiting her.

Elizabeth shed her petticoats and stays and changed into her dressing gown before gorging herself. She was famished, though until she and her aunt began their trek back to their rooms, she had given food little thought, so entranced had she been by the ball. Aunt Phillida had laughed at her. "I told you that you were laced too tight. 'Tis a wonder you had breath to dance."

Oh, but dance she had. From the slow, stately bassadance, to the serious, but more moderate tempo almain, to the lively reels and the galliard, but her favorite dance was the minuet. And she had had so many partners. Nestling down under her warm quilts, she struggled to remember all their names. There was William's friend, Lord Albin, a Lord Chardy, a Mister Sydney and a Mister Wainwright, and several other lords. They had all been charming, but she was most intrigued by and attracted to William Hayward. She danced four dances with him, two were the minuet, that flirtatious little dance where men tried to steal a kiss from their partners.

And William had tried to kiss her, but she had avoided his kiss. Not that she had no wish to kiss him, to taste his lips, but when she did kiss him, she wanted to be alone with him. She wanted to concentrate on the kiss, and she wanted to see if his kiss made the ground tremble as her cousin Timandra said it did when her husband first kissed her. Elizabeth already knew she thrilled to William's touch, and merely looking at him fair took her breath away. Actually, she did not believe any man had the right to be so handsome. She doubted few women would be able to resist his charm. He had certainly charmed her aunt as well as Annis's aunt.

Despite his charm, Aunt Phillida was not convinced he was a desirable suitor. "You are, after all, the only daughter of the Earl of Tyneford," her aunt declared. "And your father's barony at Wealdburh dates back to the Conqueror." Elizabeth was well aware of her family's illustrious ancestry. A distant ancestor had been granted the title Earl of Tyneford by King Henry VII. The estate, which was far to the north on the River Tyne, had been bestowed upon Halvor D'Arcy for fighting with Henry VII during the War of the Roses. Elizabeth had never seen the estate, though it was more extensive and provided a greater income than their holdings at Wealdburh, her home, or the other smaller estates scattered about England and Wales.

Henry VII, like kings before and after him, made certain his nobles' estates were located far apart so their power could not be consolidated and used against him. Her father journeyed once a year to the Tyneford landholdings to collect the rents and to make sure the estate was being properly managed by his steward, a distant kinsman. Her mother always worried when the Earl made the remote trip, though he was accompanied by several armed retainers. The Irish Sea was unsafe, roads were bad, and assault by highwaymen was a constant risk. Her mother claimed she could never get a decent night's sleep until her husband returned home safely.

Besides his Welsh holdings across the Dee estuary from the Wealdburh Barony on the Wirral Peninsula, her father had two small estates in Derbyshire, two in Northampton, one in Somerset, and another not a half day's ride from London, north of Wallingford in Oxfordshire. The Wallingford holding dated from the days of Edward II. Though it did little to increase their coffers, it provided her father and uncles with a retreat from the travails of Parliament.

"Mister Hayward is but the son of a yeoman, knighted by King Charles for his service to him," Aunt Phillida had continued. "And though I loved his mother dearly, William is hardly an acceptable match for you, Elizabeth."

Not in the least concerned about William's background, Elizabeth wanted to discover whether he was a caring person. Looks were nothing if they disguised a dark soul. A man needed to be gentle, and devoted to his wife and children, as was her father. He must also be brave – but she had but to look at William to tell he did not lack for courage. He had an air of authority about him despite the fact he bore no title other than the courtesy title of esquire, as merited by the son of a knight. Still, even the lords were deferential in their speech when addressing him. In admiring his brawny physique, which his fancy dress failed to conceal, she could not think many would choose to cross him.

She had no doubt William was attracted to her. And she knew he would make every effort to see her again. A tingling sensation coursed through her from the pit of her stomach to the juncture of her thighs. She squiggled as she thought of the way William had looked at her. He had been respectful, but his appreciation of her allurements had been obvious. A flush warmed her as she remembered his gaze devouring her bosom and then slowly rising to linger on her lips before lifting to her eyes. His eyes had then held her spellbound until Lord Albin had harrumphed and stated that the music had started, and he was to partner her in the next dance.

Well, she would never get to sleep if she continued to think about William Hayward. Besides, she needed to formulate her plans for the morrow. Annis was to give her aunt the slip, and they were to meet in a passageway that led to the galleries overlooking the Banqueting Hall where the King took his midday meal. When the King arrived, they would make their way down to the Hall, where she had no doubt she would be granted an audience with King Charles.

She wished the King had asked her to dance at the ball. That would have been the perfect time to present Annis's case. King Charles had danced, and indeed, he danced very well, but he had not requested her hand for any of the dances. Of course, her party had been standing at the back of the hall. Annis could not be persuaded to move forward into the crush of people. Elizabeth believed her aunt was equally pleased to spend the evening to the rear of the pressing crowd. No matter, Elizabeth felt confident she could plead Annis's case as easily while King Charles enjoyed his meal. Perhaps better, for the King could concentrate on what she was saying and would not be having to mind his step.

She smiled as sleep started to claim her. Soon Annis would be united with her young husband, Sir Jeremy. What a fine young man he appeared to be, and so much in love with Annis. She had stopped to talk with him between dances and had happily delivered his message of absolute, eternal devotion to Annis. Sir Jeremy was a baronet, third generation, and Elizabeth guessed his grandfather probably bought his title from King James or perhaps from King Charles I. 'Twas common knowledge both kings, being in constant need of money, sold titles. It was an easy way to increase the King's revenue without having to consult Parliament.

Lord Creighton was a first generation viscount. Annis believed he had purchased his title from King Charles II when Charles returned to the throne. Creighton had been a follower of Cromwell, which was how he had managed to attach some of her grandfather's estate. Annis had sneered at his changed allegiance, and Elizabeth had laughed for Annis did not manage a sneer very well. She was too sweet. Still, the man was an opportunist of the worst sort, and she was determined he would not be allowed to marry Annis. Evil should never be rewarded.

Yawning, she began to rehearse her speech to King Charles, but soon sleep claimed her, and she did not budge again until the maid, Mary, opened the curtains around her bed. Light from the leaded diamond-pained window poured in making a puddle of sunshine on the woven mat at the side of the bed. "'Tis a lovely day," the maid said. "Your aunt is up and has breakfasted and is preparing to call on a friend. She requests knowing your plans for the day."

"Actually, I requested her to ask what mischief you planned for the day," Aunt Phillida said from the doorway. "I have no doubt you and Mistress Blanchard, with all your whispering, have something on the agenda that neither I nor her aunt will approve of."

Elizabeth sat up in bed and rubbed her eyes. When she was still half asleep was not a fair time to be questioning her. She squinted at her aunt. "We are going to the gallery to see the King at his midday meal. Surely you can have no objection to that."

Her aunt tilted her head to one side. "On the surface, there would seem to be no harm in going to the gallery. You will likely encounter a number of your suitors from last night. I trust you will mind your station and will bring no shame to your family. I cannot like you traipsing off without me, but as I doubt not that Mistress Blanchard's aunt will be with you, I will allow it. However, take Mary with you. 'Twould not be fitting for you to be on your own."

"As you wish, Aunt Phillida." Elizabeth turned from her aunt to the serving maid who was stirring up the fire in the hearth. "You heard my aunt, did you not Mary? You are to be my guardian today. Means you will get little cleaning done, but I think you will enjoy the outing."

Her round cherub face aglow, Mary straightened. "Indeed, milady, I will be most pleased to accompany you."

Elizabeth smiled. She liked Mary. The girl was but a year older than she and had never been away from Harp's Ridge Hall before this trip. Other than Aunt Phillida's personal maid, Mary was the only serving maid to accompany them to London; there not being room in the coach for anyone else. Two footmen had clung to the back of the coach, a poor way to travel such a great distance to Elizabeth's thinking, but she supposed the two outriders and the coachman fared little better. Not wishing to pay for the maintenance and stabling of the horses, or the housing of the coachman and outriders, Aunt Phillida had sent them to stay at Elizabeth's father's estate in Oxfordshire until they would be needed for the journey home. The footmen, however, were housed in a men's dormitory on the ground floor. During the day they were to be ready at Aunt Phillida's beck and call, but in the evenings they were free to enjoy the delights of London.

Aunt Phillida's maid, Adah, kept Elizabeth's and Aunt Phillida's clothing cleaned, pressed, and mended, and she dressed their hair, but she did little else. Mary, besides serving as Elizabeth's personal maid, cleaned, made the beds, and ordered their meals from the central kitchen located on the ground floor. A kitchen maid, or sometimes the footmen, were they entertaining, brought the meals up to their apartment. The meals were usually cold by the time they arrived, but meals could hardly be cooked over the bedchamber or parlor hearths. Being rooms of temporary abode, the apartment was not set up for permanent domesticity.

Elizabeth knew Mary enjoyed the outings and would never interfere in her plans. When Annis and Elizabeth went down to see King Charles, Mary would wait for them in or near the gallery. No doubt she would do a little flirting of her own with the servants of the multitude of courtiers who were everywhere. Elizabeth felt a slight twinge of guilt that she let Aunt Phillida believe Annis's aunt would be with them, but at least she had not outright lied to her. Throwing back the bed clothes, Elizabeth hopped out of bed. Time to dress and set her plan to work.

🌿 🌿 🌿 🌿

Elizabeth and Mary had to wait for Annis but a short time in the darkened passageway. When Annis arrived, she appeared breathless and a bit frightened, but Elizabeth took her hand and squeezed it and promised her all would go well. Soon Annis's breathing became more normal and the bright flush left her cheeks. Hand in hand, with Mary trailing behind them, they made their way to the gallery above the Banqueting Hall. As Elizabeth had expected, they were greeted by several of her admirers from the previous night. She had rather hoped she would see William Hayward, but he was nowhere in sight.

She absently flirted with the various swains while awaiting the King's entrance. She knew her aunt would not approve of her behavior, but she was so nervous, she needed the flirtatious bantering to keep from biting her lower lip or digging her nails into her palms until they left little crescents in her skin. Annis looked even more nervous, but Mary, who was flirting outrageously with the servant who accompanied Mister Wainwright, seemed to be having a delicious time.

Mister Wainwright, his protruding grey eyes glittering, was commending himself to her. She learned he was the younger son of a fifth generation baron, and though he would not succeed to the title, he had a most comfortable income inherited from his mother's father. He assured her he was not lacking in any of the comforts. He had his own lodgings in London, and a country estate not more than a day's ride from the city. Plus he kept a fine riding stable and had his own coach and four. His bluster, however, was soon eclipsed by the plumpish Lord Albin who elbowed his way to her side. His round cheeks puffing out, he began bragging of the three principal estates and three lesser estates he would inherit when he one day became the Earl of Noseby.

Finally, when she was beginning to despair of the King's arrival, he appeared. He looked at ease despite the fact all eyes turned in his direction. If having an audience to his every move caused him any nervousness, he did not show it. A hush descended over the crowd at his entrance but was soon replaced by a noisy buzz. The crowd was there to see and be seen. Even Lord Albin hoped to catch the eye of a courtier who sat two seats away from King Charles.

"That is Lord Havenhurst," he told her. "He has the King's ear, and I have a request from my father concerning an old land claim that he hopes to gain support for from King Charles. Lord Havenhurst is just the man to plead his case."

Elizabeth noted Lord Havenhurst, but she wanted no intermediaries. She wanted to speak to King Charles herself. She was persuaded he was a romantic at heart, and was he but apprised of the facts, he would never part two young lovers. 'Twas time she and Annis went down to the Banqueting Hall and made their request for an audience with his majesty. Excusing herself from her suitors, and bidding Mary wait for them at the foot of the stairs, she grabbed Annis's hand and headed for the staircase. Annis was trembling, and Elizabeth knew how she felt, but they had to take this chance to convince the King that Annis should remain married to Sir Jeremy Danvers and should not be forced into a marriage with Lord Creighton.

Upon reaching the door to the Banqueting Hall, they found it blocked by two of the King's liveried servants. Nonplussed for but a moment, Elizabeth straightened her shoulders and stuck out her chin. "We are requesting an audience with the King," she said, adding with feigned assuredness, "I do believe he is expecting us." Knowing King Charles's reputation with the ladies, she hoped the guards would assume they were a couple of his newest conquests.

One of the footmen bade them wait while he consulted with a higher ranking attendant inside the hall. Both men looked in her direction, and she tried to adopt a haughty air. She imagined Annis cringing in fear behind her and hoped her friend's demeanor would not cost them their audience with the King. The higher ranking attendant went forward and whispered to the majordomo who stood at the end of the long table where the King dined with a number of his courtiers. The majordomo spoke to the gentleman-in-waiting standing directly behind the King. He in turn leaned forward and said something to King Charles. The whole pantomime then reversed itself, and in a matter of moments, she and Annis were being escorted into the hall and right up to the table where King Charles sat.

Both Elizabeth and Annis sank into deep curtsies until the King bade them rise. Elizabeth did so with a bright smile on her lips though she could see his majesty seemed more interested in her bosom. She had taken great care in her dress, a blue-green silk gown that matched the color of her eyes, over a creamy gauze bodice and a cream-colored petticoat with a beautifully stitched pattern of blue-green swirls. She had selected the gown precisely because it was lower cut than most of her gowns. A little distraction could not hurt, she had reasoned.

"Lady Elizabeth," King Charles said, "we have been told we were expecting you." He tilted his head to one side. "And yet we cannot recall the reason."

Elizabeth blushed. "You did say, your Grace, that you hoped to see more of me at court, and I thought, as you are so very busy and engaged in so many activities, that I might not again have the opportunity of talking with you. So we came here to see you." She indicated Annis who stood beside her, her head bowed. "This is my friend, Mistress Annis Blanchard, rightfully Lady Danvers, wife of Sir Jeremy Danvers. We have come to beg for your mercy, your Grace."

King Charles gave the sedately dressed Annis little more than a cursory glance before returning his attention to Elizabeth. "You have come to plead for our mercy?"

Ignoring insinuating comments of leering courtiers on either side of the King, Elizabeth advanced a half step and leaned forward just enough to expose more of her bosom to the King's view. "We know, your Grace, how merciful you are, and that you well appreciate the bonds of love." She reached back and pulled Annis forward. "My friend is in the most wretched condition. She has been torn from the man she loves, her legal husband, Sir Jeremy Danvers. An attempt is being made to annul her marriage and force her to wed a man she despises, Lord Creighton."

King Charles held up his hand. "We remember. We approved that annulment ourselves. We find Lord Creighton to be a most acceptable husband for Mistress Blanchard."

"But Your Majesty ..." Elizabeth began, only to have King Charles interrupt her.

"We have heard enough. We stated our decision. We will not be questioned on our judgments."

Certain she could not be mistaken in the rumors of the King's generous and tolerant nature, Elizabeth tried again. "Please, your Grace, surely you would not wish to part two young people who love each other so desperately."

King Charles's chest rose, and he inhaled deeply through his nose. "Lady Elizabeth, you try our patience," he said in a piqued voice. He looked away from them and fluttered his hand. "Be gone. We are done with you."

Elizabeth could not believe they were being so abruptly dismissed. Surely she could do something to dissuade the King from his unjust verdict. She could not fail Annis. She had promised her that her plan would work. A thought popped into her head. Might it be a matter of money? "Your Grace, what if Sir Jeremy was to tender you the same ..." She bit her lip, and her sentence went unfinished. As was often apt to happen, her tongue had rushed ahead of her good sense. King Charles, brow lowered in a scowl, turned back to her. "We said, be gone with you."

Elizabeth scrunched her shoulders as though she had been hit. The look on the King's face sent shivers up her spine. She had not known such fear since as a child a dog had bared his teeth and come near to attacking her. Her cousin Ewen, swinging a stick, had leapt between her and the dog and had chased the cur away. But Ewen was not there to leap between her and the King.

She saw attendants hurrying in their direction. Hastily grabbing Annis's hand, she started backing them up, curtsying as they went.

Chapter 5

William Hayward stood at the top of the stairs of the gallery and watched the scene below. He did not know what Elizabeth D'Arcy said to King Charles, but she had annoyed him; that, everyone in the gallery had seen. He could not see Elizabeth's face as she backed out of the hall, but he could tell by her posture and actions, she was frightened. He intended to meet her as she exited the hall. Hurrying down the stairs, he stationed himself at the doorway. He had known she would seek an audience with the King. He had seen her determined look the night before. He was sorry he had not arrived in time to try once more to dissuade her from her foolish goal.

When Elizabeth and her friend rushed past the King's guards stationed at the door, he was there to greet them. Both young women were visibly shaking. He grasped Elizabeth's hands and recklessly pulled her into an embrace. Had her aunt been present, he would never have been so bold, but then, had her aunt been present, the girl would never have been in to see the King. Her aunt, he felt certain, would not have approved of her niece's actions. He tightened his embrace, glorying in the feel of her breasts pressed against his chest.

He spoke soothingly to her. "There now. You are safe. By the time his majesty has finished his meal, he will have forgotten all about the incident. Have no fear. Nothing will befall you." He patted her back before reluctantly loosening his hold on her to grasp Annis by the wrist and pull her to his side. "That goes for you too, Mistress Blanchard. You have nothing to fear, so do stop your trembling and give me a smile, for I have a most pleasant surprise for you." He grinned broadly and released Elizabeth. "Come, let us take a stroll on the parade grounds."

He offered an arm to each lady. Elizabeth, head cocked, looked up at him. If she was embarrassed by his brazen behavior, she gave no indication. "What kind of surprise?"

He laughed. "'Twould be no surprise did I tell you." He looked at Annis. "Do I take it, your aunt is not with you?"

The girl blushed, shook her head, and looked down at the ground. So timid, he thought as he again offered his arm. She took it, but did not look up. Elizabeth placed her hand on his forearm but said, "I must collect my serving girl. She is waiting near the steps."

He glanced to where Elizabeth pointed. An innocent, yet beguiling-looking, young woman with a mass of blond hair tumbling out from beneath a neat white lappet cap was engaged in an animated conversation with a male servant who gave every appearance of being entranced by the serving wench. The girl looked in their direction, and Elizabeth beckoned to her. The wench immediately dropped a curtsy to the lad she had been enchanting and hurried to her mistress.

"Lady Elizabeth, 'tis sorry I am to make you wait. I only just saw you. Did all go well? Did you see the King?"

Elizabeth shook her head. "We did indeed see his Majesty, but all went far from well."

"Oh, I am that sorry, Lady Elizabeth. Do we go back to our lodgings now?"

"No, Mary, you must postpone your work for yet a while. Mister Hayward has a surprise for us on the parade grounds. I am too curious not to accompany him and discover his surprise."

William was pleased to see Elizabeth smiling up at him. The surprise seemed to have both intrigued her and taken her mind off her humiliating and frightening experience. He admired her resilience. Annis, on the other hand, still seemed shaken. The surprise would change that, he thought, as he steered them away from the crowd and out toward the open parade ground. They had not advanced far before a young man approached them. He was both hurrying and lagging, halting his steps then rushing forward. William had been holding forth on his opinion of a play he had recently seen when Elizabeth interrupted him.

"Oh, my, look Annis, 'tis your husband, Sir Jeremy."

Annis looked up as Sir Jeremy stopped before them. "Annis," the youth said, holding out his hands. "My darling Annis."

Grasping his outstretched hands, Annis gasped, "Oh, Jeremy, Jeremy, my love. How came you to be here? What fate is this?" Her hands in his, she was drawn into his embrace. Her head barely coming up to his shoulder, he stooped and rested his cheek on the crown of her head.

Elizabeth grinned gleefully as she looked on at her friend's joy. That approval was what William had hoped to see. He had decided the way to win Elizabeth's affection was to help her friend. He doubted he could do aught to actually prevent Mistress Blanchard's marriage to Lord Creighton, but he could appear to be trying. The bringing together of the two lovers made him look good in Elizabeth's eyes. He could not mistake the glow on her face. She was pleased with him.

"This is the surprise you promised us?" she asked.

"It is. You approve?" Effecting a smile as broad as Elizabeth's, he looked down at her.

"I cannot think of a better surprise," she answered. "But how could you have known where we would be? Or that Annis and I would be on our own?"

"When we were dancing, you asserted you were determined to see the King. I wagered you would escape your aunt's watchful eye. Last night when I could not convince you that pleading your cause to his majesty would be to no avail, I decided to meet you here. I thought you might need some perking up, so I arranged to have Sir Jeremy awaiting us on the parade grounds. I could but hope Mistress Blanchard would be with you, and without her aunt."

Elizabeth glanced up at him and back toward her friend. "Look at them. They are so much in love. If his majesty could but see them together."

William started shaking his head. "No more of that. You have tried that route. King Charles is not apt to change his mind. You must come up with some other plan. However, should you keep me informed of what events you plan to attend, or outings you mean to take with Annis, I will contrive to have Sir Jeremy present."

"Oh, how kind you are," Elizabeth said, looking up at him with glistening eyes.

Covering her hand with his, he said, "I could do no less. I, like you, wish only for their happiness." He turned back to Annis and Sir Jeremy, and tucking Elizabeth's hand in the crook of his arm, he said, "Come. Let us stroll. We should not linger. We will attract attention."

Sir Jeremy and Annis pulled apart, and Annis placed her tiny hand on her husband's arm. With her staring up at him, they started out across the green. William and Elizabeth fell in behind them, with Mary following at a discreet distance. That pleased William. He had no wish to have the maid reporting back to Elizabeth's aunt the flirtatious nothings he might choose to spout. However, Elizabeth gave him no opportunity to attempt to charm her. Her sole interest was in the ill-fated couple who, lost in each other, strolled along before them. How to thwart Creighton and his malicious plans and unite the lovers was all she wanted to discuss.

"Mister Hayward, there has to be some way to outsmart Creighton." She looked up at him with her sparkling, blue-green eyes, and he near melted into them. Now, what was this, he thought, as he forcibly restrained himself from enfolding her in his arms and kissing her until the worry crease between those eyes disappeared. His reaction to Elizabeth D'Arcy was unlike anything he had experienced. He had enjoyed his share of trysts with the fairer sex but had never felt this perplexing desire to protect, to make all things right. He thought himself quite willing to do most anything to keep Elizabeth smiling and happy. Confusing, but he did not have time to contemplate his feelings for Elizabeth was speaking again, and he gave her his attention.

"Obviously, Creighton has bribed King Charles. What if Sir Jeremy came up with a larger bribe, might his majesty change his mind?"

"First off, we have no idea whether Sir Jeremy could muster a larger subsidy."

"Oh, but you could find out from him," she interrupted.

He continued speaking as though he had not heard her. "We have no way of knowing what the initial compensation amount was, to know whether Sir Jeremy could compete." He held up his hand as she again opened her mouth to speak. "King Charles must need be approached in an inoffensive manner – after all, he has already given his word to Creighton. 'Twould have to be done most delicately, and I am doubtful Sir Jeremy would have the skill."

"Oh, but might not someone intervene for Sir Jeremy? I saw Lord Albin in the gallery today. He said he was hoping to get Lord Havenhurst to speak to the King on behalf of his father. Might we not be able to find someone to speak on Sir Jeremy's behalf?"

William silently cursed his friend for putting ideas into Elizabeth's head, even if Albin did not know he was doing so. William did not want Elizabeth involved with King Charles in any way. The King was generally quite genial, but even a beautiful woman like Elizabeth could, on occasion, push him too far, especially if his majesty thought his judgment was being challenged. Still, he decided he would not attempt to discourage her at this time. He wanted her to believe he would do all he could to help her young friend.

"Very well. I will talk with Sir Jeremy, see where his fortunes lie. Does he have the coin, or would he have to mortgage his estate? We must determine what he can muster before we start talking to anyone about speaking to King Charles on Sir Jeremy's behalf. And, of course, there will be the remuneration for the individual we ask to speak to his majesty."

"Oh," Elizabeth's free hand went to her heart. "I had not thought about that." Her mouth straightened into a thin line, and she shook her head. "Well, as you say, we must see what Sir Jeremy can muster." She looked up at him. "You will talk to him directly?"

"I will speak with him this very afternoon," William consented. "But when might I see you, that I may tell you what I have learned?" What a perfect excuse to see her again soon. The more he could keep her in his company and away from his competitors, the better.

"Hmmm. This evening we are taking supper with one of Aunt Phillida's dearest friends. No doubt we will stay for games of some sort and perhaps a musical interlude." Her lips firmed and she shook her head. "I will not be able to see you tonight." She shook her head again. "Tomorrow morning I have more fittings, and then we are to have dinner with another of Aunt Phillida's friends, Lady Canby." She twisted to look up at him. "I do believe Lord Albin mentioned she was his aunt. Mayhap he will be joining us."

William hoped not, though he did not consider Albin any real competition. His friend was affable and would one day become the Earl of Noseby, but he doubted Elizabeth D'Arcy would be attracted to his plumpish friend. She was not looking for a fortune or a title, she was looking for a romantic love like her friend and Sir Jeremy had. He could not believe Albin would fit into her dreams. Still, he would prefer to take no chances. He would make a point to see his friend and get him started gambling. Lord Albin had been known to forget all about former engagements when on a winning streak at cards, and William meant for him to be a winner.

He looked back at Elizabeth. She was chewing her lower lip. "Tomorrow evening will not work either," she said. "I could ask you to supper, but we would not be able to talk in front of Aunt Phillida, so 'twould serve no purpose."

William tried to think of some way he could convince her that having him to supper would serve a purpose, but he came up with no acceptable response. She continued talking, though more like reflecting out loud. "I can think of no engagement for the day after tomorrow. I believe 'twould be best do we meet at the steps of the gallery as we did today. At least, I will try to meet you there about the same time as today." She smiled, and her teeth gleamed white against her full rosy lips. He had to suppress his longing to gather her into his arms and crush those lips with his. "Would that work for you? Mind you, my aunt may be with me, but in the crowd, we should be able to find a moment that we can converse without her overhearing us."

"I shall be there, Lady Elizabeth. Now I think we must start back that Lady Grasmere should not be worried. No doubt Annis's aunt is scouring everywhere in search of her charge."

Elizabeth laughed. He liked her throaty gurgle. It sounded like the soft rustling of leaves. "I have little doubt her aunt is, by now, near delirious," she said. "Especially if Lord Creighton happened to stop by to see them. Not that he calls often, at least, according to Annis. When he does visit, she hides in her room and pleads the headache. However, he must approve any of the outings or events she attends, other than daily walks. Fearing she will encounter Creighton at the events he does approve, she has been on few outings. I had to near twist her arm to get her to agree to attend last night's ball. I think 'twas desperation and her deep love of Sir Jeremy that gave her the courage to slip away from her aunt to join me in our quest to see the King today."

She stopped and stamped her foot. "I cannot believe his majesty would not listen to me. Would not even consider the issue."

William shook his head. "You must forget all about that. King Charles is a practical man, but he enjoys rewarding his friends." He avoided mentioning the King's mistresses who had received a multitude of gifts, estates, and titles. "And, he is in constant need of money. So whether someone is buying a title or a spouse, King Charles is happy to oblige. For now, we will concentrate on determining whether Sir Jeremy can compete with Creighton monetarily. If he can, we will seek out who might be best to broach the King on their behalf." It will not be you, sweet Elizabeth, he thought as he headed their little group back toward the palace.

Chapter 6

Elizabeth was disappointed when she received a message from William that he would be unable to meet her as planned. He unexpectedly had to leave London. He would contact her as soon as he returned, and he hoped he would then be able to see her at her earliest convenience. Elizabeth was surprised by how much she had been looking forward to seeing him, and even more surprised at how not seeing him left her feeling melancholy and dispirited.

Her aunt had worried that she was ill, but in determining she had no fevers and no aches, she said, "Something has upset you. Are you worrying too much about that little friend of yours? There are times, my dear, when we must simply accept that we can do nothing to change the path of fate." She rubbed her palm over Elizabeth's forehead. "Come now, 'tis time you got ready for dinner at Lady Canby's. I do believe she has invited several young people, including her nephew, that Lord Albin who keeps sending you poems and posies. Arise! You are here to find a husband, not lie about on your bed."

Elizabeth did not accept that the path of fate could not be changed, but she rose and gave her aunt a hug. "You must not worry about me Aunt Phillida. I believe I am simply tired out from all those fittings this morning. I can scarce imagine needing all those gowns."

Aunt Phillida laughed. "You will be surprised how many you will need. You would not want to wear the same gown to the next ball we attend. And you must look smart as well as stay warm when you take walks. We will be attending many more dinners and late suppers with games and mayhap dancing afterward. You will be glad of every single garment we are having made for you."

Her aunt started out the door, but looked over her shoulder at Elizabeth and smiled. "Of course, I will be happy should you find the man you wish to marry within the next fortnight, and we can head for home."

Elizabeth returned her aunt's smile. "I will do my best," she answered, wondering whether she had already found the man she wanted to marry.

Mary came in to help her dress and whispered, "I have a note for you from Mistress Blanchard." She took it from her pocket and handed it to Elizabeth. "The lady said I was to give it only to you and to no one else," Mary added.

Elizabeth hastily unfolded the note. Tear stains had smudged the ink, and she had trouble reading what her friend had written. She squinted and held the blotched letter closer to the candles on the stand beside her bed. "Did she say anything else to you?" she questioned Mary.

Mary shook her head. "No, but her face was tear stained, and her hair and gown were all disheveled. She caught me right outside the door when I was returning from taking the morning dishes back to the scullery. After I promised Mistress Blanchard I would give the note to you, she hastened back down the hall."

Elizabeth tried again to read the note. From what she could make out, Lord Creighton had learned Annis had slipped away from her aunt to seek an audience with the King in the Banqueting Hall. He heard of the King's displeasure with her, and that added to his displeasure. He had threatened to confine her to her rooms, and he had had her aunt in tears as he raged at her incompetence as a guardian. And, he had forbidden Annis to see Elizabeth.

"Oh, Mary, this is horrid."

"What is amiss, milady?" The maid turned back from the trunk where she had taken out a gown and was shaking it to rid it of its worst wrinkles.

"This note says Mistress Blanchard is not to be permitted to see me anymore."

"How can that be? Poor dear seems to have no other friends. She seems so meek."

Elizabeth shook her head. "She is very timid at times, but she has been brave when necessary. I must write her back immediately, and as soon as you have helped me dress, you must take the note to her. But you must give it only to her. Do you understand?"

"I do, but milady, suppose her aunt will not let me give her the note?"

"Oh dear, I fear you may be right. I wonder might you find a way to give the note to her maid servant to pass on to Mistress Blanchard. She told me her personal maid has long been with her. Surely she is loyal to Mistress Blanchard."

Mary nodded. "I shall do my best, milady."

"Thank you, Mary. Now while you lay out my clothes, I will write a quick note." She pulled her writing desk out from under her bed and set it on the small round table that was opposite the bed. As she opened the desk and took out paper, ink, and quill pen, Mary brought over a lighted taper from the mantle shelf.

Elizabeth absently thanked Mary before turning to her note. Chewing her lower lip, she tried to think how best to reassure Annis. How could she assure her all was not lost? They would prevail. One way or another, they would see each other again, and soon. The task was not easy, and when she finally finished her missive, she was not particularly pleased with it. She had scratched out several lines, had blotched a couple more in her haste, but it would have to do. She had to get dressed. Her aunt would soon be ready and would not be pleased at having to wait for her. She sanded the letter, folded it, and sealed it with a dab of wax from the taper.

Hurrying her dressing, she completed her toilet before her aunt's maid, Adah, came in to do her hair. Long nimble fingers flying, the thin-faced maid wove a string of beads into the curls at the crown of Elizabeth's hair. The beads glimmered in the light cast by the hearth fire and the candles. "Oooh," Mary sighed, "you look lovely, milady."

"Of course, she looks lovely," Adah said, her pinched nose in the air. "Think you I would send her out to dinner did she not look her best?"

Mary giggled. She never got ruffled by the older maid's haughty attitude. Elizabeth liked that. But she, though often annoyed by Adah's snipes, admitted the woman was an artist with hair adornments. Adah had been with Aunt Phillida for years, and her aunt appreciated Adah's skills. Perhaps the maid had earned her right to be arrogant.

As Adah, back erect, head high, left the room, Elizabeth whispered to Mary, "Do your best to get the note delivered." She then hurried out to the parlor to find her aunt awaiting her. Her appearance approved, they left for the dinner party. Lady Canby and Aunt Phillida had been friends since girlhood when they had been fostered in the same household. Their bond had lasted through the years, and they corresponded regularly. Elizabeth took her aunt's arm and gave her a big smile. She knew her aunt was looking forward to this social gathering with her dear friend, and Elizabeth would not mar the occasion with a sullen face.

The dinner was being held rather late, at two of the clock. Elizabeth was used to eating dinner at eleven or twelve or perhaps one, so she was quite hungry. She hoped dinner would be served immediately, and they would not have to spend an hour socializing before going in to eat. Elizabeth had learned her aunt's friend was renowned for her gracious dinner parties, and Elizabeth was eager to see her table settings, which she had been told were exceedingly elegant. For a number of years Lady Canby had been a lady in waiting to the Queen, a great honor. Age and sore knees had ended her days in the Queen's service. A widow, and with her four children married and scattered across England, she diverted herself with lavish entertainments.

Lady Canby's apartment had its own kitchen on the ground floor, and she was noted for the meals her cook prepared. Elizabeth was pleased they went into dinner shortly after the arrival of the last guests, two young women near Elizabeth's age. They simpered a lot and seemed incapable of talking about anything other than their gowns and various entertainments they had attended. She found them rather dull but guessed they had been invited for her benefit, especially after the busty, full-buttocks Lady Canby, her bright, blue eyes twinkling, gushed, "I know the three of you will become fast friends."

Other dinner guests included two of her aunt's friends, the austere Lady Worverton, with whom they had had supper the previous evening, and the slight but bubbly Lady Bainbridge. Accompanying Lady Bainbridge was Lord Weatherford, who was quite old as well as deaf, and his grandson, Lord Holcombe, who kept raising his nasal voice in an attempt to keep his grandfather abreast of the conversation nearest him.

Lord Albin was also in attendance. His elbow resting on the ornately carved mantel above the parlor hearth, he devoted himself to amusing Elizabeth. She enjoyed his banter and jovial anecdotes, but she most enjoyed learning more about William Hayward – when she could steer the conversation around to William. She learned Lord Albin and William had been friends since their school days at Oxford. They had gone on the Grand Tour of Europe together.

"Oh, Lord Albin, how I do envy you men! I would so love to see Italy. My oldest brother, Robert, went on the Grand Tour, and what stories he had to tell. His favorite country was Italy. He said it was so warm and sunny, and the people were all so welcoming. And the incredible ruins he saw. The churches and villas, according to him, were magnificent."

"All he told you is correct," Lord Albin assured her, his chubby face abeam. He had started to tell her of the enchantments of Greece when dinner was announced. She admitted to being glad they were now to eat. Her stomach had been making most embarrassing noises.

Lady Canby had a dining chamber separate from her parlor, and Elizabeth was impressed by its splendor. The lower half of the walls had wainscot panels, and the upper half and ceilings were of plaster with ornate designs. A rush mat covered the floor, and a huge tapestry depicting a hunting scene hung over a three-tiered buffet which displayed an array of silver plate and ewers. Elizabeth was glad she was seated with her back to the elaborate tapestry scene. She could not say she found the scene particularly appealing. Joyful hunters stood over a slain stag, while a nearby servant held a pheasant dangling from his hand. Horses and dogs pranced about, and a golden sun stood boldly out in a bright blue sky. Not a scene to appeal to the appetite. Must have been selected by Lord Canby before he passed on, and Lady Canby was too sentimental to part with it. Or perhaps it was just too costly to be relinquished. Whatever the case, she pushed the tapestry from her thoughts and gazed at the lovely table setting.

She guessed the table to be at least twenty feet long and three to four feet wide. It was covered by a snow white damask table cloth, tucked up at the corners to reveal a pink cloth underneath. While two liveried footmen poured wine into exquisite, Venetian drink glasses, Elizabeth dipped her fingertips into a fragile, three-legged, glass finger bowl, before placing a pale pink napkin that had been arranged in the shape of a pleated fan on her lap. She was glad her aunt had told her she would not need to bring her cutlery pouch, as their hostess would provide all necessary flatware. And indeed, the newfangled, two-pronged fork, as well as matching knife and spoon, all of silver with ivory hafts, rested beside

45

each delicate silver plate and added to the sumptuous place settings. A silver tripod in the center of the table had three beeswax candles, and two tripods with long creamy tapers were suspended overhead. The combination of the candles, along with wall sconces and the hearty fire in the marble hearth at the far end of the room, gave the dining chamber a bright, glowing warmth.

Elizabeth was not surprised that a shield of brawn with mustard was the first course. It was a special dish, and she knew Lady Canby wanted to honor Aunt Phillida. Elizabeth liked the delicate, highly-spiced young boar meat swimming in a dark, wine sauce, and she found the fork most helpful in keeping her fingers clean.

Lord Albin, though, made no use of the fork. "Did God mean us to use these newfangled prongs, He would not have given us hands," he declared. Holding the meat down with his fingers, he cut several bites then used his knife to stab and eat them.

The second course was eel in a saffron sauce and a nutmeg custard. Roast goose, a venison pasty, a dove pie with currants and figs accompanied by a crab apple jelly, and a mutton pottage with garlic and leeks followed. When she thought she could eat no more, the servers brought in the desserts, suet pudding and gingerbread cake. Though stuffed, she could not resist a small tasting of each. The meal was finished off with cheese, nuts, and dried plums.

Feeling a bit light headed from the wine she had consumed – she was more used to ale – she wished she could lean back in her chair as Lord Albin was doing, but her stays would not allow her that comfort. She had been seated between Lord Albin and one of the young women, whose name she was trying to remember. At present the lady was yammering on about a picnic outing to Hampstead Heath, but a short ride out from London.

"Of course, you must join our party," the lady insisted, placing her hand ever so lightly on Elizabeth's forearm. "May is perhaps a bit early for a picnic, 'tis yet a mite chilly, but several of Lady Harbinger's servants are going there ahead of us, and they will have warm blankets spread out and a roaring fire going should anyone be chilled when we get there."

The young woman – Elizabeth finally remembered her name – Lady

Appolonia Silverton, leaned forward to address Lord Albin. "You plan to join us, do you not Lord Albin?"

"Would not miss it," his lordship answered. "Always attend any function Lady Harbinger arranges. Always bound to be a lark."

Lady Appolonia's younger sister, Lady Florence Silverton, who was seated across the table next to Lord Weatherford's grandson, Lord Holcombe, added her entreaty to her sister's. "Oh, indeed Lady Elizabeth, you must join our party."

Elizabeth was not at all sure she would enjoy the outing with the two sisters, but she said she would speak to her aunt about it. "And, when did you say is the day of this outing?" she asked, hoping it was a day she already had an engagement.

"Oh, 'tis not until next week," Lady Florence Silverton answered, her pale blue eyes glowing, her cheeks a bright pink from the wine she consumed. "And I am having the loveliest new riding coat fashioned for me. It is a dark green with ...."

With a silent sigh, Elizabeth smiled, but paid little heed to the new coat being described in such great detail. What boring creatures were the two Silverton ladies, she thought, before turning her attention to Lord Albin. What might she ask him to start him talking about William? Lady Appolonia solved her dilemma.

"Lord Albin, think you your friend, Mister Hayward, will join our party?"

"Is he back in town, I have no doubt he will join us. He would not miss an outing with Lady Harbinger."

Elizabeth perked up. Who was Lady Harbinger and what was her relationship with William Hayward? She realized she was feeling a prick of jealousy. That in itself was unusual. She had never before been jealous of any man's attention to another woman. She was mulling over the curious emotion when Lord Albin added, "Strangest thing. Hayward invited me to join him for a game of cards last evening, then next thing I know, he canceled, saying he had to make a quick trip out of town. Would not even tell me where he was going."

"Now is that not strange?" Lady Florence said, shaking her head and making her pearl earrings bob up and down. She giggled. "I have known men to do the most unusual things."

As Lady Florence set off on a tale about the antics of a young man who had been courting her, Elizabeth shut out the monolog and let her thoughts return to Lady Harbinger, who had apparently arranged the upcoming outing. Elizabeth thought perhaps she should go on this outing, if for no other reason than to meet the lady who seemed to have charmed both William and Lord Albin.

Elizabeth cast a sideways glance at Appolonia Silverton. The lady had asked about William, so she must know him. Was she also entranced by the ever so handsome William Hayward? Elizabeth felt no jealous pricks where Lady Appolonia was concerned. Not that the young woman was unattractive. She was pretty enough, having the same pale blue eyes as her sister, a flawless complexion, and a pouty little mouth that could quickly turn into a simpering grin. Like her sister, she was rather skinny and flat-chested, and surely no man with any acuity would long be able to put up with such inane chatter.

With dinner at an end, that being signaled by Lord Weatherford when he finally pushed away his plate and issued forth a loud belch, Lady Canby suggested they adjourn to her drawing room where she had tables set up for cards and backgammon. Afternoon passed into evening, and Elizabeth learned little more about William from Lord Albin as he was at a different table and was completely engrossed in his card game. He had, however, assured her he could provide her with a horse did she choose to join them the following week on their outing. She had learned Lady Harbinger was married to the Marquess of Harbinger. "Quite in his dotage," Appolonia said with a snicker. She guessed the Lady Harbinger was at least thirty, though still quite lovely. "And 'tis said she has had several paramours," she added in a whisper.

By the time Elizabeth crawled into bed that night, she had determined she would go on the outing. What a perfect way to get to know William better. And to discover who her rivals might be. She might also be able to think of some way to get Annis to join them. Then, of course, Sir Jeremy would join them, and the two could spend the day together. Mary had assured her the note to Annis had been safely delivered. Feeling much less gloomy than she had before she had gone to Lady Canby's, Elizabeth drifted into sleep.

Chapter 7

William paced back and forth outside the banqueting hall, his gaze flitting over the eager spectators that thronged the grounds and hall. He hoped Elizabeth had received his message, and that she would be able to meet him. He worried she might be annoyed with him for canceling their previous engagement, but he was certain once she knew his reason for absenting himself from London, she would forgive him, even praise him.

When he sighted her, the jolt of excitement that cascaded up his spine surprised him. He had never experienced such heady arousal at the appearance of a woman. Breathtakingly beautiful, she advanced toward him, her brilliant smile setting his pulse to thundering in his ears. He breathed a sigh of relief when he determined her aunt did not accompany her. Her maid was her soul companion. Stepping forward, he clasped her outstretched hands in his and bent over them. "Oh, Mister Hayward," she enthused, "I am that pleased you have returned. I have much to discuss with you and little time. I am supposed to be at a fitting, but when I received your note, I knew I must see you. I wonder, might you walk me to the manteau maker, and we may talk?"

Agreeing to her plan, he tucked her arm through his and assured her he would follow wherever she might lead. Though eager to tell her his news, he listened patiently as she recited the events that had transpired during his absence. He sympathized with her when he learned Annis had been forbidden her company. He applauded her plan to join Lady Harbinger's outing and promised he would arrange to have Sir Jeremy accompany them. He thought he might even have a plan to ascertain Annis's attendance.

Looking up at him with shining eyes, Elizabeth exclaimed, "That is wonderful! How might you contrive such a feat?"

"I do think, did Lady Harbinger herself invite Mistress Blanchard,

49

Mistress Underhill could scarce refuse her, especially should Lady Harbinger go in person to extend the invitation."

Elizabeth's eyes widened. "Think you she would? I cannot believe she knows Annis."

"No, but I know the lady well. She is a minx, a puck, always game for a bit of deviltry. I think she will be only too happy to extend a helping hand to Mistress Blanchard and Sir Jeremy."

At his words, Elizabeth gave him a look he could not discern, her head cocked to one side, her eyes narrowed. Surely she could know nothing of his relationship with Lady Harbinger. Before he could study her further, her gaze darted away, and she expressed her worry that Lord Creighton might forbid Annis from joining them. Or worse, insist on joining the outing himself. His mind racing, William said he thought he might be able to avert that crux as well.

"Could you really? Pray how?"

"That I cannot say for certain as of yet. I must speak with Sir Jeremy. But let me tell you what Sir Jeremy and I have accomplished." He had her attention, her luscious, blue-green eyes framed by thick, dark lashes widened questioningly.

"Sir Jeremy and I have been to Aylesbury."

"To Aylesbury?" Surprise evident in her voice, Elizabeth stopped.

He halted beside her and nodded. "Aye. And a hard day's ride it was. 'Tis near Sir Jeremy's home. The following morning we consulted with Sir Jeremy's uncle who has been his guardian since his father died six years ago. Having but gained his majority while in Europe on his Grand Tour, Sir Jeremy has yet to take the reins of his estate. His uncle, of course, approved his marriage to Mistress Blanchard, which had been prearranged years earlier, but the marriage settlement has not been implemented due to the annulment procedures."

Before Elizabeth could comment, her maid hastened forward. "Milady, you are late now for your fitting. Lady Grasmere is to meet you there that you may then join Lady Canby to go see the dancing dogs in St. James's Park."

Elizabeth nodded. "Yes, Mary, thank you. You are right. I dawdle." Her lovely lips took a downward turn, and she said, "Mister Hayward, we must hurry. I cannot think my aunt will be pleased am I not done with my fittings by the time she arrives. But do please continue telling me what else you have learned."

They set off at a brisk pace, William keeping a firm grasp on Elizabeth's arm as they wove around people and obstacles in their path. "Sir Jeremy's uncle called in his solicitor," he stated, after steering Elizabeth past a man paying little heed to his direction so bowed was he by a heavy cask balanced on his shoulder. "According to the solicitor, Sir Jeremy's finances are in good order, and the solicitor has been instructed to hire an advocate to plead Sir Jeremy's case in the Consistory Court, which handles divorces, annulments, and wills."

Elizabeth's voice brightened, "Oh, think you he might win in the Bishop's court? Surely their long-term betrothal cannot be so easily set aside."

"There is some chance," William answered, "but the court will be loath to go against the King's wishes. Still, I have more good news. This morning we talked with a cleric who clerks for the judge reviewing Sir Jeremy and Mistress Blanchard's case. The judge is having difficulty questioning the witnesses who were at Mistress Blanchard's wedding." William chuckled. "Seems the presiding minister says his vicar, who assists him, is away, visiting his sister in Yorkshire. The good priest claims he cannot leave his flock unattended."

Elizabeth glanced up at him but did not interrupt his dialogue, so he continued, "Lord Blanchard's solicitor, who served as witness, plus the young neighbor, local squire's son who stood in for the groom, left together for a fishing trip in Scotland. Left suddenly, actually the day the summons arrived from the Consistory Court. Neither the solicitor's wife nor the squire knows when the two will return. They claim both left before the summonses could be presented."

William chuckled again when Elizabeth gave a joyful skip and beamed up at him. The look in her eyes was making all his efforts worthwhile. He was on his way to winning her heart. Looking down at her happy countenance, his own heart did a little thud-a-thud. The thrumming perplexed him, but he had more to impart, so he pushed the curious phenomenon aside and added, "The attending physician who was the other witness has come down with a malady he claims prevents him from traveling. He is uncertain when he will recover, but he is treating himself so is confident he is in good care."

Elizabeth broke out in a peal of laughter. "Mister Hayward, what excellent news. What a good man Lord Blanchard must have been to have such loyal friends. Friends who want the evil Lord Creighton's plans to be foiled. I wish I had some way to tell Annis her fate is not doomed. Mayhap I will write her a note this very night and Mary can deliver it to her maid."

As they had arrived at the seamstress's shop, William was forced to bid Elizabeth good day, but he promised he would be back in touch after he consulted with Sir Jeremy on how best to insure Creighton could not interfere with plans for their outing.

🌿 🌿 🌿 🌿

Aunt Phillida tapped her toe and drew her eyebrows together. "I cannot think why you should not be done with your fittings. I declare, Elizabeth, you shall know my wrath are you not finished when Mertice's carriage arrives."

Elizabeth hid her smile. She knew her aunt to be exaggerating her irritation. Having spent the morning at the Exchange, the four-storied covered corridors flanked by everything from milliner and tailor shops to booths with China silks and porcelains, she no doubt was tired. "As long as I must be in London," her aunt had declared before departing that morning but after admonishing Elizabeth not to be a laggard, "I plan to do some shopping. I believe I will purchase some forks." Her mouth scrunched, she added, "Though getting your uncle to use one may prove impossible." Her face thoughtful, she tied the cord of the cloak Adah placed over her shoulders. "I hope I may find some of those delicate Venetian drink glasses. And I would like to find a decently priced, combed, worsted wool for draperies. What I really want is a matching set of velvet cushioned chairs like Mertice has in her dressing chamber."

Elizabeth's thoughts returned to the present, and in hopes of diverting her aunt's attention from her tardiness, she asked, "Had you success in your shopping?"

Her aunt's face brightened, but then her mouth turned down. "I had entirely too much success. Berold will not be pleased when he learns how much I have spent."

Elizabeth slipped out of the popinjay-blue, cambric overdress she hoped would be ready to wear to Sunday services. "Found you the chairs you wanted?"

Aunt Phillida again brightened. "I found a man willing to make the chairs for me as soon as I find the velvet I want. I hope I may find a marigold-yellow velvet. I am at thinking that would go nicely with the maidenhair-tan wool I found for draperies for our bedchamber." As Aunt Phillida chatted on, the seamstress finished a final tuck at the waist on the primrose-yellow petticoat that would go under the blue overdress. She then helped Elizabeth out of the petticoat and back into the clothes she had worn to the shop.

Mary helped Elizabeth smooth her hair and fluff the lace at her neckline and on her puffed sleeves. Toilet accomplished, Elizabeth was ready when Lady Canby arrived to take them up in her carriage. The seamstress, having completed a willow-green cloak Elizabeth planned to wear on the outing to Hampstead Heath, as well as a peach, silk night rail and a delicate, lace-trimmed, silk shawl, had them carefully bundled and securely tied with a strong piece of yarn.

Turning to Mary, Aunt Phillida said, "Take these purchases back to our lodgings. Then, after you have bespoken our supper and fetched the laundry, please, sweep up the hearths. They are in dire need."

Her face crestfallen, Mary accepted the bundle into her arms. Elizabeth knew Mary had been looking forward to seeing the dancing dogs. "Might not Mary go with us to the park?" Elizabeth asked. "She could return tomorrow to procure my clothes."

Aunt Phillida looked questioningly at Elizabeth. "Do you forget that Lady Bainbridge and Lord Weatherford and his grandson, Lord Holcombe, are coming to dinner tomorrow? 'Tis for your benefit we are entertaining. Lord Holcombe is a most eligible young man, good income, good manners, and he will one day be the Earl of Weatherford."

Elizabeth turned from her aunt to hide her repugnance. Lord Holcombe was fair enough to look upon, light-gray eyes, neatly trimmed beard and mustache, unexceptional dress and stature, but his voice ... that nasal whine. She could never endure it.

Her aunt placed a light hand on Elizabeth's shoulder. "Tomorrow Mary and Adah will have much to do readying the parlor and table for our guests, not to mention helping us dress. You cannot expect Mary to run errands for you as well."

Glancing at Mary, Aunt Phillida said, "I suppose you were hopeful of seeing the dancing dogs, but as Lady Canby said she would have her companion with her, you would have to ride atop the carriage. I cannot think that would be proper." She patted Mary's arm. "Never fear child, by the time we leave London, you will have seen plenty of spectacles. Now, do have a care. I wish I had one of my footmen to escort you, but both were laden with my purchases from the Exchange and have a'ready returned to our lodgings."

Another pat to Mary's arm, and Aunt Phillida gripped Elizabeth's elbow and bustled her out to the waiting carriage. Two liveried footmen, identical in height and weight and with the shapely calves of runners, helped them up the steps and into the golden, damask-lined interior. They were greeted by Lady Canby and her companion, the diminutive Mistress Brownly, a distant cousin Lady Canby had taken into her household when the widow had nowhere else to go. Timid and self-effacing, Mistress Brownly, ever at Lady Canby's beck and call, ever eager to please, pulled her skirt aside as Elizabeth bounced down on the cushioned seat beside her. Elizabeth pitied the woman, though she guessed Mistress Brownly was grateful to have a roof over her head and food for her stomach. A woman without means was at the mercy of a harsh world. She had seen enough beggar women since coming to London to be aware of their plight.

Elizabeth attempted to converse with Mistress Brownly, but the tiny woman's breathy, hesitant answers to questions put to her soon had Elizabeth nonplussed. Deciding the woman would be happier if allowed to blend into the seat, and with her aunt and Lady Canby deep in their own conversation, Elizabeth turned her thoughts to William. She recalled the way her pulse leapt when she received his note. She had been tense and edgy, had changed her gown and petticoat three times before deciding on the prim, dove-gray overdress with whey-colored lace trim over a maiden's-blush petticoat. She had tied a black, taffeta hood over her hair and donned her black, silk and wool blend bombazine cloak, for the air had a chill to it.

How eagerly she had sought William outside Whitehall Palace, and how she had thrilled at the sight of him. When he took her hands in his warm clasp, her heart had somersaulted. That he was endeavoring to help Annis and Sir Jeremy told her he was a kind-hearted man. That was important in a husband. A husband? Had she found the man she wanted to marry? She had yet to kiss him, but if the mere touch of his hands could set her heart to fluttering, what might his kiss do? Staring sightlessly out the carriage window, she touched her fingertips to her lips.

The carriage took a bump, Lady Canby and Aunt Phillida groaned, and Elizabeth was roused from her dreamy thoughts. The drive was short and soon the carriage drew up at St. James's Park. The footmen opened the door and let down the steps. Elizabeth and Mistress Brownly were handed out first, and Elizabeth looked around at the lovely setting.

Sundry nobility and gentry meandered across freshly scythed, verdant-green spring lawns. Blossoming trees sent heavenly scents wafting through the air. Daffodils along the edge of the lake waved their golden heads in the light breeze that blew off the river. A small crowd gathered before a low makeshift stage set under a copse of newly leafed elm trees. Elizabeth fell in behind her aunt and Lady Canby as they strolled toward the stage. Mistress Brownly followed her, and the two footmen carrying lap robes and slatted-folding chairs for her aunt and Lady Canby brought up the rear of their little procession.

Elizabeth knew the King was fond of sauntering in the park. She wondered if he might make an appearance this perfect spring day. She also knew one of Charles's mistresses, the famed actress Nell Gwynne, had a house that bordered on the park grounds. Madame Gwynne was noted for calling ribald comments over her back fence to the King. Reportedly, often to the discomfiture of those accompanying him, but Charles found her levity amusing. Elizabeth wondered which house might be Nell's, but she knew better than to ask her aunt. She should not even be curious about such things. Was Mary with them, she could learn the house's location from other servants following in their masters' or mistresses' wake.

Stopping whenever her aunt and Lady Canby paused, Elizabeth paid little heed to their conversation until Lady Canby, her ample bosom heaving, said, "Oh, Phillida, there is that horrid Lord Creighton. I hope he may not make his bow to me. Indeed, I would cut him. I find him odious. He is barely received, though he struts around as though he were a man of notable merit."

Elizabeth jolted to attention. Her gaze followed Lady Canby's. Involved in what appeared to be a heated conversation, two middle-aged men, neither looking in their direction, stalked briskly past them. Elizabeth wondered that she had never thought to ask Annis what Creighton looked like. Both men were of medium height and weight, but one was dressed in a flamboyant-blue, floral-patterned coat and breeches richly decorated with ribbons and bows. Over his massive black wig that hung down his back in a profusion of curls, he wore an excessively broad-brimmed, plumed hat with one side of the brim turned up. The other man, dressed modestly in an unadorned brown coat and tan breeches, wore a plain, brown hat over his own straight, shoulder-length hair. The hat brim drooped about his head, near hiding his face. Elizabeth guessed the second man to be a staid Puritan, but she had no idea which man was Creighton. She knew better than to ask. Aunt Phillida was still angry about her confrontation with King Charles, which of course some busy-body had been thrilled to recount to her.

Returning her attention to Lady Canby, Elizabeth strained to hear the low-voiced comments. "Rumor has it," Lady Canby said, "he made his fortune off the unfair fines, and, I shall not hesitate to say, illegal taxes levied on hapless Royalists. 'Tis said he worked hand in glove with several major-generals, including Harrison, to force Royalists to take out loans at excessive rates of interest to pay their levies. 'Twas naught but usury. Then when payments could not be made on schedule, the Royalists were forced to sell off some of their land or timber, or at the very least, take their sons out of school in order to meet their debts." Lady Canby waved a hand in the air. "Oh, the list of his deviltry goes on." Leaning closer to Elizabeth's aunt, she hissed, "I am told that when the Puritans were still in power, and Creighton being in league with them, he encountered Lady Northrop on a street in Bath, and he pulled out his kerchief and scrubbed her face with it. Said the law declared the wearing of face paint to be displeasing to God. And Lady Lorimar claims she was fined for wearing too colorful a gown."

"Oh, surely not, Mertice," Aunt Phillida said, giving a quick glance at Elizabeth. They had reached the stage and Elizabeth had no doubt her aunt wished her friend would change the subject. Aunt Phillida would not want anything to strengthen Elizabeth's desire to help Annis.

"I am not exaggerating, Phillida. Even buried in Cheshire as you are, I am thinking Lord Grasmere was heavily fined for his support of Charles I."

Aunt Phillida stiffened. "We were fined, as was my brother, Lord Tyneford, and both my husband and my brother spent time in Weymouth prison before being paroled and confined to their parishes. So yes, we felt Cromwell's heavy hand even in Cheshire."

Tucking her arm through Aunt Phillida's, Lady Canby chirped, "Now, Phillida, take no offense, for none was meant." Aunt Phillida placed her hand over Lady Canby's and smiled. "No offense taken, Mertice. Let us turn our thoughts to pleasantries. Soon the performance starts."

Chapter 8

Having urged several convivial gentlemen to step aside, the footmen set up the chairs they had been carrying to the left front of the stage. Once Lady Canby and her aunt were settled with the lap robes tucked about their knees and ankles, Elizabeth took up a position directly behind them. Mistress Brownly joined her, but as the tiny woman still seemed uncommunicative, Elizabeth turned her thoughts back to Lady Canby's stories about Lord Creighton and the Cromwellians. The accounts mirrored stories her older brother Robert had told her. As a child, she had believed every horrific detail, but she later decided he had exaggerated to make the tales more thrilling. But after listening to Lady Canby, she was beginning to think he had been more truthful than not. She shook her head in wonder. To think, the Puritans had even banned the celebration of Christmas. Had forbidden people to decorate their homes with holly or to serve a goose or brawn with mustard sauce on baby Jesus's birthday. Robert had said if the Puritans even smelled a goose cooking, they would break into a house and confiscate the bird. She had never believed that to be true, but if a woman could be fined for wearing a brightly colored gown, anything could be factual.

Well, one way or another, she had to save Annis from marrying Creighton. King Charles should have imprisoned Creighton, not sold him a title. And he should certainly not be forcing the granddaughter of a loyal Royalist to marry a rotten roundhead. She stamped her foot, and Mistress Brownly turned to look at her.

"Is something amiss, milady?" Mistress Brownly squinted up out of lackluster eyes.

Elizabeth shook her head. "Nay, my thoughts but wander. Are you warm enough, Mistress Brownly?" She noted the tiny woman's thin, worn cloak. Mistress Brownly was at least as old as Aunt Phillida and Lady Canby, mayhap older, but no chair nor lap robe had been provided her.

Mistress Brownly smiled, and though the smile failed to brighten her face, she answered cheerily enough, "I am quite warm, thank you. Such a lovely spring day. 'Tis nice to be out."

Elizabeth wondered was Mistress Brownly truly pleased to be out or might she be wishing she was back snug and warm in Lady Canby's opulent rooms. A drum roll sounded and Elizabeth's thoughts turned from the woman beside her to the stage. A man dressed in mustard-colored coat and breeches leapt upon the stage. He held a tan-colored dog under each arm and both dogs were dressed in bright, crimson-red costumes.

The man bowed and set the dogs down on the stage, the dogs, balancing on their hind legs. One dog was dressed in coat and breeches, the other in a flowing gown. The man pulled a small pipe from his coat pocket and began to play. The dogs began to dance. They hopped and swirled, drew close together then backed away from each other. Enchanted, Elizabeth cheered along with the rest of the crowd. At the end of the man's lilting air, the dogs bowed to each other, and the man, to rousing applause, scooped the dogs up and hopped off the stage.

A pert, young woman in a pale-green, low-cut gown was helped onto the stage by a youth in a multi-patched, green coat. Men in the crowd made appreciative, if somewhat ribald comments, when the woman curtsied to the audience. Her smile bright and saucy, the woman clapped her hands and a large yellow dog dressed in mustard-colored breeches, not unlike the piper's, bounded onto the stage. The woman clapped her hands again, and the dog rose up onto his hind legs and hopped around in a circle. The dog had a red scarf about his neck, and tied upon his head, a brown hat cocked up on one side and with a red plume stuck in a red hat band.

The woman grasped the dog's front paws, and the youth began to sing and to play a melody on a lute that looked to have seen better days. Yet the youth's voice was so mellow, the ballad so sweet and poignant, about two lovers parted by war, tears sprang to Elizabeth's eyes. She envisioned Annis and Sir Jeremy as the tragic couple. The woman and dog on the stage swirled and dipped to the music. The dog's bushy tail, poking out of his breeches, swished back and forth. His tongue lolled out the side of his mouth, giving the appearance of a big happy grin.

Emotionally drained when the song ended and the dancer and her dog made their bows, Elizabeth swiped a lace-trimmed kerchief over her eyes. Embarrassed by her sentimentality, she sniffled, tucked her kerchief back in her pocket, and cast her gaze out over the crowd. She was surprised to see, but a few steps away, a lovely, amber-eyed woman staring at her. A slow smile curving her generous mouth upward to display straight white teeth, and making her even lovelier, the woman nodded. Regally dressed, she wore a violet-colored gown and a deep-purple cloak with matching hood. Light, brown ringlets peeked out from the sides of the hood and framed her oval face. She was flanked on either side by two young gallants, both decorously attired. Wondering who the exquisite might be, Elizabeth returned the smile and the nod.

Another drum roll sounded and Elizabeth looked back to the stage. The man reappeared. He had three small black and white dogs with red ruffs about their necks and red pointed hats tied onto their heads. He placed three short stools on the stage, and the woman handed him three hoops. Soon the dogs were jumping through the hoops, weaving in and around and popping on and off the stools, and tearing about as though out of control. The man attempted to restrain their antics, but with no success. He would bend down to pick up one dog and another would jump on his back, making him drop the dog he had picked up. The frolicking continued to the laughter of the crowd until the large dog jumped onto the stage, rose up on his hind legs and started barking. The three little dogs fell into formation, rose onto their hind legs, bowed to the roaring crowd, then scurried down the steps at the rear of the stage.

Elizabeth glanced over at the woman who had been staring at her. No longer looking at Elizabeth, she chatted with one of her companions. Elizabeth wondered who the beguiling lady might be, but she forgot her as the youth began another ballad, his sweet voice filling the air. The two dogs in the crimson red costumes began another dance. They were joined on the stage by two white doves in bright red hats with tiny red plumes. The birds bobbed their heads, strutted around the stage, hopped in circles around the dogs, and fluttered their wings. The combination of the white birds and red costumes made a pretty spectacle.

For the final act, all the dogs and the man and woman were back on the stage. Dogs and humans twirled and hopped to a happy tune played on pipe and lute. The performance ended, and hearty applause greeted the performers as they took their bows. Coins of varying worth were tossed onto the stage. Lady Canby and Aunt Phillida each handed the footmen a sixpence to add to the collection. Pulling two pennies from her skirt pocket, Elizabeth approached the young lute player. She chose to reward him. By his shabby dress, she guessed he might not be amply compensated for his contribution to the performance. She had greatly enjoyed his singing.

Bowing, the youth treated her to a fulsome grin. She noticed light fuzz on his chin and upper lip. Too young to grow a beard, but not too young to look at her with measuring and appreciative eyes. Answering his smile with one of her own, she wished him well. She returned to her aunt and Lady Canby to find the amber-eyed woman and her two jaunty courtiers had joined them. Lady Canby introduced the woman as Lady Harbinger. Elizabeth barely contained a gasp. This enchantress was the woman William admitted to knowing well enough to ask her to personally invite Annis to go on her outing. Dazed, she collected her thoughts enough to acknowledge the introduction. Lady Harbinger, in turn, introduced her companions as Lord Millbourne and Mister Salton. Elizabeth noted both men were considerably younger than Lady Harbinger, but both seemed enamored of her. And she could not blame them. The Lady, though her age was more discernible when viewed in closer proximity, was a faultless beauty.

Elizabeth could not help but wonder if William was enamored of Lady Harbinger. Might he even be in love with her? Her thoughts swirling, she realized Lady Harbinger had addressed her. "Lady Elizabeth, I, with the aid of Lord Millbourne and Mister Salton, have planned an outing to Hampstead Heath next week. We would be honored did you choose to join us."

Lord Millbourne and Mister Salton echoed the invitation. Though their devotion to Lady Harbinger was apparent, Elizabeth realized they eyed her with an appraising speculation. She, after all, was unmarried, and though not a great heiress, she had a substantial dowry. Lady Harbinger, on the other hand, being married, was not in the marriage market.

"Indeed, Lady Harbinger," Elizabeth said, "the Silverton sisters have spoken to me of the outing. They graciously invited me to join them. And Lord Albin has offered me the use of a horse from his stables."

"Splendid. We will look forward to seeing you. Now, we are off for a stroll about the lake. I find I must need take these walks or I grow listless." Tilting her head, Lady Harbinger added, "You would, of course, be welcome do you care to join us Lady Elizabeth."

Elizabeth smiled but shook her head. "I thank you, but after an afternoon of fittings, I find I am in need of a nap before getting dressed for a supper party and an evening of backgammon or cards at Lord and Lady Wexton's. I must admit, I am not used to so much entertainment. We lead a much quieter life at Harp's Ridge, do we not, Aunt Phillida?"

Her aunt's merry laugh sounded in her ear. "Elizabeth speaks the truth. We live a much more sedate life in Cheshire. Since our arrival in London, we have scarce had an evening alone." Aunt Phillida nodded at Lady Canby. "But then, we are fortunate to have so many gracious friends in London. They have treated us to such lavish entertainments."

Lady Canby's plump cheeks dimpled, and the creases around her eyes crinkled up as she acknowledged the compliment. "We are pleased, do our meager endeavors meet with your approval, Phillida. We would not wish you to return to Harp's Ridge and feel you had not been aptly entertained." She looked back at Lady Harbinger. "We must have you to dinner ere long, my dear. I fear I get busy, and at times neglect my friends. And how does Lord Harbinger?"

A bubbly laugh issued from Lady Harbinger, but Elizabeth noted no mirth filled her eyes. "Lord Harbinger drinks and gambles. I do think he will be happy does he gamble away his entire fortune that his nephew he so despises will inherit naught but his title." A brief smile touched her lips. "Do I see him, I will tell him you asked after him." Giving a nod, she said, "Now, we must attend our walk, am I to be home in time to dress for my supper party. So pleased to have met you, Lady Grasmere, and you, Lady Elizabeth. I look forward to renewing our acquaintance."

The two courtiers made their bows and turned with Lady Harbinger to stroll toward the lake. "Lady Harbinger is a lovely woman," Aunt

Phillida said, "but I cannot think she is happy."

Lady Canby shook her head and frowned. "'Tis said she loved another in her youth, but that her parents forced her to marry the Marquess of Harbinger. He is old enough to be her father. A widower, he wanted a young wife who could give him an heir. Unfortunately for him, the present Lady Harbinger proved to be no more fertile than did his first wife. And as Lady Harbinger said, he bears no love for his nephew who will be his heir. However, he is so wealthy, he is not like to be capable of gambling away more than a pittance of his fortune." She sighed but quickly brightened. "Enough on the Harbingers. We have enjoyed a most delightful performance. 'Tis so nice to have such entertainments close to hand. I cannot begin to tell you how dull life was here in London while Cromwell ruled. All the theatres closed, half the taverns closed, spring and Christmas celebrations forbidden, not even Maypole dancing."

"Yes, Mertice, but you and your loved ones survived, as did mine, and we have had twenty years of rejoicing since Charles resumed his rightful throne. This Sunday, I shall pray that England may never suffer through such a horrendous time again. Long live the King."

"Yes, long live King Charles," Lady Canby said.

Elizabeth echoed Lady Canby, but at the same time she wondered how she could convince King Charles that to force Annis to marry Creighton was a grave injustice. As wrong as the King's forced exile. There had to be a way.

Chapter 9

William stretched up in his stirrups, taking his weight off his buttocks. Being in the saddle again after but one day's respite from his previous jaunt into the country was not to his liking, but when he pictured Elizabeth expressing her gratitude, he stifled his vexation. He and Sir Jeremy had left at the first cock's crow and had not stopped to breakfast until the sun was high in the sky. They had a long ride ahead of them, close to fifty miles all total. They had need to change horses twice were they to make their destination by nightfall. They made their first posting at St. Albans, where they had been certain of obtaining good mounts, but more importantly, their own horses would be well cared for until their return.

They were headed to Thorley Hall, the estate Annis Blanchard inherited from her grandfather. Located southwest of Bedford in Bedfordshire, Sir Jeremy assured William he had been to the hall often and would have no trouble finding it, but he admitted to being leery of their scheme. William tried to reassure him. "You are married to Mistress Blanchard. As her lawful husband, her estate is now yours. Stands to reason you would visit it, expect to see the books, express confidence the annulment will be disallowed. You will want all in readiness for your wife's and your return. Matters not Creighton was granted guardianship whilst you were abroad."

Sir Jeremy remained skeptical. He worried he would be unable to confidently confront the bailiff Creighton had left in charge at Thorley Hall. William suspected was their venture to succeed, the umbrage needed to intimidate the bailiff would fall to him. He did not mind, if all went as planned. Again he envisioned Elizabeth. Winning her hand would make his endeavors worth the effort. He looked forward to the outing to Hampstead Heath when he hoped the fair lady would reward him with a kiss. Thoughts of the outing brought to mind Lady Harbinger. She had promised to visit Annis Blanchard and contrive the lady's attendance on the outing.

Resettling in his saddle, William gave his horse his head and let him set his own pace. Sir Jeremy followed suit, and the horses galloped along at an easy gait that was not overly jarring yet would keep to the schedule William had set for them. Moving as one with his horse, William let his thoughts carry him back to his recent call on Lady Harbinger. He had been shown up to her bedchamber, a room he had visited upon numerous occasions, but this time it made him feel uncomfortable. As usual, the lady looked ravishing. Dressed in naught but a filmy chemise that clung to her body in tantalizing contours, she floated toward him, arms outstretched, her smile bright, her amber eyes glowing.

"Ah, William," she purred, reaching up to wrap her arms around his neck. "I was delighted when Brock announced you. You have not honored me with your presence for several days. I began to think you tired of me." Standing on tiptoe, she grazed his lips. He felt a familiar stirring and would normally have clasped her about the waist and reveled in the feel of her skin beneath the silky fabric. His hands would have slid upward to caress her full, rounded breasts, and he would have slipped his tongue between her soft lips to probe the depths of her sweetness, yet he held back. Cambria Elsworth, Marchioness of Harbinger, was as alluring as ever, and he could not deny the desire she kindled in him, but in his mind's eye, a pair of blue-green eyes gazed trustily up at him and squelched the flame.

Lady Harbinger's arms slid from his neck, and she dropped back down on her heels. She ran a slender fingertip down his cheek. "Mayhap you do tire of me," she said before sweeping about and returning to her dressing table.

William followed her, but kept his distance. She was too tantalizing, and he was not sure he trusted himself. "A man would be a fool who could tire of you, Cambria, but I am to take a wife. Do I win her hand," he added.

Lady Harbinger, seating herself before her gilded framed looking glass, reached for a powder puff but stopped in mid reach. She met his eyes in the glass. "Are you William? You have done Charles's bidding and have found a maiden who pleases you?"

He gave but a slight nod. "I have. Lady Elizabeth D'Arcy."

Lady Harbinger's amber eyes rounded. "Lady Elizabeth? The Earl of Tyneford's daughter? The talk of the court? The brazen beauty who annoyed Charles at his dinner?"

William checked the smile he had been forming and instead gritted his teeth. "She is an innocent who but sought to help a friend. She is in no way brazen, she ..."

"Hold, William." The lady's bubbly laugh rippled forth, and she held up a hand. "You need not defend the young maiden to me. I admit I am surprised to find you so devoted, but I hear she is breathtakingly beautiful as well as amply endowed, in ways other than her dowry." Absently picking up her powder puff, she lightly dusted her chest and the exposed swells of her bosom. Then her face hardened and her tongue sharpened. "They will never let you marry her, William. She is too far above you. No, not even does she profess her undying love for you, they will not consent to such a marriage. You would be wise to find another and save both of you eventual heartbreak."

William did not answer. He had heard the rumors about Lady Harbinger. She had loved another but had been forced to marry the Marquess of Harbinger. He knew she was bitter. In her twelve years of marriage to Harbinger, she had taken several lovers and readily admitted to her dalliances. William was her most recent inamorato, and he knew any number of swains waited at her beck and call, ever hopeful they would replace him in her bed. She often joked her husband did not mind being made a cuckold. He would be pleased did she find herself with child, for was it a boy, he would claim him as his own, so great was his desire to disinherit his hated nephew.

But so great was Lady Harbinger's hatred of her husband, she was equally determined not to give him an heir. William remembered his first bedding with the lady. Unabashedly bold, she tied a soft leather sheath onto his awakened organ. Laughing at his confusion, she said, "You must know King Charles now always wears a sheath when he strays from his mistresses to visit the London whores. He believes it protects him from the French pox. I believe it protects me from getting with child." How she knew about sheaths or the King's use of them, he did not ask. She had told him King Charles had tried to seduce her when she first arrived at court, but she maintained she had refused him, laughingly telling the King he was entirely too potent. "I will bear no bastards, your Grace, not even royal ones," she had declared. "Charles, in his usual good humor, accepted my rebuff. He has no taste for rape as do some of the court peers when they cannot win their victims by seduction," she added. "The King prefers to use his charm, and does that fail, he but turns to a more compliant courtesan."

Lady Harbinger's eyes again met his, bringing him back to the present. "So ... I can see you have no intention of heeding my advice. Have you then come to bid me a fare thee well?"

William shifted from one foot to the other. "I have come to ask you for a favor, Cambria." Looking about for another chair, he saw naught but her daybed with its gold-damask covering and silk, embroidered pillows. He decided he would continue standing; too many poignant memories might be evoked did he settle on that sensuous couch.

Surprise evident in her eyes, Lady Harbinger cocked her head. "You wish to ask for a favor? Very well William, I see no reason we cannot remain friends. And should friends not grant each other favors? What do you wish of me?"

"I wish you to invite Mistress Blanchard to join the outing to Hampstead Heath."

A wry smile touched her lips and she laughed. "'Tis easy enough done. She is invited."

"No." He shook his head and dropped down on one knee to be on a level with her. "I need you to go to her rooms, intimidate her aunt, and personally invite Mistress Blanchard in such a way the aunt cannot refuse her permission."

Eyes glinting with humor, Lady Harbinger said, "I feel there is much to this favor you are asking that you have not told me. If you desire me to do this deed, I must have the full story."

Nodding, he straightened and paced the floor. He had to decide how much to tell and where to start. He would not tell Lady Harbinger that besides Elizabeth's loveliness, her dowry had influenced his decision to make her his wife before he ever met her. He would not admit he was aiding Sir Jeremy and Annis Blanchard solely to win Elizabeth's regard. He had little reason to believe anything he or Elizabeth might do would actually succeed in uniting the young couple, but his efforts made him appear the hero in Elizabeth's eyes, and that was his goal.

He would tell Lady Harbinger all he knew about the ill-fated lovers. That would gain her sympathy. She would feel Mistress Blanchard's pain as she felt her own. She would despise Lord Creighton as she despised her husband. Yes, she would be an excellent ally.

His tale completed, Lady Harbinger asked, "You say they have not consummated the marriage?"

"'Tis true. They have been kept apart since Sir Jeremy returned to England."

"But we are to bring them together on the outing to Hampstead Heath?"

"'Twill be a gift to them, and to Lady Elizabeth who has championed their cause."

Lady Harbinger's brow puckered. "Seems to me, William, the couple needs to consummate their marriage. In fact, consummate it often enough Mistress Blanchard gets with child. 'Twould be far more difficult for Lord Creighton to force an annulment is a child involved."

William stared at Lady Harbinger. Why had he not thought of that? "But how? Where could they go?" He scratched his head thoughtfully. "Creighton is bound to set up a hue and cry. He would have all local hostelries searched then would no doubt send some belswagger to Sir Jeremy's estate. He would probably even get some beak to search my rooms."

Lady Harbinger turned back to her looking glass and picking up her comb, drew it through her hair. "I wish I might offer them a room. My husband would never know they were here, but his sister-in-law and hated nephew are to arrive next week, and his sister-in-law has her nose into everything. Vile woman. I cannot blame Harbinger for despising her and her equally vile son. They poke about the house, making note of every candle stick, every sheet in every cupboard, every chamber pot and for all I know, noting what may be in the pots as well."

William laughed. Lady Harbinger had often complained of her in-laws. Lord Harbinger tolerated their yearly visit in his home only because, whether he liked it or not, Selby Elsworth was his heir, and was

68

he denied a sojourn in London at the home that would one day be his, his mother was capable of the most scandalous behavior. Grosvenor Mayhew Elsworth, third Marquess of Harbinger, seventh Earl of Laidly, Baron of Bury St. Edmonds and of Milforde Havenstoke, abhorred scandal and wanted no shame cast upon his venerable family name. He had never forgiven his brother for marrying a commoner, let alone one Lady Harbinger described as coarse and garish. Lady Harbinger considered the nephew an insufferable fop and refused to have any but the most minimal contact with either mother or son.

William's thoughts turned away from the ignoble Elsworths and back to Sir Jeremy and his lady. Where to conceal them that Creighton would not discover them yet would be conducive to liberal lovemaking? Delicately reared, Annis Blanchard could not be expected to abide in just any accommodation. The domicile must offer a modicum of gentility and maximum privacy. He considered asking Lord Albin to house them, but he selfishly did not want his friend the recipient of Elizabeth's gratitude. He wanted no competition for Elizabeth's hand. 'Twas enough Albin would be furnishing Elizabeth with a mount for the outing. He had five days before the picnic. He would think of something.

❧ ❧ ❧ ❧

Elizabeth looked at the note in her hand. William and Sir Jeremy had again left London, but William's note assured her they would return in good time to attend the outing to Hampstead Heath. He also assured her Lady Harbinger would contrive to have Annis on the outing and would provide Annis with a suitable mount. Questions tumbled about in Elizabeth's head; where had William gone? What was his relationship with Lady Harbinger? How would Lady Harbinger gain Creighton's permission for Annis to go on the outing? Or would his permission be unnecessary because William would make good his plan to hoodwink Creighton? Having no answers, she turned to her looking glass. She needed to prepare for the opera she was to attend that afternoon.

Never having been to an opera or a play, other than local mummings or miracle plays performed on Christmas or May Day, she looked forward to the experience. A delightful tingle surged through her, and she made no attempt to curb her excitement. She did not care did she appear an innocent or a bumpkin. She and her aunt would travel to the theater in Lady Canby's coach with Lord Albin as their escort. They would be joined at the theater by Lady Bainbridge and the Silverton sisters and their escort, Lord Holcomb. Elizabeth hoped the sisters would not babble through the entire performance. She had learned Lady Bainbridge was acting as the sisters' sponsor. Their mother had the falling sickness and would no longer go out in public. Lady Canby had procured a box so they would be seated above the clamor of the pit rabble.

"You must know the courtiers in the boxes can often be more lewd than the rabble that apes them," Lady Canby had proclaimed when inviting them to accompany her to the opera. "But all is jolly and gay and seldom do disputes evolve into violent fisticuffs."

"'Tis a colorful pageant for certain," Aunt Phillida answered, "but I go to hear the music. To hear the human voice raised to such glory is inspiring."

Elizabeth wished William could be there. While strolling with her aunt that morning, she had encountered Lord Chardy and Mister Wainwright, two of her dancing partners from the King's ball. When informed she would be attending the opera that afternoon, they promised they would stop by her box to chat. Was William in town, he too could stop by, and he would have another chance to impress Aunt Phillida. How could her aunt not be impressed? William was so gallant, so handsome, so charming. And he was doing so much to help Annis and Sir Jeremy. Did that not prove he had a good and caring heart? That was important in a husband and a father.

Well, she would worry about convincing Aunt Phillida that William would make a suitable mate once Annis and Sir Jeremy's lives were settled. She was looking forward to the outing to Hampstead Heath, where she hoped to grab a few moments alone with William.

Chapter 10

William was pleased with Sir Jeremy's reception at Thorley Hall. The servants welcomed him like a savior, and Creighton's proxy, Felton Davis, was as belligerent as William had expected, and as ineffectual. A skinny man with a long narrow face and pointy chin, Davis had been lording his authority over the staff, and William recognized their resentment. Their loyalty was to Mistress Blanchard and her young husband, and they were eager to frustrate Creighton and his minion in any way they could. When Davis ranted and threatened, they ignored him and did all in their power to make Sir Jeremy and William comfortable. And when William told Davis they were expecting to have a look at the books in the morning, he near had an apoplexy.

"The books, the books! You cannot see the books!" Davis raved, his eyes bulging in their sockets. "Thorley Hall belongs to Lord Creighton, or it will shortly, and he left me in charge here to mind his interests. You have no right to see the books. You have no right to even be here."

William drew himself up to his full height and puffed out his chest. Towering over the steward who was ringing his hands in agitation, William said, "Sir Jeremy is legally married to Mistress Blanchard. The annulment has not proceeded, and we have reason to believe it will not be granted. You, sir, are the one trespassing. Tomorrow we will expect a brief accounting, then we must be on our way to Sir Jeremy's estate for a day or two, but when we return, we will want a full accounting. Do we find aught amiss, funds missing, we will hold you to account, Davis."

Turning from Davis' sputtering to address the house-steward, William said, "Sir Jeremy and I are tired after our long ride, we would like supper as soon as you can manage something. We will then go right to bed. Sir Jeremy will take the master's chamber."

"Yes sir, Mister Hayward. I will see all is put to ready." The portly steward, garbed in the Blanchard green and gold livery, turned to the housekeeper who hovered nearby. "Mistress Oakes, see to bedchambers, rooms aired, clean sheets, fires stoked, warm water for washing."

"Directly, Mister Granger." Her face creased with age, but her gray eyes twinkling, she turned to Sir Jeremy. "Do you go into the parlor, sir. The footman has started a fire, and he will bring you some port to warm you while we prepare your rooms. Once you have refreshed yourselves, Cook will have supper readied. Do you wish to be served in the dining chamber?"

Sir Jeremy looked to William, and William flashed what he hoped was one of his most charming smiles on the aged housekeeper. He wanted to keep the servants' favorable regard. They would be good allies. "We are putting you to enough trouble. We will eat in the parlor."

Mistress Oakes blushed, dropped a curtsy, and with her hand to heart said, "Oh Mister Hayward, 'tis so nice to have Sir Jeremy and you here. You are no trouble." Eyes narrowed, she looked at the steward. "We will be happy when Mistress Blanchard returns to her home with Sir Jeremy at her side as is right and proper." She then stalked off, calling to one of the maids to quit gawking at her betters and find Alice. They had work to do.

"Let me show you to the parlor, Sir Jeremy," the house-steward said, leading them to a door off the main hall. William was impressed with the house. It appeared to date from the Tudor era, but a ceiling had been added over a portion of the great hall, and a grand staircase beyond the central wall hearth led to an open gallery that looked down on the hall. The parlor was furnished with two high-backed upholstered chairs on either side of a small table with a drawer, no doubt holding cards or chess men. A larger dropleaf table and two matching, slat-back chairs with cane seats stood before the hearth. William guessed Annis Blanchard and her grandfather must often have dined in the cozy informal atmosphere of the parlor.

Warming his hands at the fire, William gazed at the brightly woven tapestries hung about the room. All were of cheery scenes, flowers and gardens, peaceful paths or streams running through forests under vibrant blue skies. It was a room that spoke of comfort and graciousness. A room to bring joy to the heart. A room that would be despoiled by the likes of Creighton. For the first time since he decided for Elizabeth's sake to help Annis and Sir Jeremy, anger gnawed at his innards. The injustice of the situation struck him like an unexpected blow. He had been but going through the motions, doing what he could to help the young lovers but never expecting his efforts to be successful. Now determination raged through him. Creighton must not succeed!

His musings were interrupted by the footman who brought in a bottle of port and two glass goblets on a tray. The footman was followed by the steward, Granger. With a slight bow, he asked, "Shall I pour for you, Sir Jeremy?"

"Yes, thank you," Sir Jeremy said, but his eyes looked to William as if asking if he had done the right thing. William gave him a slight nod, and the footman set the tray on the table before the hearth and exited. Granger uncorked the bottle and filled the goblets with the dark red liquid. "Will there be anything else, sir?"

"Yes," William said. "We need have a few words with you. Would you close the door?"

Granger looked thoughtful but obliged. Returning to the center of the room, he raised his chin. "At your service, sir."

"Mister Granger, where is Davis right now?"

"I believe he is in his Lordship's study. He went there straightway after I directed you in here. But not before ordering me to send for one of the stable hands. I have yet to send for him."

William smiled. "Then you must send for him immediately."

"Sir?" Granger looked confused and sounded concerned. "I do believe he means to send word to Lord Creighton that Sir Jeremy is here. I feel certain he means to get Lord Creighton here before Sir Jeremy can return to go over the accounts."

William took a sip of his port and nodded. "That is exactly what we want him to do. We need Creighton out of London so Sir Jeremy can see Mistress Blanchard. The sooner that messenger can get on his way, the better. We need him to go with haste and not to dawdle on his way. Tomorrow, we will be returning to London, not going to Sir Jeremy's, but only you know our plans. We are trusting you with Mistress Blanchard's future, with her happiness."

A smile spread across Granger's face, and he rubbed his chubby hands together. "You can count on me, Mister Hayward. I can think of no greater joy than to have Mistress Blanchard safely home and rightfully addressed as Lady Danvers, her marriage to Sir Jeremy assured. Your scheme is safe. I will send for the stable hand and will make certain he knows to ride hard."

"Thank you, Granger," Sir Jeremy said, taking the steward's hand and vigorously shaking it. "We will depend upon you to do all in your power to keep Creighton here once he arrives. The longer he is gone from London, the better our chances of foiling his plans."

Granger exited and Sir Jeremy turned to William. "Your idea seems to be working, does Creighton but take the bait."

William took another sip of port and stared into the fire. "I hope we were right in trusting Granger. He could be in Creighton's pay, but I saw such distinct distaste in his eyes when he looked on Davis that I felt I could not be mistaken in judging his loyalty to Mistress Blanchard."

"Granger has been in the Blanchard employ since he was a youth. Lord Blanchard trusted him explicitly. And Lord Blanchard bequeathed both Granger and Mistress Oakes ample pensions upon their retirements. No, I cannot think Granger to be in Creighton's employ."

"So all is well. Soon we will dine then go to bed. We will have a brief look at the books tomorrow morning, just enough to worry Davis, then it is back to London. And soon you and your bride will at last be united."

Sir Jeremy lifted his gaze to the ceiling. "I pray all goes as planned. But I cannot but fear the King's displeasure."

William paused in pouring himself drink. "Aye, King Charles may be angry at first, but once he knows he will be compensated for the loss of Creighton's bribe, he will be quick to forgive. 'Tis his way. You are not like to see the inside of a prison. His normal punishment is banishment from court until his humor returns. As you and Mistress Blanchard have no desire to remain at court, 'twill be no hardship on you. Be of good cheer." William hoped he was right in his assessment of King Charles's forgiving nature. He could not afford to lose the King's patronage.

Before Sir Jeremy could respond, Mistress Oakes tapped on the door. "Your bedchambers are readied. Do you wish to refresh yourselves, I

74

will show you to your rooms, and by the time you come back down, your supper will be on the table."

"Splendid," William said, again bestowing a broad smile upon the housekeeper. He was tired, and he was hungry, but 'twas little enough to endure if it won him Elizabeth's heart. Arm extended, he bowed slightly. "Lead on, dear Mistress Oakes. Do lead on."

❋ ❋ ❋ ❋

Elizabeth tossed restlessly on her bed. Normally she had no trouble falling asleep, but this night she had so many thoughts tumbling about in her head, she could not settle down. The opera had been captivating beyond compare. She enjoyed the entire spectacle; not just the wondrous voices that at first held her in breathless amazement, but the costumes and the colorful attire of the courtiers and their ladies or courtesans in the other boxes. The quarrelling and jeering antics of the audience in the pit were both startling and amusing. The wanton actions of women in vizard masks made her blush as they milled about the pit, flirting and making assignations with men who caught their fancy. Appolonia, in a loud whisper Elizabeth feared her aunt must have heard, told her that not all the women were prostitutes, some were ladies of the court. Elizabeth did not know how Appolonia would know such a thing, and she did not ask. She but wanted to bask in the grandeur, the gaiety, and the garish tawdriness that was the opera.

She had not understood the performers for they sang in Italian, but she understood the gist of their story. Another tale of lovers cleaved apart. The man in the role of the fiend who parted the lovers could not have behaved more dastardly, but his voice was spellbinding. Even the pit audience stood in awe when his voice reverberated around the theater, but they raised their voices in protest when in the end he seemed to have defeated the hero. The malefactor, his voice booming, strutted across the stage, waving his sword in the air, proclaiming his victory. But what was that – the hero moved. He struggled to his feet. The crowd gasped, then all was silence but for the fiend's pulsating voice. Barely able to clasp his sword in his hand, the hero staggeringly advanced on his foe. Somehow he gained the strength to lift the heavy sword. He raised his voice in song, and as his enemy turned in surprise, the hero stabbed him in his chest. Blood gushed forth. Elizabeth screeched, and the crowd cheered.

The evildoer was defeated. His sword clattered to the stage. He clutched at his chest, wobbled about while continuing to sing though his voice grew weaker. With a last anguished groan, he collapsed. The bloodied hero, leaning on his sword, stood over him and sang in glorious triumph. The heroine appeared. Arms outstretched, she sang a few lines and joined her lover. Their voices melded, and the crowd roared their approval as they left the stage. The lovers had triumphed, as would Annis and Sir Jeremy. Elizabeth was sure of it. And the evil Creighton would be vanquished.

The entire cast returned to take their bows to thunderous applause. The fiend rose from the dead and magnanimously accepted his jeers and hisses. Elizabeth applauded until her palms were sore. The pageant was over, but it held her in its thrall. Only her aunt's insistent tug on her sleeve got her to her feet. "Come, Elizabeth, the carriage will be waiting. This crowd will delay our arrival at Lady Worverton's and 'twill not do to keep her waiting supper."

Supper was a lively affair what with the Silverton sisters' chattering, Lord Holcomb's nasal-voiced whining, and Lord Albin expounding on the hunting merits of hawks versus falcons, but Elizabeth ignored all and remained in a daze until the meal ended. She scarce touched a bite and Lord Albin voiced his concern. "Come Lady Elizabeth, you but push your food around on your plate and do naught but sit and sigh. You have not the vapors have you?"

Elizabeth managed a smile. "Oh, no, Lord Albin, I am yet in awe of the wondrous performance we have so recently witnessed. I cannot think when I have enjoyed myself more. Did you not think it magnificent? Were you not moved by the plight of the hero and heroine?"

Lord Albin wiped his mouth with his napkin before answering. "'Twas moving, I suppose, but I grew tired of all the caterwauling."

"Caterwauling! You would call that glorious singing, caterwauling?" Elizabeth stared at Lord Albin in amazement. Could he be so insensitive?

Lord Albin harrumphed. "Never was much into singing. Cannot sing a note myself and cannot say I feel deprived. Daresay I might have cared for lullabies when still a babe. The young seem to take to such twaddle, but I have no memory of whether I was taken by them or not."

Elizabeth shook her head. "'Tis a pity, Lord Albin, you cannot appreciate music. However, at least you feel no loss, so I will not waste my sympathy on you."

"I pray you will not." Lord Albin picked up his wineglass. "Now, could I not taste this excellent claret, then I would beg for your sympathy." Taking a sip, he sighed contentedly.

She laughed, and took a sip from her glass. "I do agree, though I think I prefer sack."

They might have continued the debate over the wines – Lord Albin was embarking on his assessment of the Rhenish wine, Brabant, when mixed with honey and cloves – but Lady Worverton suggested they adjourn to the withdrawing room where her daughter would play the harp for them. Lord Albin groaned, more music. "Hope my aunt is as tired as she looks," he whispered to Elizabeth, and she looked at Lady Canby. Yes, the lady's eyelids drooped over her blue eyes, and her shoulders slumped ever so slightly. Hands on the arms of a thickly padded chair, she cautiously lowered herself onto its seat.

Lady Worverton's daughter started playing and Lady Canby's head started nodding. Elizabeth glanced at her aunt. She was attentively listening to the music, but she seemed to feel Elizabeth's eyes on her, and she turned to her. Elizabeth shifted her gaze to Lady Canby, and Aunt Phillida's eyes followed hers. She smiled, nodded, and when the song ended, though she warmly applauded the performance, she rose from her seat. "How lovely. You are truly accomplished," she told the young woman. "Neither of my daughters was particularly musical, though Timandra does have a sweet voice. Elizabeth plays the lute quite well and has a nice voice. Perhaps she can sing with you some time. Tonight, however, I fear, does Lady Canby not object, we should be returning home. I have had word my brother, Lord Rygate, is to visit London, and as we are staying in his lodgings, I must see all is made ready for his arrival."

Pushing herself up from her chair, Lady Canby declared, "I agree, we must take our leave. I am quite tired. It has been a full day." She looked to Lord Albin. "Are you ready, sir?"

Lord Albin nodded. "I have told the footman to have your carriage brought round."

The carriage ride home was uneventful. Lady Canby and Aunt Phillida conversed quietly, and Lord Albin discoursed on his preference of card games to musical evenings. Elizabeth's thoughts turned to her uncle's visit. Would any of her cousins come with him? She would have enjoyed seeing her mischievous cousin, Selena, who was her age. She had not seen her in near three years, but her uncle's letter said Selena was on her way to her Aunt Rowena's and Uncle Nate's in Leicestershire. She wondered about that. Ever embroiled in some escapade, Selena was known to keep her household in an uproar. Elizabeth shrugged. Selena must have done something to merit banishment to Whimbrel, her uncle's estate in Leicestershire.

As she crawled into bed, she wondered what impact her Uncle Ranulf's arrival might have on her plans to unite Annis and Sir Jeremy. Might he be the perfect intermediary to King Charles on the lovers' behalf? Her uncle was a favorite of King Charles. He had fought beside the King in fifty-one and had joined King Charles in his excel and remained with him until he was restored to the throne. Who better to plead their cause?

Her thoughts turned from her uncle to William. Where was he? What was his relationship with the lovely Lady Harbinger? Elizabeth touched her finger to her lips. Would she find time alone with William at Hampstead Heath? Would he kiss her? She hoped so. Her thoughts returned to the opera, and she imagined William as the hero. With his help, they would find a way to save Annis, she knew they would.

Chapter 11

The day of the outing dawned to glorious sunshine. Elizabeth was so excited she could hardly eat, but knowing she would be hungry long before they reached Hampstead Heath, she forced down her eggs and bacon and drank a small cup of ale. With Mary's help, she donned her riding habit. Coat and skirt were russet colored and looked well with her new willow-green cloak. Her black, floppy-brimmed hat, turned up on one side, had a russet plume to set it off. Looking at herself in the mirror, she approved her appearance. Could she read approval in William's eyes, she would think time spent at the seamstress's worth the effort.

She had not seen William in four days. She missed him more than she liked to admit, but she had received a note from him, assuring her that he and Sir Jeremy had returned to London and would be joining the expedition to Hampstead Heath. He also informed her Creighton had left town and Annis would be a member of the excursion. Elizabeth had already received a note from Annis telling her the same. A note of joy and wonder, it was the first note she had received from Annis that was not tearstained. Elizabeth was happy for her friend and grateful to William. She had no idea how he accomplished his mission, but she intended to find out; and thank him.

Elizabeth was ready when Lord Albin arrived with the Silverton sisters to escort her to the stables where their mounts would be waiting. Aunt Phillida bid her have a fun day and gave her a kiss on the cheek. "I shall use this day to relax. I think I may write your mother and tell her of our stay thus far, then perhaps I will nap. I may reread *Guy of Warwick*. 'Tis a lovely romance. Or mayhap I will read some of John Donne or Edmund Spenser's poetry. 'Twill be a peaceful day, and I shall not worry about you for I know you are in Lord Albin's care."

Elizabeth wondered how her aunt would feel had William been escorting her. She had not mentioned that William would be joining the outing. Aunt Phillida did not know she had seen him twice since the palace ball and would have seen him more did he not keep traipsing off with Sir Jeremy. She would not worry about her aunt's approval this day. This day she meant to enjoy to its fullest. She would see Annis, and her friend would be united with her husband. And she would see William. Hopefully kiss him. The thought of kissing him set her heart to fluttering and had her stomach turning flips. Would the ground tremble when he kissed her?

Lady Harbinger's courtyard was a bustle when Elizabeth and her companions arrived. Lord Albin had also provided the Silverton sisters with their mounts, but in an aside, he informed Elizabeth he had given her the best horse. She admitted the chestnut gelding was a fine animal, spirited, but he had a tender mouth so was easy to handle. As the horses clattered into the cobblestone courtyard, Elizabeth looked about for Annis and William. She spotted Annis and Sir Jeremy but disappointment stabbed her as William was nowhere in sight. A footman helped her from her horse and led it away, and she hurried to join Annis. "Oh, you are here. I am so glad. I feared something might go awry," she said, hugging Annis.

Annis looked happier than Elizabeth had ever seen her. She sparkled – her bright blue eyes danced, her smile shone, her cheeks glowed a rosy pink. Dressed in a gray habit with blue trim and with a small flat brimmed hat perched atop her golden hair, she joyously gripped Sir Jeremy's arm. "Dear Elizabeth, you cannot imagine how kind Lady Harbinger has been. She sent two footmen and her own chair to bring me here, and she has furnished me with a mare that she assures me is gentleness itself. Aunt Beata is utterly overcome. Yesterday, when Lady Harbinger visited to invite me on this outing, she was so grand, she had Aunt Beata near slavering."

Looking up at Sir Jeremy, Annis added, "Jeremy tells me we owe this whole day to Mister Hayward. 'Twas his scheme that lured Lord Creighton away. And 'twas he who asked Lady Harbinger to extend an invitation in person to me that my aunt could not refuse. Jeremy and I have not been able to thank him enough."

Elizabeth looked about. "Is he here? I would also like to thank him."

She not only wanted to thank him on behalf of her friend, she wanted to see him. Wanted to bask in the warmth of his smile. Wanted to thrill to the clasp of her hands in his. Oh, where was he!

"He went off with an acquaintance," Sir Jeremy said. "I knew not the gentleman, but he was intent upon asking William, ah, Mister Hayward about some coal shipment from Durham."

Elizabeth knew William styled himself a broker, but she had no idea what that meant. He told her that he helped people make wise investments, but how he determined what might be a wise investment, she could not guess. Nor did she care. She but wanted to find him. She spotted him advancing toward her. He had just left Lady Harbinger. Jealousy stung her like a wasp.

"Lady Elizabeth, you look charming. Russet becomes you," he said. His hands outstretched, he reached for hers. She let him take her hands, but she gave him no welcoming smile. If he noticed her reserve, he gave no indication. He smiled brilliantly down at her, and despite her resolve to control her emotions, her heart fluttered. She found herself returning his smile and pushing thoughts of Lady Harbinger out of her mind. Could they not be but friends?

"Mister Hayward, Mistress Blanchard and Sir Jeremy have been telling me that you are responsible for their happiness this day. You must tell me of your exploits."

"I promise to tell all do you allow me to ride beside you today. Am I not too bold, I must tell you I have missed you and have looked forward to this outing."

Elizabeth's pulse quickened. He missed her! "Yes, do ride beside me. I would have it no other way." Had she been too brazen? What did she see in his eyes? Pleasure in her words?

The clanging of a bell pulled her thoughts away. She glanced over her shoulder. A footman, swinging a cow bell, stood on the steps to Lady Harbinger's house. Arms akimbo, Lady Harbinger stood two steps above him and waited for her guests to quiet. William put his hand on Elizabeth's elbow and a tingle shot up her spine. He turned with her to face Lady Harbinger.

Elizabeth wished the lady did not look so beautiful. Her smile was radiant, her voice a seductive purr as she greeted her assembly. A peachy-yellow hat trimmed with a gold band and gold feather adorned her head. She wore a matching peach habit and had a black cloak slung over her shoulders. Her teeth gleamed white against rosy lips, and her honey-colored eyes glowed like polished gold. Everyone grew quiet to hear her soft voice.

"I welcome all of you and thank you for joining me on this resplendent morning. I prayed for sunshine, and I thank the Lord in his heaven for granting us this lovely spring day. I have asked Lord Millbourne and Mister Salton to lead us today. When we arrive on the hill overlooking London, you will find chairs, blankets, food and drink awaiting you. Warming fires will be handy to any who might be chilled by the ride. So, we are ready. Let us mount up!"

A cheer rang out, and the partiers hurried to claim their horses. William escorted Elizabeth to her horse, but Albin was there to assist her into the saddle. "Ah, Hayward, glad you have returned. Knew you would not miss Lady Harbinger's event." The lord cupped his hands to give Elizabeth a boost up. "I have loaned Lady Elizabeth Fedor. Means Divine Gift in Greek."

"And he is divine," Elizabeth said, placing her foot in Lord Albin's hands.

"I shall get my horse and be with you again in but a moment," William said as Elizabeth settled onto her side-saddle and took the reins proffered her by a footman.

"What is this," Lord Albin said, "you joining us rather than Lady Harbinger?"

"How could I desert the sun for naught but the moon," William said with a flourish of his hand. "But a moment, dear lady," he added and was gone.

Elizabeth pondered his words as she watched his tall figure move through the mass of people and horses. That he preferred her company to Lady Harbinger's was encouraging. But that Lord Albin was surprised William would not be riding with Lady Harbinger had to mean some sort of relationship other than friendship existed between him and their lovely hostess.

Lord Albin mounted his horse and said something Elizabeth did not hear due to the resounding clip clop of horses' hooves on the cobblestones as the cavalcade exited Lady Harbinger's courtyard. William drew up beside her, smiled, and together they fell in behind Lord Holcomb and Lady Florence Silverton. Elizabeth meant to enjoy the day. She would think about William and Lady Harbinger some other day. This lusty day was heaven made for fun and frolic.

❧ ❧ ❧ ❧

The ride through the narrow crowded streets that led out of the city lent little opportunity for conversation, but William was content to ride beside Elizabeth and revel in her nearness. He inwardly chuckled over Albin's discomfiture. He had outmaneuvered his friend, forcing him to ride beside Appolonia Silverton. The pulsing streets did little to halt that young woman's incessant chattering. William was thankful Elizabeth was not of that nonsensical mode, especially as he intended to make her his wife. Substantial dowry or not, phenomenal beauty or not, he would not wed a woman who could not mind her tongue.

Once they left the city behind, the road widened and Albin and Lady Appolonia edged their horses up beside William's and Elizabeth's. Their presence prevented William telling Elizabeth how he lured Creighton out of London or from discussing his next plan. But he was in no hurry. He preferred to be alone with her when he recounted his deeds that she might more readily express her gratitude for his endeavors. Glancing over his shoulder, he saw Annis and Sir Jeremy were engrossed in each other and had little awareness of anything going on around them.

"Look you there, Hayward." Lord Albin interrupted William's thoughts. "Is that not Selby Elsworth and his sister just ahead? He is on that dun horse." Albin's voice became derisive. "Poor bit of horseflesh if ever I saw such. Not an ounce of spirit to him that I can see."

William looked to where Albin pointed. "Aye, that is Elsworth."

"Well, what I want to know is what is he doing here? You cannot tell me Lady Harbinger invited him to join our outing. Know she abhors the dunderpate."

"Hard for her to hide an outing this size," William said. "Elsworth naturally got wind of it. I understand when he received no invitation from Lady Harbinger, he told her she had no interdict on the road, and he may ride where he pleases. I believe, though, that Lady Harbinger extended an invitation to Elsworth's sister."

"Hmmm, rightly so, lady is a good sort. Not at all like Elsworth or that lurid mother of his. Too bad the lady is so plain, and I hear she is bookish."

"What do you mean she is bookish, Lord Albin?" Elizabeth asked.

William heard an edge to her voice, but Albin seemed not to notice. He jovially answered, "Bookish. Always has her nose in some book. Not womanly, prefers reading, even Latin and Greek, so I have heard, to things like dancing and shopping and gossiping."

Oh, you have done it. William could see Elizabeth bristling. "And why should a woman not enjoy reading? I enjoy reading, and I have interests other than dancing and gossiping. I do believe Mistress Elsworth most fortunate did she receive an education that included more than housewifely arts and dance and music lessons. I find women's education sorely limited."

Albin coughed a couple of times and attempted to redeem himself, but Appolonia interrupted him. "Now, Lady Elizabeth, I daresay you make a point, but I cannot think a woman's mind is meant to delve into things meant for a man's stronger mind."

"You say men have a *stronger* mind!" Scorn evident in her voice, Elizabeth leaned forward to peer around William at Appolonia.

"Why yes. I knew one poor soul, who beyond all reason, insisted on burying herself in her books and even in writing. She neglected her home, and her husband finally had to lock her in a room in the attic and take all reading matter from her in an attempt to cure her. It failed. The poor dear ended up losing her wits and jumped out the attic window. Killed her, of course. Just shows a woman's mind is weak and not meant to meddle in strenuous thoughts."

"Not meant to meddle ... why, she no doubt jumped ..." Elizabeth's protest was drowned out by a shout from Lord Albin as Lord Holcomb's horse nickered then reared and pranced.

Albin nudged his mount between Elizabeth's and Holcomb's. "I say, Holcomb, mind what you are doing! Your horse near reared into Lady Elizabeth's."

Holcomb and Lady Florence, riding before them, had been absorbed in conversation, at least the lady had been, when Holcomb's horse shied. "Could not be helped," Holcomb whined. "Squirrel darted out. Startled my horse. Lucky Lady Florence's horse is placid."

William chuckled as Albin puffed out his chest. "Luck's got naught to do with it. I provided her with a solid mount. Old Rhesus could go through a storm and ne'er be perturbed."

Despite Albin's deft juxtaposition of his horse between Holcomb's and Elizabeth's, her eyes still blazed, but to William's relief, Appolonia changed the subject. "Do tell, Lord Albin, what relation are Mister and Mistress Elsworth to Lady Harbinger?"

"Bain't no relation to the Lady. Elsworth is Lord Harbinger's nephew and heir, much to the old man's chagrin. Cannot abide the tomfool."

"Why ever not?" Appolonia asked with a measuring glance at Elsworth.

William tried to silence his friend. Insults could be hard to retract, but Albin was not one to care who he might offend or what rumors he might start. His wealth and place in the peerage assured, he seldom found reason to mind his tongue. "Man is a nit for all he will one day be the Marquess of Harbinger and be one of the wealthiest men in England."

"Will he?" Appolonia glanced again at Elsworth.

"Stands to reason. Lord Harbinger has no children. Elsworth is his brother's son."

"You have not explained why you consider him a nit, or why Lord Harbinger dislikes him so intensely," Elizabeth interjected. William was pleased she no longer seemed angry, but he wished he could redirect the conversation. He did not like Elsworth. The man was a pompous fool, but he would one day have an immense amount of money and would need someone to advise him on investments. William would prefer to stay in the man's good graces.

"His father married beneath him," Albin said. "Naught but an innkeeper's daughter, so I heard, but a slyboots. The Widow Elsworth was said to have been a beauty in her youth, but now she is a cow, a harridan. Puts on airs. And her clothes, ostentatious, grandiloquent. She must dress Elsworth as well. He looks an anile fop. Look to him there." His voice animated, Albin waved his hand in Elsworth's direction.

"Look at all that lace and those ruffles. Lord Harbinger, not having given up on begetting a son, will not give Elsworth permission to use his lesser courtesy title, Earl of Laidly, but Elsworth styles himself as such anyway. Expects to be addressed as such. But 'tis not done, and I will not so address him. I tell you outright."

Not wanting to be party to Albin's disparagement, William said, "I have had no dealings with Elsworth, but surely, Albin, you cannot fault Mistress Elsworth's dress or manner."

"Nay, how she has managed with that mother, I know not, but she is a true lady, if poor-featured. Nose is too long, mouth is shapely enough, but lips are too thin. Her eyes are too pale a blue." Albin looked to Appolonia. "Cannot compare to the blue of your eyes, Lady Appolonia."

The lady simpered and thanked him but then stated, "I believe I remember meeting Mistress Elsworth last year. I would be remiss did I not renew the acquaintance. Do please excuse me. I will jog on ahead and welcome Mistress Elsworth back to London." With a light touch of her whip to her horse's flank, she urged her mare forward to join the Elsworths.

Albin's brow creased as he watched Appolonia ride away. "I find it strange she would feel the need to reacquaint herself with Mistress Elsworth at this time."

"Do you? I cannot say I find it at all strange. Note her bright smile," William said. "Elsworth may be a tomfool, but as you say, he will one day be a rich one."

"I should like to meet Mistress Elsworth," Elizabeth said. "I admire her being bookish." She cast a glance at Albin then looked at William. "You will introduce me, will you not, Mister Hayward?"

William answered in the affirmative, but he hoped this new twist would not interfere with his plans to get Elizabeth alone. He had much to discuss with her, plus, he wanted his reward.

Chapter 12

The view looking down on London and Westminster and the serpentine Thames River from the Hampstead Heath hillside delighted Elizabeth. Standing at her side, his hand on her elbow, William pointed out distant salient features from government buildings and cathedrals to parks and museums. Others of Lady Harbinger's party were also enjoying the panorama, but some were warming themselves at the numerous campfires or had gathered under white billowy canopies where tables, laden with an assortment of culinary dishes, had been set up. Jugs of wine and barrels of ale were in ample supply, and Lord Albin, professing a thirst, had hastened to procure a mug of ale. Mug in hand, he was waylaid by Lady Harbinger, and to Elizabeth's delight, William deftly spirited her away.

William's chuckle had her gaze following his to Annis and Sir Jeremy. "Those two see none of the view," he said. "They see naught but each other."

Elizabeth smiled. William was correct. The young lovers, hands clasped, were lost in a starry-eyed gaze. She envied them their love, but not the turmoil that separated them. "I should speak to them," she said. "I have paid them little heed since we left Lady Harbinger's courtyard."

William shook his head. "They need this time together. You will have much to discuss later. And I have much to discuss with you now. You would stroll with me along the lakeshore?"

Elizabeth eagerly assented. She would be alone with William. They could wander amongst the trees and be lost to the sight of prying eyes. She could scarce control her breathing, and sharp little tingles prickled up her spine. In leading her toward the lake and away from the other members of the outing, William again chuckled. "What do you find amusing now?" she asked.

"Lady Harbinger is a mastermind," he answered, and jealousy stung

Elizabeth. She attempted to cover her resentment of his complimentary statement of the lady she presumed to be a rival by stating, "Indeed, she is most kind to have helped Annis, even to providing her a horse."

"She has done more than that. I confided to her that I needed time alone with you to discuss our plan to unite Mistress Blanchard and Sir Jeremy. She assured me she would contrive to arrange it. And so she has. Look to your would-be suitors." He nodded to his left. "There is Wainwright in hot conversation with Lord Millbourne. No doubt discussing the merits of some racehorse. Both are fanatics. Lady Harbinger would have asked Millbourne to initiate the topic. Look there." He pointed to Lord Chardy. "Poor soul will be sorely tried by the time he escapes Mistress Maida Kirkwood. She is a close friend of Lady Harbinger's, and did the lady ask Mistress Kirkwood to keep Chardy engaged, that she will do. Lord Holcomb is still in Lady Florence's clutches, and Albin has been passed from Lady Harbinger to Mister Salton. So you see, your courtiers are occupied, unless you have some that have escaped my notice." He looked down at her in a way that set her pulse to racing. How observant he was to know her principal suitors. To go to that effort, he had to have more than a casual interest in her. Surely Lady Harbinger could not be involved with William, or the lady would not so readily help William in his endeavor to gain time alone with Elizabeth.

Hoping she looked provocative, she cocked her head and glanced sideways at William. "I agree, Lady Harbinger has been most accommodating, but do please tell me how you lured Lord Creighton out of London."

His half smile and sensual gaze told her she had succeeded in arousing him. Pleased, she smiled inwardly and turned her attention to his tale recounting his and Sir Jeremy's adventure at Annis's home. She praised his ingenuity and added, "Annis will be happy to know her servants are loyal to her and are eager for her to return to her home with Sir Jeremy at her side."

"They are indeed," William said, "and that brings us to our next plan. I warn you, 'tis not without its risks, but I do think 'twill further their cause."

Elizabeth stopped and looked up at him. "Do tell. I am certain Annis will be willing to do whatever she must to stop the annulment of her marriage. And can I help in any way, I will."

"The suggestion was Lady Harbinger's." He twisted his mouth and shook his head. "I should have thought of it." He paused, then looking down at her, blurted out, "They must consummate their marriage. And does Mistress Blanchard get with child, even better."

Elizabeth blushed, but clapped her hands. "What a splendid idea."

William looked relieved she had not taken offense at his immodest statement, and he rushed on. "As I said, 'tis not without risks. We may anger King Charles, and he might become even more determined to support Creighton. Or they might be found before they consummate the marriage, and Creighton could well have Annis locked in her room until the annulment is arranged. He will no doubt be returning any day now. We must act fast. Tomorrow."

"Tomorrow? Very well, but where are they to go?"

"That we have yet to determine. Lady Harbinger would offer her home were her in-laws not there. I could offer my lodgings but they are bound to be searched, as will yours. Inns will also be searched. Though 'tis far from desirable, I can think of only one person I would feel safe asking to help us. Lord Albin. But he is not apt to want to become involved. He will be worried about offending the King. That is where we must rely on you, Lady Elizabeth. I do think you could convince him to hide them, but you would then be in his debt. That I cannot like."

Lowering her gaze, Elizabeth shook her head. "I cannot like being in his debt, yet I am in yours, and I mind it not." She looked up and was pleased her words had brought a glow to his eyes. She shrugged. "Still, if I must, for Annis, I will do so." She did not want to give Albin the idea she favored his address, yet did he put himself at risk at her request, he would think he had a claim to her affection. Nor would she want any harm to come to those who were helping Annis and Sir Jeremy. "I have less fear of the King than some might, for my uncle is a dear friend to him," she continued, "and Uncle Ranulf is coming to London very soon. 'Tis his lodgings that my aunt and I stay in. I am willing to risk the King's ire, for I know my uncle will protect me from his wrath. But what of you, Mister Hayward? What peril do you risk?"

He patted her hand that rested on his forearm. "Nothing more than banishment from the court for a few months, I would think. Sir Jeremy is apt to be fined, but he can afford it."

She nodded thoughtfully. "'Tis not too drastic. Hopefully you will not be banished or Sir Jeremy fined, but I do think 'tis an excellent plan, and I will do what I must to secure Annis and Sir Jeremy lodgings. Do I speak to Lord Albin today?"

"'Twill likely be necessary do we fail to contrive another solution. We will turn to Albin as a last resort. The day is yet ahead of us. We may hit upon another plan." He took her hand and tucked it under his arm. "For now, let us enjoy the beauty of this day." He resumed their stroll, and she made no protest. They were headed toward a copse of trees that abutted the lake.

Glancing back over her shoulder, she saw others of their party strolling toward the lake. It was a glorious day, the wind was dying down to naught but a gentle breeze, the sky was a clear dazzling blue, the grass underfoot was bright and springy, and the woods they were entering displayed a medley of colorful greens. She tilted her head and sniffed the air. It smelled fresh and clean and so invigorating after the ever present scent of smoke that hung like a pall over London.

William led her down a narrow path that meandered in and out of the trees beside the lake. For a time she could hear voices in the distance, but soon the only sounds she heard were the birds singing and her own breathing. Even their footsteps were muted on the soft leafy trail. They came out into a small glade of verdant green ornamented with bluebells and tiny white daisies. The sunlight hitting the lake cast glistening diamonds across it. Elizabeth mouthed a silent, "Oh." She could not have imagined a more romantic spot for a first kiss. And William was going to kiss her. She knew he was.

Gazing out over the lake, she was very much aware of William's presence behind her. "'Tis lovely, is it not," she said, her hand sweeping out to indicate the lake, but in looking back at William, she found him looking at her. "'Tis lovely indeed," he said, his eyes meeting hers.

Lost in his gaze, she finally murmured, "I was speaking of the lake."

"Were you?" He turned her to face him. "Could you but see yourself, you would know why I meant you. The sunlight glinting on the wisps of hair framing your face under that saucy hat, your cheeks aglow with a rosy freshness, your eyes sparkling like twin jewels, indeed, you are resplendent." His eyes went to her lips and lingered there.

A fiery heat crept up Elizabeth's neck to her face. She licked her lips, anticipation nipping at her. Her eyes went to his lips. Crooked in a half smile, they were tantalizing, tempting, mesmerizing. His hands on her shoulders burned through her clothing to her flesh as he drew her against him. Of their own accord, her hands went to his chest, slipping inside his coat to his silk waistcoat. His chest felt firm, muscled, powerful. He bent, and his lips brushed hers – lightly, ever so lightly. She could almost believe she had imagined it had his lips not returned to claim a longer kiss. Soft, so soft. A luscious warmth caressed her, enfolded her. His lips firmed on hers and became more demanding. She met his demand with a compulsion of her own, her hands sliding up around his neck. She clung to him as his tongue traced her lips. She parted her lips, and his tongue slipped inside to find hers. Shock waves reverberated through her. She had no idea whether the ground trembled or not for she was floating in the air.

She could not say how long they were lost in their kiss, but eventually William groaned and loosened his hold on her. She continued to cling to him as his lips moved from hers to plant a light kiss on the tip of her nose. He kissed her eyelids, her forehead, and finally reached up to unclasp her hands from around his neck. "My beautiful love, my dear Lady Elizabeth, you cannot know the passions you arouse in me. Would I was a poet that I could express my fervor."

Still amidst the clouds, Elizabeth thought she preferred the fervor he had demonstrated to any poem he might compose. Thrilled by the passion he aroused in her, she would be quite willing did he wish to continue the demonstration, but he instead distanced himself from her. His hands knotted into fists, he beat them against his thighs and stalked around the glade a time or two before returning to her. "Though enamored by your beauty and the sweetness of your kiss," he said, "I am cognizant of the need to observe propriety. I would love naught more than to spend the rest of the day here in this mystical glade with you. I want to know you better. I want to talk of nonsensical things as lovers will do. But we will be missed. We must return to the others. First though, I must need straighten your hat." He adjusted her hat on her head, tugged at her cloak so it was straight on her shoulders, and again dropped a kiss on her nose. "Had you any idea how adorable you look, you would ne'er entrust your modesty to a rogue like me."

She ached to be pressed against him, but to her disappointment, he had himself under control. Straightening the collar on his coat, she said, "I am willing to take my chances with you any time. You have proven how trustworthy you are by all you have done to help Annis and Sir Jeremy. You have shown kindness and courage. We will never be able to thank you enough."

Taking her hands in his, he gazed into her eyes. "Tell me I may hope that someday I will have more than just your gratitude." He drew her closer, but did not take her in his arms, though she leaned forward in expectation of an embrace. "Might I dare hope to win your love? You must know you have already stolen my heart." He shook his head. "Nay, not stolen, I have given it freely, without reserve. 'Tis yours to do with as you will."

Elizabeth giggled. She could not help herself. His kiss had entranced her, but his speech was too glib. It broke the mood that had held her transfixed. "Prettily spoken, Mister Hayward, but I conceive you have used such wooing words before, have you not?"

He stared at her, then his mouth quirked. He tilted his head back in an uproarious laugh. He laughed so hard tears sprang to his eyes, and he released her hands to pull a kerchief from his pocket to wipe his eyes. His amusement at last spent, he recaptured her hands. "For an innocent, you are too astute. I may have used similar blandishments before, though I do swear to you, milady, I have ne'er before truly meant them. No doubt my felicitous tongue comes from growing up on the border with Wales. The Welsh do ever speak in such honeyed, melodious phrases, and I was often exposed to their cajolery."

"Blame whom you might," she replied. "I prefer plain speech. As to my heart, my gallant knight, you have made a good start at winning it." She smiled at the light that jumped into his eyes. He had proclaimed he loved her, but did he mean it? Yes, he was attracted to her, and yes, she aroused his passion, but did she not have a substantial dowry, would he be courting her? She had no doubt she had fallen in love with him. But she needed to be certain her love was reciprocated. She had no doubt he had had other lovers. He was too handsome and too skilled to have lived a celibate life. She decided she would be happier did she not know about them. All the same, she would let him dangle awhile yet. Slanting her eyes, she glanced up at him. "For now, as you say, we will be missed. In addition, we must make arrangements for tomorrow with Annis and Sir Jeremy. And you promised to introduce me to Mistress Elsworth. Plus, I am hungry."

"Right on all counts," he said, taking her arm and tucking it under his. "Let us return to the party and see have we been missed."

❀ ❀ ❀ ❀

Breaking from the woods, Elizabeth spied Mistress Elsworth standing alone and looking out at the sweeping vista. Insistent they take advantage of the moment, she urged William to escort her to the lady's side. Mistress Elsworth turned as they neared. She looked surprised they had chosen to join her but was gracious when William made the introductions.

As Lord Albin had said, Blythe Elsworth was no great beauty, but Elizabeth did not think her as plain as he had intimated. She was slim, but shapely. Mayhap her nose was a tad pointed and her lips thin, but her eyes, though the palest blue, were alive with humor and intelligence. "I see you are appreciating the view," Elizabeth said.

"Indeed, 'tis lovely, but I am mostly enjoying being out of London. I cannot say I like the city – the smells, the constant noise, all the people. I prefer the country, but Mother will come to London for a couple of months every spring. I believe she continues to think I will somehow find some lord, even if naught but a baron, willing to marry me."

"I would not think that too difficult, did you wish it," Elizabeth stated.

Blythe laughed. It was a sweet laugh and fell gently on the ears. "My uncle has kindly settled an adequate dowry on me, but I fear it has done little more than bring the fortune hunters to my door. I cannot expect a handsome lord to fall madly in love with me, but can I find a man who appreciates my need to expand my knowledge – a man not afraid or intimidated by what my brother, Selby, calls my bookishness, I would consider such a marriage." She laughed again and glanced from Elizabeth to William and back to Elizabeth. "Does such a man exist, he would also have to accept my injudicious tongue and my complete lack of social etiquette. I have not the art of polite conversation. Here we have but just met, and I have bored you with my personal revelations. Worse yet, I have not the good sense to be embarrassed. Selby says I am hopeless."

Elizabeth laughed. "I cannot find you in the least hopeless. Nor do I fault your honesty or desire to learn. I have often considered my education too limited. I am not sure I would want to study Latin or Greek – I struggled enough with French, but I find geography fascinating."

Before Blythe could reply, their conversation was interrupted by Lord Albin. Advancing toward them, Mister Salton in tow, he was calling to Elizabeth. "There you are, Lady Elizabeth. I have been searching all over for you."

Elizabeth turned to greet him and Mister Salton. "We were strolling along the lake. Then we saw Mistress Elsworth, and I insisted upon an introduction. And now we have met, I have no doubt we will become the best of friends. We have so much in common."

"Indeed, indeed." Albin bowed toward Blythe. "Mistress Elsworth, always a pleasure to see you. You, of course, know Mister Salton." He turned to indicate Lady Harbinger's youthful gallant who, at his lady's request, appeared to be glued to Albin's side.

Blythe had time but to acknowledge Lord Albin and Mister Salton before they were joined by Mister Wainwright and Lord Millbourne, and then by Lord Chardy and Mistress Kirkwood. Elizabeth was frustrated. Her private chat with Blythe was at an end. She was being mobbed by her courtiers. Other members of the party, people she did not know, began clustering about them. She was forced to acknowledge one introduction after another. Normally, she would have been pleased to be making so many new acquaintances closer to her own age, but she found Blythe Elsworth much to her liking and wanted to become better acquainted with her.

Finding herself the center of the group, she noticed Blythe had been maneuvered to the edge. She caught her eye, and Blythe gave her a sympathetic smile. She had felt sorry for Blythe, no one paying her any

94

mind. But 'twould seem Blythe felt sorry for her.

Elizabeth was pleased William remained at her side. His hand firmly griping her elbow, he allowed no one to come between them. Occasionally he whispered in her ear some trivial, but entertaining, tidbit about the various individuals vying for her attention. His anecdotes often caused her to laugh at inappropriate moments, forcing her to apologize to the person conversing with her. She had no idea why she had become so popular until a young woman introduced as Mistress Erwina Ogden leaned in close and asked, "Dear Lady Elizabeth, do tell us what you said to King Charles to so anger him? You must know your mettle has been all the talk this past sennight. There have been so many stories bantered about. I know I would never have the courage to confront the King at his dinner. I have been told it concerned a love you have been denied," she glanced up at William and smiled saucily, "but I cannot credit that."

William whispered in Elizabeth's ear, "Ask her who the young knave was she slipped out to meet on Lady Harbinger's balcony last night."

Though she wondered about William being at Lady Harbinger's to note Erwina Ogden's tryst, Elizabeth giggled and hissed, "Do hush, I cannot ask such a question." She looked back at Mistress Ogden. "I have naught to say concerning my foolish behavior. I have much to learn. I hope I may not again present myself as such a dunderpate."

The woman sniggered, but her next comment was forestalled by Lady Harbinger's dulcet voice. Despite its soft tones, it sounded clearly over the hubbub. "Lady Elizabeth, I have need of you. You did promise to sample the cheese and tell me is it truly Cheshire cheese. I paid a goodly sum on the assurance it was. Yet, Lord Millbourne did portend he could not be certain. Who better to give an opinion than one who is from Cheshire?" Elizabeth had no recollection of making such a promise, and a glance at Lord Millbourne told her he had no idea he had complained. Happily extricated from the assemblage, she trailed after Lady Harbinger. William maintained his grip on her elbow, and in looking back, she saw Blythe followed them.

Upon reaching the tables spread with an array of foods, Lady Harbinger said, "I know you have not eaten. You must be hungry." She looked to Blythe. "You, too." She patted Blythe's hand. "I am glad you have met Lady Elizabeth. A woman of good sense is hard come by. I feel certain you two will find you have much in common." She looked at Elizabeth. "You may confide in Blythe. I assure you, she is trustworthy, and like you, is not lacking in sensibility. Now, enjoy your meals. I will keep the mob away." Before heading off in the direction she had come, she said, "Do you seek Mistress Blanchard and Sir Jeremy, they are under that tree." She pointed to a large oak where the couple, plates of food on their laps, sat on a blanket.

Elizabeth decided to take Lady Harbinger's advice and trust Blythe with their scheme. She needed an excuse not to join her aunt's shopping expedition to the Exchange on the morrow, and rather than plead a headache, she could say she preferred to become better acquainted with her new friend. She had no doubt Aunt Phillida would be pleased with Blythe. Hand to her heart, Aunt Phillida had sworn she could not endure many more outings with the simpering Silverton sisters. Elizabeth shared her sentiments.

Their plates piled high with cheeses and dried fruits, joints of various fowl from chicken to pigeon to dove to duck, and wedges of mincemeat pie, they joined Annis and Sir Jeremy.

Chapter 13

Elizabeth and William decided they would not ask Lord Albin to house the couple until the following morning. Better they not give him the night to worry and decide he was too leery of offending King Charles to help them. Blythe, when told of the lover's plight, immediately fell in with their plans. "I shall be at your service in any way I can, Lady Elizabeth," she proclaimed.

"Thank you, and you must please call me Elizabeth. I feel we are already friends and need not stand on formalities," Elizabeth said.

Blythe gripped her hand. "I feel the same. You must call me Blythe."

By the time they finished their meals, and footmen collected their plates and refilled their mugs, they had formulated their plans. On the morrow, Annis would pretend weariness from the outing. When her aunt took her nap after their noon meal, Annis would slip out and join Sir Jeremy, who would be waiting nearby. They would then join Elizabeth and William, and unless they hit upon another idea, they would go to Lord Albin's. Once the lovers were settled, Elizabeth and William would meet Blythe outside the Whitehall Palace gallery. She and Elizabeth would return to Elizabeth's lodgings acting as though they had spent the day together. Aunt Phillida should never be the wiser.

Elizabeth was aquiver with excitement and some trepidation. She could tell by Annis's nervous twisting of the lace kerchief in her hands that she felt the same, but her friend was resolute. She was prepared to take whatever risks necessary to be with the man she loved. Her eyes glistening, Annis looked at Sir Jeremy. "My dear husband, to think that tomorrow night I shall be in your arms, never again to be parted. We can never thank our dear friends enough."

"We have been thanked enough," William said, rising and extending his hand to first help Elizabeth up and then Blythe. "Come. I see Lord Albin advancing in our direction. We must jolly him. 'Twill soon be time to leave, and we want to end this day in his good favor."

Taking William's words to heart, Elizabeth headed off, hands outstretched. "Lord Albin, there you are. I was but telling Mistress Elsworth how gracious you were in lending me such a wondrous horse for this outing." She noted Albin no longer had Mister Salton in tow. She spotted that young man paying homage to Lady Harbinger who was allowing him and Lord Chardy to escort her toward the lake.

Albin grasped Elizabeth's hands in his and beamed under her praise. "My dear Lady Elizabeth, you must know I was most pleased to provide you with a horse. Happy to be of service any time." He bowed his head to Blythe, but his gaze immediately returned to Elizabeth. "Would you care to take a stroll about the lake?"

"Oh, sir, I wonder might we instead stroll by that pond?" She gestured airily over her shoulder. "I am quite certain I saw adorable baby ducks. Shall we see are they still there?"

"Indeed we shall," Albin assented, drawing her arm through his. William took Blythe's arm and followed after them. Annis and Jeremy chose to remain on their blanket.

"We have much catching up to do," Annis said, her eyes bright with her happiness.

At their approach, the mother ducks, amidst a deal of quacking, herded their broods into the water. Elizabeth laughed and patted Lord Albin's forearm. "Hear those mothers scold us!"

Albin joined her laughter and put his hand over hers. "'Tis nice to have this time with you. I declare I cannot fathom what got into Salton today. Could not escape the man. Barely know the fellow but for some reason he insisted upon laying open his feelings to me." He leaned closer and whispered conspiratorially, "He is in love with Lady Harbinger. Told him he was wasting his time. Lady is married. Needs to find himself an unmarried woman." He shook his head. "Asked me to suggest some women to him. Now, I ask you, how should I know what kind of woman he might like. Asked him that, too, but he insisted he held me in great esteem and would listen to my advice." Albin puffed out his chest. "What could I say to that?"

"Indeed, what could you do but help the poor man," Elizabeth said, hoping she sounded suitably admiring.

"Thought to introduce him to Mistress Ogden, but no, she would not do. Nice enough young woman, I thought and told him so, but ..."

"Lord Albin," Elizabeth interrupted. She knew she needed to flatter Albin, but she had had enough of his soliloquy. "Look at all the lovely flowers. I do think we should fashion some flower necklaces. What say you?" She smiled, widened her eyes, and cocked her head. It worked. He was most willing to acquiesce to her suggestion. Blythe and William were agreeable to the proposal, so while William and Albin gathered the flowers, Blythe and Elizabeth set to fashioning garlands and wreaths. In short order, they were joined by the Silverton sisters and their escorts Selby Elsworth and Lord Holcomb and by Elizabeth's other two suitors, Mister Wainwright and Lord Chardy. They were accompanied by the Mistresses Kirkwood and Ogden.

Amidst the laughing and chattering, Elizabeth caught William's eye. He flashed her a smile. She was devoting her attention to Albin, but William would be escorting her home. As William kept his horse in Albin's stable, he would be returning with them at the end of the day. Albin would need to escort the Silverton sisters home, and William would see to Elizabeth. She hoped they would not anger Lord Albin, but did she ride beside him back to town and cajole him all the way, he should be mollified. Her other worry was her aunt. What would she say to William escorting her niece home? She had yet to bring Aunt Phillida around to accepting William as a suitable courtier. Well, she would. As soon as Annis and Sir Jeremy's more pressing problem was alleviated, she could concentrate on William's and her future together.

※ ※ ※ ※

William was pleased with the day's events. On the ride back to London, he contemplated Elizabeth's kiss. It had been as sweet as he had imagined it would be. She aroused a passion in him he had had trouble tamping down. He looked forward to their marriage bed. That he had won her heart, he had no doubt. She had been as eager for their kiss as he had been. 'Twas her heated response to his kiss that had made pulling away from her so difficult. Her fervor was undeniable, and he felt certain he could have sampled more of her favors had he chosen. But she was a maiden, an innocent, despite her amorous inclinations, and he knew better than to take advantage of guilelessness. He would not win the consent of her family did he in any way despoil her.

He disliked Albin riding beside Elizabeth while he rode with Mistress Elsworth, but he no longer feared his friend might win Elizabeth's hand in marriage. She was his but for the asking, of that he was confident. He found conversing with Blythe Elsworth pleasant, and the ride ended with minimum vexation. At least he had not been stuck with Appolonia Silverton. That young woman seemed to have fixed her interest with Selby Elsworth. To William's knowledge, she had not left the future Marquess's side all day. He pitied Blythe Elsworth did her brother someday marry the enterprising Lady Appolonia. To have such an inane babbler for a sister-in-law would be painful for anyone, more so for someone of Mistress Elsworth's sensibilities.

Upon arriving at the stables, Albin relinquished Elizabeth to William's care. Albin had a card party to attend that evening and had no wish to be late. Lord Havenhurst was to be at the tables, and Albin had hopes he could convince the lord to intervene on his father's behalf and gain the King's support for a disputed land claim. "Do you escort Lady Elizabeth back to her lodgings, Hayward. I will escort the Silverton sisters to Lady Bainbridge's apartment on the way back to my rooms," Albin said.

William assented to Albin's request. He caught Elizabeth's eye, and they exchanged a smile. The day could not have been grander, and he again had Elizabeth to himself. He hoped to claim another kiss before delivering her safely to her door. Immersed in a discussion on how best to confront Albin on the morrow, they strolled down the maze of corridors leading to Elizabeth's lodgings. Upon rounding a corner, William saw two men ahead of them. By their garb – jerkins, rough leather boots that drooped at mid-calf, and neck kerchiefs opposed to cravats, he guessed them to be seaman. He wondered what they were doing in the narrow passageway. Absorbed in an argument, the men paid no heed to his and Elizabeth's approach.

Both men were young, tall, and powerfully built. They were also good looking. William had to admit the taller of the two, with his sun-bronzed skin, slim-aquiline nose, strong jaw line, and rich auburn hair floating about his broad shoulders, was even better looking than he was. He would not want to be competing for Elizabeth's hand with that young man. Suddenly Elizabeth screeched. He started, his heart rushing up to pound in his ears. The next thing he knew Elizabeth left his side to fling herself at the taller youth. The man turned in time to catch her in his arms. He at first looked as startled as William felt, but a wide grin quickly replaced his stunned mien.

Elizabeth was laughing and crying and repeating over and over, "Oh, Garrett, Garrett, Garrett, how came you here? Oh, Garrett! 'Tis really you!"

William's stomach churned. Was this some long lost love? Elizabeth was so thrilled to see the man. Had he been mistaken in thinking she had fallen in love with him? The man she called Garrett lifted her off her feet and whirled her in a circle. He finally set her down and proclaimed, "Lord, Elspeth, we have been lost in this maze of passageways for I cannot say how long. What luck you should happen upon us. We have been searching for your rooms. Brennan said we should head down this corridor, but I was leaning toward the one you came from."

Elizabeth laughed, "You would both be wrong. 'Tis down this passageway you are standing in. Oh, but, Garrett, let me introduce you to Mister William Hayward." She reached out a hand to draw William forward. "Mister Hayward, this is my youngest brother, Garrett D'Arcy." She turned slightly. "And this knave is his friend and mate, Brennan Kilkenny."

Though William could not image how Elizabeth's brother came to be in the passageway, relief flooded him when Elizabeth introduced the handsome youth as her brother, but the lulling was short lived as the Irishman declared, "Come, pretty colleen, are you having no welcoming hug for an old friend?"

With a laugh, Elizabeth turned to embrace the Irishman. Jealousy nipped at William's innards. As bronze-skinned as Elizabeth's brother, Kilkenny was near as good looking. His hair was a brighter red, and he was not as tall, but he had a charming if crooked smile, and the roguish look in his sky-blue eyes could well appeal to a woman of Elizabeth's temperament.

When released from the embrace at her brother's nudge to his friend,

Elizabeth asked, "How is it you are here? I had no word you were coming. And where is Captain Ridgely."

"You must know, I am master of my own merchant ship?"

She nodded. "Mother, in her recent letter, did tell me Father had so gifted you."

"I am captain now, and Ridgely is my first mate." He shook his head. "Ah, make no such face. He is content to have it so. For such has he trained me. At present, he minds the ship while we came in search of you and Aunt Phillida. How does our aunt?"

Elizabeth's grimace at her brother's words concerning the non-present Ridgely, added another worry to William's mounting disquiet. Did Elizabeth favor the fellow? His earlier cockiness rapidly disappearing, William believed his presence forgotten as Elizabeth chatted gaily with her brother and the bold Irishman.

"Aunt Phillida does well, though she is eager to return to Harp's Ridge," Elizabeth answered her brother, but a concerned look replaced her look of joy. "How does our mother?"

"She has her good days and those not so good," Garrett said, his face mirroring hers. "On clear days, her breathing seems almost normal. Rainy days, the consumption saps her strength, and she stays indoors near the fire. Hannah, ever the devoted nurse, makes her drink sweet wine possets. Her granddaughter, Rilletta, cheers her, and the new baby, Claresta, brightens her eyes, but she is saddened that she can no longer sing to them. She has not the breath."

"And Eugenia, does she pine that she bore another daughter?"

"Nay. Robert complains not. He dotes on his daughters. Eugenia is healthy and strong. Robert doubts not the next birthing will bring him a son and heir to the earldom."

Kilkenny stepped between the two. "Sure an' I am at wondering might you be doing your reminiscing somewhere besides this drafty passageway? I am near dying of thirst, and I have no doubt Lady Grasmere has some fine wine on hand. Would I be wrong, Lady Elizabeth?"

Elizabeth laughed. "You would be correct, Mister Kilkenny. Would you but follow us?" She turned to William and revived his spirits by taking his arm. "Where do you stay?" she asked over her shoulder. "Will you take supper with us?"

102

"Aye, we may sup with you, then 'tis back to the ship. We will be staying aboard her. She is a grand ship, Elspeth. Mayhap tomorrow, I can fetch you to come see her. She has a goodly sized captain's quarters, and Ridgely had her bilge pumped and cleaned before we set out on this, our maiden voyage, so the smell is not yet rancid. I have named her the *Lady Alesia*."

Elizabeth stopped abruptly, jerked free of William, and whipped about to face her brother. "You have not so named her!"

Garrett stiffened. "And why should I not. Father gave his permission for me to wed Alesia, do I return from this voyage with a profit and so prove I can support a wife."

William could see this news did not please Elizabeth. She shook her head. "I cannot say I like the lady, but as you have chosen her, I will accept her as a sister." She smiled and took her brother's hand. "I am certain the lady is virtuous, and I will not slander her. Forgive me?"

"You are forgiven, dear sister. Once you know Alesia better, you will come to love her."

"No doubt," Elizabeth replied, but by the look on her face that her brother did not see, William suspected Elizabeth was none too assured of any such sentiment.

"Do we get that drink, milady, or must I be returning to the ship to reprieve my thirst?" Kilkenny asked. "I am beginning to think I will be getting a drink sooner aboard ship than with you and Garrett forever blathering."

Elizabeth stopped again and narrowed her eyes. "Where are you anchored, Garrett?"

"Off Billingsgate. We await our time at the wharf."

"You will be staying here in London for a while?"

Garrett laughed. "A good while. We must go through customs, sell our cargo, then collect a new cargo before we set off on our voyage. We plan to sail to the West Indies and mayhap the American colonies."

"And you say your ship is comfortable? You have a roomy cabin? A nice bed?"

Garrett cocked his head. "As I said, I can take you to see it tomorrow, do you wish? But what are all these questions?"

Elizabeth caught William's hand and looked up at him. "Mister Hayward, would not Garrett's ship be a much better place to hide Mistress Blanchard and Sir Jeremy than Lord Albin's rooms? No one could think to look aboard a ship." She looked back at her brother. "Garrett, we have a great favor we must ask of you." She glanced at Kilkenny. "And Mister Kilkenny, I am afraid you will have to return to your ship for that drink. Aunt Phillida must not know you are here yet."

❦ ❦ ❦ ❦

William had to admit, Elizabeth's idea to house the lovers on her brother's ship was brilliant. Her brother had needed but little convincing. "You need not house them for long, Garrett," Elizabeth pleaded. "Uncle Ranulf is due here any day, and I have no doubt he can convince King Charles that Mistress Blanchard and Sir Jeremy should not be parted."

"I am thinking 'tis a splendid idea," Kilkenny pronounced. "We Irish bear no love for the Puritans. Do we have a way to foil their goals, then I am for it."

William understood the Irishman's hatred of Puritans. In 1649 during the war in Ireland, Cromwell had condoned the slaughter of women, children, and the elderly, even those who surrendered. Livestock were killed, villages laid waste, and property confiscated. He imagined Kilkenny could well have lost property or loved ones or both.

So plans were laid. On the morrow, Garrett would have a skiff waiting at the Billingsgate main wharf to pick up the young lovers. He would see to their needs, give them privacy, and await word from Elizabeth regarding when he might hope to have his cabin back. "I understand their love," Garrett said. "Were I denied Alesia's love, I would be as desperate."

Elizabeth ducked her head, but William saw her frown. She did not approve of her brother's betrothed. He hoped her brother would not be as disapproving of him. Desirous of gaining Garrett D'Arcy's goodwill, he offered to help him secure his cargo. He knew merchants and investors and would be pleased to introduce Garrett to some. His offer was eagerly accepted. Elizabeth beamed at him, and William was confident he had advanced his campaign.

Having parted with Elizabeth's brother and his mate, they hastened their steps. "I fear we may be late," Elizabeth said. "I cannot want Aunt Phillida to think we have been imprudent. She rightfully trusts Lord Albin." Elizabeth cast a sidelong glance up at him. "She may just as rightfully mistrust you, Mister Hayward."

He laughed at her banter. She was remembering their kiss. Considering the delay, he would not get a chance at another such moment as they had shared in the woods. But the taste of her lips yet lingered with him and increased his anticipation of their next kiss. He hoped 'twould be soon.

Chapter 14

Elizabeth hid her impatience with her aunt's tardy departure. As she had surmised, Aunt Phillida was pleased she had a new friend in Mistress Elsworth and readily excused Elizabeth from accompanying her to the Royal Exchange that she might spend the afternoon furthering her new acquaintance. Even better, her aunt was taking her maid with her so Elizabeth would not have to contrive an excuse to escape Adah's watchful eye. She had but Mary to deceive. Not that she did not trust her serving maid, but if pressed by authorities, Mary might, out of fear, divulge Annis's whereabouts, did she know it.

No sooner was her aunt out the door, and Elizabeth was scribbling a note to Blythe. With escorting Annis and Sir Jeremy to Billingsgate instead of Lord Albin's apartment, she needed to change her meeting with Blythe to midafternoon. She sealed the note with a drop of wax and handed it to Mary. "After you deliver the message, you may have a couple of hours to wile away as you choose, but you are to meet me near the stairs of the Whitehall gallery at midafternoon."

Taking the note, Mary bobbed a curtsy. "Yes, Lady Elizabeth, but should I not accompany you ..."

"No. I am meeting Mister Hayward. He will bear me company until we meet later."

Mary's eyes widened, then she smiled. "As you wish, milady. I will be at the gallery as directed." She bobbed another curtsy, threw a shawl about her shoulders, and scurried out.

Elizabeth took one last look in the mirror. She bit her lips and pinched her cheeks. Satisfied with her appearance, she drew on a light cape and hurried out the door. She had arranged to meet William where they encountered her brother the previous evening. He would escort her to the Parade Grounds to await Annis and Sir Jeremy. There they could stroll without attracting undue attention. Once Annis and Sir Jeremy joined them, they would head for the river and take a wherry to the Old Swan Stairs just west of London Bridge. Having no desire to shoot the bridge, they would walk from the stairs to Billingsgate where her brother should be waiting with a skiff to take Annis and Sir Jeremy to his ship.

Annis would have to wait for her aunt to take her nap before she could slip out, so how long Elizabeth need bide with William she could not guess, but as she would be in his company, she did not care. She wondered would he take advantage of their being alone in the darkened passageway to kiss her. She hoped so. Memories of their kiss in the woods had kept her awake late into the night, but she had awakened early despite her lack of sleep. Tingling with excitement, she hastened down the narrow corridor. Such a day this would be! Annis and Sir Jeremy would be safely spirited away on Garrett's ship, and she could turn her attention to convincing her aunt that William was a worthy suitor.

Aunt Phillida had not been pleased William, instead of Lord Albin, had escorted her niece home from the Hampstead Heath outing; all the same, she courteously invited William to stay to supper. That had worked in William's favor. Aunt Phillida was not immune to his charms. He told amusing stories about his life at court, tales that included outings with King Charles. He talked of his limited memories of his mother and brought tears to Aunt Phillida's eyes. But when he attempted to explain his burgeoning business, Aunt Phillida frowned. "Mister Hayward, am I correct in remembering your father owns his land outright?"

"Yes, Lady Grasmere, he owns land that has been in our family since the time of the Conqueror, or so 'tis believed. A small parcel was added to it by King Charles when he knighted my father. All told, we now have close to nine hundred acres."

Aunt Phillida nodded. "I suppose he has a number of men and women working for him?"

William set down his fork, one of Aunt Phillida's recent purchases, and looked curiously at his hostess. "He does, some twenty permanent and seasonal workers – carters, shepherds, dairy maids, and laborers who work the fields."

Her aunt's next question did not surprise Elizabeth. "Is there a reason, sir, you choose to go into trade rather than overseeing the farming of the land as does your father?" One could not be considered of the gentry was one in trade. Though William did no manual labor, he accepted fees for his services. That put him in trade. Being in trade was worse than being the son of a yeoman farmer. Many such farmers were edging their way into the ranks of the gentry.

William smiled that beguiling smile that never failed to set Elizabeth's heart to fluttering. "My father not only oversees the work of his land, he often engages in the labor; anything from the washing and shearing of the sheep to the herding of the cows to market. 'Tis hard work, and I find I am not well suited to it." He swept his hand down the length of his body. "I prefer to be handsomely clothed, comfortably bedded without the aches and pains of a too laborious day, and I prefer the stimulating company of the court compared to the grunts of the swine and baas of the lambs. Does this disappoint my father? I think not, or he would not have encouraged my education. To maintain the style to which I have accustomed myself, I must need use my wits to my advantage. You may think my clients render me a fee for my services. I prefer to consider it an honorarium, no different than a barrister receives."

Aunt Phillida returned his smile. "You defend your dealings most elegantly, Mister Hayward. However, you are still forced to dicker with *merchants.*" Aunt Phillida's merchants sounded like a curse, so did she spit it out, though her face remained neutral, no sneer marring her comely features. "I suspect from what you have told us, you have truck with an assortment of commoners as well. All pay you a fee, or if you prefer, an honorarium, am I correct?"

William laughed, a merry, guttural chuckle. "Correct on all counts, Lady Grasmere. I have truck, as you say, with commoners and dukes alike. Even King Charles has availed himself of my services from time to time. I am honest in my dealings. I look to defraud no man. If I may, I will say I seldom have a dissatisfied client. Does my investment advice mean I have lost standing; I am no longer a member of the gentry? I have seen no such sign. I am welcome in the King's court. Have visited him in his closet, accompanied him to Newmarket. My friends and associates are attendants of the court. I have not been shunned nor cut by any courtiers. So do you worry about your niece's reputation by being in my company, I believe you can be at ease."

Aunt Phillida inclined her head. "I will withhold my judgment on that until a later date, Mister Hayward. For the present, I must say I find your discourse entertaining, and I can find no fault with your address. I will not forbid Lady Elizabeth your company."

Elizabeth let out a whoosh of air, and her aunt looked at her, though she spoke to William. "As I said, I will not forbid Lady Elizabeth your company, but I will expect all to be circumspect. I will abide no linking of your names by idle gossipers."

"Indeed not, Lady Grasmere," William said, his eyes dancing, though his mien remained sober. "I will do naught that would disparage Lady Elizabeth's good name."

What her aunt would think of William's and her current clandestine meeting, Elizabeth did not want to hazard. Hurrying her steps, she prayed no busybody would chance upon them. Rounding a corner, she saw William pacing the corridor. Upon sighting her, he hurried to her, and grasping her hands in his, pulled her to him. Out of breath, she panted as he clasped her to his chest. She loved the feel of his arms around her and nestled her head against his shoulder. He let her catch her breath, then with his finger under her chin, tilted her head up so she looked into his sea-green eyes. "So lovely," he whispered before exacting the kiss she had hoped he would claim. Blood rushed to her temples and a drumming rumbled in her ears. Did the ground tremble? So lost was she in the delicious ecstasy of his lips on hers, she had no idea.

Dazed and with her head spinning, she could do naught but cling to him when he straightened and deprived her of his lips. She stood on tiptoe in an attempt to renew the kiss, but he shook his head. "Nay, my dear Elizabeth, we dare not tarry here. As I promised your aunt, I will do naught to deprecate your good name. Take my arm and let us hasten our steps."

Elizabeth placed her hand on his forearm and let him steer her along the dimly lit passageway. She wondered if he realized he had called her by her given name. My dear Elizabeth, he had said. She loved hearing her name on his tongue, so sweet did it sound.

They had a lengthy stroll on the parade grounds before Annis and

Sir Jeremy arrived. Fearing Annis had been unable to escape her aunt's surveillance, Elizabeth greeted her friend with great fervor. Patting Annis's waist, she said, "You seem to have put on a few pounds."

Annis flushed and giggled. "I am wearing three shifts, three petti-coats, and two over gowns." She touched her head. "I have my night cap and lappet cap under my bonnet. I have three pair of stockings, two handkerchiefs, a pair of slippers, and my comb in my pockets. I dared not bring a satchel. Fortunately, Aunt Beata sent my maid to fetch more coal and to request our supper, so she was out when I slipped away. She cannot be blamed for my escape." Annis shook her head. "Aunt Beata will know Lord Creighton's wrath. I can almost feel sorry for her."

"Well, I cannot," Elizabeth said. "You are her own blood. That she should turn on you and support Creighton's dire ambition is reprehen-sible."

"Yes," Annis nodded, "but she lived in such sad straits. A spinster with no income of her own, she lived off her brother's meager charity until he died. His son, her nephew, gave her even less. Grandfather and I knew naught of her penury, or we would have had her to live with us. After my parents died, my grandfather lost contact with my mother's family. They live in Yorkshire, and it does seem so distant." Her blue eyes saddened, Annis looked up at Elizabeth. "How Lord Creighton knew of Aunt Beata, she cannot hazard. He but appeared one day at the hovel where she boarded and offered her a goodly sum to act as my guardian until he and I should be wed. She had no idea I was already married to Jeremy. Creighton seemed a savior to her. Not until we were in Creighton's coach and on our way to London did she know the truth. Then 'twas too late. She had accepted his money and signed his con-tract to act in good faith. What will become of her now, I do wonder. Creighton may well turn her out."

Elizabeth felt contrite. She pitied women who had no means of sup-port. She and her family had so much. And she had a substantial dowry that would guarantee her almost any husband she might choose. The majority of English women were not so fortunate. Feeling a similar pity for Beata Underhill as she felt for Lady Canby's companion, she patted Annis's hand. "Have no worry. Though I cannot approve of your aunt's actions, she cannot be made to suffer for her lack of income. If need be,

I will see she has the funds to return home safely."

Annis brightened, her smile giving her an angelic appearance. "Oh, Elizabeth, you and Mister Hayward have done so much for us. We will never be able to thank you enough."

"Nonsense. Just knowing we are outwitting a Cromwellian is thanks in itself. Now, we have much to tell you." Together she and William told them of the alteration to their plans. Both Annis and Sir Jeremy were delighted with the change.

"Now, 'tis certain Lord Creighton will never find us," Annis said.

"'Tis far less likely," William agreed, "but we must make haste. We must get you to Billingsgate, and we must return in time for Lady Elizabeth to meet Mistress Elsworth. Would not do for Lady Grasmere to become suspicious."

"Indeed, let us go," Elizabeth said, taking Annis's arm and heading toward the river.

Annis glanced over her shoulder at William and Sir Jeremy then looked up at Elizabeth. "Do tell, dear friend," she whispered. "Might you have a tender for Mister Hayward?"

Elizabeth offered Annis a secretive smile. "Mayhap. I do think he may be close to declaring himself. My aunt says she cannot favor him, but I think she can be brought round. Once I have her on my side, I will have no trouble gaining my father's consent." She glanced behind her and added, "That is, do I decide 'tis William Hayward I intend to marry, which I have yet to determine." She knew she lied. She had determined she would marry William even before their first kiss. She believed she had fallen in love with him the first night she met him at the King's ball. She but needed to ascertain that he loved her as much as she loved him.

They reached the river and William procured them a wherry. The tide was with them and they soon reached the Old Swan Stairs and disembarked. Sir Jeremy paid the watermen handsomely and bid them wait to take William and Elizabeth back up the river. Pudding Lane was close to hand, and they followed it to Billingsgate's main wharf where Garrett was to meet them. Elizabeth was disappointed to find instead of her brother, Sefton Ridgely awaited her. Not that she was not happy to see Ridgely. He had been her brother's teacher for the past six years. On her visits home, he had taken her with them on day cruises, and she had always enjoyed his company. He had never been annoyed by her numerous, and she guessed, foolish questions. But though pleased to give Ridgely a hug, she missed having another chance to see her brother.

"Garrett, being captain now, has more responsibilities," Ridgely said in the slight Scottish burr Elizabeth well remembered. "Customs inspector boarded the *Lady Alesia* taeday and has been poking his nose through our cargo since early morning. Wi' little more than dried haddock, barrels o' smoked cod, and some cheese for trade, you would think he would be done by now."

"Captain Ridgely," she began, but he halted her. "Nay, I am no longer the captain, Lady Elizabeth. I am the first mate, Mister Ridgely."

"That I shall have trouble getting used to, sir," she said with a smile, but then she frowned. "I have more trouble with Garrett naming his ship for Alesia, and even more trouble believing he means to marry the vixen."

Ridgely's teeth gleamed in his sandy-colored beard and his blue eyes danced. "Milady, did your mother but hear you."

Elizabeth blushed but persisted. "I will wager Mother is no more pleased."

"I am keeping my nose out o' it," Ridgely said with a chuckle. "Now, I need tae be getting back tae the ship, so let us be getting these newlyweds aboard, and we will heave off."

Elizabeth hugged Annis and patted Sir Jeremy's hand, then the two were helped into the skiff by two sailors. Ridgely doffed his hat to William, gave Elizabeth another hug, and boarded the skiff as the sailors took to their oars. Elizabeth waved and Annis and Sir Jeremy waved back until a slowly rowed barge blocked them from view. A week would pass before she would again see her friends or have a chance to visit with her brother – unless Uncle Ranulf arrived sooner.

The trip up the Thames took longer, the watermen having to row against the tide, but by midafternoon, Elizabeth and William were on time to meet Blythe and Elizabeth's maid outside Whitehall Palace gallery. William bid Elizabeth good day with the promise he would see her the following evening at an entertainment being given by Lord Chardy.

A masquerade. Elizabeth was thrilled with the prospect. She had no doubt William would pick her out, but she was eager to learn how long 'twould take him to discover her identity.

As William disappeared in the crowd, Elizabeth linked arms with Blythe. "Come, let us stroll awhile afore we confront my aunt. We must need have our tale straight ere she asks how we used our day. I hope you plan to stay to supper with us."

"I would be honored, but we must need send a message to my mother that I will be detained, and she should not send the chair and footmen for me before eight."

Elizabeth turned to Mary who trailed after them. "Have you bespoken supper?"

"Nay, Lady Elizabeth, you did give me leave to comport myself as I chose." A smile hovering about her lips, she blushed. "I went to the park with Mister Wainwright's man, Castor. They were to have various contests and footraces. Castor entered the leapfrog contest and won." She giggled and her eyes glowed. "The prize was a shiny ha'penny, and he used it to buy me a fig tart. 'Twas most tasty."

Elizabeth smiled. "I am glad you enjoyed your day. Especially after you missed seeing the dancing dogs. You know you must not mention your outing to Aunt Phillida. She would not approve your being on your own with your young man. She is responsible for your welfare and guidance as she is for mine."

"As you say, milady." Mary grinned and bobbed a curtsy.

Elizabeth glanced at Blythe. "What think you, Blythe, might we not say we strolled the park. Did we go there now, we would not be telling a lie."

At Blythe's nod of agreement, Elizabeth said, "Splendid. Now Mary, do please hasten to our rooms and let Aunt Phillida know Mistress Elsworth will be joining us for supper."

Mary bobbed another curtsy and hurried off to do Elizabeth's bidding. Elizabeth again linked arms with Blythe. "We must have something to tell my aunt of our day's conversing."

"First, do tell me all went well with Mistress Blanchard and Sir Jeremy."

Elizabeth almost skipped. "Indeed, all went better than planned due to a happy circumstance yesterday. But I will say no more on that. You must remain an innocent, do they question you."

"I am so happy for Mistress Blanchard. She is so sweet and lovely. She should not be forced to leave the man she loves and marry such an evil man as Creighton."

"Indeed she should not. Can we but keep her and Sir Jeremy hidden until my uncle arrives and can speak with King Charles on their behalf, all will be well."

"You are certain he will speak for them?"

"Oh, yes, Uncle Ranulf is a romantic. He adores his wife, though she has been crippled for close on ten years. Her coach was run off the road by a drunken stage driver. Three of my cousins were in the coach with her. Thankfully, they were uninjured but for minor scratches."

Blythe shook her head. "'Tis sad."

Nodding, Elizabeth brightened. "Come, what have we discussed this lovely spring day?"

"Flowers, mutual acquaintances, tomorrow evening's masquerade, who might be attending?"

"Yes, all good subjects, and yesterday's outing as well." She gave Blythe's arm a light squeeze. "How pleased I am we have met."

Chapter 15

Her days crammed with numerous engagements, Elizabeth marveled at how rapidly the week flew by. Her new circle of friends had her flitting from dinners to dances to suppers followed by card parties or madrigal performances. She had been to a tennis match, been bored near to tears at a new sport called cricket, and had played a game of pall mall. William had been present at near every entertainment. When he handily penetrated her disguise at Lord Chardy's masquerade and steered her out onto the balcony, they had their first opportunity to discuss Beata Underhill's frantic search for her niece.

"Mistress Underhill came to our door last evening. We had just finished supper," she said. "Mistress Elsworth dined with us, and we sat chatting over sherry. Her footmen were not due to come for her until eight. To say Annis's aunt was distraught would be no exaggeration. Aunt Phillida tried to calm her. She got her to sit and drink a glass of sherry, but it did naught to soothe her. She had awakened from her nap, but thought nothing amiss. Annis's door was shut, and she believed her tired by the previous day's outing and still napping. 'Twas not until their supper arrived, and she sent the serving maid to awaken Annis that she discovered her missing.

"Blythe and I were questioned. We expressed surprise that Annis had the temerity to flee." Elizabeth giggled. "We lied not, but we are prepared to do so does it become necessary."

"You may well need tell a falsehood once Creighton returns. He may press you most forcefully."

Elizabeth shook her head. "Nay, not with Aunt Phillida present. She will not allow a vehement inquisition. For now, she believes I spent the day with Mistress Elsworth and suspects nothing. My maid, Mary, looked at me a bit curiously, but she will say naught. Anyway, Aunt Phillida had her maid walk Mistress Underhill back to her apartment, after urging her not to worry. Annis was bound to return when 'twas time for bed.

"Of course, Annis made no such return, and her maid was at our door this morning, again asking if we had news. There is really naught Mistress Underhill can do now besides worry until Creighton returns. When do you think that might be?"

"My guess, he has determined he was tricked and is on his way back. He could arrive tomorrow, mayhap the following day." William lightly squeezed her hand. "I hope he will not frighten you."

Elizabeth smiled. "Nay, to be honest, I find the whole affair exciting. I but wish I knew how Annis and Sir Jeremy are faring on Garrett's ship. I cannot wait for this week to pass that we may visit them. And Garrett, acting as though he has but just arrived in port, can visit me and Aunt Phillida. 'Tis hard to know he is so close, yet I must be deprived of his company when 'tis well over a year since I last saw him."

"You and your brother are close?"

"Oh, yes. Naught but two years separates us in age. Before I was fostered at Aunt Phillida's, he and I were always together. He contrives to be home whenever he knows I am due to visit. Father promised to buy him a ship when he turned eighteen, did Captain ... I mean Mister Ridgely, approve his seamanship. He has been in training since he was twelve. As he now has his ship, I assume he passed whatever requisites he needed to pass."

"I believe I am not mistaken in thinking you care not for this woman, Alesia?"

Elizabeth frowned. "Alesia Hedgemont," she said with a curling of her lip. "She is the younger daughter of a neighboring baronet. "Sir Bertram is a good man, and Alesia's sister, Leona, is quite nice. But Alesia, though beautiful beyond compare, is flint hearted." She shook her head. "'Tis sad Garrett cannot see past her great beauty. She loves him not. She loves who he is, the son of the Earl of Tyneford, albeit the youngest son. He can open doors to her. Doors as a baronet's daughter, she could never enter. She has ambition." Elizabeth cocked her head. "I cannot fault her that; I can but fault her for deceiving Garrett, making him think she loves him."

"I am sorry I brought up her name. I meant not to take the smile from your face. But as you have been speaking of beauty, Lady Elizabeth, may I say tonight you are beyond compare."

Enjoying the flattery, Elizabeth laughed and batted her folded fan against his arm. "How can you say so? Am I not hidden behind a mask?" Elizabeth knew she looked good. Her gown was a pale yellow muslin over a darker yellow damask petticoat cut sharply in to accentuate her narrow waist. Her domino was golden satin, and her matching mask hid but the upper half of her face. Her hair, pulled starkly away from her face, cascaded in finger ringlets down her back. A bejeweled band circled the top of her head and was ornamented with two golden feathers.

"The gold of your mask enhances the sparkle of your eyes," William said, "and your smile, as always, is radiant. Your brilliance, this night, puts the moon and stars to shame."

She laughed again. "You wax poetic tonight, Mister Hayward. I believe you do think to turn my head." His smile and the way his eyes glistened behind his mask accelerated her pulse. She had known him immediately despite his mask, as he had known her. He wore a black domino and black half mask. She liked the black. It gave him an air of mystery. Some of the men wore scarlet, some popinjay blue, Lord Albin wore whey, a pale whitish blue. She had danced the roundel with the portly courtier and had been surprised at how light he was on his feet. When the dance ended, she had been more breathless than he, but then he did not wear stays. Her next dance had been claimed by Lord Chardy, then Lord Holcomb, and finally she found herself with William. Alone on the balcony, she hoped he would try to steal a kiss, but the chance was lost when a couple sauntered out. 'Twas Selby Elsworth and Lady Appolonia Silverton. Twittering gaily, Appolonia had eyes for no one but Elsworth, but he was looking about the balcony. William snagged Elizabeth's hand and drew her back inside before they could be accosted.

She had had two more dances with William that evening and took supper with him and Blythe, but she had no more chances at a kiss. She was beginning to believe she was winning William's heart. His concern that Creighton might verbally accost her. His notice that she did not care for her brother's beloved Alesia. The warmth in his eyes and soft tone of his voice when he flattered her. All contributed to her grow-ing confidence. She knew her dowry of an initial ten thousand pounds with an additional five hundred a year for ten years was an attractive incentive to her suitors, but was her dowry to be reduced, would her suitors cry off? Would William?

'Twould be a good test of his devotion. She cared not that he was but the son of a knight, a yeoman farmer. That he was involved in trade and was not a peer of the realm meant naught to her. He was witty, humor-ous, and caring, not to mention handsome and ever so charming. And his kisses! Her heart set to fluttering whenever she thought of the two times he kissed her. She eagerly anticipated the next time they could find a way to be alone. She hoped 'twould be soon.

She reveled in William's praise when she told him of Creighton's visit to their apartment. They were at a tennis match and had stolen away from the crowd to saunter about the park. "The man is a fop," she de-clared. "He bears no resemblance to the strict Puritan dress, nor does he exhibit the ethics he once espoused. He wears a huge wig, and the day he called on us, he wore a pease-porridge colored coat, ochre-or-ange breeches, and parti-colored stockings." She giggled. "Oh, he was a sight. Aunt Phillida could do naught but stare when the footman an-nounced him.

"His tone was harsh and he demanded I tell him where I was hiding Annis. Aunt Phillida would have none of his bombastic manner. She told him could he not speak with a civil tongue he could leave forth-with, and she called to the footman. Lord Creighton's face turned puce, and he swallowed hard a couple of times but then apologized and asked in a more polite tone did I know where he might find his betrothed, Mistress Blanchard."

Elizabeth choked on her laugh and tears sprang to her eyes. She wiped them away with a lace kerchief before resuming. "I told him did I know where he might find his *betrothed*, I would most certainly tell him, but I had no idea where said lady might be. And I cannot think I lied for in no way do I consider Annis to be his betrothed. He started getting angry again and said he wanted to search our rooms. As you may guess, Aunt Phillida would have none of that. She bid the footman escort him out. We have not seen him since. What of you?"

"You were brilliant," he said, and his warm smile sent a flush of heat coursing through her. "Yes, he accosted me. Demanded he be allowed to search my rooms. I readily acquiesced. Finding no one, he demanded to know did I accompany Sir Jeremy to Thorley Hall. I told him indeed I had, but then remembering we had an engagement in London, we returned home. He was livid." William chuckled. "I would say your description of the color of his face was most apt. He continued with his questions until I grew weary of him and kicked him out. He has not been back, but he has had a man following me. Do you look over your shoulder, you will see him even now. Man in the dull grey coat and breeches, floppy brimmed hat covering his face."

Elizabeth glanced behind her then back at William. "That cannot be good. How are we to slip away to visit Annis and Sir Jeremy with him following you?"

William laughed and patted her hand resting on his forearm. "When I am ready to be rid of him, I will lose him. For now, I prefer making it easy for him to follow me. He will grow lax, bored, and when the time comes, I will disappear and meet you at our usual spot."

"Do you think I am being followed?" Elizabeth worried.

"Nay, your rooms are in too restrictive an area. Anyone loitering about would be questioned by the King's guard that regularly patrol the maze of buildings surrounding the palace. And there are too many ways in and out to keep all entrances watched. All the same," he turned her to face him, "I think 'twould be best you go nowhere alone. I would not want you confronted by Creighton if your aunt is not near to hand."

She liked William's concern for her, and reading a sincerity in his eyes, she glowed with a warmth that radiated out to her fingertips enclosed in his strong grasp. When they resumed their stroll, she had difficulty restraining her desire to skip. Joy bubbled up inside her. The world seemed bright and wonderful – the birds' chirping had never sounded more beautiful, flowers had never blazed in such vivid hues, the grass and trees had never been greener, the sky never bluer. She wondered if William felt as bedazzled as she. She glanced up, and he smiled at her, that ever so charming smile that took the breath from her lungs. He just had to love her.

Blythe's tale of Creighton's visit to Harbinger House was equally entertaining. "Lady Harbinger refused to see him when he called," Blythe recounted. She and Elizabeth were enjoying a morning stroll along the strand, their maids following at a discreet distance. "The house steward left Creighton standing in the entry, never showed him into the parlor. When he returned and told Lord Creighton Lady Harbinger would not attend him, Creighton started shouting. That drew Mother's attention. The steward and footman were in the process of forcing Creighton out the door when Mother asked what was amiss. Creighton demanded an audience with her, and to my chagrin, Mother, being curious, consented. I should not have worried. No sooner did Creighton demand he be allowed to search the house for Mistress Blanchard than Mother became irate."

Her pale blue eyes alight, Blythe suppressed a giggle and continued, "Mother can be magnificent at times. She is tall and has put on a good deal of weight since Father died. Then with those ridiculous heels she totters around on, she is even taller and more intimidating. Drawing herself up and sticking out her chin, her eyes narrowed she glared at Creighton. 'Lord Creighton,' she says in her most haughty voice, 'was there a Mistress Blanchard in this house, I assure you I would know it. To think you would accuse Lord Harbinger's household of harboring a runaway is of the utmost insult. I demand you apologize or you will be hearing from my brother-in-law.'"

Blythe rolled her eyes. "Not that Uncle Grosvenor would deign to worry with the likes of Creighton. But Creighton could not know he would receive no more notice from my uncle than he did from Aunt Cambria, so he stammered an apology."

Elizabeth clutched her friend's hand and grinned. "Oh, do tell, did he turn puce?"

Blythe laughed and nodded energetically. "Yes. Yes, I believe that is just how I would describe the shade of his face. He looked ready to burst when Mother called to the steward to show him out. To think near a week has passed, and the lovers have not been discovered. You and Mister Hayward hid them well. Now, we but need your uncle to arrive to plead their cause."

"He keeps being delayed. His principal seat, where he resides most of the year if he is not here at Westminster, is in Surrey. Not but a day's ride from here. 'Tis a lovely estate. I was there but once. I was quite young, but I remember its beauty. Uncle Ranulf's letters have not said what keeps him, only that he has matters he must attend. No doubt he will be here soon." She did not add that once Annis and Sir Jeremy's fate was settled, she would set to work on her own.

Chapter 16

Elizabeth anxiously awaited William outside Whitehall Gallery. They had arranged a visit to her brother. A week had passed since they had spirited Annis away, and Elizabeth was eager to see Garrett. Eager to inspect his ship and excited to learn how Annis and Sir Jeremy fared. Having consummated their marriage, would they still be as enamored of each other? Would their eyes yet glow with their love for one another? She hoped so. Otherwise, her efforts would have been for naught, were they not the romantic lovers she believed them to be. After she visited with the lovers and toured the ship, Garrett was to return with her to her lodgings. She would have the whole evening with him.

Gnawing her lip, she paced back and forth, Mary trailing at her heels. Not wishing to appear immodest or be accused of unseemly conduct, she kept Mary close to hand, but her intent was to send Mary on an errand to her manteau maker as soon as William arrived. She also had a note for her aunt telling her she would be late for supper but would have a wonderful surprise for her upon her return. Aunt Phillida could not be angry when she returned with Garrett at her side.

A number of men eyed her, but the glare she imparted kept any from accosting her. She prayed she would not meet any of her new friends or acquaintances. She did not want them to see her leaving on William's arm, and Mary going off in a different direction. At last she spotted William moving with his easy stride through the meandering crowd. Her heart skipped a beat as he caught her hands in his. "Lady Elizabeth, I do hope I have not kept you waiting long."

She shook her head. "Nay, not too long. But I have been worried. Why did the King wish to see you?" He still held her hands. She knew she should pull free, especially with Mary watching, but his warm clasp helped calm her fears.

William laughed. "He wanted me to play a game of tennis with him.

He, of course, won, but I gave him a good game. Then he would talk on about a new horse he is hoping will do well at the Newmarket races. He next insisted I join him for dinner. I feared he might so insist, which is why I named such a late hour for our rendezvous. I sent a ..." He halted his sentence and looked over her head at Mary. Smiling, he said, "Ah, Mary, you are looking mighty fetching this afternoon. Have you an assignation with Wainwright's man, Castor?"

Mary blushed, giggled, and dropped a curtsy. "No, Mister Hayward, I have had me work all morning. Then I have been here pacing with Lady Elizabeth."

William looked back at Elizabeth. "Pacing? I did indeed keep you waiting."

Elizabeth frowned. "Mary exaggerates. But now she has an errand she must run for me. I am expecting a gown to be completed for Lady Worverton's dance and card party on Friday." She looked up at William. "Do you attend?"

He inclined his head. "I do. I am acquainted with Lady Worverton's son. He is but recently returned from a hunting trip in Shropshire. He extended me an invitation." Raising an eyebrow, he added, "Had he yet set eyes on you, he might not have invited me. Worverton is a fine-looking cavalier. Mind, he will try to turn your head with fancy words and flowing phrases."

Elizabeth laughed. "As do you, Mister Hayward."

A slow smile crept across his face. "I speak but the truth always, Lady Elizabeth. But are we to meet our friends, I suggest we tarry no longer."

"Indeed." She turned to Mary. "Is my gown ready, do take it home." She pulled a folded and sealed paper from her pocket and handed it to Mary. "And do give this note to my aunt. You need not tell her I am with Mister Hayward. Tell her naught but that I sent you to fetch my gown and that I told you not of my plans." Mary turned to leave, but Elizabeth caught her hand. "Tell her naught unless she presses you. I would not want you to get into trouble with my aunt."

Mary bobbed a curtsy. "Yes milady," she said and scurried away.

William took Elizabeth's arm. "Let us make haste."

"Are you certain we are not being followed?" she said with a look over her shoulder.

William grinned. "King Charles did us a favor by sending for me. My nebulous friend could not follow me into the palace. No doubt he awaits me at the entrance to Whitehall. I dined with King Charles in the Banqueting House and before leaving, I searched the crowd well. My ghostly phantom was nowhere to be seen. The King did ask if I know Creighton. Then if I knew Sir Jeremy and Mistress Blanchard."

Elizabeth gasped, "Oh no, what did you answer?"

"I said I knew all three, but would prefer not to know Creighton. Said I considered Creighton a pigeon-livered charlatan. The King laughed and said he rather agreed. I told him Creighton had accused me of concealing Mistress Blanchard and her husband, and out of courtesy, I let him search my rooms. I asked King Charles why Creighton should think I had an interest in the couple."

"Did you so! What did King Charles say?"

"He said he had no idea, but added Creighton had accused me of spiriting his betrothed away. I could not lie to King Charles, so I took my cue from you." He glanced down at Elizabeth and smiled. "I answered I would never spirit away Creighton's betrothed. Certainly a woman cannot be betrothed to one man when married to another. I have no doubt Charles will see the humor of my statement. He appreciates a cunning wit."

"I hope you are right. I would hate to have the King angry with you."

"Your concern for me gives me hope I may be winning your heart," William said, and the way he looked at her set her pulse racing. He had won her heart, but had she won his. Soon she would put his love to the test.

They reached the river, and William engaged a wherry. "I sent a message to your brother as to when he might expect our arrival. I trust he will have a skiff awaiting us."

"I have no doubt he will. 'Tis the day we set to visit him. I can scarce wait to see him. And to see Annis and Sir Jeremy. I pray all has gone well."

The tide being against them, the trip down river took longer than Elizabeth expected, but at last they disembarked at the Old Swan Stairs, hurried down Pudding Lane, and found Kilkenny awaiting them at the

Billingsgate wharf. Kilkenny swept her into his arms and planted a kiss on her forehead. "'Tis near to giving you up I was. I feared you had not escaped your watchful aunt."

Elizabeth laughed and pulled away from Kilkenny. He was a rogue, but she enjoyed his easy banter and overly familiar embraces. Her aunt would be shocked did she see such display, and she could tell by the look on William's face that he was not pleased either. Well, 'twas good for him to be jealous. He was much too confident. Better to keep him guessing.

"Our visit will be shorter than planned," she said, "but are we home before dark, Aunt Phillida will not be worried." Kilkenny handed her into the skiff, and she smiled at the young seaman who took up his oars. William settled on the seat beside her and Kilkenny pushed them off. He hopped lightly in the bow and took up another set of oars. With the two men rowing, they skimmed across the water, skillfully weaving their way around the score of various-sized boats and barges plying the river on a multitude of errands.

Garrett, Annis, and Sir Jeremy were at the railing awaiting them. Annis, waving a small laced kerchief, glowed with her joy. Sir Jeremy grinned from ear to ear. Their week together had them in good spirits, Elizabeth thought, thrilled to find them as much in love as ever. Lifted from the skiff onto the deck in a sling while William clamored up the rope netting hanging over the side, Elizabeth was swept into her brother's arms. Laughing with delight, she touched his face with her palm. "You look well, Garrett. You look the captain."

He beamed at her compliment but said, "I know you wish to greet your friends and determine they are well and happy. Then we will partake of some refreshment before I show you about the *Lady Alesia*." He swept his hand out indicating the main deck where a long trestle table had been set up under a canvas awning. Various food stuffs as well as wine bottles and goblets were assembled on the table.

"How pleasant," Elizabeth said before turning to embrace Annis. After a moment she held her friend at arm's length. "To my eyes you could scarce look happier. Tell me I am not deceived."

Annis giggled. "You are not deceived." She glanced at Sir Jeremy and blushed. "My husband has made me happier than I ever imagined possible."

"I am after thinking he must be making her very happy," Kilkenny said. "They have scarce been out of the captain's quarters but to partake of their meals."

Annis blushed a brighter pink and Sir Jeremy colored and coughed. They were spared any further embarrassment by Ridgely's arrival. He embraced Elizabeth then told Garrett he needed a word with him. Garrett directed Kilkenny to see to their guests and withdrew to the ship's stern with Ridgely. She hoped naught had gone foul.

While Kilkenny poured wine into the goblets, Annis eagerly apprised Elizabeth of her stay on the *Lady Alesia*. Foremost, Sir Jeremy was wonderful, so loving, so considerate, all she could wish for in a husband. Next, Elizabeth learned the captain's cabin and bed were comfortable. Annis loved the gentle rocking of the ship. It helped her sleep at night. She and Sir Jeremy took breakfast and supper in the captain's quarters but joined the captain and his officers for the noon meal in the main cabin. Afterward, they generally took a stroll about the deck.

The ship's cook, Annis proclaimed, prepared quite acceptable meals. "He is forever preparing treats he thinks I will enjoy," she said. "Yesterday he made a pigeon stew with mace and cloves, and the day before, for breakfast, he made me cinnamon toast. I had never had such before, and I found it delightful. Today we had barrel-cod in cream seasoned with pepper and parsley and garnished with prunes." Hopping from one subject to another in her enthusiasm, she added, "Captain D'Arcy is so accommodating. To give up his quarters as he has done and to provide us with every comfort, he is beyond generous!"

"I am pleased all goes so well," Elizabeth said. "I keep thinking my uncle will arrive any day and will plead your case to King Charles."

Her chin raised defiantly, Annis declared, "Jeremy and I have decided that even must we flee to Europe, we will not again be parted. We pray the King will rescind his order that I must wed Creighton, but does he not, we are prepared to leave England."

Elizabeth hugged her friend. She admired her new spirit and found the lovers' courage inspiring. "He will rescind it, I know he will." Feeling confident her friend's fate would soon be changed for the better, she sipped her wine and nibbled at some bread and cheese. Her eyes strayed to William and Sir Jeremy. Standing at the opposite end of the table, they talked in low voices punctuated by William's occasional guffaws. As Kilkenny refilled her wine goblet, Elizabeth said, "I have not seen Mister Fogarty. You cannot tell me he has forsaken you."

Kilkenny laughed. "Nay, he is below deck organizing the wares to be off loaded. We are expecting any day now to be getting our turn at the dock. Ne'er fear, he will be popping up afore you leave to bid you welcome."

"He will do more than bid you welcome, Elizabeth," Garrett said, rejoining her.

Hearing a despondent note to his voice, she whipped about. "What is amiss?"

"Mister Ridgely has informed me an agent interested in buying our cod wishes to meet with me this evening. We have received word we are to dock tomorrow. The agent needs to ascertain quantity and quality. Upon inspection, does he approve the cod, he will need make payment and have transport at the docks to receive it tomorrow. 'Twill save us warehousing it, and that means a bigger profit." He shook his head. "I am sorry, I cannot return with you."

Elizabeth knew she presented a deplorable appearance, droopy mouth, droopy shoulders, downcast eyes. "Oh Garrett, I had so been looking forward to spending this evening with you." Her hands flew to her mouth. "Oh! And what will Aunt Phillida say, do I return without you as escort at this late hour? She is not apt to approve, does William escort me home."

"You shall have an escort near as good as me. You shall have Mister Fogarty."

Elizabeth brightened. "Mister Fogarty!"

"Nay," Kilkenny said. "I would be happy to be escorting Lady Elizabeth home."

Garrett guffawed. "You would be no more welcome than would Mister Hayward. Fogarty will accompany her. One look at him and Aunt Phillida will have no fears Elizabeth might have been dallying. But for now," he turned back to Elizabeth, "I intend to enjoy your visit. We have much to talk about. I must tell you of your niece, Rilletta's, newest escapade. Seldom a day passes she has not her mother shaking her head and her father roaring in laughter. She reminds me of you."

Elizabeth batted his shoulder. "Say not such things. You will have Mister Hayward thinking me a hoyden." She glanced at William. He was glaring at Kilkenny. She suppressed a giggle. Kilkenny was not a man any woman with a brain in her head would consider marrying. He was all blandishments and cajolery. His eye strayed to near every woman who passed his way. To think he would ever choose to marry, or be faithful if he did, was to be a fool, and she was no fool. But William need not know all she knew about Kilkenny. Let him stew a little.

She took Garrett's arm, and with William trailing in their wake, she allowed her brother to show her about his ship.

❈ ❈ ❈ ❈

The tour of the ship complete, they were in the main cabin, seated around the table with Annis, Sir Jeremy, and Kilkenny, sipping on a sweet claret when Ridgely interrupted Garrett's tale of his first day captaining the *Lady Alesia*. "A low fog is advancing o'er the water, Captain," Ridgely said. "I believe 'tis best Lady Elizabeth left for shore. Mister Fogarty is readying the small skiff. The larger one is in use bringing the agent over." He turned to William. "Mister Hayward, I understand you were influential in directing the agent tae us. We thank you."

Elizabeth looked with surprise at William. He had offered his help, but he had made no mention of having recommended an agent. "Wait until you determine you are satisfied with Chandler's offer before you laud me," William said. "I know him to be honest, but also shrewd."

Ridgely laughed. "Captain D'Arcy will be doing the haggling on this. He has had a number o' years to perfect his trading skills, but he has ne'er bargained on so grand a scale. 'Twill be interesting to see how he handles himself."

"Do I stumble, I will have Ridgely to pick me up," Garrett said, "but now, Elspeth, let us get you into that skiff."

Elizabeth hugged Annis and promised to send word as soon as her uncle arrived. Annis, returning her hug, whispered, "I have never seen an uglier countenance than has Mister Fogarty, nor have I ever heard a sweeter voice. He sings the loveliest songs in the evenings. He is really a dear man. Always so polite." She shuddered. "Still, to look at him, he gives me the shivers."

Elizabeth looked at the bronze-skinned, black-haired little man awaiting her at the railing. He was ugly. From under a black eye patch, a red, puckered scar traced down the side of his face to turn up the corner of his mouth in a perennial snarl. Elizabeth knew the scar and vacant eye socket to be a gift from one of Cromwell's officers. She also knew Fogarty hated the English but was devoted to her brother. Those Garrett cherished, Fogarty treated with utmost respect.

His mouth half snarl, half smile, Fogarty extended his hands to her. "Lady Elizabet, by tah saints, I am after believin' ye grow more lovely each time I am seein' ye."

Elizabeth grasped his hands and bent forward to drop a light kiss on his forehead. "And you grow more like Mister Kilkenny, full of blandishments."

"Nay, milady, I speak tah trut. I leave cajolery t' Brennan. It better suits him. But here, let us be gettin' ye an' yeer gent aboard. I like not tah looks o' dat fog creepin' in."

After hugs to Garrett, Ridgely, and Kilkenny, and another to Annis, Elizabeth was plunked back on the sling and lowered into a small skiff.

Chapter 17

As soon as Elizabeth and William were settled, Fogarty took to the oars. Elizabeth found the fog thicker at the water level. Its density was a bit frightening. She was glad she was seated close to William. He had an arm around her waist, and his hand covered her hands in her lap. A lantern hung from a pole at the bow of the skiff, but the flickering light did little to dispel the gloom. Fogarty rowed at a steady pace, seeming to sense when they approached another vessel and maneuvering effortlessly around it. The river traffic had lessened; fewer small craft plied the waters, reducing the risks of collision.

They were in the middle of the river, had silently skimmed around a ponderous ship at anchor, when Fogarty raised his oars from the water and cocked his head. His one eye narrowed, he peered into the wispy fog. "Somedin's closin' on us fast," he said. Dropping the oars back in the water, he set to with a new vigor. "Lady Elizabet, do I say jump, ye jump."

Elizabeth's heart pummeled against her chest and her breath caught in her lungs. Jump into the river! She heard nothing, could see nothing, but she knew Fogarty's senses, especially his hearing, were superior to hers.

"What do you mean by that!" William demanded.

Between puffs and pants, Fogarty spat out, "Barge, I tink. Comin' fast. No lights. Could ram us."

William's hand tightened reassuringly on Elizabeth's, and she turned to him, but he was peering upriver. She looked again. Did she see something? Oh my God, yes!

"Jump now, milady!" Fogarty's words rang in her ears, but she could not budge. He still pulled desperately on the oars as if against hope they could escape the looming mass headed at them, then the boat shook and toppled as William jumped into the river pulling her with him. At
130

the same instant the numbing cold water sucked the breath from her lungs, she heard a whacking sound and knew the skiff had been hit.

A heavy object hammered against her head and shoulders, then her left arm was struck hard. She was struck again on her head, and her hand was grazed. She cried out and swallowed some of the river. Coughing, she kicked desperately, but her waterlogged skirt and petticoats, twisting about her legs, hampered her movements, and their weight threatened to pull her under. Struggling and gasping for air, she felt a tugging at her skirt. Something was trying to drag her down, drown her. She flailed wildly, batting her arms against the water. Then the weight was gone. Skirt and petticoats – gone. She could kick freely.

William popped up in front of her, at first frightening her, but as she recognized him, flooding her with a heady relief. He was alive, and she was not alone in this dark, churning netherworld. Sucking in gulps of air, he panted, "You hurt?"

Her immediate terror of drowning subsiding, she shook her head. "Not badly."

"You ... swim?" he puffed, turning to spit out some water that sloshed into his mouth.

She nodded. "Yes, but ... have trouble ... get ... air," she sputtered. "Stays bind me."

He raised a knife out of the water and waggled it. "Remedy that," he said and before she knew his intent, he slit the bodice of her gown and stays right up the middle. Air whooshed into her lungs, and she savored each bracing inhalation. "Get ... weighty ... sleeves," he added, cutting the sleeves off her bodice. She realized he had cut away her skirt and petticoats. Had he not, she had little doubt she would have drowned. Down to little more than her shift, what she had worn when her cousin Ewen had taught her to swim, she felt no shame, she felt naught but exaltation that she was not going to drown.

She had no idea how long they had been treading water, but she knew they were being carried downstream by the river's current. "What of Mister Fogarty?" she asked, praying he had survived. His warning had saved them "You ... see him?"

Bobbing along beside her, William shook his head. "Nay, thoughts ... on you. Tried ... pull you ... way from ... barge, but ... guessing you got smacked ... by ... oars."

"That is what ... kept hitting me." She should have known. "I tried to swim away, but my skirts ... dragged me down. Thank you ... for cutting them off."

"Sorry ... took so long to get to you. Had to shed ... boots ... coat or I would have gone down and ..." He spit out more water. "Been no use to either of us. Current is swift. My guess ... Fogarty ... carried down river a ways. May even have reached shore. We have dawdled to ... let you catch your breath. Now ... we swim ... to shore, or a boat, whichever we happen on first."

"Which way do we go?" she asked, her sense of direction befuddled by the fog.

"North bank. I think 'tis ... closer." He pointed to the left, and Elizabeth struck out with a strong stroke but winced as she lifted her left arm. She had not swum in many a year, but she silently thanked her cousin for her lessons. Her fear of drowning no longer paramount, she noticed the stench of the river and its nasty taste in her mouth. She hoped she had not been poisoned by swallowing some of it. Her eyes burned, and the assaults to her body began to pain her. Still, she was alive, and William was alive. These present miseries would pass.

They had to struggle against the fast outgoing tide, and she began to tire. She also became more chilled by the moment. Her head throbbed, and she kept ingesting more of the nasty water as she fought against the current. William swam beside her, encouraging her, urging her on. Then they were in the shallows. The current no longer tugged her away from the shore. Her foot kicked the river bottom, and, thrashing and gasping, she stumbled to her feet, only to flounder as her tired legs buckled under her. William grabbed her around the waist, and pulling her to her feet, near dragged her up the sloping embankment.

Barely out of the river, they fell to the muddy bank and lay puffing and panting. She coughed and wheezed and tried to disgorge some of the river she had swallowed. She started shaking violently. She was so cold her teeth chattered. "W... W... William," she stuttered, "I am fr... freezing." She was aware she had called him by his given name, but she did not think she need concern herself with proprieties at this time. At present she believed did she not soon warm up, every tooth in her head would shake loose.

Gathering her into his arms, he said, "I know no better way to warm us both." Night had fallen, and no moonlight penetrated the fog. She could not see his face, but she felt his warm breath on her mouth. Then his lips, wet and chilled, but soft and caressing, covered hers. Locked in the safety of his embrace, the enormous fright that had engulfed her began to evaporate. His kisses, so sweet, so gentle, and his body pressed tightly against hers, eased her shivering. His lips firmed, and his kiss became more heated. Was the ground trembling or was she still shaking from the cold? She did not know, did not care. He was right, what better way to chase away the chill. A burning need crept up inside her, blotting out the horrors they had endured.

William's hand slipped behind her head and tangled in her hair. His other hand cupped her breast. Naught was between her skin and his hand but her wet shift. She arched her back as his fingers caressed and fondled her. All pain was forgotten but the poignant pain between her legs. She did not fully understand what she was feeling, but she knew she was craving something only William could satisfy. His lips left her mouth and traveled to the hollow between her neck and shoulder. She gasped and clung to him. She trembled but not from the cold. Her flesh now burned, seared with a heated desire that William's roaming hand inflamed. His leg, draped over hers, was heavy yet comforting. She could feel his manhood pressed against her upper thigh and the knowledge that she aroused him despite their present circumstances increased her own desire.

His hand slid slowly down her rib cage to her waist and slipped over her hips to cup her buttocks and pull her tighter against him. She reveled in his touch, and as his lips again scorched hers, she ran her fingertips up and down his arms and torso. She marveled at his muscled shoulders, the power of his upper arms. Then he froze. He lifted his head. She almost cried out, but he whispered, "Someone is about."

🌿 🌿 🌿 🌿

William listened to the voices, quiet, stealthy voices. The men could be up to naught but mischief or something more deadly. Were he not exhausted, he might choose to fight, did the men prove malevolent, but he could not take a chance on losing, not when Elizabeth's safety was involved. And Elizabeth's safety was paramount. Until he had nearly lost her, he had not realized the depth of his feelings. When lust and desire turned to love, he did not know. But he loved her, that he did know and with a gut wrenching intensity that unnerved him to the fibers of his being. Protect her he would, did he have to drag her back into the river. He doubted the men advancing along the river embankment would want to follow them into the Thames.

Rising to his knees, he pulled Elizabeth up beside him. By keeping low, they were less likely to be seen, but they needed to be ready to spring to their feet and dive back into the river. A swinging light dimly penetrated the darkness; a lantern used to light the two men's path. Elizabeth sneezed. The swinging light stopped.

"Who is there?" came a guttural voice.

William froze and felt Elizabeth stiffen beside him.

"Who is there I say?" demanded the same voice.

William cautiously rose to his feet and, with a hand to Elizabeth's elbow, helped her to rise. The fog protected them, but at any moment they might be spotted. The lantern had been raised and was being used to search the darkness. Furtive footsteps moved toward them. Two shadowy figures appeared behind the lantern; one a normal man size, the other a mammoth.

"I see you," the mammoth said, raising the lantern higher and holding it out at arm's length. "What do you here?"

"Our skiff was hit by a barge," William said. "We had to swim to shore."

The mammoth drew closer and William gripped Elizabeth's hand, ready to make a dash for the river. The huge man squinted his eyes and poked his head forward as he peered at them. Then he shook his great head like a dog, his long scraggly hair flying about him. "Gramercy," he said, "bain't you Mister Hayward?"

William was surprised the man should recognize him, but his voice had become decidedly more friendly, so he answered in the positive. "Indeed, I am, but you have me at a disadvantage."

"Why, can you not recognize me by my size? 'Tis me, Harley Keene.

134

Me mam's Queenie Keene. You been investin' me mam's money for her and makin' her rich. Four to five more years, and she says she can sell the bawdy house and retire to the country and set herself up lack a laidy." He reached over, grabbed the collar of the man with him, and hauled him forward. "This here jackstraw be Wally Peeper." He chuckled. "You can guess how he got his name."

Tension drained from William's legs and arms. A savior in the form of this good-hearted behemoth was the answer to his prayers. "Criminy, Harley, I could not be more pleased to see you. We need help. We know not where we are and we are near to freezing." Hearing Elizabeth's teeth again chattering, he wrapped his arms around her. The embrace would also help shield her near nakedness from the two men's leering stare.

"Aye, you are but a stone's throw from me mam's. We will tike you there directly." He swatted the smaller man on the back. "Peeper, give your coat to the laidy. Can you not see she is near to freezin'?" He pulled off his own coat. "Here, Mister Hayward, you tike my coat. Be a bit big on you but 'twill keep you warm till we get to me Mam's." He shook his massive head. "I know 'tis not a fittin' place to be tikin' a laidy, but we have nowhere else to tike you. We will go in the back entrance and no one will see you."

"Thank you," William said accepting Keene's coat and passing Peeper's on to Elizabeth. "We must need protect my companion's reputation. She is a true lady." He looked down at Elizabeth as she shrugged into the coat. "Can you walk?" he asked.

"I am not certain, but I will try." Elizabeth's voice sounded tired and weak. William did not blame her. He was tired, too.

"Here now," Keene said, handing the lantern to Peeper and stepping forward. "No need for the laidy to walk. I will just carry her." Before William or Elizabeth could protest, he scooped Elizabeth up in his arms and started off with her. "Mister Hayward, you tike the lantern and light our way so's Peeper can run ahead and tell me mam she got fine guests a-comin'."

William grabbed the lantern from Peeper and hobbled after Keene, cursing under his breath as sharp pebbles stabbed his stocking feet. In minding his step, he heard rather than saw Peeper dart around him and hurry off into the darkness. He wondered the man could find his way in the fog, but guessed by his name, he had had practice skulking about in the dark.

Keene slowed enough for William to catch up with him. "Guess you must be tired out, too," he said. "Sorry I cannot carry the both of you."

"'Tis my lack of shoes," William said. "Had to shed my boots in order to swim."

"Ah," the giant said, looking down at William's feet. "I would be just as shambling without me shoes." He chuckled. "Your feet are apt to be mighty sore come morning. Get on ahead of me with that lantern. I have no mind to stumble while carrying your laidy." He looked down at Elizabeth and smiled, but a glance at Elizabeth told William, that with her eyes shut and her face pressed against Keene's chest, she did not see the big man's friendly gap-toothed grin.

Fortunately, their walk was short. William heard the raucous voices pouring from Queenie Keene's bawdy house before he saw the twinkling lights sneaking out chinks in the shuttered windows of the tap room. Then the two-storied building's shadowy form took shape. Keene directed William to an outside staircase leading to the upper story. A lantern hung from a post over the landing, but its dim light offered no aid in illuminating the steep flight of stairs. William's stocking feet made no sound on the rough steps, but Keene's clomp, clomping echoed off the side of the building. The door at the top of the stairs flung open. Light poured onto the landing until partially blocked by Queenie's magnificent apparition.

Chapter 18

"Mister Hayward, I bid you welcome. All is being readied to see to your and your lady's needs." At the sound of the ringing voice, Elizabeth opened her eyes, looked up, and stared. She had never seen a more enormous woman than the one standing on the landing, hands on her gargantuan hips. Not that the woman was fat, she was just huge. Tall, with a big horsey face, broad shoulders, and a voluminous bosom, she sported a prodigious grin.

"Set the lady down," she told her son with a swat to his shoulder as he reached the landing. "You try carrying her through the corridor, you will be banging up her knees."

Set upon her feet, Elizabeth wobbled, but the woman stuck a hand under her elbow. "Let me help you. I am Queenie Keene. I own this establishment. Bain't much by some standards, but then 'tis better than most houses of its type." Her beaming smile showed a row of large blackened teeth, but under the bright light cast by the wall sconce, her vivid blue eyes sparkled, and her cheeks glowed a rosy pink. Elizabeth glanced at William. He had been squashed into the corner railing. Queenie clucked and said, "You have no cause to be frettin' on Mister Hayward. Harley will see he is looked after." She chuckled. "But do I know Mister Hayward, him being the gent he is, he will be makin' sure you are all right and tight afore he looks to his own needs.

"So come on. I am putting you in my room. Set my gal to changing the sheets. Be some hot water up any moment. Know you are gonna want to wash up, especially your hair, after being in that river. I got some nice lavender-scented soap. 'Tis a shame a body is not safe on the river come nightfall. A shame it is. I got a warming drink for you, too."

Elizabeth let Queenie usher her to an open door at the end of the narrow corridor. The woman's hand on her elbow was surprisingly gentle and her chatter was like a soothing balm. The room was another surprise. The shimmering light cast by two wall sconces and candles atop a bureau and beside the bed chased the darkness from all but the corners of the colorful chamber. Red and gold rag rugs scattered about the floor and a garish-orange canopy over the bedframe contrasted with a bluish-green quilt resting on a bench at the foot of the bed. A young girl with eyes near too big for her pixyish face was tucking in a corner of a yellowish sheet on a fluffy mattress. The room had no hearth, but two coal braziers gave it a toasty warmth. A slightly older girl turned from a large trunk she was bending over and gasped when she saw Elizabeth.

"Gadzooks!" the girl said, "if you be not a fright."

"Cherry! Mind your tongue!" Queenie snapped. Elizabeth knew she looked a harridan; wet straggly hair, muddied shift sticking out below Peeper's coat, no shoes, mud caked on her face and hands. She could not blame the girl for voicing her amazement.

Cherry neither blushed nor looked chastened. She but held up a filmy blue dressing gown. "Will this do? Maribel is mighty peeved I took her gown, but I told her you said find somethin' fit for a laidy to put on."

Queenie nodded. "That will do. Now go see is the hot water ready."

Flipping a blond curl off her forehead, Cherry hurried out. Queenie turned to the small thin girl standing beside the bed. Elizabeth could not help but pity the little waif. She wondered what a girl so young was doing in such a place. Surely she could be no more than nine or ten.

"Jill, you go down and help Audrey serve the drinks. No doubt she is in a muddle tryin' to handle the customers on her own." The little girl hastened out, deftly weaving around William who stood outside the doorway. Elizabeth almost giggled. He looked as disreputable as she did.

"Mister Hayward," Queenie said, "you have no cause to stand at my door a-gawkin'. Go on with Harley and get cleaned up. He will find you some clothes to put on. You can come back and see your lady once I have her clean and warm and tucked into bed. Now begone with you!"

"You will be all right?" William asked Elizabeth.

She nodded. "I can tell I will be well cared for, Mister Hayward. Go see to your needs."

"Very well, but I will return soon. We must need decide how we are to inform your aunt of your safety. And we must somehow see to getting you home."

Elizabeth had not given her aunt a thought. She had been so scared by her near drowning, then so spellbound by William's caresses that had chased away the numbing cold, and finally so engrossed in Queenie and her bawdy house, she had not considered the consequences of her being in such a place. How could she be so thoughtless? Her aunt would be worried sick by now. They had to get word to her. "Yes," she said, "come back when you are freshened."

William left to follow Harley down the corridor and Queenie closed the door only to open it an instant later as Cherry called out, "We got yourn water."

Cherry, a large crock pitcher in her arms, was followed into the room by a sullen-looking girl with black hair and dark eyes. She was lugging a bucket of water, but by the way she eyed the blue gown draped across the trunk, Elizabeth guessed she must be Maribel. Both girls wore thick, pasty-white face make-up and their cheeks were too pink, their lips too red. Dark kohl on their eyelids gave them a sleepy look. Cherry was the more cheerful of the two. Maribel, obviously older, had a more developed figure. Elizabeth guessed Cherry no more than sixteen.

Queenie pulled a foot tub out from the corner of the room, and Maribel dumped the bucket of water into it. "That will do," Queenie said. "You go on back to Mister Hillock. Does he raise a fuss that you have kept him a-waitin', tell him his next drink is on me."

Maribel exited and Queenie directed Cherry to lock the door. "Want no unexpected visitors whilst we get you cleaned up," Queenie told Elizabeth, then before Elizabeth knew what they were about, Queenie and Cherry had her stripped and standing in the foot tub. They scrubbed her with soft rags and the lavender soap. Elizabeth knew she was blushing. She had not been seen naked by anyone but her servant girl since she was a child, but as neither woman commented on her discomposure, Elizabeth relaxed, and by the time they started washing her hair for the second time, she felt completely at ease. It felt so good to have the smell of the river off her hair and body. Next thing she knew they had her dried, dressed in Maribel's gown, and tucked in bed.

Queenie held out a cup to her. "This is some gin and mint. Swish it around in your mouth then spit it out. 'Twill take the taste of the river away. Then Cherry's got you a goblet of sherry. Once you drink that, I will let your man back in to see you afore you settle for the night." She held up her hand as Elizabeth tried to thank her. "No need to be thankin' me. What I owe Mister Hayward I can never repay. I was not born into this low existence. No, I was born bettern this, but my old man, Harley's father, gambled away near everything we had. By the time he died, I was lucky to still have this house. Widow with a child to rear. Naught else I could do but turn it into a bawdy house. But thanks to the investments Mister Hayward has made for me, in a few more years, I can sell the house, move to the country, and live in genteel comfort."

"And she is takin' me with her, bain't you, Queenie?" Cherry said with a bright grin.

Queenie took the goblet from Cherry and handed it to Elizabeth. "Are you not so foolish as to fall in love and get married, I will take you. You and Jill. And I suppose I will have to take Audrey. Lord knows how else that girl would survive."

"Jill is the little girl who made the bed?" Elizabeth asked before taking a sip of the sherry.

Queenie nodded. "That little mite has been a God-send. Audrey is addlepated, thick witted," Queenie tapped her head with her finger. "Jill is as quick as Audrey is slow. Young as she is, she keeps orders straight, and rights what Audrey messes up. Jill is worth ever' penny I paid for her."

Elizabeth nearly chocked on the sherry. "You bought Jill!" she finally managed.

"Aye, poor dear. Skin and bones she were with welts all over her where her father beat her or kicked her. He owed me a pretty hefty debt for his drinks. I told him I would take Jill, and his drinking debts would be settled. He agreed. Jill has been with us near a year now, would not you say, Cherry?" Cherry nodded and Queenie continued. "A bawdy house might not be the best place to raise a child, but 'tis a sight bettern the hovel she lived in. Nor does Jill mix with the customers but to serve their drinks. And speakin' of mixin' with the customers, Cherry, you best get yourself back down there and see can you rustle yourself up a man for the night."

Cherry assented but when she opened the door, William was there, his fist raised ready to knock. Cherry giggled. "Might Mister Hayward enter now, Queenie? He is right eager. Looks a sight better now than he did, even if Harley's clothes are too big on him." She waggled a shoulder. "I wonder would you be interested in havin' me share your bed tonight?" she said, looking up at William. "I would make you a good price."

"Cherry, get on with you," Queenie snapped. "'Course he is not interested in you. Cannot you see he is in love with his lady?"

Elizabeth perked up at Queenie's pronouncement. Before exiting, Cherry cast a sideways glance at William, and pouting, said, "Do you say so, Queenie."

Elizabeth's head reeled. So many experiences, some frightening, some illuminating, all needing sorting out, but Cherry was right, William looked good. His wet hair curling around his neck and forehead, and the too big clothes gave him an adorable boyish appearance. She would dearly love to cuddle him and wipe the look of concern from his face. She would like to kiss that pucker between his scintillating green eyes. She flushed. Her thoughts were carrying her back to the muddy riverbank, and she was again in his arms with his hand roaming freely over her body.

Queenie interrupted her wayward thoughts. "I will leave you two alone for a wee bit, but Mister Hayward, when I return, I will expect you to leave so as your lady can get some needed rest. The very idea, a lady should have to endure what she has been through. Bain't right," she said, giving her large head a vigorous nod.

William pulled a stool up beside the bed and took Elizabeth's hand. "How do you feel? I hope you will forgive me bringing you to such a place. I knew not what else we could have done, it being so dark and me with not a cent to my name. My purse being at the bottom of the river."

"Mister Hayward, how could you think I could find fault in your endeavors to see to my wellbeing? You saved my life." Thanks, too, for warming me up she thought, feeling another flush encompass her from head to toe. She took a sip of her sherry to bring her thoughts back in line. She knew Aunt Phillida would not approve of her being alone in a room with William with the door closed, especially with her being in bed, but she could feel no shame. "We are fortunate Mister Keene happened upon us. Without him, we might yet be stumbling around in the dark. I wonder what he might have been doing out there in that fog. Whatever, 'twas lucky for us."

William rolled his eyes. "He could have been meeting a barge of pirated goods."

Elizabeth sat up straighter. "That barge that ran into us ... it was rowed by pirates?"

He nodded. "Most likely. Dark, foggy nights are what they wait for. They slip aboard poorly guarded ships, overpower the seamen, and make off with as much cargo as they can fit aboard their craft. Ships at anchor keep lanterns burning so they will not be run into, but not wishing to be seen, the pirates use no lanterns. They just steer between the lights of the ships."

"But they ran into us."

"Small as we were, single little light bobbing on the water. They would know we were naught but a skiff. Riskier to try to go around us than through us."

"You mean they knew they would hit us!" Elizabeth stared into William's eyes. "They knew they might kill us. Mayhap, they have killed Mister Fogarty."

William's unblinking gaze met hers. "Yes, but I doubt they intended to kill anyone."

She looked down and shook her head then looked back up. "Did you say Mister Keene might have been there to meet those pirates?"

William's mouth thinned, and he heaved a sigh before answering, "Life is hard for folk not born to wealth. Tenants kicked off their land by enclosures. Desperate, they come to the city. Most have families to provide for. 'Tis hard to find work, especially steady work that pays enough to keep a roof over the family's head and food in their bellies. They find various ways to survive. Men can turn mean when straightened. Many goods sold in the market are pirated or smuggled in from Spain or France or even Ireland. My guess is your father has consumed wine smuggled into the country. Most likely you have, though you might not have known it.

"So might Harley be dealing with pirates? He might be, but I am not apt to ask him. I know Peeper's nowhere about. Harley and Queenie are good-hearted people. If Harley and Peeper are dealing with pirates, Queenie might not know it. It matters not, we owe them much."

Elizabeth nodded. She knew she was so much more fortunate than so many people in England. Poor little Jill, beaten by her father. Cherry, little more than a child, and making her living selling her body. And poor, dimwitted Audrey lucky to be serving drinks in a bawdy house, else who knows in what terrible straights she might find herself. All of them dependent on good-natured, generous-hearted Queenie.

William dragged Elizabeth's thoughts back to her own concerns. "I have taken the liberty of writing a missive to your aunt," he said, pulling a piece of paper from his waistcoat pocket and handing it to her. "I have told her you are safe. Told her what happened. Told her 'twould be best she not come here herself. She should send you clothes and a chair, not a carriage. Queenie says would cause too much tittle-tattle did your aunt send for you tonight. Many of her customers will be here drinking till after midnight. Best to come early in the morning. Fewer folk to be curious about the comings and goings. Do you approve, Harley has agreed to take it directly."

Elizabeth approved the letter, though she felt guilty about the grief she would be causing her aunt. She also approved the note William had written to her brother, but she could not fathom how she could face Garrett was Mister Fogarty dead. William seemed confident the little man had survived, but she could not help worrying. His appearance might be gruesome, but he was a dear man. She worried, too, about Annis and Sir Jeremy. Would their hideaway be exposed? Aunt Phillida would insist she be apprised of all the facts concerning Elizabeth's visit to the *Lady Alesia*. If Elizabeth told her about the lovers, would her aunt insist upon informing King Charles?

Despite her worries, she found exhaustion claiming her. Queenie returned and shooed William out. She tucked the quilt around Elizabeth like she was naught but a child, and before Queenie finished putting out the candles, Elizabeth was asleep.

Chapter 19

Garrett D'Arcy paced the deck. The hour had grown late and Fogarty had yet to return. The agent purchasing their barrels of cod had approved their merchandise, sealed the deal, and had been returned to shore, but still no Fogarty. Kilkenny assured him he had no reason to worry. Likely Fogarty stopped in a tavern for a mug and fell to telling tales, but Garrett could not dismiss the feeling something had gone wrong. Fogarty was dependable. He would be unlikely to stop for a drink, knowing his captain would be anxious to know his sister had been safely returned to her home.

Someone might have made an insulting remark about Fogarty's appearance. His second mate had a quick temper, but he could handle himself in a fight. And he had the good sense to retreat were the odds against him. No, something was wrong. A "Hallo the ship" brought his head around. A second call, "Hallo the *Lady Alesia*,", and Garrett, followed by one of his seamen, hurried to the bulwark and leaned over.

"Who calls?" Garrett hollered down.

"Would you be claiming a slubberdegullion by the name of Fogarty?"

"'Tis me, Captain," Fogarty's voice rang out clear on the quiet night air. "I promised deese rapscallions who fished me out o' tah drink dat ye would be givin' dem a shillin' fer returnin' me."

"Ye gads, how did you end up in the drink. Never mind, come aboard and I will hear all."

"Not afore we gets our shillin,'" said a voice from the boat. "Came out of our way in this fog t' bring him back t' ye, though by the looks of him, we are not knowing why ye would want him."

Garrett pulled his purse from his pocket, drew out two coins, and dropped them down. "Here are two shillings. And I thank you for returning him to me."

"Thank ye, cap'n," the man said as the seaman next to Garrett dropped netting over the side, and the wet, bedraggled Fogarty climbed aboard. Garrett's first words concerned his sister. "What of Elizabeth?"

Fogarty shook his head. "I am not knowin', sir. We were after bein' broadsided by a fast movin' barge; pirate 'tis my guess. I am knowin' Lady Elizabet went int' tah river afore we were hit for Hayward pulled her in after him. And I am knowin' she can swim, but her clothes were bein' powerful heavy. Yet, I cannot tink Hayward would be lettin' her drown. Him bein' too much in love wit yeer sister t' let aught happen t' her. I stayed wit tah skiff until tah end, hopin' t' save it, but it were smashed t' splinters."

Water dripped down his face, and he blinked his one good eye. Though other members of the crew circled around him, he looked only at Garrett. "'Tis sorry, I am, captain, dat I can tell ye no more. Me breeches got caught on a barb on tah side o' tah barge, and I was propelled a ways downriver afore I could cut meself free. 'Twas lucky I was t' be picked up when I was. I were near wore out fightin' tah current t' get t' shore."

Garrett's heart plummeted. If Fogarty had trouble trying to reach shore, how could Elizabeth have made it in that heavy gown? Yet he could not believe she was dead. Not Elizabeth, she was too alive, too vital. Kilkenny put a hand on his shoulder. "What now, Garrett? What would you be having me do? I will be going with you to your aunt's, do you wish it."

Garrett slowly nodded. "Aye, have the launch readied and wake Ridgely. I will leave him in charge." He turned to Fogarty. "Go below and get dried off and change your clothes."

"Aye sir." He started to leave but turned back. "Captain, as shure as me name is Doyle Fogarty, I am dat certain yeer sister made it t' shore. I took Hayward's measure. He would go down wit her afore he would let her drown. An' he would no' go down wit'out one hell ov' a fight. Dey aire t' shore, I will lay ye odds."

Garrett nodded then said, "Kilkenny, make sure none of this reaches Sir Jeremy and his wife. No cause to alarm them at this time of night."

"Aye, sir."

Garrett watched Kilkenny disappear through the hatch, then he turned back to the water. Fogarty had to be right. Elizabeth had to have made it to shore.

❀ ❀ ❀ ❀

Having paid a patrolling member of the King's guard to escort him and Kilkenny to Lady Grasmere's door, Garrett hesitated before knocking. Kilkenny tried to rally him, convince him they would find Elizabeth safe in her bed, having survived an ordeal she would someday revel in telling her grandchildren, but he held no such hope. His heart heavy, he forced himself to knock. The door was jerked open before he lowered his fist, and he found himself staring into his Uncle Ranulf's anxious countenance. His uncle's expression turned to surprise when he recognized Garrett.

He reached out a hand and drew Garrett into the room. "Ye gads, Phillida, look here, 'tis Garrett. What do you here boy? Pray you bring us news of your sister. She has gone missing."

Garrett was unprepared for the number of people in his aunt's parlor. Not only had his long awaited Uncle Ranulf arrived, but his Uncle Nathaniel was also there, and two women he took to be maid servants. Aunt Phillida rushed to his side and clasped his hands in hers. "Such a time as you have come. I fear your sister may have done something foolish." She glanced over her shoulder at the younger maid. "Mary has finally admitted that she last saw Elizabeth in the company of one of her courtiers, a Mister Hayward. I have attempted to discourage his advances, but apparently Elizabeth has been seeing him unbeknownst to me. Where she might have gone with him I cannot guess, but does word get out ..." Her expression completed her thought.

Garrett blinked his eyes as they adjusted from the dim passageway to the brightly glowing candlelit room. His aunt was concerned for Elizabeth's reputation. How was he to tell her his sister's reputation was of little consequence? All that truly mattered was whether she was alive or dead. He took a deep breath before reopening his eyes to look down into his aunt's worried gaze. "Elizabeth and Mister Hayward came to see me this afternoon."

His aunt blinked, and her face clouded. "They went to see you?"

He nodded. "I have been in port for a week. I was to return with Elizabeth to surprise you this evening, but my duties as captain of my ship prevented my accompanying her."

146

Looking less confused, Aunt Phillida glanced again at the serving girl. "Elizabeth gave Mary a note for me. It promised a grand surprise. You are the surprise. But where is Elizabeth?"

Kilkenny's hand clamped on his shoulder, offering him courage to impart his tale. "As I said, I had business that prevented me from bringing Elizabeth home as we had planned. I entrusted her to my third mate, a man with whom I believed you could find no fault." He drew a deep breath before continuing. "A heavy fog lay over the river. In the darkness their skiff was hit by a barge. Elizabeth and Hayward jumped overboard in time to avoid being struck, but we know not how they fared. My mate, Mister Fogarty, was dragged downriver by the barge until he managed to free himself. Two men picked him out of the river and returned him to the ship. I had hopes Elizabeth had been picked up, and that I would find her safe in her bed."

He saw his anguish mirrored in his aunt's eyes. Her hands covered her mouth. A tiny squeak emitted from her throat sounded loud in the quiet room. Garrett looked from her to his uncles. Uncle Ranulf had the D'Arcy sea green eyes and auburn hair, though his hair was lighter than Garrett's. Uncle Nate, like Elizabeth and Aunt Phillida, had dark hair and blue-green eyes. He had not seen either uncle in several years, but they had changed little. Both were tall and broad shouldered and still looked as if they could defend hearth and family should the need arise. But this was a situation that could not be resolved by physical attributes.

His Uncle Ranulf broke the silence. "I do believe Garrett must be correct. Elizabeth will have been picked up as his mate was. She will be returning home any time now." As if to give credence to his statement, a loud rap sounded at the door. All eyes turned to the door. Uncle Ranulf stepped forward and yanked it open.

A mountain of a man stood framed in the doorway. Garrett had never seen a more enormous human being. As tall as he and his uncles were, this man dwarfed them. "I be seeking Laidy Grasmere," the man said. He turned slightly, revealing the same guard who had escorted Garrett and Kilkenny to Aunt Phillida's lodgings. "Paid this guard a sixpence on the promise he would tike me to the correct rooms."

Aunt Phillida stepped forward. "I am Lady Grasmere."

The man glared down at the guard. "You would be no longer needed," he said.

The inquisitive look on the guard's face turned to alarm, and he backed away before turning and scurrying down the corridor. The mountain removed his hat and bowed to Aunt Phillida. "Name is Harley Keene, my laidy. I have a letter for you," he said, drawing a note from his pocket.

Aunt Phillida clutched the letter and gasped, "Does it concern my niece? She is alive?"

"Aye, my laidy, she is safe and well. I thought 'twas best to send that nosy guard on his way. Mister Hayward give me strict instructions to keep his laidy's identity private." He looked warily about the room, seemingly suspicious of the number of people clustering about Aunt Phillida. Garrett restrained an impulse to grab the note from his aunt as she fumbled with it before breaking the wax seal and opening the letter.

Uncle Ranulf shook his head. "Where are my manners?" He extended an arm. "Come in, come in, shameful to leave such a welcome messenger standing in the corridor." Ducking his head, Keene entered and Uncle Ranulf closed the door. "I am Lord Rygate," he said, and clamping a hand on William's Uncle Nate's shoulder, added, "This is my brother, Lord Rotherby." He then nodded at Garrett, "My nephew, Captain Garrett D'Arcy, Lady Elizabeth's brother." He shook his head, "I know not his friend. We have yet to be introduced."

Garrett hastily introduced his second mate before turning back to his aunt. "What does it say?" he demanded, his fingers itching to snatch the letter from her trembling hands.

"Here, you read it." Her face pallid, she thrust the note at him. "I cannot believe where she is! But at least she is alive. Naught else matters. But to think of her spending the night in such a ..." Her words tapered off, and she turned to Keene. "I apologize. I mean not to disparage your home, or ... or business," she stuttered, "but my niece has been gently reared, it ... it is ..."

Keene interrupted her. "You have no need to be apologizin', my laidy. I know 'tis not a fittin' place for a fine laidy to be stayin', but 'twas no place else we could tike her. She were chilled to the bone and wore out from her swim. She needed to be put into a nice warm bed afore she caught the ague. Me mam, she saw to it no one saw her. We took her in the back entrance. And no one but me and me mam knows who she be, and we are sworn on me old man's grave not to tell nary a soul. So you jest do as Mister Hayward directs, and no one need ever know your niece spent the night in a bawdy house."

Garrett scanned the note. So great was his relief, he could not control the chuckle that arose in his throat. "Elspeth, spending the night in a bawdy house. What a tale she will have." He slapped his thigh. "Here I have been near to death with worry, and she is no doubt sleeping like a babe. Naught amiss but a need for a new wardrobe. That is my sister for you. Ever in and out of scrapes with nary a scar."

Kilkenny snatched the letter from him, scanned it, and passed it on to Uncle Ranulf who read it and passed it to Uncle Nate. Garrett glanced at the younger maid. Her youthful face still showed concern. She must not have been long in Elizabeth's service, or she would know her mistress would land on her feet. He should have known it. Fogarty had.

"I am at thinking 'tis you and I should collect your sister," Kilkenny said, interrupting Garrett's thoughts. "Either of your uncles could be known, but no one will be knowing us."

"Your mate has a point," Uncle Ranulf said. "We meet at Billingsgate. Then you two go on with Mister Keene to pick up Elizabeth, bring her back to us, and we escort her home."

Mary broke in on the conversation. "Should I not go? Come morning, who is to help Lady Elizabeth dress?"

"Good heavens no," Aunt Phillida said. "'Tis bad enough Elizabeth is exposed to such a place. I will not have a young impressionable girl in my employ so exposed. Adah shall go."

"Begging your pardon, my laidy," Keene said, "but I do think 'twould be best you not send a maid. Me mam can help your niece dress. She saw to her bath and tucked her into bed tonight. She will do her up jest fine. Best you have a veil to cover Laidy Elizabeth's face. And 'twould be better you hire a local chair, not send your own."

"Man is right," Uncle Ranulf said. "No need your footmen to know about this, Phillida. Garrett and his mate can hire a chair at Billingsgate. They will bring Elizabeth to us, and we will take the wherry back up river. Mister Keene, at what time should we plan to meet you?"

"Right afore sunrise. Few folk other than fishermen will be about. Some folk will be settin' up their wares, but they will be too busy to pay you much heed." He scratched his head. "Findin' a chair that early might prove a problem, but I think I can manage one."

"If there is no chair, Elspeth can walk," Garrett said. Knowing his sister's curiosity, he guessed she would probably prefer walking so she could see the area she would be little apt to see again. "Long as she has a veil, and with Kilkenny and me to escort her, no one will guess who she is. And, as Mister Keene says, few will be about to see her."

"'Tis settled," Uncle Ranulf said. "Mister Keene, we cannot thank you and your mother enough for all you have done on behalf of my niece. We will see you are suitably rewarded."

"I will not turn down a reward," Keene said, revealing a gap-toothed grin, "but we done it for Mister Hayward. A fine man he is, a fine man."

🌿 🌿 🌿 🌿

Garrett lingered but a short while after Keene left. "I need to get back to the ship," he said, embracing his aunt. "Mister Ridgely will be anxiously awaiting word of Elizabeth."

"I never met your Mister Ridgely," Aunt Phillida said, "but your father praised him highly." She looked Garrett up and down. "And by the looks of you, young Captain D'Arcy, I would say he has done a fine job with you. However, I know full well there is more to this escapade of Elizabeth's than I have been told. I will expect you for supper tomorrow evening to recount all that has transpired. Elizabeth should have recovered from her ordeal by then."

Knowing he looked guilty, Garrett agreed to return for the inquisition. "No excuses," Aunt Phillida added. "I am certain Mister Ridgely can handle any emergencies." Garrett acknowledged his first mate's capabilities, but more guilt assaulted him. They were to dock on the morrow, and between retrieving Elizabeth and returning to his aunt's for supper, many duties that should be his would fall to Ridgely. He should have known better than to become involved in one of his sister's schemes. Still, he liked Sir Jeremy and his shy little wife, and he hoped his uncle could convince King Charles to reconsider the annulment he had mandated.

"Nate and I will walk you through this maze," Uncle Ranulf said. "Easy to get turned around in the corridors, especially at night. Best not to have the King's guard stopping you."

"We would appreciate that. Kilkenny's no better at finding his way around here than I am," Garrett said, stepping into the dank, musty smelling passageway. Every ten paces a wall sconce gave off a smoky glow along with the noxious odor of burning fat. Garrett was glad not to be stumbling around trying to find his way in the dimly lit corridors. As they turned a corner, he said, "Uncle Nate, we were not expecting you. Or at least Elizabeth made no mention of your imminent arrival. What brings you all the way from Leicestershire?"

Uncle Nate harrumphed. "I came to assure Ranulf that Reginald's new bride is a most acceptable young woman. He need have no concern the lad has acted rashly."

"Reginald is married?" Uncle Ranulf's second oldest son, four years Garrett's senior, had but recently returned from his Grand Tour of Europe. Garrett remembered as a youngster trailing after his older cousin at family gatherings. Light-hearted but clear-headed, Reginald was not one he would expect to behave impulsively.

Shaking his head, Uncle Ranulf took up the tale. "Reggie met the young woman whilst escorting Selena to Nate's." He said in an aside, "My wife seems to think Nate's wife will be able to turn Selena into a lady, so she may someday find a suitable husband."

Uncle Nate chuckled. "My wife is no miracle worker, but can anyone curb Selena's waywardness, she can. Before I left, she had the girl in a gown and her hair out of that queue. When not dressed like a hoyden, Selena is quite pretty." He looked at Garrett. "She reminds me a bit of Elizabeth, same dark hair and bluish-green eyes."

Garrett pitied his aunt. Trying to tame Selena would be like trying to tame the wind or make a stream flow uphill. Selena made Elizabeth seem docile by comparison. Well, Selena was not his concern. His concern was to get Elizabeth home, her reputation unsullied.

Turning his thoughts back to his uncles, he asked, "What of you, Uncle Ranulf? Elizabeth says she has been expecting you for over two weeks, but she knew not why you were coming."

"I have come to London to tell King Charles that Giles, my eldest son and heir, is betrothed. Charles is his godfather, and I wanted to tell him in person. After all, Charles was so benevolent as to bestow upon me my lands and title, Earl of Rygate, that will some day pass on to Giles. Reggie and Selena's adventure, which I shall not dwell upon, delayed their arrival to Nate's. Consequently my departure continued to be postponed as I awaited word of them. Now, I learn I will be telling King Charles of Reginald's marriage as well."

"And as is oft quoted, 'all's well that ends well'," said Uncle Nate. "So, Garrett, what can you tell us of this Mister Hayward? Phillida says she cannot approve of him for Elizabeth. Is he a varlet? Keene seemed to have high praise for the man. And truth be, I know his father well. He rode with me when I was forced to play the highwayman."

Garrett was surprised by his uncle's question. But more surprised Hayward's father had been one of his uncle's highwaymen. He was honored his uncles would be interested in his opinion. Pushing thoughts of his cousins' adventures and betrothals out of his head, he answered, "I find Hayward most likeable. He styles himself a broker and indeed has helped us increase our profit by finding us a buyer for our barrels of cod. I cannot find fault with him. Especially as he seems to have saved Elizabeth's life."

"Well, we will meet him on the morrow." Uncle Ranulf said. "I intend to invite him to supper. I want to judge for myself. If Elizabeth is seeing him on the sly, my guess is she has made her choice. But is Phillida wary, we must heed her assessment." He stopped at a door and opened it onto a courtyard. "You should be able to find your way from here. We will see you at Billingsgate just before sunrise." He patted Garrett on the back and nodded to Kilkenny.

"Aye, Billingsgate before sunrise," Garrett said and stepped out into the night. Wisps of fog swirled around glimmers of light skittering out from various windows. In the distance he saw dim twinkling lights on the river. He and Kilkenny needed to catch a wherry. He did not trust his knowledge of the London streets in the dark. He had been to London only once before, in his youth. He had found it exciting then. But with trying to make his way through the crowds and bustle, he better understood why his father dreaded being called to Parliament sessions.

Chapter 20

Elizabeth slept soundly through the night and awoke to Queenie's gentle shaking of her shoulder. Feeling surprisingly refreshed, though slightly disoriented, she opened her eyes to find the large woman looming over her.

"I brought you some mulled ale," Queenie said. "'Twill warm your insides and perk you up for your trip home. Your brother has come to claim you, and he brung you some clothes." She held up an arm looped over with various pieces of clothing.

Blinking, Elizabeth sat up in bed. "Garrett is here?"

"Captain D'Arcy, he says he is. And as handsome a fellow as I ever set eyes on. So is the fellow with him, even if he be an Irishman. Good thing my girls are still abed. They would be vying with one another to bide with them whilst you get readied. So here now, pop up and I will help you dress. Best you are all out of here afore the rest of the house wakes up. We want none other than Harley and me to know your identity, Lady Elizabeth."

Elizabeth sprang from the bed, gulped down the ale Queenie pressed on her, and with Queenie's help donned the apparel her aunt had sent. A dark sober gown and a black veil made her look to be in mourning. After eyeing Elizabeth judiciously, Queenie opened the door to find William waiting in the corridor. To Elizabeth's surprise, he looked quite dapper. Green coat, tan breeches, and brown buckle shoes. "A loan from your brother," William said when he noticed her stare. "Having met Harley at your aunt's, he guessed I would be needing clothing more my own size. Most kind of him. I rather dreaded making my way through the streets of London in Harley's duds." He held out an arm. "Shall we go? Your chair awaits you, milady."

Slipping into the low-heeled shoes her aunt had sent, Elizabeth lowered the veil over her face. "Yes, I am ready." She turned back to

Queenie. "How can I ever thank you for all you have done. To take us in as you did. To ..."

Clucking, Queenie interrupted her. "Nonsense. I was happy I could oblige. And I must tell you," she reached in her skirt pocket, pulled out a small leather bag, and hefted it in one hand, "I have been amply compensated. Now, no more dawdling. Let us get you out of here."

Queenie herded her and William down the corridor and out the same door they had entered the night before. The sun was not fully up, but Elizabeth recognized her brother waiting for her at the foot of the steps. Next to him stood Kilkenny, and behind them were two men and a sedan chair. She hurried down the steps and into Garrett's open arms. He hugged her tight against his chest. "Lord, Elspeth, you put the fear of God in me," he whispered.

When he finally released her, she asked, "What of Mister Fogarty?"

Garrett smiled. "That is my Elspeth, first thought is always for the wellbeing of others. Fogarty is fine. He was picked out of the river and brought back to the ship. Was he told us what transpired, and I went immediately to Aunt Phillida's."

Elizabeth ducked her head and looked up sideways at her brother. "Is she terribly upset?"

"You will be at finding that out when you return, do you e'er return," interrupted Kilkenny. "Ne'er knew any two people to go yammering on like you two. Do get in the chair, milady, afore you wake the neighborhood."

Elizabeth flushed and Garrett said, "He is right." He handed her into the chair and told her to pull the curtains. She knew all was being done to protect her reputation, but she felt cheated. She had seen next to nothing of the bawdy house and was now to see none of the less reputable sections of Tower and Billingsgate Wards. Pulling the curtain aside, she waved to Queenie, and to Harley, who had joined his mother. "Thank you!" she called, noting again how imposing they were. William and Garrett both looked small beside the mammoth pair.

Though she peeped out the curtained window, Elizabeth saw little of the streets they took to Billingsgate wharf where her uncles awaited her. William walked on one side of the chair and Garrett on the other, blocking much of her view. She saw enough to know the streets were dark and narrow, and the upper floors of the houses on either side of the street nearly met overhead. The stench was wretched, and all manner of offal littered the poorly cobbled street. Hogs, dogs, and pigeons rooted around in the filth, and the pall of smoke hung in the air as the awakening populace stirred their hearth fires to life. Doors banged and shouts and squabbles echoed up and down the street. Babies cried, dogs barked, and children squealed and yelped. A whole world she knew nothing about careened around her, and she thanked God she was not a part of it.

¾ ¾ ¾ ¾

The raucous cries of the fishmongers rose above the cacophony of sounds announcing their arrival at the wharf. William helped Elizabeth from the chair and Garrett dismissed the porters Harley Keene had roused from their sleep to carry her to the wharf. Elizabeth wrinkled her nose at the variety of odorous aromas assaulting her. The smell of fish hung heavy in the air and made her empty stomach a tad squeamish. Before leading Elizabeth to her uncles, Garrett warned her to say nothing of her visit to his ship until he arrived for supper. "If you must, pretend you are exhausted from your ordeal and keep to your room."

Elizabeth agreed to comply with his instructions, and with William's hand firm on her elbow, and Kilkenny bringing up the rear to guard against miscreants, she followed her brother through the teeming morning crowd. Serving men and women doing the day's marketing of fish, fruits, and vegetables, sailors enjoying shore leave and ogling the women, Customs' Officers gauging barrels and crates of goods, porters carting cargoes from ships to warehouses, and vendors hawking their wares bustled and jostled about them as they made their way to the arcade of open shops and stalls that lined the west bank of the harbor.

Elizabeth was pleased to learn her Uncle Ranulf had arrived and was happily surprised her Uncle Nathaniel was also in London. That could mean help for her campaign to convince Aunt Phillida that William would make a suitable mate. After all, William's father had ridden with Uncle Nate's gang of highwaymen. She felt certain Uncle Nate would find no fault with William. And she had no doubt he would support

Annis and Sir Jeremy's bid to remain married. He knew well the pangs of forbidden love. He and Aunt Rowena had been forced to wait almost two years before they could wed. Had Aunt Rowena's first husband not died of the apoplexy, they would have been forced to wait indefinitely. Uncle Nate would sympathize with her friends.

Heartily greeted by both uncles, Elizabeth felt consumed in warmth despite the morning nip to the air. Garrett and Kilkenny bid her a hasty farewell, though Garrett promised he would see her at supper. William was introduced, and Uncle Ranulf extended him an invitation to supper. William readily accepted and also accepted a wherry ride back up river. "We will be unable to discuss your ordeal," Uncle Ranulf said. "Those oarsmen have sharp ears. After going to this great effort to insure no one knows Elizabeth did not sleep the night in her own bed, we want no minor slip of the tongue to undo our endeavor."

"I understand," William said. "I would think 'tis best none of us mention our names."

"I am in agreement," Uncle Nate said, "but first, tell me Hayward, might you in truth, as Phillida says, be the son of Caleb Hayward of Heronscross in Cheshire?"

"Indeed. He is my father," William answered with a smile.

Uncle Nate slapped his knee. "I knew it. You are his spitting imagine. 'Tis those eyes that give you away. How is your father? I have done a poor job keeping up with him."

"Father is well. He prospers, but he works too hard."

Uncle Nate nodded. "That would be Caleb. By the by, I recently saw your Uncle Cyril. 'Tis a long story I will not attempt to tell at this time. He, too, seems well. Exuberant as ever."

William chuckled. "Aye, that would be Uncle Cyril. Ever ready to fight the good fight."

Elizabeth was thrilled with how well William and her uncle were getting on. She knew nothing of William's uncle, but if Uncle Nate had recently seen him and approved of him, that too was to William's advantage. A tingle of excitement made her want to skip, but she controlled the urge. A skipping widow would attract attention.

They arrived at Old Swan Stairs, and Uncle Ranulf hailed a wherry. Conversation would be at a minimum until they docked upriver. Elizabeth looked down at the murky water and shivered. If not for William's quick actions, she would now be at the bottom of that river or else floating out to sea. She turned to him and placed her hand on his forearm. "I cannot remember thanking you for saving my life."

He smiled down at her. "'Tis a life well worth saving. And you did your part. 'Twas lucky for us both you know how to swim."

She glanced at Uncle Nate. "Ewen taught Flavia and me to swim, and Uncle Berold gave him a tanning for it. Did he e'er tell you about it, Uncle Nate? I owe Ewen much for those lessons."

Uncle Nate laughed. "My son would not be apt to so confide in me, but Flavia is ever willing to tell tales on her brother. So yes, I knew of the lessons, and I approve of them. I doubt not that when Phillida tells her husband how useful were those lessons, he may offer Ewen an apology."

"Enough," interrupted Uncle Ranulf. "Our wherry comes."

Uncle Nate clamped a hand on William's shoulder. "We must bide our tongues for now, but we thank you most earnestly our Elizabeth suffered no serious injury. We will look forward to hearing in detail at supper this evening all that transpired."

The wherry pulled up to the stairs' landing and William held out his hand to help Elizabeth into the craft. She gathered a deep breath before stepping into the boat. It wobbled but a fraction, and she gripped William's hand tighter. "Easy," he said, "you have naught to fear." He helped her sit and arrange her skirts, then he sat down opposite her, allowing her Uncle Ranulf to sit beside her. She would prefer having William next to her. She would like to hold his hand, to have his arm around her waist. She felt safe with him, but she knew her uncles would not consider such an arrangement appropriate. Did they but know the intimacies she and William had shared the previous night, they would be looking askance at her and at William.

Hiding a tiny smile, she glanced up at William from under her lashes. She wondered if he had been as besotted by their wanton embrace as she. The remembrance of his hand roaming her body, fondling her breasts, then traveling up her thighs brought a tingling sensation to her innards and started her heart beating a rapid tattoo. His kisses and caresses had created sensations she had never imagined, and she longed to again experience such rapture.

Her uncle patted her hand and brought her thoughts back to the present. She smiled at him then looked up at the awakening sky. To the east, the sun was a shimmering ball sitting on the river. The fog was gone and the sky was clear. All was well with her world.

Chapter 21

After a tearful reunion with Aunt Phillida, Elizabeth did as Garrett suggested and retired to her room complaining of a debilitating headache. Aunt Phillida was not only solicitous, she refrained from pressing for details. "What you need is rest. I am guessing you barely slept a wink. 'Tis no wonder your head hurts. 'Twill be lucky do you not come down with the ague. When you have recovered from your ordeal is time enough to tell us all that transpired." Directing Mary to fetch Elizabeth some hot broth, she tucked Elizabeth into bed herself.

Elizabeth let her aunt fuss over her, though a twinge of guilt assailed her. She actually felt exuberant and alive and would prefer being up enjoying her uncles' company and hearing about her cousins. Instead, she must spend the day closeted in her room, waiting for reinforcements in the form of her brother and William. Her aunt would not chastise her in front of William, and he and Garrett would lend her support in securing her uncles' aid for Annis and Sir Jeremy.

Hugging herself, she let her thoughts drift. Having come so close to dying, she had a new appreciation of life. Its beauties and joys should not be taken for granted. She was blessed. She lived a bountiful life, but she had seen a sordid side of life she had not known existed. True, she had seen beggars on the street, but she had paid their environs scant heed. So many people outside her insulated world lived in dismal circumstances. William seemed to understand their world. He neither condoned nor condemned their means of survival, he but accepted them.

Her thoughts carried her back to the icy cold river. Fear and panic returned, and she did not want to be alone. Ready to throw back her bedding and call to her aunt, she managed to steady her breathing as the memory of William's deft actions calmed her. He could have left her to her fate, saved himself. But he had placed his own life in jeopardy to save her. Did his heroism mean he was in love with her, or would he have done the same for anyone struggling to survive in the depths of the river? She thought he might. At the same time, she believed he would have gone down with her rather than give her up to the dark, nether world of the Thames.

She sat up in bed and shook her head. These murky thoughts would never do. She was well, she was alive, and she was going to marry William whether her family approved or not. The world was full of misery, but she would not sink into its recesses. She was no sorceress who could wave a magic wand and right the injustices of the world, but she could insure her own existence did not lack the main ingredient needed for her happiness. William was that ingredient.

The sudden opening of the door sent her slipping back under the coverings. She breathed a sigh of relief when Mary entered with the hot broth. Thankfully, her aunt had not caught her sitting up when she should have been nursing her headache. "Oh, Lady Elizabeth," Mary said as she hurried around the edge of the bed, "you cannot think how worried I have been. 'Twas only when Lady Grasmere was near to pulling her hair over her worry for you that I told her of your meeting with Mister Hayward. I do hope you are not angry with me."

Elizabeth sat up again and offered Mary a cheerful smile. "I am not angry, Mary. Have no fear. But I am starving. Is there any meat in that broth?"

Mary pulled up a stool. "Mayhap a few strands. Would you have me feed you, milady?"

Elizabeth shook her head. "Nay, give me the bowl, but stay near to hand and tell me all that has happened since I was missed. But first, where is my aunt? Is she apt to walk in on us?"

"Lady Grasmere is entertaining Mistress Elsworth. She called and upon being told you had the headache, meant to leave. Lady Grasmere, though, invited her to stay and have a sherry."

"Oh dear, are my uncles with them?"

"No milady. They left to pay a call on King Charles."

"Oh dear." Elizabeth had little doubt but what her aunt invited Blythe to stay that she might quiz her.

"Is aught amiss, Lady Elizabeth?"

Elizabeth heard the concern in Mary's voice and noted the crease between her brows. That her servant cared for her made Elizabeth feel warm inside. "No, Mary, naught is amiss, so do wipe away that frown and tell me about last evening while I eat, 'ere I starve to death."

Settling on the stool, Mary recounted the previous evening's events; Lady Grasmere's anxious worrying, the arrival of Elizabeth's uncles, then her brother and his mate, and finally the awe-inspiring giant who brought word that Elizabeth was alive and well. "Lady Grasmere did cry with relief when we had word you were safe. Though I cannot think what terror you must have known when you were in the river. The Lord must have seen to your survival."

Elizabeth shook her head. "Mayhap the Lord had a hand in it, I cannot say, but 'twas Mister Hayward who saved me." Elizabeth looked over Mary's head then back at her. "Mary, he was wonderful, fearless. Indeed, I owe him my life."

Mary nodded. "I thank the Lord he was with you." She then leaned forward and resting her elbows on her knees, asked, "What was the bawdy house like?"

Elizabeth giggled. "For shame, Mary, what would my aunt say did she know you asked such a question. You should have no interest in places of that ilk."

"That I know, milady, and my mother would box my ears did she know I shamed her by asking you about bawdy houses. All the same..." Mary's plaintive voice tapered off.

Elizabeth smiled then frowned. "I saw very little of it. I was taken in through a back door and led to Queenie's room. Queenie is the owner. I was given a bath, a goblet of sherry, and put to bed. This morning I was taken out by the same door. I saw nothing more than the corridor and Queenie's room. Oh, and a couple of the girls who work there."

The look of disappointment that had settled over Mary's face disappeared and she sat up straight. "Do tell, Lady Elizabeth, what were they like?"

Laughing again, Elizabeth nodded but drained her bowl of broth before describing Cherry, Maribel, and the little waif, Jill. "Ah, but Queenie, she is an incredible sight," Elizabeth said, handing the empty bowl to Mary. She tried to do justice to her gracious hostess but feared her portrayal was inadequate. "A kind-hearted soul, yet not someone you would want to cross. I would think few of her patrons would dare rile her."

Mary sighed. "What an adventure you have had."

"I hope never to have such an adventure again," Elizabeth said. "Now, Mary, I am still hungry. Aunt Phillida thinks I am laid up with the headache, but do I not get more to eat, I will of a certain have a headache. You must sneak me in some bread and cheese, or I may well perish."

"Mayhap you would like to start on this." Mary pulled a kerchief from her pocket, and unwrapping it, revealed a gingerbread man. "I saved it from last evening's supper. I know how hungry you are when you return from your outings."

Elizabeth leaned over and hugged Mary. "Oh, you dear! Thank you." She snatched the gingerbread man, and, biting off his head, rolled her eyes as the spicy flavor tantalized her tongue. Between mouthfuls she said, "Can you get me some ale or wine, I would be pleased."

Mary returned with a goblet of sherry and reported Mistress Elsworth had left and Lady Grasmere had laid down for a nap. "She says she slept poorly the previous evening worrying about you," Mary added.

"Poor Aunt Phillida," Elizabeth said, "I am afraid I have ever been a trial to her. No doubt she will be pleased when I am wed and no longer her responsibility."

"Are you going to marry Mister Hayward?" Mary asked then clamped a hand over her mouth. "Oh, Lady Elizabeth, I am that sorry. I was too bold."

Elizabeth slanted her eyes. "I think mayhap I shall." She put her finger to her lips. "But say naught to anyone. He has not yet asked me to marry him, though I think he may soon do so."

Mary clapped her hands. "I hope so. I do like Mister Hayward. And he is so very handsome."

Elizabeth agreed. William Hayward was so very handsome. And so very brave. Setting the sherry goblet aside, Elizabeth slid back under the coverings. Did she have to spend the day in bed, she could wile away the hours dreaming of William and his sensuous caresses of her body.

Elizabeth took great care dressing for supper. When her aunt peaked in on her in the midafternoon, she was up, having stayed in bed as long as she could endure, and had Mary curling her hair. She assured her aunt she no longer had a headache. "Truly, Aunt Phillida, I am quite refreshed, and I am eager to hear what brings my uncles to London. We had no chance to chat on the wherry for fear of giving ourselves away. Are they returned from their visit to the King?"

"Nay, I would not expect the King to deprive himself of their company until near sunset. No doubt they took dinner with him, but he might insist they join him for a private supper."

Elizabeth tried not to let her disappointment show. She needed her uncles to be at the evening meal while she had William and Garrett to help her persuade them to act on Sir Jeremy and Annis's behalf. Yet, did King Charles command their attendance, they would have to submit. To her relief, her fears had been for naught. Her uncles arrived in goodly time to refresh themselves before supper. From her room, Elizabeth heard her aunt shush them when they told her the King had plans to visit one of his ladybirds that evening. "Mind your tongues. Elizabeth is not hard of hearing. She should not be exposed to such ribaldry."

Both uncles laughed, and Uncle Ranulf said, "Lord, she spent the night in a bawdy house."

Aunt Phillida hushed him. "Better we never mention that again. What her mother will think of me does she hear of this adventure. She will rue the day she left the girl in my hands."

"Nonsense," Uncle Nate said. "Blanch would ne'er think ill of you. She knows Elizabeth is no angel. Just be thankful 'tis not Selena you have on your hands."

"Aye," Uncle Ranulf agreed, "my daughter makes Elspeth seem a model of perfection." Elizabeth wondered what her cousin had done now, and would she be able to coax it out of her uncle. Mayhap, did she want her uncle in a good mood, she would be better not to risk angering him. She decided against pressing him. Annis and Sir Jeremy's plight must first be resolved.

Garrett and William arrived together. They seemed to enjoy each other's company. That boded well for her future plans, Elizabeth thought. They were laughing over some mishap Garrett experienced while docking the *Lady Alesia*. "Oh, naught anything of great concern," Garrett assured her. "Just my inexperience. Ridgely soon had all straightened out. Now, how about supper. I am near starved. Had little to eat this day. Too busy from dawn till near dusk when I stopped to dress for this evening."

They were soon seated around the table enjoying the elaborate supper Aunt Phillida had ordered. Her two footmen, called in to serve the meal, limited conversation. They were not to be made privy to Elizabeth's exploit. The conversation instead centered on Garrett and his ship and new command, and on Uncle Ranulf's son Giles's betrothal and his son Reginald's sudden marriage. Uncle Nate again assured all that the young woman Reginald married was a paragon of virtue. The marriage had been kept simple and quiet because the girl was still in mourning. It had been arranged in haste because Reginald insisted he was unwilling to wait any longer before paying the license fee and making Mistress Bowdon his bride. "Never saw a lad so much in love." He chuckled. "Excepting myself. Fell in love with Rowena the moment I set eyes on her."

"Anyway," Uncle Ranulf interrupted, "Reggie will be bringing Amaryllis to meet the family after they have had a chance to settle in at his estate."

Elizabeth had a feeling if Selena was involved in her brother's romance, there was much more to the story than her uncles were telling, but she doubted she would learn the extent of the adventure until she next saw Reggie and met his new wife.

Abruptly changing the subject, Uncle Nate turned to William and asked him about his life in London. William explained his burgeoning business, and Garrett chimed in on how helpful he had been to him. Uncle Nate then began reminiscing about his escapades as a highwayman with William's father.

"King Charles was grateful for every pound you sent him, Nate," Ranulf said. "Just knowing you were depriving the Puritans who drove him from his throne of their riches always gave him a good chuckle. I do believe he would have liked to join you."

Uncle Nate shook his head. "We were a motley band until Rowena joined us," he said in an aside, and William assured him his father had told him much about Lady Rotherby.

"She gave us a flare we were lacking," Uncle Nate added, his eyes taking on a faraway look. "A lucky man I am. 'Tis not every man privileged enough to know such an abiding love." He looked at Phillida. "Nor are many women so privileged. We know well your devotion to Berold. But then we D'Arcys are not apt to settle for less than true love. Do I not speak the truth, Ranulf? Is your Angelica not the only woman you could imagine spending your life alongside?"

"You speak the truth," Uncle Ranulf said, raising his wine goblet. "To our spouses. May our children and nieces and nephews know the joys we have been blessed to know."

Elizabeth raised her goblet and looked over its rim at William. He inclined his goblet toward her before he took a sip. Elizabeth sipped then looked at her aunt. She had seen the exchange, but Elizabeth did not care. She believed her uncles would take her part. Love was paramount in their relationships with their wives. Her uncles would want no less for her.

With the meal ended but for the dried fruits and nuts, Aunt Phillida dismissed the footmen. They would cart off the supper dishes and remains then retire for the evening. Uncle Ranulf and Uncle Nate dismissed their personal servants, giving them the evening to enjoy the enticements London had to offer. "But be back here in the morning to ready us for Whitehall," Uncle Ranulf said.

With none but Adah and Mary in service, conversation no longer needed to be guarded. To the accompaniment of Aunt Phillida's gasps and the uncles' approving nods, William described their ordeal in the river, including the cutting away of Elizabeth's garments, then their desperate swim to shore and subsequent rescue by the Keenes. With William's tale completed to the approbation of Elizabeth's uncles, she immediately launched her barrage in support of her friends. Using theatrics resembling those she had witnessed at the opera, she hissed, "Annis must be rescued from the evil designs of the dastardly Creighton." Eyes wide, she leaned forward. "Annis and Sir Jeremy must be allowed to enjoy life as husband and wife. They are in love and must not be parted." She looked to her uncles. "No more than you would wish to be parted."

"I should have known you had something to do with her disappearance," Aunt Phillida said. "That girl has no gumption. She would not have run away on her own. But 'tis done, and because of your part in it, your uncles will have to plead their cause to save you from the King's ire." She turned to William. "And you, Mister Hayward, you were a part of this scheme I perceive."

"I fear I was. 'Tis hard to see two people so in love and not wish to help them."

Aunt Phillida harrumphed, but Uncle Nate nodded. "I can see where you could do no less. Especially did you wish to please Elizabeth. And you did wish to please Elizabeth, am I not correct?" Eyebrows raised questioningly, he looked at William.

William smiled and nodded. "I cannot lie to you, Lord Rotherby. I did indeed wish to ingratiate myself with Lady Elizabeth. At first that was my only motive. But as I came to know Sir Jeremy and Mistress Blanchard, I realized I was doing it as much to help them, as to please Lady Elizabeth. They are deserving of our efforts. That you will ascertain when you meet them."

"Garrett?" Uncle Nate said. "What reason give you for falling in with their scheme?"

Garrett coughed on the wine he had sipped and set his goblet down. He glanced at Elizabeth then back at Uncle Nate. "I am obliged to tell you I cannot think of any times I have not fallen in with Elspeth's schemes. She has a way of making all she wishes to do seem reasonable. In this case, I had but to consider how I would feel was my desire to marry Alesia denied. Then to think, 'twas a damned Puritan we could thwart, ... Well, it seemed reasonable."

Uncle Ranulf laughed. "So it does to me, too, but I have had Selena and her machinations to deal with all these years, so I may not be the best judge of what is sane and reasonable. But that brings us back to you, Mister Hayward. What are your intentions in regard to our niece?"

Elizabeth was shocked by her uncle's question, and one look at William told her he was, also. So, apparently, was Aunt Phillida. She demanded, "Ranulf, what kind of question is that?"

"A most sensible one I would say," spoke up Uncle Nate. "Look at the two of them. They are obviously in love." He held up a hand. "I know you cannot think him a suitable match for the Earl of Tyneford's daughter. So Ranulf will ask Charles to knight him or make him a Baronet. Easy enough done. Do think, Phillida, these two spent the night together in a bawdy house. Did word leak out, Elizabeth's reputation would be in shambles. Think, too, what she was wearing. Mister Hayward had to cut away her dress. You had to send her clothing."

Elizabeth flushed. She had been in a state of near nakedness, and they all knew it. Mayhap they believed she had been compromised. Was it her uncle's plan to force them to wed? Well, she would not be forced into marriage. Nay, not even to William. Not unless she knew he loved her.

�});🌾 🌾 🌾

William noted the stubborn set to Elizabeth's lips and the lift of her chin. He had seen that look when Albin had called Blythe Elsworth bookish. He had to forestall an outburst. Words spoken in haste could end his hopes of winning Elizabeth's hand. Despite her uncles' support of his suit, he could tell her aunt was not convinced 'twas prudent. Did Elizabeth declare any resistance, any misgivings, her aunt would pounce. He had no doubt Elizabeth loved him. And since their struggle in the river when he had feared he might lose her, he had come to realize he loved her more than life itself. Life without her would hold little meaning. He could not let her destroy their chance at happiness.

Scraping back his chair, he rose. "Might I have a moment alone with Lady Elizabeth? She and I know that no improprieties transpired." Not unless he counted the pleasurable fondling on the river bank. "And I could never expect her to marry me just to stop tongues from wagging. However, I do wish to marry her, and I would like very much to give her what I hope she will find a more acceptable reason to accept my hand."

His eyes met Elizabeth's. The stubborn look changed to one of wariness. He held out a hand to her. She cocked her head to one side and slanted her eyes but rose.

Elizabeth's aunt started to protest, but Uncle Nate interrupted. "Give the lad a chance to say his piece, Phillida." He fluttered his hand. "Go on Hayward. Step out into the corridor do you need some privacy. And you, Elspeth, get off your high horse and hear the man out."

William was not sure Elizabeth's uncle's comment helped his cause, but Elizabeth did take his arm and let him lead her out the door.

Chapter 22

Alone with William in the corridor with the flickering light from the wall sconces forming puddles of illumination on the dappled walls, Elizabeth's anger drained away. William had proclaimed to all he wished to marry her. She had dreamed of this moment, though she had imagined more romantic circumstances. Still ... she looked up at William, and he clasped her hands in his. "My dear Elizabeth, you must know of my love for you. This is not how I envisioned my proposal, here in this dank, smelly corridor, but I feared you might think your uncles meant to force me into a marriage not of my choosing. Naught could be further from the truth. I have but been waiting for Mistress Blanchard and Sir Jeremy's fate to be determined ere I sought your hand. I have come to believe you hold me in esteem." He shook his head. "Esteem, nay, 'tis too dispassionate. No, my lovely Elizabeth, I have come to believe you return my love with an intensity equal to mine own." He drew her closer, and she felt his breath on her lips. "I pray thee, hold me not in suspense. Tell me my suit is not in vain."

Did she read true love in his eyes? Passion, desire, yes, but love? She had to know. She looked down then back up. "I may say yes, but my father may say nay. As you know, Aunt Phillida has doubts. Does she express those doubts, my father may not consent to our marriage. I will be twenty-one in four months. I could then marry you. But I would have no dowry."

William's lips quirked in a crooked smile. He released her hands and encircled her in his arms, trapping her hands against his chest. "Dear Elizabeth, when we were in the river, and I came close to losing you, I promised God did He spare me your life, I would do all in my power to make you the most loved woman in existence."

He had vowed that, had made a promise to God! His words left her breathless. He kissed the tip of her nose then brushed her lips, and a

169

scintillating prickle tingled up her spine. His eyes held hers, and his voice softened. "You are my fate. You are my soul. I cannot fathom life without you by my side. Indeed, you are my reason for living. Must I wait four months, four years, a life time, I will wait, for I can never marry another. You are inside me, a part of me."

He again brushed her lips, and she ached to have him claim a longer kiss. Enthralled by his words of love, she wanted to wrap her arms around his neck and feel his passion match her own, but he was not done convincing her of his love. "I cannot feel your father would be so cruel as to disavow you, and I admit, your dowry would make our life more comfortable, but 'tis not needed. I can support you. My client list is ever growing, and I will someday inherit my father's estate. We may not reside in a house on the strand, but we will not be paupers."

Wrapped in ecstasy, she breathed, "Oh, William, how I have longed for this day that I might speak your given name and hear mine own name upon your lips and none can say 'tis improper. Yes, I will marry you. 'Tis long past since I did give you my heart. To know I hold yours brings me greater joy than e'er I have known."

She noted the light in his eyes that her words evoked. To her delight he seemed content to end his speech and convince her of his love with his kiss. She managed to extricate her arms and creep them up around his neck that she might hold him tight and ensure a longer kiss. His tongue found hers, alleviating her greedy thirst, and she quivered with her need to know more of this man who had won her heart. Clinging to him as he gripped her hips and pressed her against his manhood, she reveled in his need for her. So heated was their passion, she believed they could burst into flame and soar away in smoke and ashes. Then he forcibly pulled away from her.

Keeping her at a distance by holding her upper arms, he said, "Ye gads, Elizabeth, you are near to driving me mad. We must need return to the table..." Looking down he shook his head. "And I am not fit to walk through that door. Nor do I think are you. With your cheeks aflame, your passion shows on your countenance."

Swallowing, she tried to calm her racing pulse. She smiled. "Mayhap 'tis a good thing does our love show. Aunt Phillida can never hold out against you does she know the fervor of our love. She has too compas-

170

sionate a heart. Come, let us tell them of our betrothal."

Elizabeth blushed as she resumed her seat. All eyes were on her. Chuckling, Uncle Nate looked at William. "May I assume you have convinced my niece to accept your proposal, Mister Hayward?"

※ ※ ※ ※

The remainder of the evening was a blur to Elizabeth. At Garrett's and her uncles' urging, Aunt Phillida consented to write to Elizabeth's father to tell him Elizabeth had found the man she wished to marry and had accepted his proposal, subject to her father's approval. She promised to portray William in the best manner she could. Elizabeth's uncles also promised to write her father and state their favorable views on the proposed marriage.

Neither Elizabeth nor William wanted a long betrothal. They hoped to set a wedding date as soon as they heard back from Elizabeth's father. Elizabeth could well understand her cousin Reginald's eagerness to wed if he was anywhere near as in love as she. The question was where to hold the ceremony. Should they have a small quiet wedding in London, or a large gathering and invite all the D'Arcys to her father's estate in Oxfordshire, or should they go to Wealdburh and have a quiet ceremony with just William's father and Elizabeth's immediate family?

"The question revolves around your mother," Aunt Phillida said. "You know she cannot make the trip to London or to Oxfordshire. Do you wish her present, you must need go home." She took Elizabeth's hands. "You have determined you will marry William Hayward. I am not blind. I see the love you bear one another. I could wish you had fallen in love with a Marquess, but as you have not, I can now only consider what will be best for your happiness." She gripped Elizabeth's hands more tightly, and her eyes filled with unshed tears. "My dear niece, I love you as I love my own daughters. This pains me to say, but for your sake, I urge you to marry quickly here in London, then travel as husband and wife to introduce Mister Hayward to your parents."

She blinked and a tear slid down her cheek. Elizabeth leaned forward. "Aunt Phillida, what is wrong. Why do you cry?"

Aunt Phillida shook her head and brushed away the tear. She offered a wan smile. "'Tis so hard to say this, my dear, but you know your mother is dying."

Elizabeth sat up straight and jerked her chin up.

"There now," Aunt Phillida said. "I knew I would upset you, but I must warn you, do you not marry before your mother dies, you will be in mourning. No doubt you would feel obliged to wait a minimum of a year before you marry. If not, you would have to be married in black as apparently Reggie's young bride may have had to do. Your wedding celebration would need be small and quiet. I cannot think you wish that or to wait a year."

Elizabeth knew her aunt was right. She wanted her wedding day to be joyous. Wanted it to be the happiest day of her life. She raised her gaze to meet William's. Yes, her mother was dying, but she never wanted to face it. Soon she would have to, and when her mother did die, she wanted William at her side. His eyes were warm, sympathetic. He had lost his mother at an early age. He would understand her pain. She looked back at her aunt and nodded.

"Phillida's right," Uncle Nate said. "Knowing your mother, she will want what will make you happy. When I write your father, I will remind him of the urgency. Kenrick will understand. He will be a lost man without your mother. I will need go to him. Mayhap I will accompany you and Hayward to Wealdburh. It has been near five years since last I visited the home of my childhood."

"Did I not have a wedding of my own to plan, I would join you," Uncle Ranulf said. "As soon as we have the mess with this Sir Jeremy and his wife cleared up, I must need return home. Then I am up to Nottingham to meet Reginald's bride. But let me know when you set the date for the ceremony, Elizabeth. I plan to attend."

"Thank you, Uncle Ranulf. You are most kind," Elizabeth said.

He patted her shoulder and bent to kiss the top of her head. "All will be well, little Elspeth. Is that not what I would tell you when as a child you angered your father or in some manner injured yourself? And was I not always right?"

Remembering the family gatherings, she smiled up at him. She and Garrett and her cousins had oft been in various scrapes when the families sojourned together every fourth summer at the Wallingford estate

172

in Oxfordshire. Her mother had not attended the last gathering, and might not be alive come the one scheduled for the summer the following year. Tears welled in Elizabeth's eyes. She was glad Garrett had left before Aunt Phillida brought up the subject. He could well be far out to sea when his mother died and would not know of her passing until he returned from his voyage. No reason to take the joy of his first command away from him now.

But she would take her aunt's advice. When her father gave his approval, and she had little doubt but that he would acquiesce to her wishes, she would start planning the ceremony. She looked again at William. Nay, she would start planning the ceremony immediately.

❀ ❀ ❀ ❀

Entering a darkened stretch near his lodgings, William lengthened his stride. He was making enough, he should find himself a better abode. A place in a more savory neighborhood. No, that would be a waste of money as he would be moving to much nicer lodgings when he married Elizabeth. He could wait the couple of months until they were wed. He did need to start looking for an acceptable apartment, or better yet, a house, for his soon to be bride. Elizabeth. His bride. He could not remember ever feeling so exhilarated. Being in love was grand. He could well be floating on air.

He could thank King Charles for his present bliss. Had his sovereign not commanded him to marry, he would never have set his sights on Elizabeth. He would never have been at the ball to meet her, or if he had been, he would have been accompanying Lady Harbinger and likely would never have noticed Elizabeth. Well, he might have noticed her, but he would have made no move to meet her. Before needing to seek a wife, he had given maidens a wide berth.

He had been instantly attracted to Elizabeth. Admittedly, at first, just to her beauty and her fortune, but he had soon come to admire her spirit and vivacity. He respected her courage, clearly evident when she braved King Charles at his dinner to aid her friend, and when she battled the River Thames' deadly current, never giving way to the exhaustion that consumed her. He found her interest in learning intriguing. A wife he could discuss business with would be far more stimulating than an addlepated woman of Appolonia Silverton's ilk. Did Elizabeth have a fault, 'twould be an overly loving, caring, and sympathetic heart. He feared at some point he would again be drawn into some scrape did Elizabeth decide to befriend and defend someone she considered to be in dire straits. He accepted that.

A happy smile curving his lips, he sensed rather than saw a movement to his right. Ducking, he narrowly missed a blow to his head. A whack from a club fell across his shoulders instead. He staggered then twisted away from a hand that grabbed at his coat sleeve. He could hear breathing, panting, his own and at least two others'. He struck out with his fist and connected with a stomach, or so he thought as an ooff sounded upon impact, and he felt and smelled sour breath on his face. Instinct guided his left hand, and he landed a glancing blow on his assailants chin. Hearing a footstep behind him, he hunkered down and heard a whoosh above his head, and a yowl ripped through the air.

"Criminy, you tomfool, watch where you swing that club, you hit me 'crost the nose. Near broke it, I am thinkin'."

The voice gave William a target. Both fists raised, he pummeled his quarry; face, belly, face again. He heard the impact of his fists squish against lips and an already injured nose, felt and smelled sticky blood on his knuckles. So rapid was his attack on the cutthroat, the man was unable to utter little more that grunts and oaths before he sank to the street.

A blow to his upper arm had William whipping about in time to grab the club before he could be struck a second time. Wresting the club free, he heard a curse then the thudding of running footsteps fading into the night. Coward, he thought, tossing the club onto the street. It clattered to rest, then all was quiet but the muffled groans of the man at his feet. Grabbing the man by the collar, he hauled him down the street toward a dim light peeping out from a poorly shuttered window. The man, his butt and heels bumping along on the cobble stones, bawled and pleaded for mercy. "For God's sake, sir, I can scarce breathe. Ye have mashed me nose o'er to the side of me face. Me gut's near ready to heave. Have some pity."

"Aye, like you would have had for me had you knocked me over the head with that club."

"We aimed not to kill you, sir. We were but to deliver a message, a strong message."

They reached the light, and William thrust the man up against the wall. "All right, let me hear the message." He had no sympathy for his assailant, though the man was covered in blood and more oozed from his smashed nose and from a cut above his eye. William knew, had he not reacted quickly, he would be the one battered and bleeding. Alert to the possible, though unlikely, return of the second man, William squatted over his defeated foe.

"What is your name," he demanded. The man blinked, glanced to one side, then said, "Smithy." The thin stream of light streaking down the peeling-plastered wall showed William the man who had been following him for over a week. He doubted the ruffian had told him his true name, but it would suffice. "I assume the message is from Creighton," he said.

Smithy wiped a bloodied sleeve across his swollen lip then grimaced and coughed before answering. "Aye. He said to tell you he wants his betrothed back or worse will befall you and mayhap your fine laidy as well."

Heat stung William's face, and his pulse pounded in his temples. He grabbed the man's collar and jerked him forward. "Creighton dared to threaten Lady Elizabeth!"

Smithy wheezed, his breath so foul, William shoved him back against the wall. "I haf no knowledge who the laidy be," he whimpered. "I am but tellin' you his lordship's message."

"Well, you are to take a message back to Creighton. Tell him does he or his paid assailants come near Lady Elizabeth, he is a dead man." He thumped Smithy's shoulder. "You got that?"

Smithy grimaced but answered, "Aye, I will tell him."

William again grabbed Smithy by the collar but did not pull him close enough to offend his nose. "And tell him the next assailants he sends after me, they are dead. They will not be delivering any messages." He looked into Smithy's uninjured eye. "You understand me, Smithy, I see you again, you are dead."

Smithy gulped and nodded. "Aye, sir, you will ne'er see me again."

Standing, William looked out into the dark. He would have to be more careful from now on. Maybe keep his sword with him, hire a lantern boy on moonless nights. He would not have guessed Creighton to be so ruthless, but then the Puritans were not known to be cowards. They had fought bravely, had repeatedly defeated the Royalists, and had subdued the Irish and the Scottish. Creighton might look the fop, but no doubt he was battle scarred. William would not again underestimate his antagonist. And he would keep a closer watch on Elizabeth.

Leaving Smithy slumped against the wall, William, his senses vigilant, struck out down the street. Did all go as planned, Elizabeth's uncles would soon win a reprieve for Annis and Sir Jeremy. The couple would pay King Charles a handsome bribe or fine, whatever the King might choose to call it, then go home to Thorley Hall to live out their lives in peace. But Creighton could well seek revenge. William suspected that revenge might be directed at him and Elizabeth rather than Creighton's escaped prey. Still, he would urge Sir Jeremy to be on his guard.

As he neared his lodgings, his racing pulse slowed, and he became aware of a throbbing ache across his shoulders. The night air stung his knuckles, and a pain in his right hand from a blow he landed on Smithy's jaw had him guessing the hand would be swollen come the morrow. He would have to soak his hand before going to bed if he meant to have the use of it the following day. He was glad he had learned the sport of bare-knuckle boxing. His training had served him well this night. He had no wish to alarm Elizabeth, but he would tell her uncles of the incident. He had no doubt they too would take measures to insure her safety. All the same, he would be counting the days until she was under his protection.

Chapter 23

Elizabeth wished she could chew her fingers, as she had as a child when she was frightened or nervous about being called to account for some misdeed. Her uncles were closeted with King Charles in his private chamber, while she, Aunt Phillida, William, Garrett, and Annis and Sir Jeremy waited in the audience chamber. Her uncles had returned the previous morning with word the King wished to see the lot of them. According to her uncles, King Charles gave no indication as to how he might view Annis and Sir Jeremy's supplication or Elizabeth and William's part in the couple's elopement.

Pacing back and forth over the floor's woven rush matting, she carefully avoided the red ornamented carpet spread out under the only chair in the room, a type of throne for the King. Its six-foot-high, intricately carved back and curved arms and legs of polished maple set off the plush, purple seat cushion and matching footstool. She would normally have exclaimed over the florid design of the wallpaper and the gilded window frames, but with her pulse pounding in her head, she could not find the heart. Even a dancing pattern of sunlight pouring in through diamond-pane windows failed to brighten her mood. She cocked her head. Did she hear laughter coming from the King's chamber? That could be good.

She looked at William. Talking to Garrett in a quiet voice, he did not look nervous, but Annis and Sir Jeremy clung to each other. They had been reluctant to come, thinking perhaps they should instead book passage on the first ship leaving for Europe. William had convinced them they had naught to fear. He was confident King Charles would bear them no grudge, especially as they were willing to royally compensate him. She prayed William was right.

Her face a mask, Aunt Phillida's countenance showed none of her inner conflicts. Elizabeth knew she was prepared to do whatever might be necessary to deflect the King's wrath against her niece. But she had also expressed her aggravation at being placed in such a defensive position. "Your father knows well I was leery of bringing you to London. You have ne'er been good at disciplining your speech or actions. I had little doubt but what you would land yourself in some type of mischief, but I never dreamed it would involve the King."

Elizabeth apologized for causing her aunt grief, but, secretly, she could not be sorry she had tried to help Annis. Women were at the mercy of men. 'Twas important to marry a kind and loving man. She believed she had found such a man in William, and she had no doubt Sir Jeremy was devoted to Annis. Now, would King Charles but be the kind and understanding King she had always believed him to be, all would be well.

The door to the King's chamber opened and King Charles, followed by Elizabeth's uncles, strolled into the audience chamber. As always, she was struck by how tall and dark the King was, but was she not mistaken, his dark eyes were twinkling. She, her aunt, and Annis sank into deep curtsies. The men swept off their hats and bowed low.

"Arise, all of you," the King said. He went first to Aunt Phillida and took her hand. "Lady Grasmere, it pleases us to see you again. We are thinking you will have an interesting tale to take back to Lady Elizabeth's father."

"Elizabeth was ever spoiled by her parents. 'Tis no wonder she at times acts before she thinks. She has been with me ten years, and I have yet to break her of the habits formed in her youth."

The King chuckled. "Were she a man, we think she would make a courageous soldier, could she but learn to follow orders." Elizabeth flushed at the King's rejoinder. "As is," he continued, "we understand, does Lord Tyneford give his consent, she will no longer be your concern."

Before Aunt Phillida could answer, King Charles turned to William. "You aimed high, young Hayward. When we told you to find a wife, we had not expected you to choose an Earl's daughter, and one with a liberal dowry at that. You are to be congratulated."

Elizabeth shot a dumbfounded glance at William. The King had told him to marry! He did not want to get married, he had been commanded to marry. Why King Charles would make such a demand, she could not guess, but she had no intention of marrying a man being forced to take a bride. Heat stung her ears, and she barely heard the King's next words.

"Considering the lady's precedence, and at the urging of her uncles, we have decided to make you a baronet. You will receive your letter of patent once my steward has it drawn up. We considered knighting you, if for naught but to have you kneel at our feet, but we could think of no accolade. Besides, Lord Rygate seems to think you will have sons and will wish your title to be hereditary. So, you shall be Sir William Hayward, but expect no gift of land with this title."

William looked surprised by his new title, but he again bowed low. "I thank you, Your Majesty. You are most generous. I am undeserving, but for Lady Elizabeth's sake, I am deeply appreciative." He glanced at Elizabeth then dropped to one knee before the King. "I kneel before you now, Your Majesty, because I can never thank you enough for commanding me to take a wife. Did I look the world over, I could never find a woman the equal of Lady Elizabeth. Had I not met her, my life would forever be incomplete, unfulfilled. I could never love another as I love her, could never enjoy the camaraderie I share with her with any other living soul. That you have granted me a title is an honor, but that you have given meaning to my life is the greatest gift ever bestowed on a mere mortal." With head bowed, he took the King's hand and kissed it.

"Did I have doubts about your choice of a husband," Aunt Phillida said in Elizabeth's ear, "William Hayward has vanquished them. I cannot think any other man would hold you so dear."

Elizabeth agreed with her aunt. He had erased her doubts about his wish to marry her. He loved her with an intensity that matched her own. Even King Charles was applauding his fervor. As were her uncles, and Annis clapped her hands like a child before she became self-conscious and hid her face against her husband's chest.

"Arise, Hayward," King Charles said. "You have proclaimed your love in a manner befitting a poet. Such a speech must surely bind your lady's heart. We find we approve of this jointure and will write the Lady Elizabeth's father and tell him so, but now we must turn to this other matter." As William rose, King Charles directed his gaze to Annis and Sir Jeremy.

"We have been told you two have an abiding love, and though you were married by proxy, you have spent the past week consummating said marriage." Before either could speak, the King continued. "We have also been told your betrothal is of long standing. That the marriage was arranged by your families, while you were still near infants, but that you each confirmed your consent at the appropriate ages. You, Mistress Blanchard, at the age of twelve, and you, Sir Jeremy, at the age of fourteen. Are we correct on this?"

"Yes, Your Majesty," Sir Jeremy answered firmly, Annis, timidly.

"We believe we were not given an accurate accounting of the situation by Lord Creighton. A serious transgression that merits at the least a remunerative forfeiture. However, we can but think mayhap he was not made privy to the longstanding betrothal and but sought to insure Mistress Blanchard would not be left unprotected after her grandfather's death."

Elizabeth snorted then clamped a hand over her mouth. The King glanced at her, and his mouth twitched. He was making excuses for himself and for Creighton, but then, he was known for his leniency. According to Elizabeth's father, King Charles, upon his restoration, had attempted to confine revenge to as few victims as possible. He could not pardon surviving regicides, but he could ignore them, did they commit no new offenses. Likewise, by proclaiming he had been given faulty information by Creighton, the King had found a way to keep Creighton's bribe as a fine and in lieu of more severe punishment. Elizabeth guessed King Charles would extract compensation from Sir Jeremy as well. His next words confirmed her assumption.

"We have been considerably vexed by this entire misunderstanding. We met with Lord Creighton and Mistress Blanchard." He looked at Annis. "Mistress, you might have told us then of your long standing betrothal and saved us all this aggravation."

"But, Your Majesty," Annis began in a small voice, only to have King Charles wave her to silence. Elizabeth knew Annis had been given no more chance to voice her complaints at her first meeting with the King than she was presently being given. Again he was waving aside his own infraction as he continued, "We sent word to the bishop to look into an annulment. Now, we will need send word to discontinue the proceedings. The investigation, of course, entailed expenses ...," he paused, and Sir Jeremy blurted out, "Your Majesty, I will be pleased to cover any and all the court's expenses as well as compensate Your Majesty for the aggravation you have endured."

King Charles smiled. "Your recompense will do much to ease our discomfiture regarding this muddlement." He scratched his chin. "We should think four hundred marks should cover the Consistory Court expenses and render adequate reparation for our time sorting out this pother."

At the sum the King announced, Elizabeth caught a gasp in her throat, and Annis's eyes grew wide, but Sir Jeremy hastily inserted, "Indeed, Your Majesty, I will tender said sum as soon as I see my solicitor and then my banker. My wife and I cannot thank Your Majesty enough for recognizing our marriage as being valid and for setting aside the annulment proceedings. Does it please Your Majesty, I would like on the morrow to take my wife home."

King Charles waved his hand airily. "Depart when you wish. We have sent for Creighton and will inform him of our decision." He turned from them, in effect dismissing them, and directed his gaze on Garrett. "Come here young Captain. We wish to get a good look at you. We do believe you greatly favor your father, but for the color of your hair and eyes."

As Annis and Sir Jeremy bowed and backed up toward the door, Garrett stepped forward. "Your Majesty," he said, bowing low. "'Tis said I favor my father in temperament as well as looks. My dear mother is patience itself, but I, like my sister, am known to act in haste. I do profoundly regret any trouble my actions may have inadvertently caused Your Majesty."

King Charles chuckled. "You have a glib tongue like your father. We are pleased he so often uses his eloquence on our behalf and not against us." He sobered. "How fares your mother? When last we saw your father, he said she was in ill health, and he was eager to return to her."

Tears sprang to Elizabeth's eyes at the mention of her mother, and she saw Garrett swallow hard before answering. "She is kind and loving as always, but she grows weaker with each winter." He brightened. "However, spring is upon us. The warmer air should perk her up."

"When we write to your father concerning your sister's betrothal, we will commend our good wishes to her," King Charles said before turning to Uncle Ranulf. "You and Lord Rotherby will take supper with us tonight?" Though phrased as a question, Elizabeth knew her uncles had no choice but to join the King for their evening meal and most likely some ribaldry at Nell Gwynn's afterwards. Elizabeth would miss them at her own table, but nothing could spoil her joy. Annis and Sir Jeremy were united. The King himself approved her betrothal to William and would write her father. No one but Creighton was to be punished, and with naught but a fine in the form of confiscation of his bribe.

Before returning to his inner chamber, King Charles took Aunt Phillida's hand and raised it to his lips. "As always, Lady Grasmere, we are pleased to see you. Give our good wishes to your husband when next you write to him."

"I shall do so, Your Majesty, and thank you," Aunt Phillida said, sinking into a curtsy and bowing her head. Elizabeth and Annis followed suit, and the men bowed at the waist until the King disappeared, and the door was closed behind him.

When Elizabeth rose from her curtsy, she grabbed Annis and gave her a tight squeeze. "Did I not promise you all would be well?"

🌿 🌿 🌿 🌿

Supper was a joyful occasion with much laughter and merriment. Sitting at the table between William and Garrett, Elizabeth believed she had never been happier. Across from her, Annis beamed with joy. She kept touching her husband as if she were afraid he might vanish. She cherished being addressed as Lady Danvers and could talk of little but how eager she was to return home. She had decided to take her aunt, Beata Underhill, with her.

"Poor thing," Annis said. "She wanted not to harm me, but she was more afraid of Lord Creighton than was I. She has no place to go, and Creighton has given her until tomorrow to vacate our lodging. She is, after all, family. I can hardly see her cast out on the street."

"I know you are right," Elizabeth said, "but I cannot think I would be so generous."

Annis laughed. "Oh, say no such thing. I know well how kind a heart beats in your bosom. I would not now be here with Jeremy but for your generous nature."

"My wife speaks the truth," Sir Jeremy said. "We owe our happiness, nay our very lives to you, Captain D'Arcy, and Sir William." He referred to William by his new title. Elizabeth liked the sound of it, but she cared not whether William had a title or not. She simply loved him.

"Your kindness and generosity can never be repaid," Sir Jeremy continued, "but you will all ever be welcome at either of our homes. We mean to divide our time between our two estates, but you will not be apt to see our faces here in London e'er again, can we avoid it."

"Now there I cannot say I blame you," Garrett said. "The hustle and bustle, the noise and the crowds have me longing to return to the sea as soon as I may. And the smells! Why, much of London smells worse than a ship that has not had its bilge pumped in over a year."

William chuckled. "Your stay here has been too brief. Once you have lived in London for a year or more, you can think of nowhere else on earth you would ever want to live."

A chorus of groans greeted his sally, and Elizabeth took his right hand. "But look at your hand, my love. 'Tis raw and swollen. That a gentleman should be attacked on the streets speaks poorly for your beloved London." She shook her head when he started to speak. "Nay, I know we will be making London our home. And I know we will be living in a safer district. All the same, I cannot but think Garrett has less to fear from pirates than do innocents who chance out upon London streets at night."

"I agree with my niece," Aunt Phillida said. "But the other day, one of my footmen, who ventured into a roguish area by mistake, was accosted by several ruffians and barely escaped a thrashing. Fortunately for him, he is fleet of foot and outran the miscreants. I will not rest easy until I know Elizabeth will be settled in safe lodgings, and that she will have at least two footmen to accompany her does she mean to venture outside Westminster."

"Tomorrow I set about searching out appropriate lodging," William said. "I would not have her anywhere near my present lodgings. I would also be happy to start interviewing for a coachman as well as for a steward unless Elizabeth, under your supervision, chooses to do such."

Elizabeth looked to her aunt. Aunt Phillida nodded and narrowed her eyes. "You are wise, Sir William, I will say that for you. Yes, I do think 'tis best Elizabeth and I interview applicants for the various household positions. We will let you deal with whatever stable hands you may deem necessary. You will also need a coach and four or mayhap six horses. However, until we receive word from Elizabeth's father consenting to the marriage, 'twould not be seemly to start such procedures. Until his consent is obtained, we may not even announce the betrothal."

William glanced at Elizabeth and smiled. "Waiting will not be easy. Now I have found the woman I love, 'tis hard to be apart from her, but we will abide by your wishes. I trust to your judgment in these matters, Lady Grasmere."

Elizabeth returned William's smile. He knew exactly how to placate her aunt. Of course, her aunt knew William meant to disarm her, but she seemed to enjoy their jousting.

When the supper party broke up, Annis hugged Elizabeth and promised to write her as soon as she was home. She apologized that she would not be present for Elizabeth and William's wedding, but she could not bring herself to return to London. Too many sad and fearful memories would lie in wait for her. "Say you forgive my lack of courage," Annis said.

"I understand your conflict, dear friend," Elizabeth said. "Had I lived in such anguish as you were forced to endure, I would not wish to revisit the scene of my travails." She patted Annis's hand. "Happen we plan but a small wedding anywise. As neither my parents nor William's father, owing to a recent back injury that bars him from riding any distance, will be present, we plan to wed as soon as my father sends his consent. I have hopes Garrett will still be here. Uncle Ranulf goes home to Rygate on the morrow, but he promises to return for my wedding, but my family and most of my cousins, as well as William's family, are too distant to attend at such short notice. We mean to keep the ceremony intimate. We will then visit William's father on our way to visit my parents."

"You have already done much planning," Annis said. She glanced at her husband and a wistful look crept across her face. "How drab was my wedding with my grandfather dying and a proxy standing in for Jeremy." She brightened, a smile lighting up her eyes. "I am being foolish. We are together. I can ask for little more."

Hugs were exchanged and Annis and Sir Jeremy left with entreaties to their friends to visit them. Garrett left shortly afterward, and William, amidst Elizabeth's protests, followed him out the door. Had Aunt Phillida not been present, she knew William would have kissed her. Her lips ached to have him take the kiss awaiting him, but her craving went unfulfilled. Feeling hollow inside, she clutched at her stomach.

"Whatever is the matter, Elizabeth, your face is all scrunched up!" Aunt Phillida declared.

Elizabeth could not help herself. She burst into tears and stumbled into her aunt's arms. "Oh, Aunt Phillida, I had no idea love could be so painful. When I am in William's presence, I feel complete, but when I am away from him, I feel so desolate. Did you feel this way before you married Uncle Berold?"

Aunt Phillida wrapped her arms around Elizabeth and patted her back. "Why, my dear niece, I feel that way even now with Berold so far away. I often lie awake at night, longing to be cradled in his arms. To ache for the one you love gives both pain and pleasure. May you always know the love you are experiencing now. May the ache never die."

Sniffling, Elizabeth pulled away from her aunt and stared into her misty eyes. "Oh, I had no idea you felt so aggrieved at being parted from Uncle Berold. You are doubly kind to have brought me to London." She squeezed her aunt in a tight hug. "How selfish I have been. Never giving your feelings a thought."

Aunt Phillida laughed and extracted herself from Elizabeth's embrace. "That is enough. 'Tis time we went to bed. We have a busy day tomorrow preparing for Lady Worverton's ball."

"Oh my, so much has happened, I had forgotten all about it. Yes, and I have my new gown to wear. I can scarce wait to see the look in William's eyes when he sees me. I do think the crimson striped overskirt hitched up at the sides sets off the brownish pink underskirt to perfection." She did not mention that she believed William would be more impressed with the gown's tight-fitting, small-waisted bodice and low décolletage encircled with lace frills, but she had little doubt but what her aunt knew well what would entice a lover. All the same, with the mention of the dance, Aunt Phillida had banished the painful ache in her heart and innards. She would see William on the morrow, and she would glory in the look in his eyes.

Chapter 24

Lady Worverton's dance and card party was a grander affair than Elizabeth had anticipated. The Worverton home, though aged, had been beautifully renovated in the latest mode, and was perfect for entertaining. The great hall, which Elizabeth had but passed through on previous visits, was festooned in colorful streamers and flowers. A group of musicians were tuning up in the gallery above the ornately decorative screen, and at the opposite end of the hall, she could see through an open door to the parlor where several men were seated at an array of card tables.

Cushioned benches lined the walls of the hall, and Aunt Phillida, upon detecting Lady Bainbridge, immediately settled down beside her friend. Elizabeth spotted the Silverton sisters, but before she could think how to avoid them, they rushed to greet her with their latest news. Did she know William Hayward had been made a baronet? Yes she did, Elizabeth replied, looking about for William or for Blythe Elsworth or anyone who might save her from the chatty sisters.

Appolonia whispered in her ear. "Have you yet met the Marquess, Lady Worverton's son?"

Elizabeth shook her head. "I have met but her daughter, Lady Byrenum, the night she played the harp for us. The night of the opera, remember?"

Appolonia wrinkled her nose. "Could I forget? Her choices were so languorous, she near put me to sleep. I do believe she did put Lady Canby to sleep. And her own husband, Lord Byrenum, was definitely dozing." She giggled. "Florence claims he was snoring until Lord Holcomb nudged him. Am I not correct, Florence?" Appolonia turned to her sister for collaboration.

Florence nodded enthusiastically, causing the feather arrangement in her hair to bob about. "I was seated next to Lord Holcomb and saw him nudge him. I could scarce control a giggle when Lord Byrenum snorted and gazed around for but an instant then fell right back to sleep."

Elizabeth sighed. She needed rescuing. Plastering a smile on her face, she tried to respond suitably to the sisters' inane chatter, but she was growing weary of the baleful gibberish. Appolonia reclaimed her attention. "Anyway, wait until you meet Lord Worverton." She rolled her eyes upward and fanned herself. "He is as handsome as his sister is plain."

"Yes," Florence piped up, "but they say his only interest is in hunting. They say he can but stumble through a few dances, and that he spends most of his time at parties playing cards."

Elizabeth wondered who 'they' might be but decided not to ask. Besides, Appolonia was again whispering in her ear. "They say when he is in London, he keeps company with some actress. I imagine that has his mother distraught. She wants him to wed and produce an heir."

"No doubt he will oblige her," Elizabeth said, a lightness lifting her heart as she spied William advancing toward her. And just in the nick of time. She was near ready to scream. A broad-shouldered, slightly shorter man walked beside him, and Appolonia, turning in the direction Elizabeth gazed, gushed, "That is Lord Worverton. Did I not tell you he was handsome?"

Elizabeth cared not whether Lord Worverton was handsome, she but wanted to feast her eyes on William. She acknowledged the introduction to the Marquess and smiled at his gallantries but paid them little heed. She wanted to revel in William's presence, bask in his smiles. When his hand touched hers, her skin sizzled. The looks he gave her told her he appreciated her new gown, and she exulted in his approval, a warmth spreading to engulf her body in a molten heat.

Vaguely aware the music had commenced, she started when Lord Worverton asked for her hand to lead her out for the first dance. Being asked for the first dance by the host of the party was an honor, but she had expected to be at William's side. With all eyes on her, she placed her hand on Lord Worverton's forearm, and forcing herself not to look longingly back at William, let Worverton lead her to the center of the room. All traces of a central hearth had been removed, and in its place the Worverton coat of arms, artfully crafted in tiles, decorated the floor.

She smiled up at Lord Worverton. He was handsome, in a rough kind of way. His skin was as weathered as Mister Ridgely's. She guessed because he spent so many days outside hunting. His nose was large, but it did not detract from his looks. It gave him a primordial look, suggesting confidence and reliability. His brown eyes looked bright and intelligent, and he had an open smile and a ready laugh, which quickly surfaced as he stumbled through the stately pavane.

"Do I step on your toes, do forgive me, Lady Elizabeth," he said, leading with his right foot when he should have led with the left. "Hayward assured me you would be kindhearted and would not spurn me for my poor attempt at mastering the opening dance. As the host, I must need lead out a lady to start the dancing, but once this dance is over, I may retire to the tables until supper."

A twinge of anger pricked Elizabeth. William had known Lord Worverton meant to ask her to dance. She had been hungering to be with William, and he, without a thought for her wishes, had committed her to dance with the Lord of the house. She could well imagine the speculative questions being bandied about. The Silverton sisters would think she had set her cap for Lord Worverton. Every matriarch lining the benches would be certain the ties of friendship binding Aunt Phillida and Lady Worverton insured she had been the one honored with the opening dance, and their envious daughters would be hankering for her blood. She wished she and William could announce their betrothal. That would put an end to any malicious gossip.

Again Lord Worverton led with the wrong foot, causing both of them to stumble. He apologized profusely, and she glared at a grinning William. At least he had not asked anyone to dance. When the dance ended, Lord Worverton escorted her to William's side. "I understand," he said, "that the next dance is promised to you, am I not correct, Sir William?"

"You are correct," William said, not giving Elizabeth time to answer. "I will see you later for a hand or two. But remember, you have promised to join Lady Elizabeth and me for supper."

"I will not forget. And thank you again for the dance, Lady Elizabeth."

Elizabeth acknowledged his thanks, but she was looking up at William through slanted eyes. When Lord Worverton walked away, she hissed, "How could you so cavalierly consign my hand for the first dance? Did you not think I might want a say in whom I might choose as a partner?"

The music started and William proffered his arm. "Do me the honor, and I will explain all."

She cast him a disgruntled look, but put her hand on his arm, and they joined the other dancers. As they paraded around the floor, Elizabeth relaxed beside William's expert maneuvering. She need not worry her foot would be trounced, but she was still piqued, and William's chuckle when he looked down at her did little to mollify her temperament. "Pray, still your anger, dear Elizabeth, and do accept both mine and Worverton's gratitude for your patience with the poor man. He cannot dance, as of course you found out. Nor has he any wish to learn. He is a man who loves the outdoors and abhors the confines of London. However, he must pay periodic visits to his mother. And she will insist on giving these huge affairs in his honor."

The dancers they were following stopped, and they halted. A toe point here, another there, a pause, then off they went again. "The trouble is," William resumed his apology, "any lady that Lord Worverton leads out for the opening dance will get ideas he is fixing his interest in them. 'Tis unfair to the lady. For the past couple of years, to avoid giving false hope to any young lady and her mother, he has led out his sister or his mother. This year his mother informed him neither would accept his hand. He confided his dilemma to me."

"So you suggested he dance with me," Elizabeth snapped. "And now everyone is thinking his interest is fixed with me."

"Yes, but you and I know you have not fixed your interest on him." He smiled the smile she loved so dearly, and her anger melted away as he leaned in closer. "Your interest is fixed on me. And soon we tell the world, 'tis so."

"Until then, I shall have to endure back stabbing stares and sniggering remarks," Elizabeth said with a frown.

"For that, I am sorry, but you did Worverton a great service, and he never forgets those who come to his aid. He will, at some point, find a fitting way to thank you."

Elizabeth fluttered her hand. "Oh, do tell him he is not to worry. He must be a good friend, do you wish to help him. And is he your friend, so shall he be mine. One must oblige a friend. But you might well warn him the gossipers say his mother expects him to wed and produce an heir. So does he have no wish to wed, he had best be alert to the traps that will be laid for him."

William laughed as again they paused and elegantly pointed their toes to left and right. "Worverton knows well his mother's plans, and he endeavors to stay one step ahead of her," William said when they resumed their march. "He has no plans to wed and has no concern about his cousin succeeding to his title. The cousin's a fine young man with a lovely wife and two sons. Neither Worverton's title nor name will be besmirched in any way."

"His mother must feel differently," Elizabeth said as the dance ended.

"Mothers are like that. Think but how your mother would feel does your older brother have no sons. At least she has your brother Garrett, 'tis better than a nephew who carries none of her blood in his veins."

Elizabeth stopped and wrinkled her nose. "No, Robert must have a son. Garrett is not next in line. I have another older brother, Julian. He is heartless and vile," she spit out then shook her head. "I will not ruin this evening talking of him. So yes, I think I can understand how Lady Worverton feels. But at least you say Lord Worverton's cousin is a good man."

He nodded. "Indeed, a very good man."

"Then let us hope Lady Worverton will not be terribly disappointed does her only son choose not to marry," Elizabeth said before William left her with her next dance partner.

She danced a number of dances with various courtiers before William again claimed her hand. 'Twas the dance before supper was announced, and when it ended, he escorted her upstairs to the great chamber. True to his promise, Lord Worverton joined them, as did Blythe Elsworth. Lord Worverton might not know his way around the dance floor, but off the dance floor, he was every bit as charming as William claimed. He not only told witty anecdotes, but flirting outrageously, he lavished scintillating compliments on Elizabeth. She had no doubt people would soon be saying he was taken with her. She could just hear his mother joyfully twittering away to Aunt Phillida who would not be able to tell her friend of her misguided perceptions.

She was both amused and annoyed by Lord Worverton. He was near as flirtatious with Blythe, and after what William had told her about Lord Worverton's aversion to marriage, she worried Blythe might think Worverton fancied her. She hinted as much to Blythe who laughed and said, "Lord Worverton flirts only with women he knows have no interest in marrying him. He and I determined years ago we would not suit. We are but friends. He is entertaining in small doses, but can you imagine what life with him would be like? He can talk of little but his hunting experiences. He has had any number of exciting and amusing escapades, but he cannot remember when he last read a book. He hunts, cleans his guns, plays cards, races horses, and from what I have heard, often visits the theater. Does he someday decide to marry, I do pity his poor wife."

Elizabeth giggled. Blythe had aptly described the man so many ladies would sell their souls to marry. 'Twas fortunate he knew he would make a poor husband and had no mind to inflict himself on any woman. He might be a Marquess, but he in no way measured up to her William.

❋ ❋ ❋ ❋

Elizabeth was wondering when William might again claim her hand for a dance when she heard his voice in her ear. "Meet me by the terrace doors." And he was gone. Lord Holcomb had asked for hand for the upcoming dance. She feigned weariness, and he offered to get her a glass of sherry. She thanked him, and as soon as he was out of sight, she worked her way to the doors opening out onto a broad terrace with steps leading down to a garden that descended to the river. Despite its size, with all the bodies packed into the hall, the air inside was stifling. Stepping out onto the terrace, Elizabeth inhaled deeply of the cool night air. The smell of spring flowers, sweet woodruff, bluebells, and the creamy-white flowers of the Hawthorn bush scented the air, overpowering the occasionally odiferous smells that floated up from the river.

Torches lit the terrace and some of the wider garden walks, but narrow unlit paths led off into the darkness. Elizabeth felt a hand on her elbow and looked up to find William grinning down at her. "Come, my dear Elizabeth, 'tis a lovely night for a stroll." He took her hand, and without another word, they hurried down the steps and into the garden. William chose a path that led them away from the brightly lit walkways. The ground was soft under foot, and she smelled the aroma of thyme and mint as they tripped across the herb planted path. Music and laughter from inside the hall floated on the soft breeze, and the crunch of gravel or sand underfoot as others trod darkened paths told them they were not alone in the garden. William steered them away from a light stream of giggles, and they found themselves in a pleached bower, the clipped and trained tree branches sheltering them, and the scent of rosemary encircling them.

Under the tightly intertwined branches of elm and cherry trees, the moon and stars were hidden from view, as were the glittering lights from the Worverton mansion and flickering flames of the outdoor torches. William pulled Elizabeth into an embrace, and his lips found hers. His kiss was light, delicate, undemanding. She ached to have him press her tightly against him, but he instead continued to deliver airy, tantalizing kisses that fanned the embers smoldering within her innermost being. Nibbling gently on her lips, he teased her, enticed her to demand more, and she did. Tracing his lips with her tongue, she probed the parted space between his lips. The tip of her tongue met his, and exalting in her conquest, she tightened her hold on him, molding her body to fit snuggly against his. Clinging to him, she firmed her lips and pressed her advantage. He was lost. His arms tightened around her, his lips opened to hers, and with their breaths mingling, they explored the heady sensations of their rapturous love.

His hand crept to her breasts, his fingers tracing the swells then dipping below the soft lace trim around the bodice. Her heart stopped when he stooped to plant velvet kisses on each breast before lightly flicking his tongue over and into the cleavage exposed to his featherlike touch. She gasped in wanton bedazzlement at her heated response to his caresses. What enchanted, magical wonders yet awaited her? She wanted this mystical moment to go on endlessly, but her senses told her this was but a stolen interim in time. Reality could reclaim them at any instant. Until it did, she meant to lose herself in the heavenly bliss of William's tantalizing lovemaking.

"Dear Elizabeth, what things you do to me," he whispered in her ear. "You tempt me beyond all reason. I love you so much, I can scarce wait for our marriage bed. Your father's consent had best come soon, or I may well go mad."

She laughed, thrilled by his admission of his need for her. "I feel the same needs as do you, my dear William. When apart from you, I feel I am but half a person. You make me whole."

"I do think I must be the luckiest man in all of England. Nay, in all the world. I cannot wait until I can tell the world you are mine." With that statement his lips again sought hers with a hunger that left her swooning. Had he not been holding her so tightly, she felt certain her legs would have crumpled beneath her. Oh, dear Father, she thought, I do hope you send your consent by rapid messenger. I cannot think how we can survive until we are married.

When William drew away from her, she grasped the collar on his coat and tried to pull him back. The ground was trembling, and she needed him to steady it. "Nay, my beauty," he said, "we must return ere we are missed. Besides, I cannot take much more. Another moment with you in my arms and I am apt to spirit you away to Fleet Street and a clandestine wedding."

The thought of an immediate marriage to William sent a heat wave spiraling down her body from head to toes, but she knew she could not so shame her family. No, she and William must sneak back into the hall, and she would find Lord Holcomb and chastise him for not bringing her the sherry. He would sputter and swear he had searched for her. She almost giggled at the thought. At least she had had this marvelous interlude with William. She could survive the rest of the evening traipsing around the dance floor with her other suitors. Soon they would all know of her betrothal, and she and William would no longer have to hide their love.

Chapter 25

Elizabeth and William had no need to sneak back into the hall. No one noticed their entrance or saw her straighten her gown or William pluck a leaf from her hair. King Charles, with his mistress, Louise de Keroualle, accompanying him, had deigned to attend Lady Worverton's ball. The hall was yet in an uproar as the King and his entourage paraded in and everyone bowed low before him. King Charles bid everyone rise and resume their merriment, and Elizabeth, spying Lord Holcomb, a glass of sherry still in his hand, blew a pantomime kiss to William then worked her way over to her discomfited courtier.

Before she could say a word, Holcomb started apologizing in his nasal whine that grated on her nerves. "Lady Elizabeth, you must think me addlepated." He rolled his eyes and shook his head. "I was on my way back to you with your sherry when they announced the King was arriving. I knew not what to do. Should I wait for his entrance, should I hurry across the floor and mayhap spill the sherry, and the King might step in it. I stood twisting and turning, and finally decided I should wait for the King's entrance." He held out the glass of sherry. "Dear Lady, do say you forgive my tardiness."

She took the glass and thanked him. "Of course, you are forgiven. I too stood still in amazement," she lied, well only half lied. She had been swept up in amazement, but by William's kiss, not the King's arrival. "I thank you for procuring the sherry for me. Now, do you please excuse me, I see the Lady Harbinger is in attendance, and I have yet to speak with her."

Lord Holcomb bowed, saying, "Indeed Lady Elizabeth, of course, of course. And again, my apologies for keeping you waiting."

Elizabeth felt almost, but not quite guilty for deceiving Holcomb. He was a nice man, but such a worrier. So afraid he would do something improper and people would laugh at him. Her thoughts turned from him to Lady Harbinger. Without her help, they would never have been able to arrange for Annis and Sir Jeremy to be together at the Hampstead Heath outing. And Lady Harbinger had been the one to suggest spiriting the young lovers away to consummate their marriage. Elizabeth wanted not only to thank her for her help, but to tell her the happy couple were on their way home.

Lady Harbinger greeted Elizabeth as though she were a dear friend. Her golden eyes twinkled and her smile radiated warmth. She embraced Elizabeth and whispered, "Do tell me, will we soon be hearing wedding nuptials are to be announced between you and that rogue, Hayward?"

She laughed, "No, you need not tell me, your blush says it all."

Elizabeth knew she was blushing, and she hoped no one had heard Lady Harbinger's quiet question. She also wondered the lady would call William a rogue. It spoke of a familiarity she guessed at but would never ask about. What was in William's past should remain there. He retained a friendship with Lady Harbinger, that she knew. She had even seen him dancing with her earlier in the evening, and a twinge of jealousy had pricked her when he had thrown back his head and laughed at something she said. But when she looked into the lady's eyes, she saw naught to cause her concern. Lady Harbinger seemed genuinely happy for her.

Leaning forward, Lady Harbinger again whispered in Elizabeth's ear. "I look forward to the day I can congratulate you and the new baronet." Her eyes took on a faraway look, and her smile became wistful. "How fortunate you are to have a family that loves you more than they love court connections and great wealth." For an instant Elizabeth thought she remembered having seen such a faraway look on someone else, but then Lady Harbinger shook her head and laughed her bubbly laugh, and the memory vanished.

"I understand from Blythe that you and she are to be part of an outing to St. James Park on the morrow," Lady Harbinger said. "I would consider joining you, but as the Silverton sisters are to make up part of your party, Selby is certain to go along. He seems much taken with the elder sister." She crinkled her nose and a wry smile twisted her mouth. "I find them most suitable to one another. They could both do worse."

196

"They are often in each other's company," Elizabeth admitted. "My guess, Lord Laidly will be joining us in our stroll. I am told the flowers are magnificent this year. And though Mister Hayward, I mean Sir William, will not be joining us, I look forward to seeing the display."

"You need not address Selby as Lord Laidly," Lady Harbinger said. "But I do find his appropriation of the title amusing as it so annoys Harbinger." She smiled her lovely smile, and her golden eyes glowed with mirth. "Here now, you will think me disparaging, a backbiter. Though I assure you, I say nothing I would not say to Harbinger or Selby in person."

Elizabeth returned her smile. "I could never think you guilty of backbiting, Lady Harbinger. I find you kind and caring and most entertaining. Your smile and laughter brighten up a room. And without your kindnesses, Annis and Sir Jeremy would not now be on their way home. They and I can never thank you enough for your help and advice."

"What a sweet one you are," Lady Harbinger said, giving Elizabeth a peck on the cheek. "No wonder Sir William loves you so desperately. Now, as you and Blythe are friends, so must we be friends. Henceforth, do please call me Cambria, and so shall I call you Elizabeth."

"I am honored, Lady ... I mean Cambria. So shall I cherish our friendship as I cherish Blythe's." Elizabeth did feel honored. To be on a first-name basis with the Marchioness of Harbinger was an unexpected thrill. She could hardly wait to tell her aunt. As she and William would be living in London, having such a friend would make being away from her family less painful.

Trumpets sounded and Elizabeth turned with her new friend to see the King was leaving. He could not have stayed above a quarter of an hour, but his attendance would make Lady Worverton's ball the entertainment to top. Everyone bowed low as King Charles and his party exited. When all were out the door, the music started up again, and Elizabeth was delighted to find William at her side. He bowed to Lady Harbinger, she gave him a nod and a smile, then he swept Elizabeth onto the dance floor.

She told him of her new friendship with Lady Harbinger. "You will enjoy her company," he said. "She is a highly intelligent woman, well read. I understand your disdain for those who are interested in naught but frivolous past times. Such can be amusing but are more enjoyable when peppered among more enlightening and stimulating entertainments."

For an instant Elizabeth was again pricked by jealousy, but when she looked up into William's eyes, she forgot her doubt. William loved her. He admired Lady Harbinger, and so did she. She would not let whatever might have been in their past sully the future.

Chapter 26

Elizabeth looked about, hoping to spot some means of escape. Her companions' babble was near driving her to distraction. What with Holcomb's whine, Selby Elsworth's pontificating, the Silverton sisters' non-stop drivel, and Erwina Ogden's hiccupping giggles, she could scarce enjoy the beauty of the day. And it was a beautiful day. The sun was bright overhead, the park flowers, especially the tulips, were as lovely as she had expected, and she believed, could they but have a bit of peace and quiet, she would be able to hear the birds singing.

She had been sorely disappointed when she received a note from Blythe telling her she was indisposed and would be unable to accompany her on the outing that afternoon. Not only would she miss Blythe's bright company, she would have no one of any sense to talk with. She had contemplated making some excuse herself to avoid the outing, but she knew her aunt would not approve. "Once fabrications are set in motion, they are hard to control," Aunt Phillida often reminded her. "The truth is always the safest option."

Elizabeth sighed. Not even Lord Albin was along to relieve the tedium with his regaling wit. William was visiting clients. "Do we wish to live in a style befitting you, and befitting my new title," he told her, "I must insure I have numerous and satisfied, clients. When they make money, we make money. I am also looking at lodging for us. No sooner do we receive word from your father agreeing to our marriage, and I will take you to look at a couple of suites I have in mind."

Eager to see the lodgings, Elizabeth had pressed him to take her to view them that afternoon after he attended his clients. He but chuckled. "Nay my dear, wait you must. We cannot yet have our names linked. I will not incur your aunt's wrath."

Well, her name was not being linked to William, she thought dryly. It was being linked to Lord Worverton. Erwina Ogden and the Silverton sisters had been persistent in their questioning. What had she and Worverton talked about when dancing? Had he asked to see her again? "He was certainly flirtatious with you," Erwina said. "During the supper break at the ball, I heard him compliment your hair, your gown, even your voice." No matter Elizabeth's insistence Worverton had no interest in her, they thought she was being coy.

Florence Silverton's squeal brought Elizabeth's attention back to her companions. Florence pointed to two lovely black swans on the lake. "Oh, let us do go see can we get a closer look at them," she cried, starting down a hard packed path with Lord Holcomb at her heels. The remainder of the party followed after them, Erwina's hiccupping giggles wafting on the air as she grasped Selby Elsworth's arm. With a glare at Erwina, Appolonia took his other arm and sidled up closer to him. Her presence forgotten, Elizabeth stared after them. A smile crept across her face. Could she but lose them for a short while, she could enjoy the park as it was meant to be enjoyed on such a lovely day, in peaceful solitude. Having no escort nor even her maid with her, she knew she should not wander far on her own, but a short reprieve from her present company would be such a blessing.

Heading off down a path lined by tall leafy bushes and blossoming horse chestnut trees that shielded her from view, she hurried her steps but stopped when the path opened onto a field strewn with tiny violets and other wild flowers. Inhaling deeply, she listened to the quiet. Glorious. After a moment she could distinguish faint sounds, the whispering of the tree leaves in the slight breeze, the buzzing of bees in the blossoms overhead, and at the sound of a rustling in the bushes, she looked down to see a small grey squirrel dart across the path. A bird called and another answered. Looking across the meadow, she spied several couples ambling arm in arm. Soon she would be able to enjoy the park with William. He would understand the pleasure of reflecting on the beauties of nature and would not abuse the park's sanctity with frivolous chatter. Hearing the crunch of pebbles behind her, she stepped out into the meadow so she would not be blocking the path. She should return to her group, but she wanted one more moment to enjoy the loveliness of the park before returning to her party.

"Ah, Lady Elizabeth, my eyes have not deceived me. I was correct 'twas you dashing away from your companions."

Surprised at being addressed by name, Elizabeth jerked around, but until he stepped from the shadows of the trees, she did not recognize the speaker. When she did, a tiny prick of fear stabbed her heart. Hoping her eyes did not betray her fear, she gave a slight nod and said, "Lord Creighton. Do excuse me, I must return to my party. They will by now have noticed my absence."

Before she could retrace her steps, he stepped in front of her. Shaking his head, he said, "Nay, I have decided you will be accompanying me."

Raising her chin, Elizabeth said, "Indeed sir, I shall not. Now do step aside."

"You will accompany me, Lady Elizabeth," Creighton said, drawing a pistol from the pocket of his coat and aiming it at her heart.

She gasped. "Sir, you cannot think to shoot me."

A fleshy man with a swag belly, he smiled an ugly twisted smile that sent shivers up her spine. "As I said, you will accompany me unless you wish your friends to find you with a bullet between your lovely eyes. Look about you. I could shoot you now, and no one would ever know who did the shooting."

She glanced from side to side. No one was close enough to recognize her or Creighton. For the moment, she had no choice but to do as he bid. "I see I must accompany you, but when I tell Sir William and my uncle what you have done, you will wish you had never approached me."

He chuckled and nudged her in the ribs with the gun. "Head across the meadow toward those Cypress trees. My carriage is not far from there. And think twice about calling out to anyone. Much as I would prefer to marry you, I will not hesitate to shoot you."

"Marry me!" Elizabeth stopped so suddenly Creighton rammed her in the back with the pistol, and she came close to falling. "Ow!" she cried.

He caught her arm. "Watch yourself. Yes, I intend to marry you. Today when first I saw you in the park, my anger near overwhelmed me. I thought could I but find the right place to get a good shot at you, you would be dead. A proper revenge for costing me Annis as my bride. I could not believe my good fortune when you set off down the path away from your party. But then as I followed you, I had a better idea.

Why not marry you?"

"You must be mad! I will not marry you." Elizabeth stared into Creighton's icy blue eyes.

His loathsome smile returned. "Oh, but you will marry me. In fact, I have no doubt your family will insist you marry me after running away with me."

"I am not running away with you!"

He inhaled deeply through his nose and nudged her again with his gun. "You try my patience, Lady Elizabeth. Keep walking. Can you not understand your reputation will be in tatters? Especially after I put it about you ruined my chance with Annis because you wanted me for yourself."

Elizabeth turned around again. "You are mad!"

An ugly red spread across his face. "Have a care not to anger me. I may decide I would rather see you dead even more than I will enjoy ravishing your body."

She recoiled at his words, but his gun to her ribs set her stumbling across the meadow. She knew her parents would never force her to marry Creighton even did he besmirch her reputation. But William, how would he feel about her did Creighton despoil her? Men set such a store by a woman's chastity, though few of them were chaste themselves. Would William still want her? She must not think such dire thoughts. She must instead be alert to a means of escape.

"I do hope you are not prone to seasickness, Lady Elizabeth."

"Seasickness!" Once again she stopped and once again he nudged her.

"Yes, we will be taking passage on whatever vessel is sailing out of Dover. A few months or a few years on the continent, perhaps a child or two. Oh, yes, your parents will be most happy to have you marry me. And I will insist upon that ten thousand pound dowry."

Not wanting another nudge, Elizabeth did not stop, but she said through gritted teeth, "They will kill you for this."

Creighton chuckled. Then he snarled, "What is that?"

Elizabeth heard a voice calling, "Milady, milady, do wait." Looking over her shoulder, she saw a youth in a patched green coat loping toward them, a large yellow dog following at his heels. She could not believe the youth would be calling to her, yet no one else was near. As he drew closer, she recognized him. He had sung the sweet ballads at the dancing dog show she had attended. So sweet had she found his voice, she had given him two pennies.

"Be off with you!" Creighton demanded as the boy drew near.

A bright grin on his face the youth doffed his cap. "Kind sir, I ask but a moment of your time. You cannot be in so great a hurry on this lovely day? My dog has learned a new trick I wish t' show your pretty lady, whose kind words and generous bounty were such a blessin' t' me."

"Be gone, I said!" Creighton nudged Elizabeth. "Tell him to be gone."

Fearing for the youth's safety, Elizabeth said, "Another time might be best. Lord Creighton seems in a hurry this day."

"But watch, then we will be gone," the youth said, putting a hand on his dog's head. Then smiling, he commanded, "Sit, Goldy, sit!"

The large gold dog did not sit. He leapt forward and flew through the air to land on Creighton with all four paws. The impact knocked Creighton off his feet. Hitting the ground with a heavy thud, Creighton yowled and the gun fell from his hand. The dog, teeth bared, but tail wagging, straddled his chest. The youth grabbed the gun, cocked it, and aimed it at Creighton.

Everything happened so quickly, Elizabeth could do naught but stare first at Creighton on the ground, then at her savior, gun in hand, standing over Creighton. Any move Creighton made was greeted by a snarl from Goldy. "Get him off me, get him off me!" Creighton cried

"Milady," her savior said, "I was of the impression you had no wish t' be in this man's company. Am I wrong, I do treat you t' accept my apology for disturbin' your walk and showing off Goldy's new trick."

Her eyes on Creighton, her heart pounding against her rib cage, Elizabeth moved to the youth's side. "You are correct. Lord Creighton meant to abduct me. I will never be able to thank you enough for coming to my rescue." Had the boy not needed to keep the gun pointed at Creighton, she would have thrown her arms around his neck. "But what do we now?" she asked.

"We will see you back t' your friends." He patted his leg. "Goldy! Here!" The dog bounced off Creighton and joined his master. "Good dog," the youth said with a pat to the dog's head. "Now, sir, I think 'tis best do you continue t' rest upon the ground until we are across the meadow. That is unless you want Goldy t' demonstrate another of his tricks." At the sound of his name, the dog yipped and looked up with adoring eyes at his young master. Creighton made no move to rise, and the youth began backing away. "Let us go, milady."

Elizabeth followed after him, and not until they were a safe distance from Creighton, did the youth turn his back on him and slowly release the hammer on the pistol. "What is your name?" Elizabeth asked, looking over her shoulder to ascertain Creighton did not try to follow them. Her heart had returned to a near normal beat, but her legs still felt shaky.

"I am called Dicken does it please you, milady."

"It pleases me greatly. I am Lady Elizabeth D'Arcy, and I owe you a greater debt than I shall ever be able to repay."

"Nay, you owe me naught. You were kind t' me. I but returned the favor."

"What made you know I needed help?" Elizabeth asked. They were nearing the path she had followed to the meadow, and Dicken pointed to a clump of nearby shrubs.

"Goldy and I were havin' us a nap in them bushes. I awoke at your voices and heard all betwixt you and that dastard. Then, when I recognized you, I determined a plan t' help you. As we are always lookin' t' add a bit of humor t' our performances – pleases the crowds you see – we hav' been working on Goldy's new trick, havin' him do the opposite t' his command. I could not be certain he would do it right. We have been practicin' but a couple of days, but he could not have done it better."

Elizabeth agreed with Dicken. The dog had given a masterful performance.

They reached the path and Dicken stopped. "Best you not be seen with the likes of me, milady. 'Twould be talk." He held out the pistol to her. "You best take this too. Was it found on me, I would be accused of stealin' it."

Elizabeth took the gun and tucked it down in the pocket of her skirt. Heavy, it pulled on her waist band and felt hard against her thigh. She could throw it away in the bushes, but Creighton had put such a scare in her, she decided she would feel safer having the gun with her until she could return home.

"How might I reward you, Dicken?" she asked, wishing she had words to express her gratitude.

The youth tugged at a lock of his light brown hair that straggled across his brow. "But give me the same lovely smile you gave me when you told me how much you enjoyed my singing, and I will be more than thanked, milady. Few take the time t' give me notice. You did."

She smiled but before she could think of some other way to thank him, she heard voices calling her name. He heard them too. "I will be off, milady," he said, thrusting his cap back on his head, and with a scratch to his dog's ear, he and Goldy bounded off.

Back with her party, Elizabeth pleaded a headache and asked Lord Holcomb to escort her home. She could scarce wait to be safe in her aunt's arms. Just wait until she told William and Uncle Nate about what Creighton had tried to do. They would thrash him, and she knew not what else, but he would be made to regret his action.

Chapter 27

William and Uncle Nate scoured the city, but found no trace of Creighton. He had checked out of his lodgings and left no word of his destination. William sent a runner to Creighton's estate in Bedfordshire, but he had not returned to his home. "Mayhap he went to the continent," Elizabeth said. "'Twas where he thought to take me."

"Mayhap," William said. "'Tis well does he stay there, for do I see him, he will wish he had ne'er been born." Taking Elizabeth's hand, he once more made her promise she would never again go about unaccompanied.

"I do so promise," she declared without hesitation. She had been so shaken after her near escape from Creighton, when she rejoined her party, she had no trouble convincing Lord Holcomb he should escort her home. For two days, she had not stirred from her lodging. Lord Holcomb and the Silverton sisters had called to inquire after her health, but she had not been up to receiving them. They had no idea what had transpired at the park; they but thought her sorely indisposed and left their sympathies for her with Aunt Phillida.

When Blythe called, Elizabeth eagerly received her and poured out her story to her friend. Telling Blythe helped restore her confidence. Unlike Aunt Phillida, Blythe applauded her courage, claiming she would most likely have fainted – not that Elizabeth believed her strong-willed friend would have done any such thing – but she appreciated the praise. Her aunt, having assured herself Elizabeth suffered no physical harm, had chastised her for so foolishly straying from her party. "I do hope you have learned from this episode, Elizabeth. You cannot be running off on your own as you do. You were most fortunate that youth helped you as he did. I shudder to think what Creighton might have done to you had he got you into his coach."

William had been almost as fierce in his criticism of her behavior, but he had held her so tightly and kissed her so passionately, she had forgiven him his harsh words. She knew he and her aunt reacted out of fear for her, but she found Blythe's ready understanding of her motive, the need to escape her twittering companions, more comforting.

Uncle Nate had been less gruff, but the glint in his eyes when he learned the full tale told Elizabeth that Creighton had made a life-time enemy. Tweaking a curl of Elizabeth's hair, her uncle said, "The man is a bold dunce. He will be made to pay for his affront to you, my niece, but you now need to put the incident from your memory. 'Tis not fit you should waste another thought on such as Creighton. Dwell instead upon your upcoming marriage. Your Uncle Ranulf assures me he and several of your cousins will be in attendance. Mayhap your Aunt Angelica, is she up to it."

"Oh, I do hope so. I have not seen her in any number of years." Elizabeth pitied Uncle Ranulf's wife. Such a beautiful woman, but due to a drunken stage driver, she was unable to walk, forever bound to a chair or a bed.

Elizabeth was cheered greatly when the eagerly awaited letter from her father arrived consenting to her marriage. She also received a letter from her mother. It was full of love and good wishes and an eagerness to meet the man who had captured her daughter's heart. Elizabeth's joy was boundless. She and William could at last announce their betrothal. He could openly escort her to the park, to shops, to look at potential lodging, and anywhere else they might choose to go. She felt safe in his company, and the incident with Creighton receded from her thoughts. She and Aunt Phillida began planning her wedding. Uncle Nate would stand in for her father and give the bride away. Lady Worverton, though aggrieved that her hopes Elizabeth would marry her son had been dashed, offered her home for the wedding celebration after the ceremony. Elizabeth realized that between her aunt's friends and William's and her friends and acquaintances, the number of guests would be more extensive than she had initially imagined.

Besides plans for the wedding, furnishings for their home needed to be selected, and a staff hired. "You will need at least two footmen," Aunt Phillida said. "A housekeeper as opposed to a steward I should think, a cook and a scullion, and I believe, as Mary has determined to remain with you as your personal maid, two chamber maids should be sufficient. Mertice says one of her footmen has a younger brother that she highly recommends. We shall interview him first." She sighed and added, "I fear finding a suitable cook will prove our greatest task."

Amidst the daily flurry and scurrying about through mercer, furniture, and draper shops, Elizabeth interspersed visits from well-wishers. First to call were the Silverton sisters. "You are the sly one," Appolonia declared after taking a sip of the sherry she had been served. "All the time making us think you were interested in Lord Worverton, and here 'twas Sir William caught your fancy." Elizabeth recalled trying to convince the sisters she had no interest in Lord Worverton, but they had been determined to believe otherwise.

Appolonia widened her pale blue eyes and batted her blond lashes. "I will say, Sir William is a most handsome man, if not of great fortune or title."

Elizabeth bristled. "We need neither great fortune nor title. We are in love, and we will have sufficient income to live comfortably. We can ask for nothing more." She wanted to add, at least I am not chasing after the likes of Selby Elsworth, a tomfool ninny if ever there was one. His wealth and title will never change that. But she held her tongue, though with great difficulty when Appolonia added, "Yes, well at least 'tis fortunate you have a sizable dowry. 'Twill certainly add to Sir William's and your comfort." It was said in such a way, and with such an arch look, as to hint Elizabeth's dowry had influenced William's proposal.

As if sensing her sister's indecorous comment had been incitive, Florence giggled nervously and chirped, "We are most happy for you and Sir William, and envious, are we not, Appolonia?" She patted her sister's hand. "To marry for love; nothing could be more romantic."

Nodding, Appolonia agreed. "Indeed, 'tis like a romance novel. May you live happily ever after." She smiled while deftly rearranging her silken skirt over the seat of the tufted couch she shared with her sister. "I am sure your other admirers must be sorely disappointed."

"I cannot think any formed any great attachment to me as I gave them no reason to do so, therefore, I cannot believe any will feel any particular grief."

"Oh, I do think Lord Albin formed a tender for you," Florence said.

She glanced down. "And mayhap Lord Holcomb as well."

"Oh, no," Elizabeth said. "I think Lord Holcomb is taken with you." Florence had attempted to soothe her feelings, and Elizabeth wished to return the favor. Florence was pretty and less grasping than her sister. Had Florence set her interest in Lord Holcomb, Elizabeth hoped he would recognize her attributes; main one being she seemed not to mind his perpetual whine.

Blythe was second to call. "Oh, Elizabeth, how grand. I just knew you had a tender for Sir William and he for you. I am so happy for you both. I suppose you have received your father's blessing, else you would not have announced the betrothal."

"My father and mother have given their loving consent and are eager to meet William. We set off to visit his father and then my parents not a sennight after our wedding. Aunt Phillida and Uncle Nate will bear us company and will have a visit with my parents before returning to their homes. We will be gone for a couple of months. William worries about his business dealings and hopes he will not lose any clients, but he is determined I shall have a good visit with my parents before we return to London." She smiled. "He is so loving. I feel so very lucky."

Blythe hugged her. "You are lucky. But you are also courageous. You have chosen to marry for love, and you refused to let anyone deter you from your goal. I applaud you."

"Dear Blythe, you always know exactly what to say. Tell me, my friend, will you still be in London when I return?"

Shaking her head, Blythe frowned. "I think not. Mother hates London in the summer and besides, Uncle Grosvenor closes his house and removes to one of his country estates in the summer. But I will give you my address, and you must write me the moment you return, and I shall answer you the instant I receive your letter."

"Well, at least I have this time until my wedding to enjoy your company," Elizabeth said, taking her friend's hand. "I wonder, might you accompany Aunt Phillida and me on some of our shopping excursions. 'Tis grueling and exasperating, but I would value your opinion on my various selections."

Blythe beamed. "Will I not be in your way, I would be delighted to accompany you. Does your aunt approve, of course."

Lord Albin was Elizabeth's next caller. He had but the day before returned from a hunting trip to Rutland. Bowing over her hand, he said, "I rushed over when I heard the news, Lady Elizabeth. Accept my felicitations."

She smiled. "Thank you Lord Albin. I trust we will retain our friendship. I value your humor and your candor, as does Sir William."

He cleared his throat. "You must know, Lady Elizabeth, I entertained the notion of asking for your hand myself, but after my visit to Rutland, I have to say I am glad 'tis Hayward you favored." His mouth in a frown, he shook his head sadly. "For more years than I can remember, indeed since I was a puddin'-headed youth, I have hunted with my cousin. His family has as grand a lodge and as fine a woods as any true hunter could wish for. Last year my cousin got married. Mind you, the bride seemed a lovely, delicate girl. But when I arrived, ready for our usual hunt, the girl set up a caterwaul. They had this commitment and that entertainment, and he had promised to escort her. Poor fellow got no more than one day free to hunt. Dashed boring on my own. Came back early. Not meaning to offend you in any way, Lady Elizabeth, but I told my cousin Edward, I would be thinking long and hard afore I looked to take a wife."

"How dreadful for you," Elizabeth said, stifling a chuckle, "and for your cousin, did he no longer have the option to enjoy a good hunt." She was pleased Albin seemed relieved he had not offered for her hand. For him, hunting held precedence over marriage.

Cocking his head, he looked at her and narrowed his eyes. "Hayward has oft accompanied me to my cousin's. You would not be like Edward's wife and keep your new husband from enjoying a good hunt, would you?"

She laughed, "Nay, at least not did he promise to take me with him. I have cousins in Leicestershire. I would enjoy visiting them while he goes hunting with you."

A broad grin spreading across his face, Albin said, "Splendid, splendid, I knew you were par excellence. Told Hayward I thought so the first night we met."

"Thank you, Lord Albin. Now, might I have Mary pour some sherry?"

He shook his head. "Nay, though I do thank you, but I have much I must attend, as I have been gone more than a fortnight. Amazing the correspondence that can build up in that time. And, I at last have an appointment with Lord Havenhurst that I might discuss with him the matter of my family's land claim. Does he plead our cause to King Charles, we could well have a chance of having the land returned to us." He swelled out his chest. "My father will be greatly pleased do I accomplish such a goal."

"And well he should be pleased. You have certainly been persistent. I wish you luck."

Each day brought more callers; Aunt Phillida's friends, Elizabeth's former suitors, Lord Chardy, Mister Wainwright, and Lord Holcomb, and even Lord Worverton came by with his sister. He was more subdued than he had been the night of his mother's ball, but she still found him overly flirtatious. He even flirted with Aunt Phillida. Her aunt laughed at him and declared was she not madly in love with her husband, he could well capture her heart.

Elizabeth smiled. How fortunate she was to have a vibrant, witty, and tolerant aunt.

🌿 🌿 🌿 🌿

Her wedding day growing closer by leaps and bounds, Elizabeth vacillated between nervous trepidation and tingling excitement, especially when thinking about sharing a bed with William. Most of their staff had been hired, and furnishings for their home had been purchased, but they had yet to find lodging they liked. Garrett visited as often as his captain's duties allowed, and his brotherly teasing eased her fretting, but when he left, her perturbation returned.

Blythe sympathized with her, Aunt Phillida clucked, patted her hand, and told her not to worry, all would be well, and William, joining them for supper most evenings, sent shivers racing up her spine when he held her in his arms and assured her her concerns were all for naught, but still she fretted. Did they have no other guests, and was Uncle Nate out for the evening, Aunt Phillida would discreetly withdraw, though she left the door to her bedchamber open. Seated on the tufted couch, and with William's arm around her, Elizabeth once again voiced her frustrations.

"My beloved," William said with a kiss to her nose, "have no fear, we will find just the right home, and our wedding will take place as planned. Yes, we will have more guests than we initially thought, but are we not fortunate to have so many friends and well-wishers. Come now, give me your bright smile."

She smiled and cuddled her head against his chest, but said, "Until we have a home of our own, I fear I cannot feel content. Might we not search again tomorrow?"

Chuckling, he ran his hand up and down her arm. "Will it make you happy, we will look again tomorrow. But not until mid-afternoon. I have several appointments in the morning, and I am treating a potential client to dinner tomorrow at the Green Lattice Tavern. Does he invest in a tollroad trust some men have recently conceived, I could make a tidy sum." He kissed the top of Elizabeth's head. "'Could pay for that mahogany veneer inlaid table you so admired."

Elizabeth pulled back so she could look up at William. "Oh, you would not tease me would you? Might we truly be able to afford that lovely table."

"Indeed, does it bring the glow back to your eyes, I do think we must have it."

"You are too wonderful. I have never seen such a beautiful piece of furniture. And to have it in our home where I might admire it and touch it every day would be such a delight."

He tilted her chin up and softly kissed her lips. "So sweet, so sweet. I can scarce wait until we are wed. When I am with you I can think of nothing but that blissful day. And so tomorrow we will search again for just the right lodgings. I think we shall look at some houses at St. James Square. 'Tis farther from my business haunts, but 'tis a safe, clean area. When I leave home, I will have no fear for your safety."

"St. James Square? Surely we cannot afford such. I would not want you going to debtor's prison," she teased.

William laughed. "I meant to surprise you, but I suppose 'tis time to tell. I received a most satisfactory marriage portion from my father. Ever frugal, he has apparently been saving for my wedding day. He is

212

settling thirty-five-hundred pounds on me. With what I have saved, and with naught but a thousand from your dowry, 'tis enough to buy a house outright do we choose, or to make annual payments do we decide to go with a leasehold."

"Oh, William, how grand of your father. I know you have not wanted to use my dowry to purchase our home. I understand you want no one to think you are marrying me for aught but love. Indeed, 'tis ever so sweet. But what are we to do with the rest of my dowry? I have spent little more than five hundred pounds on our furnishings. I know, do we select a house, we will need more. All the same, 'tis a vast amount left over even after purchasing our coach and four."

"Rightly so." He looked at her in a way that sent a heated warmth to her cheeks. "I suspect we will have several children. We will want to provide suitably for all of them. Your dowry will help ensure none are lacking." His ensuing kiss told her they would indeed be having a large family. Finally drawing back and loosening his cravat, he said, "Back to St. James Square. Your uncle knows the Earl of St. Albans who was granted the freehold by King Charles. He says St. Albans guarantees the houses are well built. Your uncle and I have looked at a house we think you will like. It offers an appealing classical style yet is economical in space. There is an informal parlor and a grand parlor as well as a grand dining chamber and a number of bedchambers. Do you wish, he can take you there tomorrow, and I will meet you there after dinner. What say you?"

Nodding, Elizabeth smiled, and kissing William, said, "Yes! We will look at the house."

Chapter 28

Elizabeth's thoughts were on what gown she would wear for her meeting with William that afternoon when Mary announced she had a morning visitor, Lady Harbinger. Both surprised and pleased, Elizabeth hurried from her room to greet her guest. She asked Mary to serve some sherry, and once assured Lady Harbinger was comfortably situated on the couch, Elizabeth sat beside her. Aware of the honor such a visit implied, Elizabeth hoped she would not break any codes of etiquette. She wished her aunt had not gone out. She would like her guidance.

"I hope the sherry is to your taste, Lady Harbinger," Elizabeth said. "My aunt does like a sweet sack."

"The sherry is delightful, but I really must insist you call me Cambria," the lovely Marchioness said, "else how can we become dear friends."

Elizabeth laughed nervously. "I will not forget again – Cambria." The informality felt strange on her tongue. The Marchioness carried herself with such dignity, to use her given name seemed disrespectful. That the lady wanted to be her friend, Elizabeth found most flattering. She liked Lady Harbinger, respected her, and was eager to accept the proffered friendship. Mayhap 'twas as William said, Lady Harbinger appreciated having a woman friend who could discuss more than the latest court gossip. She would enjoy getting to know the Marchioness better.

"Now, tell me," Cambria said, "have you heard from Lady Danvers?"

Nodding, Elizabeth pulled a letter from her skirt pocket. "Indeed, just this morning I received a long letter from Annis thanking me and William, my uncles and Garrett, and you for all our help and support." Elizabeth tapped the paper. "She sends her deep gratitude for rescuing her from Creighton's clutches and for restoring her to her beloved

Sir Jeremy. She assures me she and Sir Jeremy could not be happier." Chuckling, Elizabeth added, "And she was pleased to report that her grandfather's friends, who went to such lengths to avoid testifying in the annulment proceedings, have been able to resume their normal lives. The solicitor and the squire's son returned from Scotland, both well pleased with their fishing excursion, the minister's capable vicar returned from his visit to his sister, relieving the minister of his multiple tasks, and the family physician seems to have miraculously cured himself."

Joining in Elizabeth's mirth, Cambria said, "My part in Lady Danvers rescue was small, but I am immensely happy for her, as I am happy for you, Elizabeth. Are plans for your wedding progressing as you would wish?"

Feeling more at ease after the shared laughter, Elizabeth rolled her eyes. "I never dreamed putting together a household, not to mention my wedding plans, could be so exhausting. So many decisions to make, but I am nearing the end of my fittings for my wedding gown." She smiled and sighed. "I do hope William will like it."

"Tell me about it," Cambria said, patting Elizabeth's hand.

Elizabeth needed no further encouragement. She was thrilled to get Cambria's opinion. "The bodice and overskirt are to be a rich burgundy velvet. The sleeves of the gown are to be tight fitting to just above the elbows then at the elbows they will flare out in gold lace intertwined with burgundy ribbons. The bodice will slope to a deep point at the waist." Elizabeth looked at Cambria's gown. "As is the cut of your bodice." Plucking at her skirt, she said, "The velvet overskirt will be pulled back to display a peacock blue silk petticoat, and that will be pulled back to reveal a gold satin petticoat, the same gold as the lace at the sleeves. Oh, and I will wear pink silk gloves." She looked expectantly at her new friend. "What do you think?"

"It sounds lovely."

Elizabeth frowned. "The only trouble is the neckline. I cannot decide whether to have the décolletage cut horizontally and trimmed with burgundy or gold binding or with the gold lace matching the lace at my elbows. Or perhaps the décolletage should be rounded or v-shaped." Putting a hand to her head, she shook it. "I feel quite the dunce fretting over such a minor detail, but I do so want the gown to be perfect."

"Nay, you are not a dunce. To want your wedding gown to be perfect is as it should be." Cambria smiled and her lovely golden eyes brightened. "Would you like me to have a look at the gown? When is your next fitting?"

Elizabeth caught her breath, and with her hands to her heart, breathlessly said, "Oh, Lady Harbinger – I mean Cambria, would you look at it? You know what is or is not fashionable. You could keep me from looking a dowd."

Cambria laughed the bubbly laugh Elizabeth found so charming and said, "You could never look the dowd, but indeed, I will be happy to give my opinion." She held up a hand. "But I will not be offended do you decide you cannot abide my suggestion. So, when do we meet?"

"I have an appointment with Mistress Abbot late this afternoon - after William and I look at a house in St. James Square. Mistress Abbot hopes to have the overskirt and both petticoats completed by then. 'Tis why I must make a decision about the neckline. She will be ready to start on the bodice. She is already finished with the sleeves."

"The timing is perfect. You will look at your house, and I have a dinner engagement with my dear friend, Mistress Kirkwood. I do think you would like Maida. At some point, I will have you both to dinner that you might become better acquainted. I should have Blythe as well. Anyway, I should easily be able to meet you at your mantua maker's. Now, I must be going." She rose as she spoke and Elizabeth rose with her. "I shall see you this afternoon."

After Cambria left, Elizabeth chuckled drolly. Did Cambria truly seek her out that she might engage in a stimulating discourse, she must have been hugely disappointed this day with conversation limited to little beyond Elizabeth's gown. Still, Elizabeth hugged herself, Lady Harbinger was noted for her fashion sense. Her advice would be invaluable. She smiled. She might well make a decision on both her gown and her house that very afternoon.

❧ ❧ ❧ ❧

The rectangular brick house with its high-pitched roof, long perfectly

216

spaced windows, and minimum of external decoration was superior to anything Elizabeth had imagined. Her Uncle Nate, having escorted her to the house, offered her his arm, and she ascended the broad steps to be greeted at the door by William. Upon entering the hall, she stood transfixed. A staircase with a gleaming white balustrade wound up to a balcony overlooking the hall. Double wide doors under the balcony opened into the grand dining chamber, but William took her arm and led her across the hall to a room lined with shelves.

"The library," he said with a smile. "We will need to accumulate some books."

She stared at him. "A room just for books? Now I know how my dowry will be spent."

He chuckled. "Well, I am thinking I may also use it as an office. I have ne'er felt comfortable conducting business from my lodgings off Fleet Street. But come, let me show you the informal parlor. 'Tis a good size to accommodate a small dining table as well as the sofas we have chosen. And the fireplace is centrally located to provide heating to both areas."

He led her back across the hall and into what was meant to serve as both dining and sitting room for less grand occasions. The wainscoting extended waist high on the wall and the remainder of the wall was plastered and painted a soft gold. The mantel piece was a creamy carved marble, and the hardwood flooring gleamed in the sunlight pouring in the multi-pane windows. Despite the summer sunlight that streamed in through the multiple high windows, the bare rooms were a tad chill. Draperies, floor mats, and tufted furniture would do much to add warmth to the house. She liked the refurbished house smells – fresh paint, newly sawed wood, varnished flooring. So different from the aged, musty halls she had grown up in.

"The servants' quarters are in the garret," William said, bringing her back to the present, "but for the cook's quarters, which is in the cellar next to the kitchen and a servants' hall. And, there is a small room for the steward or housekeeper here on the ground floor."

Again he took her hand. "Wait until you see the size of the grand dining chamber. Your uncle says 'tis large enough to seat your entire D'Arcy family."

"He is right about that," her uncle quipped. He had been trailing along behind them from room to room. Elizabeth enjoyed seeing William so excited about their future abode. The fact that he obviously loved the house made it even more appealing to her. No sooner did she admire the grand dining chamber than he was showing her the grand parlor. Then he was drawing her up the stairs to the bedchambers on the first floor.

"And this will be our room," he announced, a gleam in his eyes as he stepped into a room looking out on the rear of the house.

The look he gave her sent a delightful tingle to the nape of her neck, and she reached up to rub it. Flushing, she glanced to the windows. "Oh, will we have a garden?" she asked walking over to stare out at a barren courtyard.

William came to stand behind her, and she felt his warm breath on her ear. "Do you wish it, we will have a garden, and mayhap a fountain and a flagstone courtyard. You can see trees have been planted to block the view of the stables and coach house. In three or four years, we will see naught but the roof tiles." He put his hands on her elbows. "Do you wish to see the second floor? It has plenty of room for a good-size nursery and school room."

His intimation of their future intimacies again had her neck prickling. Her mouth dry, her pulse racing, she could do little more than nod, and off they went up the next flight of stairs. Elizabeth found the house enchanting. It was a far more commodious home than she had thought they would be able to afford. She had to admit to being thrilled.

"I told William you would like it," her uncle said. "Now, we must be leaving. William to escort you to your mantuamaker, and me to join a friend for supper and a game of chess. Do you remind your aunt I will not be at table this evening."

"Yes, Uncle Nate, and thank you for escorting me here this afternoon." Elizabeth was pleased her uncle was on a first-name basis with William. It could only mean William had been accepted as family. And soon he would be family. Their wedding was but a month away. Thank the lord they had found a home. William would make the arrangements to purchase the house, and she could start having the furniture they had ordered delivered. Windows would need to be measured for drapes, but other such decorative accoutrements would have to wait until after the wedding and their return from their visit to William's father and her parents.

As soon as the furniture was moved in, the staff she had hired could start putting the house to rights. She liked the housekeeper Lady Canby had recommended. A cheerful widow, Mistress Hall had raised a family and had managed her own household until her husband's untimely death left her in need of a means to support herself and not be a burden on her children. Elizabeth was also pleased with the cook. The cook had, in a manner, been recommended by Blythe's mother.

"If there is one thing Mother knows," Blythe said with a laugh, "'tis who can or cannot cook well. She is forever popping into the kitchen. Makes Uncle Grosvenor's cook crazy. Every year he threatens to leave, and Uncle Grosvenor must offer him higher wages. This year, he just told Cook to hire someone in his stead until Mother leaves and take himself off to Harbinger Hall, Uncle's principal country estate. Mother likes the new cook so much, she tried to convince him to return with us to Castonbury Park, but he refuses to leave London."

And so Elizabeth and Aunt Phillida interviewed the man, and Aunt Phillida pronounced him most suitable. Later with William, Elizabeth had laughed, "Oh, wait until you meet him. He is but a small man, and his voice is near a squeak, and he flutters his hands about, but when he describes the meals he has prepared, especially the pastries... Well, he had my mouth watering. He is very clean, too. Aunt Phillida noted his scrubbed nails and neat appearance. He is quite expensive, and he insists on an assistant and a scullion, but Aunt Phillida says even must we cut back somewhere else, we would be fools not to hire him. So I did. Hope you approve."

"Do you like him, I approve. So how much will he be costing us?"

She hesitated, looked down then back up. "Thirty pounds a year."

William rubbed his chin. "For that he best be good. I am paying the coachman but twenty."

They discussed the other servants she had hired, and the traveling coach William had ordered. It would be ready by their wedding, and William had already seen to its licensing. Her mind whirling from the house to the staff to past conversations, she missed William's question.

He laughed. "Your mind is far afield, that I can tell. I asked would you have me hail a chair or a hackney coach? 'Tis a way to walk."

She shook her head. "Nay, I rode over in a hackney with Uncle Nate. And the coach smelled. I prefer to walk. 'Tis not that far, and I am used to walking. At Harp's Ridge, my cousin Flavia and I walked near every day, did the weather permit."

"Then walk we shall, though 'tis near a mile, I am thinking. But it gives me more time in your presence. Seems strange not to have Mary trailing along behind us."

Elizabeth chuckled. "She is to meet me at the mantuamaker's. After dinner, Aunt Phillida sent her on several errands. If you can believe it, Aunt Phillida said she saw no reason, as you and I are now betrothed, that you could not escort me without the need of an attendant."

"I applaud your aunt's common sense. I do believe she has come to accept me."

Elizabeth smiled up at William. "Indeed, she has. She recognizes your intense love for me and mine for you. She might wish you were an Earl or a Duke, but she would never stand in the way of my happiness. Besides, neither of her daughters married Earls. They both married Barons. And they are both gloriously happy. As am I," she added, gripping William's arm with her second hand and drawing closer to his side.

To Elizabeth's thinking, the walk to the Exchange took far less time than she liked for all too soon they arrived. On their leisurely stroll, they had discussed their new home, the furnishings she had already purchased, and that they had yet to buy, and William told her of the four horses her Uncle Nate had helped him select for their coach. He had yet to hire a postilion, but he was hopeful Lord Albin would be able to help. "Albin's groomsman seems to have innumerable connections. He helped me find our coachman and our groomsman, and he has put out the word I am in need of a postilion. He will know if a man can be trusted or not. Good man is Thompson."

"Oh, Lady Elizabeth, you are here!"

Elizabeth looked to her right and saw Mary give a winsome smile to Mister Wainwright's man, Castor, before hurrying to Elizabeth's side. "I began to think I was wrong about where I was to meet you, milady.

I was telling Castor, mayhap I was to meet you at our lodgings and escort you here, but then I knew that could not be correct, so I thought ..."

"Mary," Elizabeth interrupted her maid, "you did fine. I was but enjoying my stroll here from our new house."

Mary clapped her hands. "Oh, you liked the house! How wonderful!"

Mary's enthusiasm was infectious, and Elizabeth laughed gaily. "But wait until you see it, Mary. 'Tis perfect. We will have much to do to see to the necessary furnishings for it. 'Tis far larger than I had been planning for."

William joined in the laughter. "Aye, with a house so grand, I am thinking I will be in need of a valet. One with experience. Think you Castor might be willing to leave Mister Wainwright's service, Mary?"

Mary's eyes widened. "Sir William, do ... do you say you mean to hire Ca ...Ca ... Castor," she stuttered.

"I think is Castor willing, and would Mister Wainwright not be too upset with my usurpation of his man. Yes, I do think he would serve me well."

"Oh, he would, I know he would," she said. Glowing, she looked over her shoulder, but Castor had departed. Disappointment fleetingly surfaced but was quickly replaced by a wide grin. "Mister Wainwright most like will not be pleased to lose Castor, but I feel certain, he will not begrudge Castor a new employ. He is a nice man, a gentleman."

Elizabeth agreed with Mary. Wainwright was a nice man despite his blustering, and he could not help that he had protruding eyes. At least his wealth made him a likely catch for some lady. He had said all that was courteous when he had learned of Elizabeth's betrothal, and she hoped he would find a lady who would appreciate him. For Mary's sake, Mary having obviously formed an attachment to Castor, Elizabeth hoped Wainwright would be willing to release Castor from his obligations to him.

"I will speak to Wainwright at my first opportunity," William said before turning back to Elizabeth. "Now, let me escort ..." He was cut off by a youth in ragged, dingy attire who thrust a folded paper at him. "Note for you, Sir William."

"What?" William took the paper, but he looked warily at the boy.

"From that chuff over there." The youth pointed to a slovenly dressed man with a hat pulled low over his forehead so his face was hidden in shadow. "Paid me a ha'penny to give you that paper and tell you you best read it quick."

As William opened the paper, the boy ran off. Elizabeth looked over William's shoulder. The note was brief. It stated naught but, 'follow me do you wish to see the boy, Dicken, alive.' William crumpled the note in his fist. "Elizabeth, go to your fitting. I will see you later this evening."

"But William, what does the note mean? What does it mean, see Dicken alive?" She put her hand to her mouth. "Does it concern my Dicken, the boy who saved me from Creighton?"

Chapter 29

"Go to your fitting," William again ordered before heading with a purposeful stride toward the man in the slouch hat. The man took off at a jog.

Elizabeth hesitated but a moment and took off after William. "C'mon Mary," she cried. To avoid tripping, she hiked her skirt up higher than Aunt Phillida would approve, but she could not afford to lose sight of William. She heard Mary's footsteps tap, tapping at her heels.

"Milady, ought we not be going to your fitting?" Mary gasped. "What will Sir William say?"

Casting but a brief glance behind her at her servant, Elizabeth said, "I care not what he says. He might be in danger. This has ... something to do with ... the boy who saved me from Creighton. I am ... certain it must," she managed while hurrying her steps. "William could be headed into some kind of peril because of my carelessness." She drew in a deep breath then rasped. "I cannot let anything happen to him, or ... or to Dicken because I foolishly wandered off by myself and was near abducted by Creighton. And my guess is Creighton is behind this."

"Yes, milady, but might we not be in the way?"

Elizabeth nodded, but did not answer. Her maid was right. They could make matters worse. She could be in the way, but her instincts told her she could not let William face the unknown threat alone. She could not live with herself were anything to happen to him. The pace increased, and she had to hurry her steps. She heard Mary panting behind her, and she thought she heard someone call her name, but she could not look back; she had to keep William in sight.

Fear gripped her heart as William disappeared around a corner. They had entered a more unsavory area, and she realized she was not safe in such a neighborhood, but she pressed on. Rounding the corner, she saw William and near wept with relief. She received curious stares from less than genteel-looking people she brushed past, but she paid them no heed. A couple of shoddily dressed men staggering down the narrow, malodorous alleyway called to her, and one reached out as if to grab her, but she and Mary fled by them so fast, they caused the second man to stumble. She guessed the men were doddering drunk or they might have pursued her.

Stumbling along on the uneven cobblestones, her breath coming in gasps, her side aching, she wished she had not worn the too tight stays that hampered her breathing. She knew she could not continue at the same rapid pace much longer, yet she could not tarry in this disreputable region. She would have to call to William, and he would have to escort them back to a safe haven. And what would then happen to Dicken? What a fool she had been to so rashly race after her beloved. What did she think she could do? Naught. She could do naught.

William stopped. He hesitated, then he stepped inside a dilapidated looking house. Elizabeth slowed her steps enough to catch her breath and picked her way along the lane strewn with moldering filth. Creeping to the door which had closed behind William, she peered through a crack between the ill-fitting door and the jam. She could see naught but William's back, but she could hear voices. She thought she recognized Creighton's sardonic intonation. Turning to Mary, she whispered, "Go get help, anyone. Offer them 10 pounds, a hundred pounds, just bring help."

Mary looked confused and frightened, but when Elizabeth pushed her and hissed, "Go!" Mary scurried off at a run, and Elizabeth turned and placed her ear to the crack. She had to hear what Creighton was saying.

※　※　※　※

William knew the moment he passed through the doorway he had made a mistake. The man he had followed vanished, but left the door to the miserable abode wide open. In peering into the shadowed room, he saw a youth tied to a chair behind a rickety table. The boy's head was bowed and his hair hung down covering his face. Creighton stepped from the shadows, grabbed the boy by the hair, and yanked his head up.

The boy's groan, prompted William to enter.

Still holding the boy by the hair, Creighton raised a pistol in his other hand. "Welcome, Sir William. Come in." Looking past William, he ordered, "Bates, close the door."

Glancing over his shoulder, William saw the man he had been following step from a corner of the room to shut the door. Uncertain of Creighton's intentions, he decided to be the aggressor. "What is the meaning of this, Creighton! What are you doing to that boy? Release him!"

Creighton chuckled – a nasty, cold chuckle. "I heard rumors you have been looking for young Dicken here." He pulled the boy's head back sharper, and William took a step forward, but Creighton cocked his pistol. "Easy, Sir William."

Halting, William remained balanced on his forward foot. His smile more a sneer, Creighton said, "That is better. You cannot imagine the trouble I had tracking this young rapscallion down for you. Seems the company of vagabonds he travels with had gone off to Southwark. But find him I did. Yet, somehow you seem not to be pleased, Sir William."

William heard the man behind him guffaw. "Put up a fight he did," the man said, "but after a bit o' persuasion, he came along right enough."

Amidst work, house hunting, and wedding plans, William had been searching for the boy. He wanted to thank and reward him for coming to Elizabeth's aide, but he had not been successful in finding him. Creighton had. Dicken, his face bruised and bloodied, his blood-stained clothing hanging in shreds, had been grossly beaten. The boy's eyes looked pained. His swollen lips were set in a grimace. Barely able to control his anger that these men should beat up a youth, William said through clenched teeth, "So, you have brought him to me. Now release him."

"Oh, not so fast. For my efforts, I expect to be compensated," Creighton said.

"Very well, you shall have a reward. How much do you want? I have not a large amount on my person, but my word is good for whatever sum we agree upon."

Creighton narrowed his eyes and said in a syrupy voice, "'Tis not money I need from you, Sir William. 'Tis but a note. A note to your dear friend, Lady Elizabeth."

A new anger possessing him, William felt a searing heat seethe up his neck to his face. "You leave Lady Elizabeth out of this."

Creighton released Dicken and placed both hands on the gun he pointed at William. "Smithy," he snapped, and a slovenly dressed man came through a door behind Creighton. William recognized the man as one of the two men who had attacked him. He guessed Bates to be the other man who had run away. The man shot William a wary look, and answered, "My lord?"

"Bring in my writing desk."

"Yes, my lord." Smithy answered and scurried to do Creighton's bidding.

"Recognize him, Sir William?" Creighton said. "In case you are wondering, he repeated your message to me. You can see I paid heed, huh?" A loathsome smile twitched his lips.

"Yeah, I recognize Smithy and his smashed nose. And my guess is he remembers well my warning." By the look Smithy gave him, William had no doubt Smithy remembered he told him if he saw him again he was a dead man. He had also told him to pass on a message to Creighton to stay away from Elizabeth, but his warning had gone unheeded by both men.

Smithy returned with a sturdy cherry wood writing desk, set it on the table, then positioned himself on the opposite side of Dicken. Creighton lifted the slanted lid of the box with one hand and said, "In the desk you will find paper, pen, ink, and blotting sand, Sir William. You are to write a love note to Lady Elizabeth asking her to join you at the Alabaster Inn ..."

"I will do no such thing," William stated angrily.

Ignoring the interruption, Creighton continued, "You will tell her you have the most wonderful surprise for her. Only you will not be there, I will be the surprise. You will be here with Bates and Smithy. Bound, I must add."

"You are mad or a fool," William snapped. Could Creighton really think he would give Elizabeth over to him?

Again Creighton ignored William's outburst. "As I said, you will be bound, but once I have the lovely Lady Elizabeth safe in my custody, I will send word to Bates, and he will release you and the boy." His voice became colder. "Now, Sir William, write the note."

"Do you intend to shoot me, you had best do so, for I will write no note." William tried to suppress his anger. Was he to come out of this pother alive, he needed his wits intact, not muddled by wrath. Would Creighton really risk shooting him? Mayhap, the man could well be mad. Perhaps he should charge Creighton, take him off guard. It might cause him to miss his shot. He could see Bates out of the corner of his eye. Would the man jump into the fray, or run?

Creighton recalled his attention. "I have no intention of harming you, Sir William, not unless you do something foolish. I assure you, I am most competent with a gun. I served with Cromwell and bested many a Royalist, so put any such thoughts of heroism away. I mean you no harm." A sinister smile curved his lips, and his eyes narrowed. "'Tis the boy who will suffer."

William's gaze flew to Dicken. "They have a'ready beat me, sir. I can take it," the youth said, sticking out his chin. "Write no note. I fear them not."

Creighton chuckled. "We mean not to beat him." He shook his head. "No. First we will cut out his tongue." Dicken blanched and William's stomach sickened. "Then we will cut off his fingers, one by one," Creighton continued. "Never will he sing or play his lute again."

"No!" came a cry from the door. To William's horror, Elizabeth burst into the room.

"Elizabeth, go, run!" William yowled. She instead darted to his side and grabbed his arm.

Creighton smirked. "Have you been out there all along, Lady Elizabeth? Had I known you had been so rudely left alone in this unsavory neighborhood, I would have immediately invited you in. Ah, but you are here, and I could not have hoped for a more pleasant surprise."

"Yes, I am here. Now release Dicken. Oh, and look at him. You have hurt him."

Creighton shook his head. "'Twas but a bit of pay back for his intrusion in the park. Such brazenness should not go unpunished. I trust he has learned not to again molest his betters. But enough talk." Raising his pistol to point at William's chest, he said, "Seems we no longer have a need for you, Sir William."

Elizabeth stepped in front of William and screamed, "No!" at the instant the loud report of a gunshot echoed around the room. Blood gushed from Creighton's chest, the gun dropped from his hand, and he crumpled to the floor. The smell of gunpowder smoke hung in the air. Smithy gaped, then fear leapt across his face, and followed by Bates, he raced out the back door.

In the same instant, William had Elizabeth in his arms and turned with her to the entrance. A well-dressed man stood in the doorway. A pistol in his hand, his head cocked to one side, the man said, "I had no time to do ought but dispatch the knave." He raised his gaze from the contorted form on the floor to look at Elizabeth. "Are you all right, Lady Elizabeth?"

William could feel Elizabeth shivering in his arms, but her voice was strong, if surprised, as she answered, "I am well, Lord … Lord Abercar. I cannot think how you come to be here, but I could not be more grateful."

"Oh, milady, milady!" Mary pushed past Abercar and grasped Elizabeth's hand. "Thank God Lord Abercar saw you running down the street and chose to follow. I had not gone far when I ran smack into him. He saw at once I was frightened and asked how he could help. All I did was point and say you were in danger, and he followed me here."

"Then, 'twas you I heard call to me?" Elizabeth questioned.

"I did. I could not imagine what would have you running down the street in such a fashion, but I could not think it a good sign."

One arm still around Elizabeth, William said, "May I also offer my thanks to you, Lord Abercar and introduce myself. I am Sir William Hayward."

"Oh, William, I am sorry. I should have made you known. I am sorry, Lord Abercar."

Abercar bowed slightly at the waist. "'Tis of no moment, Lady Elizabeth. The stress of the moment must preclude such formality." He looked at William. "Sir William, I am Gaston Abercar, recently become fifth Earl of Bretherton. Now, I think before the crowd outside increases, we should get Lady Elizabeth away from here."

William looked past Abercar and out the door. The gunshot had brought a growing crowd of curious spectators. Though none had yet had the courage to demand an explanation, several had crept close enough to try to peer inside. Looking back at Abercar, William said, "Do you please escort Elizabeth home, I will deal with matters here."

Elizabeth pulled away from him and hurried to Dicken's side. "I will go nowhere without Dicken," she stated. "Please, help me free him." Placing a hand on the boy's cheek, she said, "Dear Dicken, look how you have suffered for coming to my aid."

"Allow me," Abercar said, and drawing his sword from its scabbard, he sliced the ropes.

A sharp voice outside drew William's attention. "What is this! Back up! Move away!" the voice demanded, then a tall, broad-shouldered man peered in at the door. William first recognized the Harbinger silver and blue livery, then the footman wearing it. The man took in the scene, including the body on the floor, and looking back over his shoulder said, "Dewey, keep them dunderpates back. They got no call to be prying."

He looked back at William. "Sir William, 'tis glad I am to see you. From her coach window, Lady Harbinger saw Lady Elizabeth running down the street. Concerned, she sent me and Dewey after her in case ought was amiss. 'Pears there was some trouble."

"Your timing could not be better, Baldwin. I need you to help Lord Bretherton escort Lady Elizabeth back to Lady Harbinger's carriage. She must need be shielded that her name is in no way connected with this happening. And I would be grateful would Dewey continue to keep the crowd at bay until a constable arrives. I would think by now one has been sent for."

"We are at your service, Sir William."

"Thank you, and thank Lady Harbinger for me. Oh, and tell Dewey as soon as the constable arrives, he is to leave. I would not want Lady Harbinger's name linked to this either."

"As you say, sir," Baldwin answered, before stepping to the door to have a word with his fellow footman. William breathed easier. Elizabeth's reputation would be protected.

Chapter 30

With William's assurances she had no need to fear for his safety, Elizabeth found herself insistently ushered out the door by Mary and Lord Abercar. No, Lord Bretherton. Abercar was no longer the viscount who months ago had courted her at Aunt Phillida's home, he was now an earl. His grandfather must have died. She must remember to offer him her condolences at a more suitable time. Wedged between her two defenders, Elizabeth knew her identity was concealed from the curious gazes of the crowd. Lady Harbinger's footman had Dicken in his care, and his authoritative voice kept any churls from blocking their path.

Allowing herself to be hurried through the narrow streets, Elizabeth tried to grasp all she had witnessed. Creighton was dead – almost at her feet. Never again would his evil machinations harm innocent people. Yet, the suddenness of his death, the violence of the scene, had her feeling stunned. Relief flooded her when she spotted Lady Harbinger's coach parked outside her mantuamaker's shop. The coach appeared a sanctuary amidst a state of carnage and confusion.

Lady Harbinger's coachman opened the door to the coach and Abercar handed Elizabeth up the steps. Falling into Lady Harbinger's open arms, Elizabeth gasped, "Oh, Cambria, you can never guess all that has transpired. I am so grateful you sent your footmen to help us."

Her friend patted her back, but she said nothing. Elizabeth looked up at her. Cambria was staring at Abercar. "Oh, I am again remiss," Elizabeth said. "May I present Lord Bretherton."

Her face expressionless, Cambria said, "Lord Bretherton and I are old friends." She nodded to Abercar. "Gaston, I heard of your grandfather's passing. I am sorry. I know how close you were."

Abercar inclined his head. "'Tis good to see you again, Cambria. You look well."

"Do I? 'Tis good you cannot see inside my soul. 'Tis quite black, I do think."

"Oh, never," declared Elizabeth. "You are kindness itself."

For the first time, Cambria looked at Elizabeth. She smiled wistfully. "What a dear, sweet heart you have, my young friend. But here, I must get you home. I can tell something terrible has happened. You may tell me all or nothing according to your wish."

Cambria looked back at Abercar. "Do you join us, Gaston?"

He nodded. "I thank you." After assisting Mary up the steps, he started to climb in, but Elizabeth said, "What of Dicken? Where is he?"

"He is here, milady," the footman said. "I was set to put him up with the coachman."

"Oh, no," Elizabeth said. "He is too badly hurt. He must ride in here with me."

The footman looked to his mistress. "Lady Harbinger?" he questioned.

"By all means," Cambria said. "Is the boy injured, then he must ride with us."

The footman helped Dicken up the steps, and Abercar followed after him. The door was closed, and the carriage leapt forward. Still nestled in Lady Harbinger's arms, Elizabeth smiled at Dicken. Sitting up straight between Mary and Abercar, Dicken gazed with large, round eyes at the coach's plush interior. He looked uncomfortable until Abercar forced him to lean back against the gold cushioned backrest.

"I took the liberty of changing your appointment with your mantua-maker," Cambria said. "I told her you were detained and sent word to reschedule the fitting. I set your time for tomorrow afternoon, but I am sure if that is too soon ..."

"No, no, that will be fine," Elizabeth interjected. "I am certain I will be recovered by then. Will you still be able to join me and give me your opinion?"

Cambria smiled. "I may have to change an appointment or two, but I shall be there."

"Thank you, and thank you again for sending your footmen to help me ... and for waiting for me to return. I cannot yet put together all that happened, but perhaps Lord Abercar, I mean Lord Bretherton, can tell you of his part in rescuing William and me and Dicken."

Looking again at Abercar, Cambria said, "This sounds most intriguing, Gaston. Mayhap you would care to join me for supper and tell me of your heroism."

Elizabeth saw a look flash across Abercar's face – a look of what? Love? She looked from Abercar's genial blue eyes to Cambria's golden eyes. The two seemed lost in each other. Could they be in love? She remembered a faraway look in Abercar's eyes when she had told him she wanted to feel the ground tremble when being kissed. She had guessed he had once loved and lost. Could Cambria be his lost love?

As if sensing Elizabeth's interest in her and Abercar, Cambria turned to her. "Gaston and I grew up together, Elizabeth. We are old friends. I can vouch for his discretion. If telling us of your ordeal would help you, you may rely on our complete confidence. But is the memory yet too painful to discuss, just rest here in my arms until we have you safely home."

Feeling a sense of obligation to both Abercar and Cambria, as well as to Dicken, who had suffered much on her account, she decided to fill in the details of Creighton's chicanery, starting with his attempts to force Annis to marry him. She wanted Abercar to know of Cambria's part in helping frustrate Creighton's evil scheme, and though Cambria disclaimed any credit, she looked pleased by her friend's generous praise. Elizabeth next told of Creighton's attempted abduction of her in the park and of Dicken's heroism, and both Abercar and Cambria applauded the boy until they had him blushing beneath his bruises. Elizabeth ended with Creighton's use of Dicken to again attempt her abduction. She then looked to Mary. "I must not forget how brave Mary has been. With no thought to her own safety, she stayed with me through those hideous streets, and then set off on her own to find help."

Mary too, blushed "Oh, milady, you could not think I would let you come to harm. Not after how good you are to me."

Elizabeth smiled at her maid and after a deep inhale, continued. "Had Lord Bretherton not arrived just when he did, my ... my dear William might now be dead." The memory set her heart to pounding in her ears, and she felt faint.

Cambria squeezed her hand. "You were very brave, dear. I know you will be compelled to retell your tale to your aunt, but then you must put the memory behind you. Sir William is alive and well, and you need never fear Creighton again. You must concentrate on your wedding, and the wonderful future you and Sir William will share. Do I not speak the truth, Gaston?"

Abercar nodded. "Listen to Cambria, Lady Elizabeth. She gives you sound advice. Today was a frightening experience, but soon it will be naught but a dim memory. Look to your future. And may I congratulate you on your upcoming nuptials." He grinned quizzically and asked, "Do I guess correctly that Sir William's kiss makes the ground tremble?"

Surprised Abercar would remember her romantic qualification for a lover, Elizabeth giggled, her fear momentarily dissipating. "I do think he must, but as I am generally floating in the air, I cannot be positive."

Abercar's hearty chuckle was joined by Cambria's bubbly gurgle. "Ah, the sweet love of youth," Cambria said and glanced at Abercar. "I remember it well," she added, her golden eyes returning to Elizabeth.

The coach came to a stop, and Cambria said, "We have arrived, my dear. My footman will escort you to your lodgings. That is unless you would feel better did I accompany you."

"Oh, no," Elizabeth said. "You have done so much already. And I have Mary with me. Thank you, thank you so much. We will forever be in your debt."

Cambria laughed. "I did little." She kissed Elizabeth on the cheek as the footman opened the door. "I will see you on the morrow. And remember, put this experience behind you. 'Tis over. No need to dwell upon it." She looked to her waiting footman. "Baldwin, see Lady Elizabeth to her lodgings. And help the boy does he need it. Oh, and I need not tell you or Dewey that this matter will not be told about."

"Indeed, milady." The footman bowed his head. "No one will hear anything from us."

She smiled and nodded, and Abercar exited to hand Elizabeth, Mary, and Dicken out, then with a bow to Elizabeth, he re-entered the carriage.

"Lady Elizabeth?" the footman said, holding open the corridor door. Elizabeth entered, but she looked back as Cambria's coach rolled away.

Were Abercar and Cambria naught but friends, or were they cruelly parted lovers? Turning back to lead the way down the corridor, Elizabeth thought how lucky she was. She was to marry the man who when he kissed her set the ground to trembling. She was blessed.

🌿 🌿 🌿 🌿

With the arrival of the constable, relief surged through William. He knew the man. He was one of his clients. "Ah, Farr, 'tis good to see a face I know."

"Sir William, what has happened here?" The constable, a middle-aged man with a slight paunch, looked at the body on the floor.

William shook his head. "I wish I could tell you. I heard a shot. The door was open. I looked in and saw two men running out the back. And this man was dead as you see him."

"Do you know him?"

"Am I not mistaken, 'tis Lord Creighton. I cannot say I have e'er heard anything good of the man. My understanding is he made his fortune during Cromwell's rule by persecuting Royalists in various ways from taxes to land confiscation. When King Charles returned to the throne, Creighton used his ill-gotten gains to purchase his title." William had hopes the constable, a former soldier for the King, would be incensed by Creighton's unscrupulous conduct. Did he think poorly of Creighton, his investigation might be less thorough. William hoped he would not have to mention Sir Jeremy and Annis, and consequently his own connection to Creighton.

"The man who came to tell me of this shooting said a woman was involved. Do you know of any woman?" Farr asked.

"Ah, I do believe a woman and her escort were passing by and peered inside as I did. The woman near fainted and had to be helped away by her escort and a servant. Oh, and there was a youth." William wanted to turn the constable's thoughts from the woman. "I cannot tell you, did he know any more than I. He looked to be ill to me. I think he may have mumbled something about getting a constable. Mayhap he was the one who sought you."

Farr shook his head. "Nay, 'twas an older fellow." He looked over his shoulder and beckoned to a man peering in at the door. With Lady Harbinger's footman no longer there to keep the crowd at bay, the gawkers, thick behind the messenger, pressed forward.

The man entered the room. "You came to fetch me and did mention a woman," Farr said. "Would you know the woman or recognize her again?"

The man's small beady eyes narrowed to slits. "Ne'er saw her face. Had her back t' the door." He pointed to William. "And that gemman had his arms 'round her."

William shook his head. "Could not have been me. You must have mistaken me with her escort." William looked back at the constable. "Light is dim in here."

Farr looked around the room. "Aye, so it is. Could you have mistaken Sir William for the woman's escort."

Again the man squinted up his eyes. "'Tis possible. I cannot see as well now days. Me eyes do play me false at times."

So far, so good, William thought as the constable turned to the door. "Any of you other people know the woman or her escort?" No one answered immediately but then a slovenly dressed man pushed his way to the front. "Saw a couple o' women looked t' be in a hurry. Tried t' stop 'em t' see did they want t' have a drink with me and me chum, but they rushed past us. Near knocked me chum over."

"Aye," spoke up a woman shoving her way forward. "I seen two women – looked scared. Fancy-dressed for this neighborhood. Hurried past like they was on an errand. Neither had an escort. Seems to me they fled past not much after the gent there." She pointed to William.

"Uh, Sir William," the constable turned back around. "What might you have been after in this section of town?"

William laughed. "What am I usually after, Farr? Making a profit for my clients and thereby a profit for myself. I took a wrong turn though. My mind was on my upcoming nuptials and my soon to be bride." He winked at the constable. "You know how that can be."

Farr grinned. "Aye, been chaste a spell have you? Well did you notice any women in your wake? Mayhap they saw or heard something."

William shook his head. "Nay, they must have turned off. When I realized I was headed in the wrong direction, I turned back. Were any women in sight, I must have seen them, but I saw none. I think you should be looking for the two men I saw run out the back. I do think I heard shouting before I heard the gunshot."

"He would be right there." A man with a rogue eye and an overly large ear stepped forward. Been in one too many fights, William guessed. "O'er the last fortnight," the man said, "I seen a couple o' flea-bitten clods comin' an' goin'. Always looked t' me lack they was up t' no good. Slinkin' in an' out is what I would say."

"Aye, I seen 'em two," another man said. "Looked t' be bullyhuffs to me."

"Aye," another man agreed, and the constable started nodding his head. "Seems I am dealing with some reprehensible characters. Can anyone give me a description?" He looked to William, but William shook his head.

"Sorry, Farr, not I. I saw but the backs of their heads as they exited."

"Always kept their hats pulled down low," the man with the large ear said. Others agreed. "And their clothing – dirty, threadbare, poor fitting – no different than any other man's from this section o' London." His statement got a self-deprecating chuckle from the crowd.

"One other question," Farr said. "I thought I saw a man in livery when I arrived. Anyone recognize the livery or know the man?"

"He just disappeared all sudden like," the woman who had spoken earlier said. "There was two o' 'em in a blue an' silver livery. One left with a youth who looked t' be ill, barely able to walk. T'other acted like he was in charge an' kept us back from the door until you arrived. Big yawners, the both o' 'em."

William took a chance. "Harbinger livery is silver and sapphire blue."

Farr made a face. "Right. Lord Harbinger's footmen are going to be here in this part of London. What are you thinking, Sir William?"

William smiled. His tack had worked. Harbinger would never be suspected. "Mayhap they wore the livery of a guild," he suggested. "With over a hundred guilds here in London, one might think one of them uses blue and silver. Or," William held up his hand, "mayhap they are from an actor's troop, but passing through London."

"'Twould seem they did no harm," Farr said, "though I wish I could question them or the woman and her escort." He looked down at Creigh-

236

ton. "Now, I must deal with the body. Do any of you know his place of residence?" He looked first to William and then to the crowd.

William shook his head. "I have no idea."

Others were shaking their heads, and Farr heaved a sigh. "Guess I will need to get him to an undertaker. Would you happen to know does he have any kin?"

Again William shook his head. "Nay, and do you have no other questions for me, I would as lief be on my way. I have business to attend."

Farr nodded, then in a quiet aside, said, "How is that investment in the coal barges doing? Do you still recommend it?"

"I do, and do you wish, I will stop by to see you next week and tell you more about it."

"Aye, do that. Now, go ahead. Be on your way."

As William exited, pushing his way through the thinning crowd, he heard Farr say, "Here now, you and you. Help me with this body. And does anyone know the name of the owner of this building?" William did not hear the answer. He was in a hurry to get to Elizabeth. She would no doubt be in shock after the killing as well as worried for him. He wanted to hold her in his arms, calm her fears, and assure her she need have no worries of any repercussions.

※ ※ ※ ※

William's welcome was all he could have wished for. He got to hold Elizabeth in a tight embrace, even got to kiss her without her aunt objecting. When Elizabeth finally released him, he bade her sit, and he would tell all. She sat on the couch beside Dicken. The youth, bathed and bandaged, sat wrapped in a blanket. Sheepishly grinning, he awaited clean clothing.

"I cannot think I have e'er been so clean," Dicken said, glancing at Adah. "She had the footmen bathe me in Lord Rygate's own tub. Lined with linen it be." He blushed. "Then she checked me over from head to toe afore she would let me sit on anything. Afeared I had bugs." He laughed. "Right she would be had the footman not scrubbed me 'til me skin was raw." He nodded. "Took care of all me cuts and bruises, too, she did. Now, I wait for the footman to return with something for me to wear. Me own duds being too torn and bloodied to e'er be worn again."

"Dicken is to bunk with the footmen until he is healed," Elizabeth said. "In the meantime, word has been sent to his friends, that though injured, he is alive and will rejoin them when he is able. The story we have told the footmen," she added, "is that Mary and I saw Dicken beaten and unconscious in an alley we were passing. Taking pity on him, we brought him home."

Raising her brows, Lady Grasmere added, "Neither footman questioned the tale."

William would not have questioned the tale either. That Elizabeth would ever be lending a hand to those in need, he had come to expect. He just hoped future instances would not lead them down paths fraught with so much danger.

"I cannot bemoan the death of such an evil man," Lady Grasmere continued. "That Elizabeth should have witnessed his slaying, I regret, but many of us saw worse during the war, and we survived. So will Elizabeth. Now, Sir William, do tell us what happens next."

William told what transpired after Constable Farr arrived and was pleased when Lady Grasmere nodded her approval. "Think you they will catch Creighton's two cohorts?" she asked.

"Nay. Most likely the two will leave London, at least for a while. The constable will know that. His job will be to find someone to collect Creighton's body and see to its burial. Whoever is to inherit Creighton's estate will need be found, but none of that will concern us. I may be questioned again, but as no one can dispute my story, naught should come of it."

"Good. I should not want a scandal attached to Elizabeth's name."

"None will be, Lady Grasmere. Rest easy." Turning from Elizabeth's aunt to Elizabeth, his breath caught in his lungs. Naked love shone in Elizabeth's eyes. He longed to again take her in his arms. That she had placed herself at risk to prevent him from injury left him in awe. He prayed he would never fail her, never disappoint her. She was his life. How such a miraculous thing had happened he could not say, but he thanked all in heaven for giving him Elizabeth.

Chapter 31

As William predicted, though he was questioned again, no repercussions concerning Creighton descended upon them, and Elizabeth recovered more quickly than she might have expected from the harrowing incident. With her wedding plans to complete, her house to furnish, and decisions on her wedding gown to finalize, she had little time to dwell on what might have happened had she not followed William, and had Abercar not arrived when he did.

They owed their lives to Abercar, and William had presented him with a gold pendant with the Bretherton coat of arms etched into it as a token of his gratitude. He and Elizabeth had hopes they would see much more of their savior when they returned from their visit to their families.

"I like the man," William told Elizabeth after an evening spent in his company at the Rose and Crown Tavern. He chuckled. "I admit to feeling fortunate, though, that he failed to find favor with you."

Elizabeth looked through lowered lashes at William. "Oh, he found favor with me. I even let him kiss me." She laughed as William eyed her more closely, and tilting her head, said, "But his kiss gave me no thrill as do your kisses."

To her delight William gathered her into his arms. "Let me keep that thrill alive," he said, his lips claiming hers. She was thankful Aunt Phillida had withdrawn to her bedchamber as was her usual when William came calling. Her aunt seemed to recognize their need for time alone.

� � � 🌪

Once Dicken recovered from the worst of his injuries, William saw him amply rewarded for his assistance to Elizabeth. He had the youth outfitted with new clothes from his shoes and stockings to a hat with a jaunty plume and turned up brim. Dicken beamed when Elizabeth praised his appearance. She wanted to give him a job working in their new home, but he insisted his heart was in his music.

"I cannot think how I would go on could I not perform, Lady Elizabeth," Dicken said. "You are most kind to offer me a permanent position, but I fear I would serve you poorly."

William solved that dilemma. "Lord Worverton has a friend who is quite successful on the stage. And Worverton yet owes you a favor, Elizabeth. Remember? For dancing the first dance with him at his mother's ball. I am certain his friend can help Dicken find more permanent, as well as lucrative, performances. Dicken may well prove a triumph upon the stage."

Elizabeth remembered Appolonia had intimated the Marquess kept company with an actress. No doubt the actress was the friend who would help Dicken make his debut upon the stage.

"I am to play my lute and sing during the intermissions," Dicken said when he again visited. "The stage manager says he likes my voice, and that there may be a part for me in the next play do I learn to read. He says he might even write in a part for Goldy and mayhap my friends. Mistress Blessing is so beautiful and so good to me, and she says she can help me learn my parts until I can learn to read." He blushed and hastily added, "She is a wonderful actress."

"I have no doubt she is," Elizabeth said, smiling. "I will look forward to seeing her performance, as well as yours, when Sir William and I return from visiting our families."

Elizabeth and William decided to have but a few select guests in attendance as they exchanged their vows, but a large assembly would join them at the Worverton mansion for their wedding breakfast and the following festivities. They extended invitations to Cambria and Abercar to attend the private ceremony. But the two were not to join them at their wedding. Elizabeth received a note from Cambria offering her apologies. She and Lord Bretherton could not join the marriage celebration. They were running away together.

'You have been such an example to me,' the note read. 'You let nothing stand in the way of your love. I admire and applaud you. Fourteen years ago, instead of following my heart, I succumbed to the will of my parents and married Lord Harbinger. I made both his and my life miserable, as well as Gaston's. I now have the chance to rectify the situation. The love Gaston and I bear one another has not died. If anything, it has grown stronger. No longer are we willing to live our lives separately. We are claiming our chance at happiness. I care naught for the scandal I may cause Harbinger or my family. Gaston and I are leaving tonight for the continent. We will travel about for a while, but when we settle, I will write you. Your devoted friend, who thanks you for showing me the path I must follow, Cambria.'

Elizabeth had been shocked, but not completely surprised by Cambria's action. When Cambria had met her for her gown's fitting, she glowed. Never had Elizabeth seen the lady look so happy, so alive. Could be naught but love. Elizabeth told no one of her suspicions and showed Cambria's note to no one but William. Yet, news of Lady Harbinger's elopement spread quickly. Lord Harbinger retreated to the country away from gossiping tongues and ordered the closing of his London house. To Blythe's joy, but to her brother, Selby, and her mother's chagrin, they had no choice but to prepare to return to their home in Hertfordshire.

"I am happy for Cambria," Blythe said, "though I shall miss her. There is no telling when Uncle Grosvenor will recover from the disgrace and decide to return to London and open his house again, but other than not seeing you, I will not mind do we forego a few year's visiting here. I have never been particularly fond of London. I prefer the country."

"But you will come visit me, will you not," Elizabeth said.

Blythe smiled. "Indeed, at your first invitation, I will be on my way."

Hearing of the scandal from Selby Elsworth, Appolonia hurried to Elizabeth's side. Having received no commitment from Elsworth despite her best efforts to wrest a proposal from him, she was distressed. "I cannot understand him," she told Elizabeth. "So, I come to you for advice, dear friend. How did you get William to propose? What ploy did you use."

Seated on the parlor couch, a glass of sherry in her hand, Elizabeth stared openmouthed at Appolonia. First, she had never thought of herself as Appolonia's dear friend. Second, she had used no ploy to force William to propose, and so she informed her guest. "William loves me and I love him. I am certain does Lord Laidly love you, he will make you a proposal. No doubt he has much on his mind, having to suddenly prepare to leave London."

"I cannot believe Lady Harbinger could do such a horrid thing," Appolonia declared. "She is a Marchioness. What else could she want."

"Love," Elizabeth answered.

"You would take her side. Well, let me tell you, there were plenty of rumors about her amours. Lord Bretherton is but one of many. No doubt she will tire of him as she has the rest."

Heat rose to Elizabeth's face. "You know not of what you speak. Lord Bretherton and Lady Harbinger are in love. Their love has endured over many years. Rumors are but rumors and you would be wise not to rely on them. They can be false."

Appolonia blushed and tears welled in her eyes. "I came to you as a friend. I meant not to offend. I had not realized you had such a fondness for the Lady Harbinger. But I must still suffer the consequences of her actions does Lord Laidly leave without even hinting he has formed a partiality for me. We have been together so often these past three months. I cannot believe he has no feelings for me." Blinking, a tear spilled from her eye to her cheek.

Not knowing what else to do, Elizabeth took Appolonia's hand and patted it. "As you say, you have spent a great deal of time together. He must have some feelings for you. Whether 'tis love, only your heart will know. Mayhap you could invite him to visit you at your home."

Appolonia shook her head. "Nay, Mother is not well enough. We no longer entertain."

Elizabeth thought of her own mother and could not but feel some empathy for Appolonia. She wondered if Appolonia had any love in her heart for Selby Elsworth, or did she but wish to marry him for his future title and wealth. And what might Elsworth feel for Appolonia? "Do stop crying, Lady Appolonia. I will speak with Blythe, Mistress Elsworth, and see does she know her brother's feelings. Now, as I said, trust your heart. Your heart should ne'er steer you wrong."

Appolonia smiled wanly and thanked Elizabeth. She left without ever once asking Elizabeth if her wedding plans were progressing as she wished. No concern but for herself, Elizabeth thought, but she did consult Blythe about her brother's feelings.

Her friend sighed. "I fear I will be stuck with Lady Appolonia as my sister-in-law. Selby has asked Mother to invite the Silverton sisters to our home this summer. Mother hates to spend her own money on entertaining, but I have no doubt Selby will convince her. He seems truly fond of Lady Appolonia. Do tell her she may expect an invitation once we are settled back in at Castonbury Park."

Elizabeth laughed. "Will their visit be a great hardship on you? Do they stay overly long, you could always come up to London to visit us. I expect we will not be gone more than two months. We must return before the fall rains start or the roads will be impassable."

"Thank you, but fortunately Castonbury is an extensive estate. I have found many secret retreats over the years. In addition, the minister and his wife are always welcoming, and I am allowed to enjoy their rather extensive library at my leisure. However, I will look forward to visiting you once you are returned and have had time to settle into your new home. I know you will have much to do to put all to rights ere you start entertaining."

As expected, Appolonia was exuberant at Blythe's assurances. Hugging Elizabeth and promising her undying friendship, Appolonia swore she could not be happier. Elizabeth pitied Blythe should her brother marry Appolonia, yet she believed Appolonia and Elsworth to be well suited to one another. Selby liked being fawned over, and Appolonia was good at fawning.

With Appolonia's angst quieted, Elizabeth was able to concentrate on her house. Drapes were being hung, and furniture set in place. Mistress Hall, the new housekeeper, and two maids moved in to start readying the house for occupation. "I know we lack many items yet," Elizabeth told William when giving the house a tour, "but we have beds and linens, tables and chairs, and pots and pans. 'Tis enough to keep us comfortable until we can find the other furnishings we need. I have no wish to rush our purchases and then wish we had not been so hasty."

William kissed the tip of her nose. "I bow to your wisdom, my dear. Do we have a bed, and you say we do, I am content."

Laughing, she batted him on the arm. "Oh, William, did I not know better, I would think you had naught but our wedding night on your mind."

His smile lascivious, he asked, "What makes you think I have else on my mind?"

Heat suffused her cheeks, and she said, "Do stop such talk and walk me home. I must need go over our wedding breakfast repast with Aunt Phillida.

Chapter 32

Elizabeth fairly danced down the street. Not but a week until her wedding and all seemed in readiness. She had had her final fitting on her wedding gown, and it was to be delivered on the morrow. She had received another warm letter from her mother and a lovely gold locket on a delicate gold chain. She remembered her mother wearing it, treasuring it because it had belonged to her mother's mother. And now it was hers. Hers to some day pass on to a daughter of her own.

She reached back to clasp Mary's hand. "Oh, let us hurry. I am so excited. I cannot wait to see William this evening. I have so much to tell him."

"Yes, milady," Mary said, hurrying her steps. "Just wait until Sir William sees you in that gown on your wedding day. You look like a fairy princess, you do."

Elizabeth glanced back and smiled. "Thank you. It is a lovely dress, is it not? I think ..." she began, but stopped short as a man stepped in front of her. Mary bumped into her, stepped on her heel, and almost dropped the package she carried.

"Oh, milady, I am that sorry."

"That is all right, Mary, 'twas not your fault." Elizabeth raised her chin and glared at the man blocking her path. "Kindly stand aside, sir."

The man did not move. "You be Lady Elizabeth?" He peered at her with calculating eyes.

Elizabeth surveyed the man more closely. He was no beggar. He looked too fit and well fed. And his clothes, though worn, were those of a gentleman. "And if I am?"

The man looked from Elizabeth to Mary. "She your servant?"

Mary tugged at Elizabeth's hand. "Milady, let us go round him. You have no call to be talking to strange men."

Elizabeth agreed with Mary, but before she could step around the man he said, "You will listen to what I have to say or find your fine Sir William in jail."

"What do you mean by that!" Elizabeth demanded, her heart thumping against her chest.

The man grinned. "Ah, now you be ready to listen."

"No, Lady Elizabeth, pay him no heed." Mary urged, again tugging at Elizabeth, but Elizabeth ignored her servant's entreaty.

"What do you mean Sir William will go to jail?"

The man looked at Mary. "What I got to say is for your ears. Send her on her way."

"I will not leave you, Lady Elizabeth. Nay, no matter what you may order," Mary said.

Elizabeth knew Mary to be adamant, and to be honest, she did not want to be left alone with the man. His breath reeked of fish, and his body odor hung heavy in the air. "I trust my servant. Whatever you have to say to me, you may say in her presence."

The man glanced once more at Mary then sneered. "So be it. I seen you at the murder of Lord Creighton. I know you was there and so was your maid. You followed Sir William, and I followed you. I knowed you was up to something. A lady like you in them parts. Not normal."

Her heart in her throat, Elizabeth said, "I have no idea what you are talking about. Who is Lord Creighton, and what has he to do with Sir William?"

"Play no games with me, Lady Elizabeth, or 'tis off to the constable I be. I can get other witnesses who saw you there. Witnesses who heard Sir William say he knew you not. Lying to the constable he was, impeding the investigation. I know not what you were doing there, but you were there and no doubt the constable will want to know why. And he will want to know why Sir William lied. That is an offense against the law."

Elizabeth's mind swirled. This man's word alone would not stand up against William's, but if he brought forward other people who had seen her mad dash down the back lanes and alleys following in William's wake, could William be called to account for deceiving the constable? His only goal had been to protect her reputation, but would the magistrates look askance at such a reason? Might William go to jail, go on trial? She could not allow that.

"What do you want?" she demanded.

He smiled a sleazy smile that said he knew he had won. "Two hundred pounds will buy my silence, milady. A mere pittance to you from what I hear."

She gasped and stared at him. "I have not that kind of money, not in coin."

"Well, you best get it, and by tomorrow, or I go to the constable."

"Tomorrow! Where do you think I can come up with that kind of coin in a day? Even my aunt could not grant me that sum at such short notice. We would have to go to the bank ..."

"Nay, this bargain is betwixt you and me. Do you tell anyone else, I go to the constable. I will not have anyone say I too was impeding the investigation. Did I not need such a sum, I would not now be offering you this proposition. I would already have gone to the constable. I be a law-abiding citizen. You can ask anyone who knows me."

In no way did Elizabeth believe the man to be law abiding, and Mary's huff told her Mary did not believe him either. However, she was afraid to cross him. "I still have no way to get such a vast sum," she said. "I need a few days to think, to come up with a plan."

"I have not a few days to wait. I need the money now." He looked at her throat. "You have a pretty bauble about your neck. That and a few other of your trinkets should bring a tidy sum." He reached toward her. "I could take that now, and you can bring me the rest on the morrow."

Elizabeth's hand went to her mother's locket, and she stepped back. She had worn the locket that day to see how it would look with her wedding gown. "Stay away from me," she hissed. "I will get your money must I pawn some items myself."

"Oh, no, milady," Mary said, but the man ignored her and, looking at Elizabeth, said, "Now, you are being sensible. I will meet you here on the morrow at this same time. You have the money, or I go to the constable. You tell anyone, and I go to the constable. You have anyone with you other than that maid." He glanced with disgust at Mary. "And I go to the constable. You understand?" Eyes narrowed, he looked at Elizabeth.

She nodded. "I understand."

"Good." He started to leave but turned back. "Remember, you tell anyone, you may get me in trouble, but Sir William will also be facing the law. And there goes your wedding, huh?"

"I will tell no one," she answered.

The man smirked. Gave her a nod and left.

"Oh, Lady Elizabeth," Mary said, "you cannot mean to give that horrid creature two hundred pounds? You would not pawn your jewels?"

"Mary, I will do anything to keep William from jail. Mayhap the man lies and there are no other witnesses, but I cannot know that. Mayhap William would be in no trouble, but mayhap he would be in terrible trouble. I cannot chance it. We must hurry home and sort through what jewelry I have that may bring enough to satisfy the man. I cannot think I have two hundred pounds worth of jewelry, but no doubt the beast will take what I offer."

"I cannot like this, milady. We should tell your aunt. Ask her advice."

Elizabeth grabbed Mary's wrist. "Nay! That we must not do. Aunt Phillida would never countenance this. She would advise I ignore the man. That I not meet him on the morrow. She might even call the constables on him."

"And she would be right to do so," Mary said.

Elizabeth shook her head. "No, Mary, think. The wedding is but a week away. Even did no harm come to William, think of the scandal. I want nothing to mar that most important day in my life. And think what such a scandal might do to William's business. No, I must pay this demand. But once the thief has his bribe, and William is safe, I will tell Aunt Phillida, and we will get the money from the bank and retrieve my jewelry. William need never know of the whole affair.

"But I need your help. You must find out from Castor where I might find a reputable pawn shop. Do you see him tonight?"

"Yes, milady, but will he not think it strange do I ask about a pawn shop?"

"True ..." Elizabeth chewed her lower lip and cocked her head. "I know, you must tell him you want to get a gift for your mother to take when we go home for a visit. Tell him you heard you can get very nice things for most reasonable prices at pawn shops."

"You want me to lie to Castor?"

Elizabeth shook her head and rolled her eyes. "Oh, Mary, 'tis but a little lie. And besides, we can buy something for your mother, and then it will not be a lie."

"I tell you again, I cannot like this, milady."

"Nor can I, Mary, but I think I have no choice. Now, come, let us go home."

🌱 🌱 🌱 🌱

Elizabeth did little but pick at her supper. She had no appetite. She attempted to respond to her aunt's musings, but she initiated no conversations. Her mind kept going to her jewelry. She had not that many articles – four rings, including the one William had given her which she wore constantly and would never part with, a silver ribbon-shaped broach with a diamond at the knotted center, a gold broach shaped like delicate rose petals, tiny pearl earrings, her gold pendant earrings with the shimmering sapphires, two gold link bracelets, the rope chain necklace with the apple-shaped pendant, and the gold filigree choker studded with tiny rubies that her parents had given her on her eighteenth birthday. Would those items bring enough to satisfy her extortionist? She had also the gold locket her mother had sent her, but she could not pawn that.

"Elizabeth! Whatever is the matter with you this evening?" her aunt demanded. "You have barely touched your meal, and you have scarcely said a word since you returned from your fitting. Is aught wrong with your dress? You said it looked lovely."

"I am sorry, Aunt Phillida. I seem to have no appetite. Must be nerves. My gown is lovely, but I cannot but wonder did I pick the right fabrics for my drapery. 'Tis playing on me," she lied. She was glad William had sent a note that he would not be joining them for supper. He had an important meeting with a client he hoped to convince to join the tollroad enterprise he was promoting for one of his more affluent clients. William would see through her lies. He would know something more than new drapes troubled her.

She glanced at her aunt. Aunt Phillida did not appear particularly convinced either. Forcing a smile, Elizabeth said, "You must not fash yourself, dear aunt." 'Twould not do for her aunt to become suspicious. Elizabeth needed complete freedom on the morrow was she to pawn her jewelry and meet the hideous creature by midafternoon. Thankfully, she had no major dinner engagement. Lady Canby would be joining them, but she and Aunt Phillida would start reminiscing and that would make Elizabeth's escape easier. Elizabeth had already told her aunt she meant to visit Blythe. Her dear friend was in the midst of packing to return to her family's country home. The Elsworths would depart the day after Elizabeth's wedding. Much of Lord Harbinger's house was already being shut down by his staff, Lord Harbinger having departed mere days after his wife deserted him for Lord Bretherton.

"I do have a bit of a headache." Looking down, Elizabeth swirled the sherry in her goblet and absently watched the dark red color dance in the candlelight. "Mayhap I shall lie down until William comes by." She looked back up and, hoping she appeared convincingly happy, again smiled. "I have much to tell him. I found the perfect candelabra for our parlor. And I cannot but think he will be pleased with the chess set I purchased. Do you not find it charming?"

Looking less concerned, her aunt nodded. "I think you made a good purchase. A man needs a chess set. Many men spend too much time playing at cards these days. Too much time gambling. Chess requires skill and intellect. I cannot but think Sir William will be pleased. Now, my dear, go lie down for a bit. Nap if you wish. I will awaken you when Sir William arrives."

Elizabeth eagerly made her escape. But once closeted in her room, she could not rest. Pacing the floor, she beat her fists together. Was she doing the right thing? The thought that William might spend even one night in jail she could not abide. Drawing in deep breaths, she tried to calm herself. She could not appear so agitated when William arrived. He would immediately suspect something. She hoped his meeting would go well. That would put him in a good mood, and he might not notice her lack of vivacity.

She prayed Mary would be able to get the name of a reputable pawn shop dealer from Castor. Despite Aunt Phillida's chiding that she allowed her servant too much free time, she had given Mary the evening off. "You will spoil the girl," her aunt had declared. "You must be careful how you handle your servants. Are you too lenient, they will think you weak and will take advantage of your generous nature."

"I will mind your advice, Aunt Phillida, where all my other servants are concerned, but Mary is devoted to me, that I know. Had she not returned with Lord Bretherton, William might have been shot by Lord Creighton. No, I owe her William's life. I will not deny her time with the man who has captured her heart."

"Aye, Mary is a good faithful servant, I will grant you that. But you must remember that you are responsible for her moral integrity. When Mary's suitor starts working for Sir William, and they are living in the same household, you must not let her slip into immoral conduct."

Elizabeth smiled. "I will heed your warning. Must I see them joined in wedlock to preserve their virtue, so will I do."

Aunt Phillida frowned. "You scoff, Elizabeth, but you must guide your staff along a path of righteous decency. Their souls are in your care. You are young, but I hope I have instilled in you the ability to discern what is proper decorum amongst those in your employ."

Elizabeth hugged her aunt. "You have, and I have taken your lessons to heart. I give you my word. But fear not for Mary's soul. Trust me that I know my servant."

She did trust her servant. Mary would not fail her. She would return with the name of a pawn shop dealer. Mary might not think the plan wise, but she would abide by Elizabeth's wishes. With a sigh, she sat down in front of her looking glass. She looked wane. William would notice. She could plead the headache with him as she had with her aunt. He would be most sympathetic. He was such a dear. She was fortunate to have found a kind and caring man. And a man who set her soul on fire. Thinking of William's kisses brought color to her cheeks. She smiled at her reflection. Yes, that was better. She but needed to concentrate on William, forget about the morrow for the time being. Feel William's love encompass her, and all would be well.

❦ ❦ ❦ ❦

Elizabeth rose up on her elbow when Mary tiptoed into her bedchamber. "Goodness, Mary, what is the time? Are you not dreadfully late?"

"Oh, Lady Elizabeth, you are awake. I thought for certain you would be asleep. Indeed I am late, but through no fault of my own. And Adah has given me such a scolding for keeping her up. She could not retire until I returned as she had to let me in. I know I will hear more from her about this on the morrow. But I swear, 'twas Lady Appolonia's fault, not mine."

"Lady Appolonia's fault? Whatever can you mean?" Elizabeth peered at Mary. In the dim light cast by the candle on the mantelpiece, Mary's gown appeared mussed, her hair disheveled.

"Castor took me to see a puppet show in the park." Mary clasped her hands together. "Oh, it was such fun. I cannot think when I ever laughed so hard." She put her hands to her cheeks. "I know I must be blushing. It was a bit ribald. For that, I assure you, Castor apologized. All the same, it was funny. He then bought me a mincemeat pasty from a vendor for my supper. It was delightfully tasty. When we were done eating, we walked over to the Exchange and poked about in some of the shops." Smiling, she drew closer to the bed. "It was a wonderful evening."

"But what of Lady Appolonia? How was your tardiness her fault?" Elizabeth was beginning to feel a tad exasperated, especially as she had yet to learn if Mary had gained the name of a pawn shop dealer.

"I am sorry, milady, I was coming to that. We were returning home, at a very decent time, when we chanced on a splendid-looking coach that had lost its wheel. It looked to have collided with a water cart. We were skirting the melee when I heard someone calling to me. 'Twas Lady Appolonia. She had been on an outing with Lord Laidly, but upon returning, the accident occurred. Lady Appolonia was frantic. Lady Bainbridge was having a small card party this evening, and Lady Appolonia had promised she would return from her outing in time to attend the function. One of Lord Laidly's footmen had secured her a chair, but with the hour growing late, she could not think it proper she had no woman companion. She insisted I bear her company. And, so I did. Castor, of course, accompanied us and then escorted me home. Lady Appolonia promised she will send you a note on the morrow explaining her predicament and excusing my tardiness."

"And your disheveled appearance? Your rush home caused that?"

Mary grinned. "No, milady, that would be Castor's doing. He was so obliging to see me home, I had to see him rewarded."

Elizabeth eyed Mary. After her talk with Aunt Phillida, she thought she might have need to have a talk with Mary. But this was not the time for it. "Very well, you are forgiven your late return. But did you get the name of a pawn shop dealer?"

Frowning, Mary twisted her hands in her skirt, thinned her lips, and nodded. "Aye, I have the name and the directions. Castor said he would prefer to escort me, that area not being a fit place for a proper-raised, young woman to go on her own. I lied and told him I would not go without him." Her lower lip protruding, she added, "I cannot like lying to him."

"I cannot like this deceptive game we must play either, Mary, but play it we will. By tomorrow afternoon, it will all be over. William will be safe. No scandal will mar our wedding. Now, I know you must be tired. Do go to bed. And thank you, Mary."

"Good night, milady," Mary said, and started to slip into the closet off Elizabeth's bedchamber, but she turned back. "Milady, what if after you give this jackanapes the money, he still goes to the constable? Or else he may demand an additional sum at a later date."

Knitting her brow, Elizabeth said, "I cannot think he will. He would have no reason to. 'Twould bring questioning down upon him – such as why did he wait so long to come forward. I cannot think he wants that. And does he demand more at a future date, I will have to tell him to do his worst, but that he should not expect my uncles to be forgiving of his fraud."

Mary brightened. "Could you not threaten him with your uncles' displeasure and not give him the money at all? As he knows who you are, he must know you have powerful uncles?"

"Nay." Elizabeth sighed and shook her head. "I simply will not chance it. As I told you, nothing must mar my wedding day. Now, go on to bed, and thank you for getting the information."

Elizabeth flopped back on her pillows. All was now set to put her plan into action. She but had to get through the morning and dinner, then she could slip away, pawn her jewelry, pay the extortionist, and have a final end to yet one more horror wrought by Lord Creighton. Thankfully, William had believed a headache accounted for her despondency, and he had been all sympathy. She had tried to appear vivacious, but he had seen through her mask. Though exuberant about the sale he had made, he had noted her pallor. With his comforting arms around her, she had come close to telling him about the extortionist. Only her fear that William would thrash the man then take his chances with the law kept her silent.

Thinking she needed her rest, William had left after but a brief visit. "My dear one," he said, "you are trying to do too much in what time remains before our wedding. I want you to give me your word you will rest tomorrow. You will pamper yourself."

She had promised. "I will do naught tomorrow morning but write some letters, then after dinner, I go to visit Blythe." She had not precisely lied, she had but omitted telling the whole of her plans. She would stop briefly by her friend's, still, she felt guilty. But she did not think she had a choice. Dear God, she could scarce wait for the morrow to be ended.

Chapter 33

"Mistress, are you certain you wish to pawn all these items?" The pawn shop dealer eyed Elizabeth over the rim of his spectacles. She wondered if he might think the pieces had been stolen. She had not given him her name, but surely the richness of her gown, her overall appearance, the fact she had her maid with her must tell him she was no thief.

"I must need pawn these items today, but I will reclaim them to-morrow. On that I do swear. Now, please, sir, what do you give me for them?"

He took his time going over each piece of her treasured jewelry. His hands were small for a man, almost delicate, and his pointed nose seemed to quiver each time he brought an item closer to his eyes to examine it. He almost seemed to be sniffing them, and he did stick his tongue out and lightly lick her gold broach. He was tidy in appearance, and his shop was neat and orderly, if dimly lit. The only light coming from the candles next to him on his counter and what light could creep in through a single multi-paned window. The shop smelled musty, but it did not stink of waste as did the streets she and Mary had warily traversed to get to the shop.

She wondered at the hodgepodge of articles stacked about the shop – largest items, tables, chests, and a throne-like chair nearest the door – smaller and more valuable items, a gold clock, a delft-blue china bowl, a crystal goblet, behind the counter. She noted a set of gold-handled forks. Mayhap when she returned for her jewelry, she might purchase the forks. She could not but feel saddened by the contents of the shop. So many poor souls had been in need and had been forced to part with beloved treasures. She thanked God she would be able to retrieve her jewelry on the morrow. She need not fear any of her jewelry would be sold. The dealer assured her he never put any new articles out for sale for at least a week.

"I can give you one hundred ninety-five pounds," the dealer said, interrupting her thoughts.

She almost sank to her knees in relief. Her hand went to the locket at her throat. She would not have to pawn that prized possession. Resolved, she stiffened her back and cleared her throat. "I will take it." The extortionist fiend would have to accept what she gave him and be happy with it or, she was determined, she would let him do his worst. Not that she for a moment doubted he would quibble about the lack of five pounds.

"Very well," the dealer said. "I must get the sum from my safe. I will be but a moment." He turned from her and called, "Brody, watch the shop while I am in the back."

A man with broad shoulders, heavily muscled biceps, and hands the size of anvils arose from a stool in a back, darkened corner. Elizabeth had not even noticed him until he stood, and Mary's gasp said she had not seen him either. The man's black eyes looked tiny in his big round face and his thin lips offered no smile. He wore a horse pistol tucked into a rope tied around his waist, and he had a large knife sticking out of one of his huge leather boots. Elizabeth imagined few thieves would be tempted to try to rob this shop with the bugbear, Brody, on duty. He had her quivering, and he had done naught but stand up.

She waited, nervously tapping her toe and occasionally casting glances at the pawn shop guard. His gaze seldom left her and Mary, though he did glance in the direction of the window if anyone lingered too long outside. Elizabeth was glad no other customers were in the shop. She would not have wanted anyone to see the jewelry she was leaving in the dealer's care. Though, now that she knew about Brody, she did feel her jewelry was safer. She had little doubt but what the man slept on a cot inside the shop. She believed few men would want to encounter Brody in the middle of the night in the darkened shop.

At last the dealer returned and counted out the coins into Elizabeth's hands. She thanked him, again swore she would return the next day for her jewelry, plunked the coins into a leather bag, and tucked the bag into the pocket of her skirt. "I hope you have considered all your options, Mistress," the dealer said as she turned to leave.

She turned back. "My options?"

The dealer nodded. "I cannot but feel you face some kind of trouble. Have you no man who can help guide you down another path, no father, brother, husband?"

Elizabeth raised her chin. "Your worry is misplaced, sir, but I thank you for your concern." 'Twas to save her man that she faced this dilemma, and she would succeed, where, was William consulted, he might cause a confrontation that could result in any number of harmful or embarrassing resolutions. No, she needed no man to resolve this problem.

Turning back to the door, she near bumped into a small middle-aged man with a taller, younger man in tow. "Why, Lady Elizabeth, whatever do you here?" the little man squeaked, and Elizabeth recognized her new cook. What could she possibly say to explain her presence in the pawn shop? Lifting her brows and widening her eyes, she decided she did not have to explain her presence. In fact, he had no right to even question her.

"Indeed, what do you here, Wardell?" she asked, looking down her nose at him.

The little man was immediately humbled, and he fumbled with the hat in his hands. "Begging your pardon, milady. I am here seeking cookware. You did say to purchase whatever I might need. Oft times, quality goods can be found in these shops and costs will be lower. Oh, and might I present my new assistant, Claude." He looked over his shoulder at the youth behind him and nudged him in the ribs. "Your hat, dunderpate." The youth, Elizabeth guessed him to be in his late teens, jerked the cap off his head and smiling sheepishly, said, "Honored, milady."

Elizabeth nodded then looked again at Wardell. "Very well, you may carry on with your shopping." Still attempting to be haughty, she half smiled. "I will not forget your attempts at saving us some coin. I will report your forethought to Sir William."

Elizabeth started to sweep past him, but he said, "Milady, where is your escort? You cannot think to walk through this neighborhood without an escort."

"I have my maid. That will suffice."

The little man plopped his hat back on his head, and in his high-pitched voice, proclaimed, "Oh, indeed not. Claude and I will escort you at least as far as Covent Gardens. Do you wish it, to your door. I cannot think who thought this a proper area for you to come, let alone without an escort." He waved his hands about. "No, no, I insist."

Elizabeth sighed. Did she not allow his escort, most likely he would tag along at her heels. She could see his concern for her was real. And, as she looked about at the shoddy buildings, unkempt people passing by, and the refuse-littered street, she thought she would actually welcome his escort. His assistant was a strapping youth, and though his round face had a sweetness to it, she felt more secure having the two men with her. Claude walked respectfully behind her and Mary, Wardell strutted ahead, warning people to step aside, which to Elizabeth's surprise they did. Men even courteously doffed their hats. Elizabeth could not imagine who they thought she might be, or what they thought she might be doing in their neighborhood, but she held her head high and followed after her cook.

She was pleased when Covent Gardens and its vegetable stands came into view. There, she would insist she no longer needed Wardell's escort. She could not have him trailing after her when she met the extortionist and handed over the money in her purse. She could not help putting her hand in her pocket and feeling the coin bag. It weighed heavy against her leg but at least was hidden from prying eyes.

When they reached the piazza, Elizabeth called to Wardell. "You need not accompany us any further. I mean to browse a bit and then stop in at a stand or two. Thank you for your escort."

Wardell swept off his hat. "My pleasure, Lady Elizabeth." He looked around as if assessing the surroundings. Then he nodded. "As you have your maid, I will leave you and return to my shopping." He bowed his head. "Good day to you, milady."

"Good day to you." She nodded then watched him strut away, Claude at his heels. She sighed, looked at Mary, and started to giggle. "What do you think he is thinking about our being in that pawn shop? Is he not the strangest little man?"

Mary giggled. "Indeed he is, but milady, I admit to being glad for his escort."

"I too. But now we must hurry."

Mary's smile drooped. "Oh, Lady Elizabeth, do you not think this a mistake? Might we not go back home instead and tell your aunt all?"

Elizabeth shook her head. "Nay, Mary, I am determined. I will pay the man. Only after the deed is done will I tell my aunt. Now come. Let us not tarry."

"Lady Elizabeth! Halloo! Halloo!" A lilting voice called to Elizabeth and her heart sank. Appolonia Silverton was waving to her. Had she not looked up when she heard her name being called, she could have hurried away, but Appolonia had seen her look in her direction. Elizabeth could do naught but wait for her.

"Dear friend," Appolonia gushed. "I went by your home this afternoon, but your dear aunt said you were out. I explained to her, as I must to you, why your servant," she nodded at Mary, "was late returning last evening."

"Mary has already told me. I have no need for you to confirm her story," Elizabeth said, hoping to avoid a lengthy explanation. Her hopes were in vain.

"Oh, but you must be wondering why I should be out with Lord Laidly without my maid." A disgusted look on her face, Appolonia turned to her servant. "'Tis all Bessie's fault." Standing behind Appolonia, the young woman, burdened with packages, had watery eyes, a red and sniveling nose, and flushed cheeks. "She would claim she was not well, and she would not stop coughing and sneezing. Lord Laidly found it most annoying. He was prepared to call off our outing, but knowing I would have few other chances to see him before he departs for the country, I suggested we instead set Bessie down and continue on."

'Twas plain to see Bessie was not well, and Elizabeth wondered where Appolonia set her maid down, and how far the sick woman had to walk to get home. "We went to watch a tennis match." Appolonia chatted on, apparently having given nary a thought to her distressed servant. "Lord Laidly had a wager that his friend, Lord Padstow, would win. And of course, he did, and Lord Laidly was most pleased."

Appolonia's ramblings about the match and the people she saw there had Elizabeth's insides writhing. She had to go. The extortionist might think she was not coming. He might even now be on his way to speak to the constable.

"Well, anyway, you can understand why, when Lord Laidly's coach met with the accident, I needed a maid servant to see me home. Could well have been a scandal had I arrived at home in a chair and with naught but men accompanying me. And none of them a gentleman."

Elizabeth's attention returned to Appolonia when she realized she was expected to respond. "Oh, indeed, most fortuitous Mary happened along."

Appolonia lightly grasped Elizabeth's wrist and pulling her closer, whispered in her ear. "I cannot think it wise that you let your maid go round on her own with young men. She could find herself in an awkward situation." Appolonia gave Elizabeth a knowing look, and Elizabeth was hard pressed not to roll her eyes. Especially as Appolonia had gone off alone with Lord Laidly. "I never let Bessie go out like that," Appolonia continued. "Mother has always said 'tis best to keep servants busy. They get into less trouble that way."

"You must do as you think best, and so will I. But now, I must be going."

"Which way do you go? Mayhap we can walk together."

Elizabeth feared whatever direction she named, Appolonia would be going that way. She glanced skyward, hoping for an answer. Several birds flew by overhead, and she remembered the merchant who sold brightly colored and ornate feathers. "Do forgive me, I near forgot. I mean to find a small gift for Aunt Phillida. Mayhap a feather to replace the one the rain near destroyed last week."

Appolonia's face registered surprise, and she gave her head a little shake, before saying, "Oh, how, er, how sweet. Sorry I may not join you and help in your selection, but I must be getting home. Good day to you. Come Bessie." She started to walk away, but stopped, and again grasped Elizabeth's wrist. "Now, that you know why I had not my maid with me, you can understand 'twas not scandalous. All the same, no reason the incident should be bandied about, do you think? Lady Bainbridge, as my guardian, does have some concern."

Elizabeth assured Appolonia she would remain mum, as would Mary. Her guess that Appolonia would not wish to join in her shopping expedition had been accurate. Appolonia would not wish to shop for anyone but herself. Now Elizabeth just had to get to her dreaded appointment. Surely she would encounter no more hindrances.

❀ ❀ ❀ ❀

Elizabeth spotted the extortionist pacing back and forth in front of the haberdasher's shop where he had first accosted her. When he turned and saw her hurrying toward him, he stopped. Arms akimbo, he frowned at her, and as she drew near, he snarled, "I was nigh set to head for the constable."

"Meeting your demand has not been easy," she snapped in return. "I had many trials."

"Never mind that, have you got the coin?"

"I have one-hundred ninety-five pounds. 'Twas all I could raise."

A smile crept across his face. "'Twill do. Hand it here."

Elizabeth straightened her shoulders. "What guarantee do I have you will not go to the constable? That you will never go to the constable?"

The man's voice became more wheedling. "I am a man of my word. We have us a deal. Do you fulfill your part of the bargain, so shall I." He put his hand over his heart. "My honor."

Your honor, ha, she thought, but said, "Very well." She reached into her pocket, but before she could pull out her purse, she again heard her name being called. "Lady Elizabeth, what happenstance we should meet you here."

Elizabeth groaned inwardly. Not another chance encounter. Was everyone she knew in London out and about this day? She turned to find Lord Albin approaching her, and the man at his side, she recognized as Lord Havenhurst. When they reached her, Albin said, "Lady Elizabeth, allow me to present to you, Lord Havenhurst. I think you have ne'er been introduced."

Lord Havenhurst swept off his hat and bowed slightly at the waist. "Lady Elizabeth, I am honored. I know your father well. I pray you remember me to him?" Attempting to act nonchalant, Elizabeth acknowledged the introduction with a smile and promised she would remember him to her father. Thus far neither man seemed to have noticed the extortionist who, with hunched shoulders, had turned away and seemed to be interested in the shop window.

"I was but just telling Lord Havenhurst about Sir William's need for a postilion," Lord Albin said. "He says he has just the man. A youth, but he knows how to handle horses. Havenhurst's own postilion's son. You must tell Sir William I will send the lad to see him, does he so wish it."

"Indeed, I shall tell him. I am certain he will be interested." She looked to Lord Havenhurst. "I thank you, Lord Havenhurst." In his fifties, yet still captivating thanks to a devilish twinkle in his silver-blue eyes, he had the King's ear. Elizabeth knew that meant much to Lord Albin. She hoped Havenhurst would plead Lord Albin's case to King Charles, and that Lord Albin's father's land claim would be upheld.

"Might we escort you somewhere, Lady Elizabeth?" Albin asked with a glance at the extortionist. "You were not being accosted by yonder fellow were you?" Eyes narrowed, he squinted suspiciously at the man who now seemed almost to be cowering.

"Oh, no, he but asked directions." Elizabeth blurted out the first thing that came to mind.

"Such as he has no call addressing a lady, no matter the reason," Albin asserted, puffing out his chest. "You, what mean you by accosting a lady on the street?" He addressed the extortionist. Keeping his head lowered, the man peered around at Albin.

"I am certain he meant no disrespect, Lord Albin." Elizabeth tried to turn attention away from the man. Fear gnawed at her insides. What if he were to run? Run right to the constable.

"Wait here now," Lord Havenhurst said. "Healy! Is that you, Healy? Look up here man."

The extortionist turned. Fear discernible in his eyes, he swept off his hat. "Aye, my lord."

His eyes cold, his lips firmed, Havenhurst pointed his cane at the man he addressed as Healy. "Did I not warn you to leave London? Did I not say I would see you hanged did I e'er set eyes on you again?"

Elizabeth's hands went to her mouth. The man had crossed Havenhurst. She held her breath. Would Healy try to save his neck by telling on William?

"I am leaving this very night, my lord. You will ne'er see me again, I ... I give you my word. I but needed to collect a debt owed me, but 'tis

262

done and I am leaving, leaving now."

He attempted to back away, but Havenhurst brought his cane down hard on Healy's shoulder. Healy cringed. "Do I find you have in anyway offended Lady Elizabeth," Havenhurst said, his voice icy, "I will not wait for the noose, I will run you through with my sword."

Healy shook his head, "Nay, nay, my lord, ask the lady. I have not offended her." He turned pleading eyes on Elizabeth.

She shook her head. "He did naught to offend me, Lord Havenhurst. Does he purport to leave London, do you please let him go." Did Healy leave London, he could take no tales to the constable.

"You are a quacksalver, a scoundrel of the worst sort, Healy. You will get no more chances after today. Be gone and let me ne'er see your ugly face again."

Bowing repeatedly, Healy said, "Thank you, my lord. Thank you, milady." Turning, he hurried off down the street.

Elizabeth watched him scurry away but brought her attention back to Albin when he stated, "I must say, Lady Elizabeth. I know you to be an innocent on the ways of London, but you must not speak to the likes of Healy." He turned to Mary, who, with eyes widened and mouth open, had been watching the whole confrontation. "I know you, too, are unfamiliar with the ways of London, but you should know to never allow such boors to address Lady Elizabeth."

Mary's mouth snapped shut, and she dropped a curtsy. "No, my lord. 'Twill ne'er happen again. I do so promise."

"Nay, Lord Albin, blame not my servant. She did urge me to ignore the man and pass him by." Elizabeth felt guilty. Mary had done her best to steer her away from Healy, yet Mary was being blamed for the incident.

"Next time," Havenhurst interrupted. "Pay heed. Men such as Healy prey on the innocents that come to London. He looks the scum now, but he can polish himself up to appear a gentleman. He took a youth from one of my villages for his entire inheritance. A letter from the youth's poor widowed mother took me to his rooms. I found him drunk and with pistol in hand. Shamed, he meant to put an end to his life. I paid his bills and packed him back home on the stagecoach. I gave Healy fair warning I would see him hang for the thief he is did I e'er see him again. You, Lady Elizabeth, saved him his life. Worthless life that it is. So pay heed to Albin."

"I will heed your warnings. And I thank you for your concern. Now, I must be going. I mean to stop by to see Mistress Elsworth."

"We will walk with you," Albin said. "Just to be certain no one else accosts you."

Elizabeth smiled. "As you wish, though I am certain Mary will ne'er again let such as Healy address me."

Chapter 34

Euphoric, Elizabeth wanted to skip down the street. Healy had been banished from London. She did not think he would dare cross Havenhurst and risk staying in town to make charges against William. William was safe, and she still had the money she had borrowed. She could return to the pawn shop on the morrow and retrieve her jewelry without ever having to tell her aunt about the reprehensible incident.

She chatted amiably with Albin and Havenhurst as they ambled down the street and thanked them again when they made to leave her outside the Harbinger residence. To avoid having lied to William and her aunt, she had need to stop in for a brief visit with Blythe. "Indeed, you need not walk me to the door," she said. "You have gone enough out of your way. You are promised to Lord Millbourne and Mister Salton for cards and supper. You must not keep them waiting."

"Aye," Albin agreed, looking up at the Harbinger mansion. "They have both been inconsolable since Lady Harbinger ran off with Lord Bretherton. I would ne'er have guessed it of the lady."

"I cannot say it surprises me," Havenhurst said. "She and Harbinger were ill suited to one another. I knew her when she was but a young maiden. Beautiful, healthy, full of life. Cannot blame Harbinger for desiring her, but 'twas no love match." He glanced at Elizabeth. "Begging your pardon, Lady Elizabeth. I mean not to carry tales."

"I have great regard for the Lady Harbinger," Elizabeth said. "I can but hope she finds the happiness she has so long been denied."

Havenhurst inclined his head. "'Tis a hard road she and Bretherton have chosen. Forsaking family and friends. They are now outcasts. But is their love strong enough, no doubt they will survive the scandal." He half-smiled. "Good day to you, Lady Elizabeth."

Still buoyant, Elizabeth smiled brightly. "And to you, Lord Havenhurst, Lord Albin."

Once out of earshot of her two saviors, she allowed the laughter she had been withholding to bubble out. "Oh, Mary, do think, I was so upset with Lady Appolonia. She delayed us, and I feared the nasty fiend would be on his way to the constable. But had we arrived sooner, I would have given him the money for we would not have met up with Lord Albin and Lord Havenhurst. Is fate not ever so beguiling?"

Mary was not laughing. "I am but glad 'tis over, milady."

Elizabeth sobered. "I too, Mary. But tomorrow, we must return to the pawn shop and buy back my jewelry. And we will buy that gift for your mother so you will not have lied to Castor. However, we will take a footman with us. He can wait outside the shop and be none the wiser about our transaction."

A smile again brightening her face, she traipsed happily up the stairs to rap on the door. It was immediately opened by a stiff, and she thought overly formal, footman, but she was used to the man. She was but surprised he had not retired to the country with Lord Harbinger. "Mistress Elsworth is in her room," he said. "Do you wait in the parlor, and I will inform her you are here."

"No, you need not do that. I will run up to see her. Come Mary," she said and brushing past the footman, she skipped up the marble staircase. She had been to Blythe's room often enough to know her way around the multi-roomed house.

Blythe was delighted to see her. "I had thought you would be stopping by. I received a note from your aunt asking were you here. I sent back that you were not, but I expected you."

Elizabeth frowned. "I wonder what Aunt Phillida wants. I suppose I must hurry home. Mayhap my uncle and his family are to arrive sooner than planned. Anyway, I but stopped by to tell you of my gown. It should be finished and delivered this evening. It is lovely."

Blythe clapped her hands and said, "Oh, I am that glad you are pleased with it. Now, do tell me of your plans for the wedding breakfast." Elizabeth obliged her then said she must be returning home. "As it grows late, would you have one of your footmen escort us. I would not want Aunt Phillida to be concerned."

Elizabeth, knowing she had two hundred pounds in her pocket, was not wanting to again be stopped by any would-be extortionists. A footman would insure no one approached her. She dismissed the footman at the door to her apartment. He bowed and turned to retrace his steps. Smiling brightly, she opened the door. She had expected to find no one but her aunt, but to her delight, William was there. Then her mouth dropped open. Sitting on a chair, his nose twitching nervously, the pawnshop dealer raised his gaze to meet hers. What could he be doing in her aunt's parlor? She glanced from William to her aunt. William had risen at her entrance and in an instant was at her side and had her in his arms.

"My dearest love, we have been so very worried. Only your aunt's calm reasoning kept me from raising a hue and cry and from setting up an immediate search for you. When I received Lady Grasmere's note that I must come at once, I cannot tell you the fear that gripped my heart." He pulled her closer, squishing her ear against the rough fabric of his coat collar. "Whatever could have possessed you to pawn your jewelry? I could only imagine an indescribable calamity. Had Mister Truesdale not assured us you seemed under no undue duress, I think I might have gone mad with worry for you."

"Do release her, Sir William, and let her talk," Aunt Phillida said. "She can hardly explain herself with her mouth muffled against your chest."

William loosened his hold on Elizabeth, and she straightened her shoulders. She was in trouble. That, she knew, but she also knew the pawnbroker must not be made privy to her dilemma. She looked directly at the little man. "Sir, I cannot think what you are doing here. I wonder you do stay in business do you so divulge the transactions of your customers."

"Think not to turn the subject, Elizabeth, by attacking Mister Truesdale," her aunt said. "He came to me after he learned your name from your new cook who made some purchases in his shop. He came because he believed you to be in some sort of trouble. 'Tis kind of him. And, he has brought your jewelry with him."

Elizabeth extricated herself from William's arms and reached into her pocket to pull out her purse. "Well, that will save me a trip back to his shop on the morrow." She held up the bag. "I have the money here. I told him I would be returning for my jewelry."

"But why, Elizabeth, why did you need pawn your jewelry?" William asked.

She looked up at him. "I will tell all over a glass of sherry, my love. I have had a busy day, and I am tired. But now, might I buy back my jewelry and let Mister Truesdale return to his shop. No doubt he has lost sales whilst he has been away."

Mister Truesdale seemed eager to depart. Clutching a soft pouch in both hands, he sprang from his chair. "Yes, I had to lock up when I came here. My assistant makes a good guard, but he cannot handle the business." He held out the pouch. "Milady, your jewelry." When Elizabeth reached for it he coughed nervously. "Ah, mayhap 'tis best we put your jewelry on the table. I would not want you to think any has gone missing. Uh, we might also count out the money."

"Perfectly sensible," Aunt Phillida said. In short order, the exchange was made, and Mister Truesdale was on his way, his pocket a bit plumper with a token of thanks from William.

"Now, young lady," Aunt Phillida said, "you will explain yourself."

"Might I not have that glass of sherry first."

"Mary, get Lady Elizabeth a sherry and one for me and Sir William as well."

Mary bobbed a curtsy. "Yes, Lady Grasmere."

Elizabeth sat on the couch, and William sat beside her. His face still showed his concern, and she touched his cheek. "My dear William, look not so worried. I was never in any danger. 'Twas my fear for you that compelled me to act as I did."

"Fear for me?" He both looked and sounded startled.

"Yes, my love," she said, accepting a glass of sherry from Mary. "Let me but have a sip, and I will begin my tale."

Once Aunt Phillida was seated on a tufted chair opposite Elizabeth, and she and William had their sherries, Elizabeth began her narrative. She had not progressed far into her story when Aunt Phillida interrupted her, "You should have listened to Mary. You should never have allowed the man to address you."

"But Aunt Phillida, the man threatened that William might end up in jail."

"Surely you could not have thought his word would be believed over

Sir William's?"

"He said he had other witnesses."

"My dear Elizabeth," William said, pulling her closer to him, "that you have such a great love for me leaves me in constant awe. But in the future, do you please trust me. Had you told me of this rapscallion, I could have put your fears to rest. I would have had no trouble refuting any charges such as this Healy might have made, whether he drummed up witnesses or not. But 'tis not likely he would have gone to the constable. He would not risk being charged with libel."

"Yes, Elizabeth, he took a chance he could frighten you, and you would be fool enough to believe he could do Sir William harm," Aunt Phillida said.

Elizabeth nodded her head. "Yes, I see now you are right. Lord Havenhurst did say Healy looked to innocents to deceive. I suppose I am yet too ignorant of the machinations that go on in London. But I shall learn."

"What has Lord Havenhurst to do with this?" William asked.

"Do you both allow me to continue, I will tell you."

"Continue," her aunt said. "I shall hold my comments until you have explained all."

Having no additional interruptions, Elizabeth completed her account, concluding with her joy that Lord Havenhurst had frightened the extortionist off with the threat to run him through with his sword. "He and Lord Albin then walked with us to Harbinger House. I was glad of their company as I still had the money in my pocket."

William chuckled. "Seems I owe Albin and Havenhurst a debt, yet I cannot well repay them without telling them more than we could wish them to know. I will think of something." He cupped Elizabeth's face in his hand. "Promise me, my love, you will keep no more such secrets from me. Our marriage must be based on trust."

"Oh, I do so promise, William. I will never again keep any such secrets from you. I will trust you, and I want you to feel you can trust me."

"Splendid," Aunt Phillida said, "now we must hurry and dress for supper. Your Uncle Nate is bringing a guest this evening. What with Ranulf and his family due to arrive on the morrow, 'twill be our last quiet supper until after your wedding."

❀ ❀ ❀ ❀

Elizabeth tucked her jewelry back in the delicately carved jewelry box and closed the lid. She had much to learn about life in London, but with William at her side, she had no fear of her new home. He would protect and guide her, but she would still rely on her own instincts. She could not think she had been wrong to help Annis, or to follow William when he went to save Dicken, or to believe the extortionist's lies had some merit. After all, she had been at Creighton's decrepit hide-away. Had been witness to his death. She must have been noted by many. Her mistake had been to think the word of a person of the meaner sort would hold any weight against the word of a gentleman, and in particular a baronet known to enjoy the King's favor.

Well, she would learn all the intricacies revolving around her new life. And she would trust William, but she had a suspicion, that from time to time, she might not confide all her secrets. She would be running the household, and he would have no time for nor interest in the minute details of everyday events. A broken lamp, a stained table cloth, any number of trivial household tribulations would occur that he need not, nor would he expect to be made privy to. Nor need he be privy to her intent to find a suitable husband for her dear friend, Blythe. But that was a future project. Now, she needed to prepare for the onslaught of her Uncle Ranulf's family.

❀ ❀ ❀ ❀

The apartment having but three bedchambers, Elizabeth's aunt moved in with her that Uncle Ranulf and Aunt Angelica might have the larger chamber. Uncle Nate planned to stay with a friend so Uncle Ranulf's sons could have the chamber he had used. Arrangements had to be made for their servants as well. With the need to house Angelica's maid, Adah and Mary would both be squeezed into Elizabeth's closet. Elizabeth might have pitied Mary being forced into such close company with Adah, but Mary laughed and said, "Oh, have no worry for me, Lady Elizabeth, Adah may grump, but as you say, 'tis but for four nights, and then we will be in your new home. I shall manage fine."

It was a squeeze, but Elizabeth loved seeing her cousins and her Aunt Angelica. She had not seen them for near three years. Artemas was now attending Oxford, though Elizabeth had a suspicion he was not of a scholarly bent. Ten-year-old Thayer, on the other hand, was already portending to be a scholar. His father said he feared his youngest meant to be a lawyer.

Elizabeth talked with Giles about his wedding plans and learned it would be a grand affair. As the heir to his father's earldom, he would be expected to have a lavish wedding. "Though Caroline and I would prefer a smaller affair," he said. "Caroline is rather retiring."

"I will look forward to meeting her," Elizabeth said and listened graciously while her cousin expounded on his betrothed's virtues. Elizabeth hoped Caroline was not the paragon Giles painted. Were she, she would have trouble adjusting to Uncle Ranulf's and Aunt Angelica's raucous brood.

That night Elizabeth went to sleep with a smile on her lips. She was fortunate in her friends and her family, but she had come to London to find adventure and love. She had found both, and they were embodied in the man she was to marry.

Chapter 35

At last the day of the wedding was upon them, and Elizabeth could not have asked for a more beautiful day. The sky was clear, the morning sun shone brightly. Elizabeth's Uncle Nate escorted her down the aisle of the lovely Lady Chapel in Westminster Abbey. "You look radiant," he whispered, taking her hand and tucking it into the crook of his arm.

She smiled up at him. The only thing that could have made this day more perfect would have been to have her mother and father present. But she knew her mother was too ill, and her father was loath to leave her side. Still, she had her dear Aunt Phillida, her Uncle Ranulf and Aunt Angelica, and three of their sons, Giles, Artemas, and Thayer. Blythe was her attendant and witness and Lord Albin stood by William. Garrett had been joined, at her express invitation, by Kilkenny and Ridgely. Fogarty sent his regrets. Someone had to mind the *Lady Alesia*. Elizabeth guessed the little man had volunteered for the job. He would think his appearance might be offensive to her other guests and would want nothing to spoil her day. A lovely soul he had. 'Twas sad more people could not see it. She would ever be grateful to him for his warning that had saved her and William's lives that foggy night on the Thames.

Mary and Adah were in attendance, as was Dicken, though he was not a member of the household. After the ceremony, they would return to the apartment where a wine punch and a fruitcake with marzipan icing awaited the servants' celebration of Elizabeth's wedding. Aunt Phillida's footmen and Elizabeth's uncles' servants would be invited to the festivities, as would be Mistress Hall, Elizabeth's new housekeeper, and Castor, William's new valet de chambre, Wainwright having graciously acquiesced to William's request to purchase Castor's contract.

"You must always remember to include your household in your important celebrations," Aunt Phillida instructed her. "Marriages, births, even funerals. It helps insure their loyalty, do they know they are valued."

Elizabeth's thoughts returned to William. Awaiting her at the altar, he looked so handsome, her heart skipped a beat, then another. His love for her shown in his sea-green eyes and in his sensuous smile. The look he was giving her made her long for the wedding and subsequent festivities to be ended that they might escape to their new bed in their new home. Thinking of William's kisses sent her senses reeling with promises of greater thrills, and she eagerly anticipated experiencing those additional delights.

Nothing marred the quiet, traditional ceremony, and before Elizabeth realized it, she and William were pronounced man and wife. As they walked back up the aisle, Elizabeth clung to William's arm. They now belonged to one another.

When they arrived at the Worverton mansion, they were greeted by their many well-wishers. Lady Worverton and her son escorted them to the expansive breakfast table set up in the great hall. William was seated at the end of the table, and Elizabeth at his side. The Worvertons took their seats at the other end of the richly decorated table. Silver candelabras with white candles aglow and bright floral arrangements on a gold damask tablecloth added warmth and elegance to the large formal hall. Crystal goblets, embossed silver trenchers, and rose-colored napkins adorned each place setting.

Elizabeth was grateful to the Worvertons for hosting the festivities. Her father would be paying for the celebration, but the Worvertons had gone to a lot of trouble seeing all was set up properly, and that the cooks had the breakfast ready in a timely fashion. The meal consisted of tarts and muffins, peaches poached in sherry, a beef steak and kidney pudding, pheasants with apricots, chicken stuffed eggs in mushroom sauce, and codfish cakes. They had the traditional fruitcake as the wedding cake, but they also served little 'maids of honor' jelly cakes.

When selecting the dishes to be served, William insisted on the steak and kidney pudding. "The men will need something more substantial than the delicacies you have selected."

The champagne flowed freely, and the revelers offered toast after toast to the newlyweds. Looking down the table at all their guests,

Elizabeth was amazed at the number of friends and acquaintances she had accumulated since coming to London. She knew all the guests but for a couple of merchants and their wives that William felt compelled to invite due to his lucrative trade with them. Kilkenny and Ridgely were seated next to the merchants, and Elizabeth noted them deep in conversation to the apparent annoyance of the merchants' wives. Garrett, engaged in conversation with his cousins, was likely telling them about his ship. Busy with preparations before his departure, he had not had time to visit with his cousins before Elizabeth's wedding. Elizabeth was grateful he delayed his voyage that he might attend the marriage ceremony.

Seated at the opposite end of the table, next to Lady Worverton, Aunt Phillida looked resplendent in an apple-green gown. Catching her beloved aunt's eye, Elizabeth raised her goblet to her and took a sip. Her aunt acknowledged the salute. Her duty to Elizabeth was completed. The night before, when tucking Elizabeth into bed for the last time, she admitted to being content, even pleased with Elizabeth's choice. "I have no doubt he will stand you in good stead, my dear. And as handsome as he is, you should have beautiful children."

Blythe drew Elizabeth's attention back to the present. "Look to Lady Appolonia and my brother," she whispered. "The lady is all gush and goo. But that seems to appeal to Selby. I understand her dowry is adequate, and I am guessing, does the visit to Castonbury Park go well this summer, Selby will ask her guardian for permission to address her. Her father was an Earl so his peerage is acceptable. Her mother's problem with the falling sickness is a worry to my mother, but Appolonia's mother's family dates back to the Conqueror, and that appeals to Mother. Her own ancestry being something we are not to discuss," Blythe added with a smile.

Elizabeth laughed. "Just remember, you will always be welcome in our home does Lady Appolonia's syrupy sweetness become overbearing."

Elizabeth's attention was next drawn to her Aunt Angelica. Her name suited her well. Always pleasant, always ready with a smile, she never complained about the fate that left her a cripple. "Have I not the most wonderful husband any woman could ask for," Elizabeth had once overheard her telling a well-meaning friend when offered sympathy. "Many women have far worse fates than mine. My husband adores me. I have five lovely, healthy children. I want for no comfort. I can do little but praise the good Lord for all my blessings." An heiress of four major estates and a number of small manors, she had married Uncle Ranulf while they were both in exile on the continent with King Charles.

Leaning forward, Angelica told Elizabeth she looked lovely. "I cannot think when I have seen a more beautiful bride," she said, her dulcet voice reaching across the table. Her pale golden hair, hiding any signs of gray, cascaded in ringlets around her neck and ears. Her sapphire-blue eyes alight, her shapely lips curved in a sweet smile, Angelica looked entrancing despite her forty-odd years. Elizabeth thought her uncle a lucky man. "I am sorry Selena could not be here," Angelica continued. "You, at least, seem to have outgrown your penchant for impetuous calamities. I hope Rowena will be able to guide Selena along the same path you have taken."

Though she smiled, Elizabeth blushed. Her Uncle Ranulf must not have told his wife about Elizabeth's several misadventures. For that she was grateful. After all, she was now a married woman, and she needed to act with more decorum. For Angelica's sake, Elizabeth hoped Selena would allow herself to be molded by her Aunt Rowena, but she very much doubted it.

William recalled her attention to him. He rose to propose a toast to all their many friends who had joined them in their wedding celebration. After taking a sip, he looked down at Elizabeth. "And to my lovely bride." Another sip amidst applause. William remained standing until all was again quiet. "As many of you know, Elizabeth and I will be visiting our families, but when we return, we hope you will all call on us. Our home will always welcome you." More applause, and he sat down, but his eyes remained on Elizabeth. Leaning closer, he whispered, "How long do you think we need remain at our celebration before we may leave?"

Widening her eyes, she said, "Why William, whatever can you mean? Desert our wonderful friends. What would they think of us."

He leaned closer. "That we are in love and have better things to do."

"Mmmm. That sounds promising." She tilted her head and gave him what she hoped was a seductive smile. "I look forward to those..." she paused, then added, "better things."

Either the smile or the words had their desired effect. He cleared his throat and said in a loud voice, "If all are finished eating, I suggest we get on to the dancing."

People laughed and chairs scraped – breakfast was ended. While guests gathered in groups and chatted, the servants cleared away the remains, removed the table to a corner, and lined up the chairs along the walls. The music started, and William led Elizabeth out to the middle of the hall where but a little more than a month earlier she had been led by Lord Worverton to start the dancing for his mother's ball. Now, she danced as Lady Elizabeth Hayward.

Chapter 36

Propped against a multitude of fluffy pillows, Elizabeth awaited her husband. She could hear him in the adjoining closet. Castor was helping him don his sleeping attire. William had waited in his library while Mary and Mistress Hall helped Elizabeth shed her wedding apparel and don the silky golden night shift Aunt Phillida had helped her select. Glancing at the tripod of candles glowing on the stand by the bed, she felt a nervous prickle at the nape of her neck. She knew basically what to expect. Aunt Phillida had explained much to her. She knew she could experience some pain, but she was not afraid. She just did not want to disappoint William.

In an attempt to calm her racing heart, she thought back to the ride home. With Aunt Phillida's and Worverton's help, they had been able to slip away from their guests, thus avoiding the semi-social bedroom rituals. Settled into the new coach with its plush cushioned seating, and with William's arms around her, his lips devouring hers, she had floated dreamily. Knowing that he hungered for her increased her confidence. Yet he was so experienced. His kisses, his caresses told her so. Could she possibly measure up to his other lovers? Not that she was jealous. His past was his past. And she was the one who had won his heart. Still, she wanted to make him forget all his previous lovers.

She shook her head. This worrying was no good. Sending her thoughts off in another direction, she thought back to her first meeting with William – at the King's ball. Annis had been at her side. Dear little friend. Though her friend had not attended the wedding, she and Sir Jeremy had sent Elizabeth and William a beautiful wall tapestry of a sea of flowers and a brook and a lovely blue sky. William said he had seen it hanging in the parlor in Annis's home. He guessed it to date from pre-Tudor days. It now hung in their parlor and was a prized possession.

Elizabeth's dear friend, Cambria, also not at the wedding, had sent a gift of twelve amber colored wine goblets, twelve silver tong forks with ivory handles, and twelve matching spoons. She sent, as well, her loving wishes for a glorious future for Elizabeth and William. So many wonderful gifts from friends and family, but the gift Elizabeth prized the most was the tiny miniature of William given to her by Blythe. How Blythe had managed to get William to sit for the tiny portrait, she could not guess, but the miniature was the perfect size to put in the treasured locket her mother had given her.

Elizabeth would miss Blythe when she adjourned to her house in the country, but they would correspond, and hopefully Blythe would soon come for a visit. Elizabeth wondered that more men were not attracted to her friend. By rights, she should be courted by any number of men – but not that just any man would do for Blythe. She would need someone who appreciated her intelligence, encouraged her learning. Surely such a man existed.

She began going over the men of her acquaintance when the opening of the closet door halted her rumination, and she turned to look at her husband. Quietly closing the door behind him, William advanced into the room.

The gold, leaf-patterned silk banyan he wore over his white ruffled nightshirt, shimmered under the glow of the candlelight. Mesmerized by the look in William's eyes, Elizabeth could do naught but sigh in wonderment. William was a gorgeous man, and he was her husband. Stopping short of the bed, William smiled the smile she loved so dearly. "You could not look more lovely my bride," he said, "there in your frilly gold shift and with your silken hair floating about your shoulders. I am a fortunate man. Were I a painter, I could not ask for a more delightful subject."

Elizabeth reveled in his words. They had waited for what seemed an eternity for this day, this moment in time. But now it was here and soon they would be as one. Eager for William to join her in the bed, she started to blow out the candles, but he stopped her. "Nay my love, the flickering light of the candles will but enhance our love feast. Our banquet of tastes and sights and delectable sensations." As he spoke, he kicked off his slippers and slowly untied the sash of his banyan.

He removed the banyan and draped it over a nearby chair, then with his eyes glued to hers, he slipped his night shift off over his head and tossed it aside.

Elizabeth stared in awe at his hard, lean body, the taut muscles of his legs and arms, and his manhood, already at attention. Candlelight cast dancing shadows across his chest. He held out a hand to her. "Come to me, my bride."

Enraptured, she silently obeyed. When she stood before him, he drew her into an embrace, crushing her to his chest. His lips seared hers, and she gasped as his tongue found hers. She answered his hunger with a fervency of her own. The sensuous feel of the thin layer of her silky shift between their bodies added to the tingling sensations coursing through her. William's hands roaming up, down, and all around her body ignited fiery sparks that sent her reeling, breathlessly spinning until his hands cupped her buttocks and pressed her against his throbbing manhood. Then she knew what she wanted, desperately needed. But he had other plans.

He pulled the shift off over her head, but with his hands on her shoulders, he held her at arms' length. "God, you are beautiful," he whispered, his gaze meandering over her body. She felt no abashment under his direct gaze. She instead felt exhilarated, titillated, and loved. Slowly he drew her back into an embrace, bare skin against bare skin. His lips lightly grazed hers, while one hand held her against him and the other caressed her breasts. Waves of passion rose in her, swelled, and demanded compliance, yet William's tantalizing touch and smoldering kisses continued to tease and torment her in a resplendent torture. Not until she was dizzy with a desire she could not control, and she dug her fingers into his shoulders did he relent and scoop her up in his arms and carry her to their bed. But there he again tortured her, his hands and lips exploring and tasting every inch of her.

Repeatedly he brought her to a near peak of a delight she could not yet fathom, not yet understand, but knew she craved, only to let her slide gently back down to near drown in a pool of molten passion. When she thought she could endure no more, he moved over her and at last she possessed him. The pain she felt as he broke through her barrier was miniscule, nothing compared to the urgency obsessing her, the driving need to be one with the man she loved with a fiery ardor. She would ever know an insatiable hunger for this man who took her to wife.

She clung to him and together they soared beyond the known world. They reached heights Elizabeth would never have dreamed possible. The colors of the rainbow danced before her eyes and mystical music serenaded them. And when she finally reached that peak, she cried out in naïve wonderment before rejoicing in her husband's ardent fulfillment.

The candles had burned down to nubs, their blackened wicks trailing down the tripod when William extinguished them and drew Elizabeth into his arms. What a lover she had married. Cradled in his arms, her head pillowed on his shoulder, her hand resting on his chest, she felt completely satiated – for the present. But she had no doubt the hunger, the thirst would return with a greater craving now she knew what to expect. She was truly blessed to have such a wondrous husband.

🌵 🌵 🌵 🌵

William was enthralled with his wife. Her responses to his lovemaking had near undone him. He had been determined to pleasure her, to make her first experience with him a joy, a delight, but her ardent passion had near overcome his will power. Lying with her body curled next to his had his heart again pummeling. His desire for her again stirring. He heard her soft breathing, and thought she had drifted into sleep, but she surprised him with a question.

"Do you not think Blythe Elsworth an attractive woman?"

"What makes you think of Mistress Elsworth now?"

"She is my dearest friend, and I would like her to be as happy as I am."

He kissed her forehead. "Are you happy, my love?"

She sighed and reached up to touch his face. "You must know I am. But you have not answered my question."

"What question is that?" he asked, pushing aside her hair that he could caress her breast.

She gave a little gasp, but persisted. "Is Blythe not an attractive woman?"

"I suppose she is in her own manner. Not beautiful as you are, but attractive, yes." He nuzzled Elizabeth's neck and felt her shiver.

Her voice became more husky, and she stuttered, "She is in...intelligent...and caring...and... Oh," she breathily groaned as he placed tiny kisses along her jaw line. "William, I do... think any... man would be... lucky..." Another, "Oh," ended her sentence, and he believed the conversation to be over, but she pulled away ever so slightly.

"Do you not think Blythe would be a wonderful wife for the right man?"

"Yes, for the right man, she would be the perfect wife. But now I have better things for us to do than talk of Mistress Elsworth." He punctuated his sentence with a lingering kiss.

As he had hoped, Elizabeth responded by draping a leg over his and cuddling closer. "Have you?" she purred.

He tilted her chin up with his fingertip and found her lips. "Indeed I have," he murmured against her lips. His hand went to her buttocks and drew a little gasp from her as he pressed her closer, and she discovered his hardened manhood. Her lips parted, and reveling in the feel of his bride's sensuous body, William deepened the kiss. The silky feel of her bare skin, the softness of her mounds and curves, the sensations her light touch sent coursing through his body were mystical. Lord, he was a lucky man, and well he knew it. Heart and soul, he belonged to her and she to him. With a joyful heart, he turned to pleasuring her before seeking his own release.

🌱 🌱 🌱 🌱

Elizabeth melded her body into her husband's. That he again wanted her, thrilled her. For a brief instant her plans for Blythe held her, but as her husband's lips found hers, she forgot all but her love for the man caressing her. Indeed, he set trumpets blaring, angels singing, and the ground to trembling. She could scarce ask for no more. Nor did she as, pushing all other concerns from her mind, she surrendered to her desire.

The End

Look for my Next Novel!

Excerpt from
Perfidious Brambles

Chapter One

Northumberland, England 1673

In the day's dying light, Lady Timandra Lotterby peered out the coach window at the dark and shuttered house and wished she had never offered to accompany her friend, Eliza Tilbury, to Perfidious Brambles. A cold shiver crept up her spine, and she squiggled uncomfortably on the padded seat cushion. Eliza's trembling hand slid over hers, and Timandra felt instant shame. She was here to support her friend, not give way to silly, baseless fears. Yes, the estate grounds appeared unkempt, and the house foreboding, but an old man living on his own might find little need to keep up appearances.

"Holy Mary, would you be looking at that house," Timandra's Irish maid said in breathless awe. "Nary a light peeping from nary a window. Be you after thinking anyone is to home, Lady Timandra?"

Timandra drew her lips into a thin line and spoke in a firm voice meant to chastise her outspoken maid. "Mind your tongue, Finola. Indeed, I do think someone is home. We are expected. We sent a message from our lodgings last night that we should be arriving today. I've no doubt all will be ready for us." She smiled at Eliza and patted her hand.

"You will see, dear friend, all will be well. Your great Uncle Percival's steward wrote that your uncle was graciously giving you and your siblings a home. Tomorrow in the light of day, when we are not so tired, all will look brighter. There now, give me a smile."

Timandra had seen the letter Percival Seldon's steward had sent. There had actually been nothing gracious about it. It simply stated Eliza's uncle recognized and accepted his office of guardian to his nieces and nephews and would fulfill his duties. Their uncle expected them to make their own travel arrangements to Perfidious Brambles. Should further communications be necessary, they should apply to him, the steward, Mister Eustace Colyer. Their uncle had not bothered to address even a short note to his new wards. Of course, he was old, and mayhap had failing eyesight. Or he might have suffered an apoplexy and be debilitated. Still, he might have expressed some sympathy to the Tilburys for the loss of their father.

Eliza blinked her large brown eyes, and her soft pouty lips tried to muster a smile, but she failed so miserably, Timandra had to laugh. Her pretty friend with her perfect little nose and her perfect little white teeth, her naturally pink cheeks and glowing complexion, not to mention a sweetly curvaceous figure, was going to need a lot of reassuring. Until three months ago, Eliza's life had been that of a fairy tale princess. Pretty and pampered, but with a sweet disposition, she'd been betrothed to a handsome, charming prince. Overnight, all had changed.

Timandra was glad she had been with her friend when Eliza received word of her father's sudden death and her world crashed down around her. They had been planning Eliza's wedding. Eliza's mother having died when Eliza was fifteen, Eliza asked Timandra to help her with the wedding arrangements. 'Twas to be a Spring wedding. The invitations had been addressed. Plans for an opulent wedding breakfast were being organized. Eliza's gown of burgundy with a cream-colored petticoat with gold embroidered roses had had its final fitting. Her thick golden hair was to be curled and interwoven with burgundy ribbons and gold roses. The third announcement of the wedding banns were set to be read in the village church the following Sunday. Then the messenger from London arrived.

Over the next few weeks, the initial shock turned to horror as first the details of Vincent Tilbury's death – he died in the arms of his mistress, a woman his family had no knowledge of – then the sad state of his financial affairs surfaced. After his wife's death five years earlier, Tilbury turned to drink and took lodgings in London. He fell into the company of what his solicitor termed a scheming woman who introduced him to London's increasing number of gambling houses. What with his drinking, gambling, and numerous exorbitantly expensive gifts to said woman, along with his neglect of his estate, he fell deeply into debt. By the time all his obligations were settled, little was left for his children.

The Tilbury estate, Merrywic, was sold to pay off the mortgage Tilbury had taken out. Most of the house furnishings, as well as some of Eliza's mother's jewelry, needed to be sold to cover other debts. To Eliza's dismay, her mother's pearls, which she had planned to wear on her wedding day, were missing. Tilbury's solicitor Andrew Kenelm, an older partner in the firm of Kenelm and Severin, had hemmed and hawed, then despite a frown from the younger partner, Bartley Severin, had said he believed they'd been given as a gift to her father's mistress. He'd seen the woman wearing a lovely string of pearls mere days before Eliza's father's death.

Later that evening, Timandra rocked a weeping Eliza in her arms. Hands over her face, Eliza squeaked, "I cannot believe Father would take Mother's pearls. He was home for such a short visit. I went over the wedding plans with him. He was so jovial. He went riding with Herman and Bennet, and he kidded Charissa and Delilah that they would soon be making their wedding plans. He seemed happier than I had seen him in years. He had not been so gay since before Mother died. He visited with Ralph's parents and finalized our nuptial contract." Eliza took several convulsive gulps, hiccupped, then wept, "And all the time he knew he could not honor the contract."

"Mayhap he had no knowledge his financial affairs were in such disarray." 'Twas possible, Timandra thought. Tilbury's excessive drinking could have fogged his brain. "As you say," she added, "he was so happy. He certainly never thought he would be dying so suddenly."

"But to take the pearls and give them to that woman! Oh, Timandra, how could he!"

To that question, Timandra had no answer. She could do naught but continue to rock and croon to her friend.

The coach coming to a stop nudged Timandra's thoughts back to the present. She noted the ragged, overgrown island in the rutted circular drive then looked out at the house. It was huge, and ugly. It had been added on to a couple of times, but with no thought to art or symmetry. The main section of rough stone was old. She guessed it dated back to Henry IV or earlier. With its two projecting corner turrets, it must at one time have been a fortified keep. The circular drive might have been a moat. A wide stone staircase of some twenty steps led up to heavy oak doors. One of her footmen raced up the steps to knock while another opened the coach door and let down the steps. Descending onto the drive, Timandra looked up at the west wing of the house. H-shaped and timber-framed, with brick and plaster infill, it harkened back to the time of Queen Elizabeth with its multitude of windows and spiral chimney stacks. It reminded her of her aunt and uncle's home where she had been fostered for ten of her twenty-two years.

The east wing appeared more classical in design, mayhap dating to Charles I. It was similar in some ways to her own home. In 1630, her grandfather tore down the old Harp's Ridge fortified house dating from the days of Henry IV and built a beautiful new home for his family. Her father had made few changes to the elegant house. Timandra looked forward to exploring the various sections of Perfidious Brambles. It would give them all something to do and would hopefully dispel some of the eeriness surrounding the house.

Eliza alighted and Timandra reached for her hand. "Come, dear friend, let us mount these steps and have done with it. I am dead tired and can think not even an ogre of the worst sort can keep me from my supper and bed."

Not waiting for a footman to open their door, Eliza's two younger brothers scrambled from their coach the moment it drew to a stop. Eliza had to restrain them from racing up the steps. "Herman, Bennet, calm yourselves. You must need want to make a good impression on Uncle Percival. We cannot have him think he has invited two bully-huffs to move into his home."

"Eliza is right, boys. Wait for your sisters," Timandra said. Over the past three months, she had learned the youths paid more heed to her than to their older sister. She guessed her imperious visage gave her an advantage. Tall and stately, she had her mother's dark hair, high forehead, and blue-green eyes, and her father's slim aquiline nose, wide, thin-lipped mouth, and strong jutting chin. To her mind, the combination melded poorly, and despite her mother's assurances she had a regal appearance, she could not consider herself beautiful.

Emerging more slowly from their coach, Charissa and Delilah seemed far less eager to enter their new abode. Clutching each other's hands, they gazed wide-eyed as the sound of a heavy bolt being drawn aside echoed off the stone steps. Timandra looked back around in time to see one of the heavy oak doors grate slowly open. The footman stepped aside to reveal a stooped, wizened old man standing in the doorway. Behind him a woman holding a candle peered over his shoulder.

"Be you the Tilburys?" rasped the old man.

Eliza at Timandra's urging stepped forward. "I am Eliza Tilbury," she reached back a hand, "and this is my friend, Lady Timandra Lotterby, who has accompanied us and provided us with a much needed second coach."

"I have no knowledge was the master expecting an extra person," wheezed the old man. "He made no mention to me, but no matter, you best all come in." He stepped aside and Timandra followed Eliza inside. The only light came from the flickering candle and the last rays of sunshine filtering in the high windows above the doorway, but Timandra, peaking around a beautifully carved dark wood screen, could see they had entered a grand old hall. She could tell at a glance few changes had been made to the hall. Not even the central hearth had been replaced by a wall fireplace.

"I am Mistress Weston, housekeeper," the tall, lean woman with the candle said. "That is Old John Orvin. Used to be the house steward, now he just ..." She shrugged. "He does what he can." She turned to the old man, and speaking loudly said, "Old John, you show the footmen where to take the baggage and point the coachmen the way to the stables. Guess they will need a light. Best give them a candle from the entry so they can light a lantern."

Old John shuffled out and Mistress Weston looked back at Eliza. "We never use this section of the house, but Old John and I thought you might come knocking at this door, so we were on the alert." Turning, she said, "Well, follow me, and I will see you to your rooms. You are late you know. Mister Seldon has a'ready retired. We keep early hours here." She looked back over her shoulder. "Mind your step and make sure to close the door. Old John will see it is bolted when he has seen to your baggage."

Timandra waited to insure the door was closed properly, and to make certain Herman's and Bennet's tutor regained control of his young charges. Ernest Knolles, barely out of school, had replaced the boy's older tutor who had not wished to continue in the Tilbury's employ at reduced wages. Nor had he wanted to travel from Warwickshire to Northumberland. For that Timandra could not blame him. It had been a long, tedious trip. Over two weeks of bumping, bouncing, and jostling about in the coach, combined with poor food and poorer beds whenever they were forced to lodge at inns rather than stay with families of Timandra's father's acquaintance, the trip could be considered naught but an ordeal. The nagging fear of highwaymen waylaying them should they be delayed reaching their evening's stopover added a strain to the already stressful situation.

Grateful to her father for providing not only his coach and six as well as the postilion, extra footmen, and an outrider, Timandra could not help but wonder that her parents had acquiesced to her wish to accompany Eliza. She could but think her Aunt Venetia must have persuaded them to permit her to take the extensive journey. Eliza's mother having been Aunt Venetia's dearest friend, next to her cousin, Delphine, Aunt Venetia would want to help her departed friend's children in any means she could.

With the door secured, Eliza's brothers in an orderly line in front of Mister Knolles, her sisters in front of them, and Finola and Eliza's young maid, Audrey, bringing up the rear, Timandra fell in behind Eliza. They passed from the great hall into a narrow corridor then into a small chamber with a narrow staircase leading up into darkness. Mistress Weston paused before a large oak door, and handing her candle to Eliza, used both hands to lift a stiff iron latch and pull the door open. Taking the candle back, she said, "We will be entering the west wing where Mister Seldon lives, and where you will live. The west wing 'twas built during the reign of good Queen Bess," she added, reverence in her voice.

"What of the east wing?" Timandra asked. "Is it not newer?"

"Aye, but Mister Seldon keeps it locked up. No one is allowed into the east wing."

Timandra found Mistress Weston's statement intriguing, but as the housekeeper failed to elaborate, she decided not to press for details at the moment. She was tired and hungry and the mysteries of the house could wait.

Descending a stone staircase, Mistress Weston tossed back over her shoulder, "Be certain the door is closed." Timandra again waited to make sure all were in line and Mister Knolles had the door firmly shut behind them. The staircase ended at another door which Mistress Weston swept open with one hand, and they followed her into a well-appointed parlor. Large windows covered two walls, but heavy draperies were drawn over them, shutting out any lingering daylight. A large fireplace on the wall opposite the front windows showed no sign of use. Either Mistress Weston kept a very tidy house, or a fire was seldom lit. Timandra guessed the later. Still, it could be a bright comfortable room that would catch the morning sun.

When they were all assembled in the parlor, Mistress Weston counted noses. "My, you are more than I was expecting. Three girls and two boys, that is what Mister Seldon told me to prepare rooms for. He said the boys were young so I was expecting a nanny and I had the nursery made up for them."

"The nursery!" ten-year-old Herman yelped. "I will not stay in a nursery."

"Surely 'tis but for one night, Hermie," Eliza said.

"I will not stay in the nursery either," stated the seven-year-old Bennet, though he had been out of the nursery for less than a year. His lips in a pout and his arms folded across his small chest, he added a stomp of his foot.

"Now boys," Mister Knolles said, "if I can stay in the nanny's room for one night, you can manage the nursery. We cannot ask Mistress Weston to make up new beds at this hour."

The boys again started to complain, but Mistress Weston said, "Girl what does the beds is gone home. She is the daughter of a tenant. No one else here to make up new beds. 'Tis the nursery or nothing."

"You heard Mistress Weston," Timandra said. "Herman, Bennet, you may sleep in warm beds in the nursery for this one night or you may make your own beds in a room you think more acceptable. And you may not think Mister Knolles will make the beds for you. He is tired like the rest of us, and after his supper, he plans to sleep in the nanny's room. 'Tis your choice."

Having an eight-year-old brother, Timandra was used to the vagaries of young boys. Herman and Bennet were tired and hungry and that would make them cranky. Their world had been turned upside down. Orphaned, they had been forced to leave the only home they had ever known. They had no control over what was happening to their lives, and they needed to make a stand. Controlling a chuckle, she watched the emotions wash over Herman's face. Bennet was watching him, too. He would follow his older brother's lead.

Herman firmed his lips and ran a hand through his dark brown hair. "Oh, I suppose does Mister Knolles sleep in the nanny's bed, we can sleep in the nursery for one night." His brown eyes alight, he looked up and stated, "But 'tis for only one night."

"So be it," Timandra said. "Mistress Weston the crisis is resolved, do lead on."

"What of these two?" Mistress Weston indicted Finola and Eliza's maid. "We have made up no beds for them."

"Finola and Audrey are our personal maids. Do you but give them linens, they will make up their cots in the closets next to our rooms or on trundle beds, whichever you may have for them."

"Got a cot in the closet off Mistress Tilbury's room, and one in the closet off the young misses' room," Mistress Weston said. "Should serve, I suppose. Master has not entertained for near on thirty years except when his sister used to visit, and she died ten years back. I fear, Lady Timandra, you will be needing to sleep with Mistress Tilbury. I had no knowledge the young mistress was bringing you, so I made no arrangements." She looked to Charissa and Delilah. "I put the two young misses together. We got but one girl does the cleaning. Only so much she can be expected to keep up with."

Timandra wondered that Eliza's great uncle had not informed his staff that she would be accompanying Eliza. She had seen the letter Eliza had written him giving the approximate date of their expected arrival. Mayhap they should have written the steward instead, but that would have seemed discourteous. Seldon's age must have made him forgetful.

"Sharing a bed with Eliza will be no hardship," she said, smiling at Eliza. "Certainly we have shared beds this entire trip. And when fostered at my aunt's, we shared a bed and many a secret."

Eliza returned her smile. "Indeed, 'tis no hardship to share a bed with my dearest friend."

Timandra expected sharing the bed was for the better. She doubted Eliza would want to be abed alone this first night in this strange house. And it was a strange house.

Biography

Celia Martin is a former Social Studies/English teacher. Her love of history dates back to her earliest memories when she sat enthralled as her grandparents recounted tales of their past. As a child, she delighted in the make-believe games that she played with her siblings and friends, but as she grew up and had to put aside the games, she found she could not set aside her imagination. So, Celia took up writing stories for her own entertainment.

She is an avid reader. She loves getting lost in a romance, but also enjoys good mysteries, exciting adventure stories, and fact-loaded historical documentaries. When her husband retired and they moved from California to the glorious Kitsap Peninsula in the state of Washington, she was able to begin a full-fledged writing career. And has never been happier.

When not engaged in writing, Celia enjoys travel, keeping fit, and listening to a variety of different music styles.

Visit my web site at:
cmartinbooks.kitsappublishing.com

CPSIA information can be obtained
at www.ICGtesting.com
Printed in the USA
FSHW011249250820
73286FS